The Sorrowsmith

Andy Monk

Let us drink and sport to-day,

Ours is not tomorrow.

Love with youth flies swift away,

Age is nought but sorrow.

Dance and sing,

Time's on the wing,

Life never knows the return of spring.

Three Airs For The Beggar's Opera, Air Xxii

John Gay

Prologue

I fell in love with Owen James in the autumn of 1911.

I should be able to recall the exact day. Such things are important, after all, but I must confess I don't.

Time passes, but the memories do not always hold.

What I never forgot, however, was the joy of being with Owen. My days in Camelot, as I came to think of them. The love we shared stayed with me throughout my life, a defiant flame to hold against the darkness to come.

The war changed my world. That was the start of it. But from there, the fault rests with me. The choices I made, the things I refused to see, the love I allowed to bind me.

The life I am going to tell you about wasn't the one I would have chosen; it is the one my choices made for me. Lived in a bleak hinterland of washed-out colour, where the wind howls for days without end, and the salt corrodes everything, including your soul. Frank, the children, the grey cottage overlooking the grey sea, the loneliness, the empty place inside me where love once resided. The thing that lived in the furthest corner of my eye, whispering in the dark.

Grief, pain, heartbreak, loss, fear. Sorrow.

No, I would never have chosen that.

Often, on the nights Frank left me alone, I would close my eyes, listen to the sea's song and try to live in Camelot once more.

Owen and I stealing every moment to be together, lips and hands always touching the second we thought no one was looking. The sun forever on my face, dappled through summer boughs.

I remember laughing as we ran through ripening barley. I remember giggling and drinking cider. I remember scoffing Dad's sandwiches atop Cleeve Hill, the Cotswolds stretching so far away around us it seemed we could see all the way to the edge of forever. I remember sprawling in the long grass, babbling endlessly about our future whilst we watched the clouds racing above us.

Marriage, children, our home, growing old together.

How strange and exciting such possibilities seemed.

Above all, I remember being happy. So, so happy. Then the war came.

And I was never truly happy again until the day I died for the second time.

Part One

Sloightly on Th' Huh

1920

I had only seen the sea a handful of times before Frank brought me to Grey Gull. I was twenty-four years old.

I saw it every single day for the rest of my life.

The sea - agitated, powerful, endless – quickly unnerved me in my new home. Or I thought it did. Even then, I knew it was really Frank who frightened me, but I didn't want to articulate or acknowledge that fear. So, I convinced myself it was the incessant beating of the sea upon the shore outside my bedroom window that kept me awake every night, rather than my growing concerns about the man whose child I was to bear.

Over the years ahead I would come to realise there were other things to be afraid of here too...

Grey Gull cottage. Though I always thought of it as the Castle. A hard and foreboding outpost of humanity in a place that had never welcomed the intrusion of man.

In time, the Castle became my prison. The sea formed a barrier on one side, my husband no less impassable on the other. Two restless creatures, both capable of quickly turning to rage and violence. They became my cage, restricting my life to a bleak margin of brittle shingle and brackish marsh.

Cloud kissed the earth the day we arrived, the sea only occasionally visible behind misty veils. I sat on the splintered bench of Mutt Harris' cart, wedged between the old man and Frank's burly frame. My belly swollen enough to be visible even under the heavy coat I huddled in.

I had naively wondered what the locals would make of a newlywed already showing for all to see. As it happened, the gulls and terns didn't appear concerned about my shame. And as for the sheep, well, they clearly couldn't didn't give a hoot.

"It's a place, isn't it, Sweetness?" Frank grinned and patted my knee.

I stared at the pile of stained, damp stone emerging from the mist and tried to find a smile. It certainly was.

Frank's inheritance. Frank's good fortune. Frank's dream. A run-down, rectangle of pitted stone slabs and cracked, lichen-flecked slate the weather had been trying to wear down to sand for centuries.

"Home sweet home..." Mutt chuckled out of the side of his mouth.

That had been the autumn of 1920. Nine years after I'd fallen in love with Owen. I couldn't remember the day that had happened (not all memories hold, as I said earlier), but I thought it might very well be nine years to that very day.

The universe, I'd begun to suspect, did things like that.

Nearly four years had passed since Owen's parents received the telegram. *Missing, presumed dead.* That was a date I would never forget. 14th October 1916.

The day Owen's dad phoned me at the secretarial college in Birmingham and told me the love of my life was gone. I hadn't timed the telephone call, but I doubt it lasted twenty seconds before the line went dead.

It took me a long time to accept Owen wasn't coming home and my days in Camelot were over. My heart never genuinely believed it until Frank found me and told me what happened. Told me that Owen wasn't missing at all; they just never recovered his body from the German lines. That day, I finally accepted, he was gone. In a smoky Charing Cross pub, Frank still in his uniform across the table. I cried. Again. Frank handed me his handkerchief and, later, rested his hand gently on top of mine.

He'd seemed kind then.

Later that evening, I sat on the bed in my lodgings and twisted off the engagement ring Owen had saved for over a year to buy me. When I went down to breakfast the following day, Mrs Hollister, who ran a lodging house for respectable single women fortunate enough to have obtained employment in the Civil Service, and who never missed a thing when it came to her charges, took both my hands. She squeezed them and said if I needed anything, I only had to ask. I nodded, thanked her, and told her I would.

The next thing I knew, I was sobbing in her arms. Mrs Hollister, not a woman who easily succumbed to bouts of emotion, held me tight and stroked my hair. For a moment, I think I loved that stern old woman as much as anyone in my life.

That had been 19th May 1919. The day I finally believed, beyond my foolish heartbroken hopes, that my Owen was never coming home.

I stopped believing a lot of things during my time with Frank. Over the years, the greater reality of our marriage eroded most of my truths. Eroded them as surely as the wind howling off the sea ceaselessly wiped away the structures of man, but I continued believing Owen died under German fire right through until 23rd October 1954

Which was the day the love of my life came back from the dead to help me kill my husband and save my son.

1921

Francis was born on 9th January 1921.

I wanted to go to hospital for the birth, but Frank wouldn't hear of it. The weather eventually made it impossible, regardless. The snow came thick and hard out of the north. And it kept on coming for days, turning the grey world outside white.

"We'll manage," Frank sniffed, staring out the window at the alien place the marshes behind the Castle had become. What he meant, of course, was that *I'd* manage.

I'd never been more scared in my life.

"I don't know what to do..." I whispered, as much to myself as my husband.

"Sure you do," he didn't turn around, "the midwife... what's her name?"

"Janet."

"Yes, Janet. She told you all about it. Didn't she, Sweetness?"

"She said she'd be here."

Frank sighed, "People let you down, my love; that's a sad fact of life..."

As I lay in that cold room with no curtains, making patterns out of the watermarks on the ceiling, I didn't blame Janet. The snow was knee-deep and drifting, the wind strong enough to rattle the Castle's windows in their blackened frames.

Janet advised Frank to get me to the maternity ward in good time, the winter's storms were coming. Most years, the weather cut off the isolated farms scattered along this stretch of coast at some point. Frank looked at her like she was a fool and said we weren't going to leave Grey Gull. The hospital was miles away. It was the midwife's job to be here. That was what he was paying for, after all.

Janet relented in the end; she couldn't force me to go. Even though I wanted her to. She gave me a strained smile before she left, "I'll be back on Wednesday," she assured me, but the snow arrived on Tuesday, and there was no sign of Janet after that.

"The baby's coming..." I hissed through my teeth.

Frank carried on looking through the window. After a while, he nodded, "I'll go boil some water."

Ten minutes later, he returned with a chipped enamel bowl of lukewarm water and a couple of threadbare towels, which he placed on a stand next to the bed. Leaning over, he stroked back my hair and kissed my forehead.

"Everything is going to be alright, Sweetness," he smiled as I groped for his hand.

Then he walked out of the room and left me to it.

1924

I found I had fallen pregnant again on Valentine's Day 1924. The fact that the baby would be due before winter set in was the only joy the realisation brought me. Perhaps I would have someone to help me this time.

I told Frank immediately. Me knowing something he didn't was one of the many things Frank didn't like. He'd looked up briefly. Blood-red paint slashed his cheek as if a knife had elongated his mouth, "Another son would be good," he nodded, as if ordering lunch, then returned to his painting.

I was dismissed.

At least pregnancy would spare me his visits to my bedroom for a few months, I assumed. He hadn't with Francis, and in the years since our son's birth, his visits had decreased in frequency. However, they had also increased in unpleasantness.

It was as if each time he finished his business, he hated either himself or me a tiny bit more.

Like many things in my life, however, I was wrong.

Frank came to my room every night for the next week and did what he pleased with me. On the fourth night, after he'd finished with a snarl and a hiss of stale air in my face, he didn't push himself off, clean his bits with my sheet and leave like he normally did. He stayed atop me, panting slowly, regarding me with glistening eyes in the lamp light.

"Why has it taken so long for you to be with child again?" he asked as he shrivelled and slipped out of me.

"I don't know," I replied, truthfully. I hadn't wanted another tie to bind me to Frank and Grey Gull, but I'd done nothing to prevent it. I'd assumed he would eventually tire of me as he tired of most things, save his ghastly paintings.

"Francis came quick enough," he said, still propped on his arms, "we only did it the once."

It sounded like an accusation haunted Frank's voice.

"Mother nature works in mysterious ways," I tried to smile, but all I wanted was to shrug him off me. I knew he wouldn't take kindly to that, so I forced myself to remain still beneath the weight of his body and dark eyes.

"It is mine, isn't it?"

That was beyond absurd. The only other person I spent time with was our son, Francis, "Frank, that's ridiculous!"

He'd hit me before, but only when in a rage. This time he eased up onto his knees. He looked down on me with something akin to distaste, mulled over whatever was going through his head and then slapped my face. Hard.

"Don't laugh at me, Beatrice; this isn't funny. If you ever let another man fuck you, I'll kill you. And him. Do you understand me?"

"Yes, Frank, I'm sorry..." I nodded, eyes wide, face stinging.

Satisfied, Frank dropped his hand. Then he cleaned himself with my sheet and left.

I extinguished the lamp once the door to Frank's room clicked shut. Then I lay in the darkness, one hand pressed against my smarting cheek, the other on my belly.

Not for the first time, I stared into the night and thought about how I could run away from my husband.

1914

Men in uniform look somewhat dashing if you believe women of a certain opinion. Owen, however, looked ridiculous in his ill-fitting blue *Kitchener's Uniform*, topped off with a cardboard badge on his cap. He looked more like a postman. If someone had to make their own costume for a fancy-dress ball. In something of a hurry.

I'd wanted to be angry at him for running off and volunteering. In fact, I was bloody furious, but I couldn't help laughing when he jumped off the train. He'd blushed and looked down at himself, "The Kaiser's quaking in his boots..." then he'd grinned that self-mocking grin of his and anger squirmed further from my grasp.

That had been 2nd November 1914. The day I first saw Owen in uniform. Not a *real* soldier's uniform, of course. There weren't enough of those for all the mad fools who had rushed to volunteer after Lord Kitchener insisted their country needed them.

The army whisked Owen and his friends to a camp near Bristol. From what he said, training hadn't involved much more than running, marching and getting his hair cut. He'd seen a rifle but hadn't touched one yet. Like real uniforms, guns were in terribly short supply.

I hadn't liked his new military haircut, but missing his unruly curls was the least of my worries.

"You shouldn't have gone," I'd said as we sat on a bench outside *St John's*. It was possibly the millionth time I'd told him since he'd announced he would volunteer once he'd helped his dad get the harvest in.

Owen dragged his boots (his training seemed to have taken in boot polishing, too) back and forth through the fallen autumn leaves spread at our feet.

"I had to, Bea... everyone else was going. It was the right thing to do," he'd replied, possibly also for the millionth time.

"And if everyone else were going to jump off a cliff, I dare say that'd been the right thing to do too, wouldn't it, Private Owen James?"

"What's done is done... let's not argue, eh?" Owen sighed. As you may have gathered, it was a path we had travelled many times since he'd marched himself down to the recruiting day at Milford Conservative Club.

Owen reached out and placed his hand on top of mine. I resisted the impulse to jerk away from his touch and gripped it firmly instead.

I knew my anger was born of fear. He hadn't done a bad or selfish thing. It was brave and noble, but I didn't want him to go to war. I wanted him with me. I was eighteen years old, and my life had been neatly arranged very much to my liking until the Kaiser stuck his big nose in. Now nothing was certain.

"It'll all be over by Christmas, Bea. I'll probably never even get to the front..."

I looked at him then, in his baggy pretend soldier's uniform, with his silly cap and cheap cardboard badge. Looked into those large, expressive eyes I'd been gazing into at every opportunity since I'd fallen in love with him on a particular day in 1911 I could no longer name. I saw he was as scared as I was.

From the outbreak of war in July, people had been saying it would be over by Christmas and the allies would eat their turkey in Berlin. Summer had turned into autumn, and we were now on the cusp of winter. The British and French were nowhere near Berlin. The regular army crossed the English Channel and halted the German advance at Marne, but the war still raged. The British army was now engaged in fierce fighting around a place called Ypres. The papers talked of valour, heroism and glory. But they also talked of heavy casualties and sacrifice too. The boasts of being in Berlin for Christmas were fading.

"I know it won't last long..." I said, trying to sound confident.

It's always best to sound confident when you're telling a lie, whether you're sitting outside the house of God or not.

1924

Wednesday was market day in Creethorpe, and Frank allowed me out to walk the three miles across the marshes and windswept fields on my own to do the weekly shop. My pregnancy was no reason to inconvenience himself by going instead. He was far too busy.

Running away from your husband is no small matter, especially for someone brought up to believe in the sacredness of marriage vows. But by the spring of 1924, I'd become too worried by Frank's behaviour to care. The practicalities of running away when you had one small child and another on the way had become my chief concern.

Part of me wanted to wait, have the baby and let Francis get a little older. But, of course, I might well be with child again by then. Frank expected me to bear him as many children as possible. I didn't know why; he had precious little time for Francis.

Now and then, he would spend a few minutes throwing his squealing son into the air or running with him on his shoulders before ignoring him again for days.

However, it wasn't my place to question Frank's reasoning. Opening my legs at the appropriate moments was all my husband required of me.

I had no family or friends to fall back upon; Dad had died in 1919 and my mother passed away when I was little, so young I only have the haziest memories of her. I have no siblings and no cousins. I'd lost contact with my old friends when I'd moved to London to escape my grief for Owen and made no new ones in my time there. In Grey Gull, I barely saw anyone, let alone made a friend.

I was on my own, save for Francis and the baby in my womb.

It was a terrifying prospect, but it gave me one advantage, there would be no trail for Frank to follow. No telegrams to send, no letters to write, no relatives to call unexpectedly upon. He wouldn't know where I might go other than back to Hollscombe or London. Despite the appeal of London's size and anonymity, I had no intention of escaping to either. There were other cities to lose myself in, and I would choose one to rebuild my life away from Frank's brooding presence, mood swings and violence. Any city would do, so long as it wasn't near the sea.

All I needed for my new life was money. Not a fortune, just sufficient for decent lodgings until the baby came and was old enough for me to work.

I had no idea how much I required for this, but as I'd lain alone in the darkness, one hand on my smarting cheek, the other on the child growing in my belly, I'd decided the amount I had would have to do.

I'd saved most of what I'd earned in the Civil Service before meeting Frank, and this had been swollen by my inheritance from Dad. I'd withdrawn some to help us move to Grey Gull, but the bulk remained earning interest in the *London & Midland Bank* account I'd opened when I'd started work.

My savings were not a fortune, but they amounted to a tidy sum all the same. I was not sure how straightforward withdrawing the whole balance at once would be; I had no intention of leaving any in that account in case Frank, somehow, managed to trace my location through later withdrawals.

So, my plan was to get the money and hide it until Frank went to London on one of his occasional trips to promote his work, then, I would take Francis and go.

One son, one unborn baby, one suitcase and a purse full of bank notes. I'd decide where we were going only when free of the Castle. It wasn't a fear I would give breath to, but deep down, I was scared if I thought about my plans within the dank confines of Grey Gull, the cottage would whisper those thoughts urgently in Frank's ear.

It was totally irrational, but Grey Gull was so much his domain I could not shake the idea those salt-corroded walls would betray me if I gave them the opportunity.

And, by then, I'd already started to notice the strange things that happened in that house…

So, I confined planning my escape solely to when I was outside, playing with Francis on the beach or on my long walks to market.

9th April 1924 was the day I meekly entered the Creethorpe branch of the *London & Midland Bank* to withdraw my life savings.

Frank had grandly announced he was taking his new work to London on Friday and would be gone for a few days. He had that excited gleam in his eye he got whenever he went to tout his work around the galleries and art agents, confident that, this time, they would recognise his talent.

It was a doubly auspicious time to leave because his mood always blackened each time he returned, seething and resentful at the ignorance of others. Frank's genius was something only apparent to himself.

I waited my turn to see the teller, heart thumping and convinced at any moment, someone would demand to know what the hell I thought I was doing.

By the time the clerk smiled, looked over the top of his glasses and bid me good morning, sweat dampened the back of my neck, and my cheeks were aflame. I have never been a bold soul, but my years with Frank had turned me into a mousey creature I barely recognised, unable to achieve the simplest tasks without my husband's direction.

Beatrice, you know you'll never amount to anything without me, don't you, Sweetness?

Frank's long, exaggerated sigh echoed in my ear as the clerk continued to look expectantly at me.

I cleared my throat and thought of a life that didn't involve waking up every morning and wondering which man my husband would be today. In a small, faltering voice, I explained I wished to close my account.

The clerk took the necessary details, ran an eye over them, and told me to come back in an hour to collect my money as it would need to be authorised by the bank manager.

He hadn't demanded to know what I wanted the money for, what I thought I was doing or that I was a stupid little woman who should know where her place was. He just smiled a pleasant smile, adjusted his glasses, and bid me a good day.

I'd let the surge of relief carry me, blinking, out into the sunshine.

It was mild and sunny. Cherry blossom decorated the trees around the market square, and nobody paid me much attention, save a gentleman who smiled at me from behind an enormous, well-tended moustache as he tipped his bowler hat in my direction.

I blushed, sat on a bench, and tried not to feel like a harlot. Frank hated other men looking at me and would, likely as not, have vented steam in my direction if he'd seen such a thing.

Soon, I thought. Soon I wouldn't have to be scared any more. I had no idea what I wanted to do with the rest of my life, save bring up Francis and the baby to the best of my ability, but I was sure I would have a life of some kind. A life of worth and value. Perhaps not a life in Camelot, but still a life, with God's grace, that would have no small amount of love contained within it.

An hour later, I went back to the bank, where the stony-faced manager demanded to know why I was trying to withdraw money from an account my husband closed two years earlier...

1943

By the summer of 1943, I was living alone.

Frank, much to his disgust, had been called up.

"I've been through this once already; I don't want to do it again," he'd fumed when the letter arrived. He was forty-six and considered himself too old and unfit to fight the Nazis. However, the Secretary of State for War thought otherwise and posted him to an anti-aircraft emplacement to the east of London.

Francis had joined the navy before he could be conscripted. His father's occasional tales of the trenches had persuaded him the last place any sane man should be during wartime was in the infantry. His brother Simon was in the infantry.

I constantly prayed I wouldn't lose another young man I loved to war. Frank, however, could damn well look after himself.

Francis was on a destroyer protecting shipping somewhere in the Atlantic, Simon was chasing the Germans out of North Africa. Frank was probably down the pub.

Without Frank to tell me not to, I cycled into Creethorpe every weekday. With the men away, there was plenty of work, and I was happy to do my bit for the war effort. Most of what I earned went into my running away fund.

I knew I would never use it. I'd become too scared of Frank to leave him long before 1943. Every day I wished I'd left him years ago, that Dad's money had been still waiting for me in my bank account the one time I'd attempted to run. I never tried again and doubted I now ever would. Frank had bound me so tightly for so long, I still felt the chain around my ankle despite the fact I was free of him for months at a time and leaving would have been easy.

I still daydreamed of another life. The one I might have had with Owen for the most part. But Frank had made me his prisoner, and freedom was never more than a soaring bird glimpsed through iron bars. He had cowered me and broken me, used my love for Francis and Simon to keep me here, kept me isolated from the rest of the world with no means of running away. And then there were the other things he did. The rages, the spite, the casual violence he hid from everybody.

The money I squirrelled away in an old coffee can hidden under a loose floorboard was simply my rebellion. My heart quickened, and I always looked over my shoulder whenever I prised the board up, even when Frank wasn't home. It was my secret. The only little sliver of excitement and hope I had in my life.

Until I met Tom Dupree.

1951

I met Merry on 23rd October 1951.

That day was a Tuesday and a fine one for the time of year. The Castle was empty, and I went out to lose myself amidst the whispering hiss of surf on stone.

I didn't expect to see anyone. Maybe a fishing boat or one of the grizzled locals who grazed their sheep on the wetlands. Few visitors came here even on a sunny summer's day, given the poor state of the local excuse for a road.

I walked far enough for the Castle to have long since disappeared behind the restless banks of shingle before stopping to stare out to sea, as I often did. Holding my hat atop my head I peered into the light. I had never quite lost the daydream that if I stared long and hard enough on a fine day, I might catch sight of Camelot's towers upon the hazy horizon.

Of course, I never did.

When I turned back to the shore, however, I noticed a man astride the sun-bleached remains of a tree trunk ahead of me.

A couple of thoughts bubbled up. The first, inevitably, was of Tom Dupree. This man had no sketch pad, was much older and looked nothing like him, but my breath caught in my throat all the same. I half expected him to look up and wink at me.

But the stranger didn't. He remained hunched forward, one leg on each side of the log as if it were an idling motorbike. Hands clasped together, he stared at the horizon with a furious intent.

Maybe he was looking for Camelot, too?

The second thought was that I had no recollection of a washed-up log on the beach before I'd turned towards the sea. It wasn't a small tree, either. The log must have been at least fifteen feet long, two feet across and bleached to the colour of old bone. Presumably, it was lumber lost from some storm-tossed ship years ago.

The man sitting on the log looked like he might have been washed off with it.

I toyed with turning around and heading home, but I had no desire to listlessly float about the Castle any sooner than necessary.

As I walked again, the man's head swivelled in my direction; he had a thick dark beard marbled with veins of grey. His hair hung to the shoulders of a faded leather brocade coat with a mandarin collar and silver buttons. He wore once-white linen trousers and sandals.

A smile cracked the beard. He sprung from his perch, "Hail, fair maiden! Come rest your weary bones upon my gentle steed!"

He indicated the white log with a flourish. When I didn't reply, he produced a handkerchief from his sleeve and wiped down a bit of the driftwood.

I'd intended to walk on by, but to my surprise, I stopped. I smiled. Somewhat foolishly, no doubt.

"She is a docile beast and won't bite..." he nodded towards the log again, turning the handkerchief over in his hands, "...at least these days..."

Sitting on a log next to a strange man who had clearly misplaced a marble or two was not the kind of thing a respectable married woman should do. But, once again, my legs came to a different conclusion to the rest of me and took up the offer.

I tucked my skirt under me and lowered my bottom with the dainty care of a debutant.

He sat astride the log again, eyes fixed on me. I blushed; his gaze was unusually intense. Still, women my age, particularly those who happened to be a vicar's daughter, shouldn't be blushing in public. I glanced at him, intending to return my attention to the beach immediately, but found myself speared by his regard. I noticed his eyes were the same colour as the sea rippling and swelling behind him.

"A lovely day..." I muttered, not knowing what else to say.

"For now," the man nodded, raising his eyes to the sky, "but it will rain soon. An hour, maybe two. You should be home by then."

"There's not a cloud in the sky."

"Trust me," he leaned in closer, "I know about these things..."

Taking him for a vagrant, I'd expected him to smell of sweat, alcohol and tobacco, like old Monroe, who occasionally washed up at the Castle offering to do odd jobs for beer money. Instead, he carried the earthy scent of a deep, dark wood.

"I've never seen you here before?" I ventured.

The man straightened his back, and looked first left, then right along the deserted shingle beach, "I've been to a lot of places. But I've never been here, as far as I recall."

He had an accent, faint and textured, but I couldn't place it.

"Where are you from?"

"Oh, a long, long way from here, beyond the kissing point."

I raised an eyebrow, I'd never heard of Kissing Point and assumed it must be much further up the coast, but he didn't elaborate.

"I'm Merry," he declared before adding, "That's my name, not my mood!"

"Beatrice, a pleasure to meet you."

He nodded vigorously enough to set his hair dancing and beamed at me.

"You're from this shore, Lady Beatrice?" he asked, still smiling beneath the tangles of his beard.

"Further along the beach," I waved a hand in the direction I'd come from.

"An empty place..."

"Not many people come here, no..."

"Have you had a happy life, Beatrice?"

His sea-grey eyes fixed upon me, making my gaze fall to the shells about my feet.

"I've had blessings and my sadness, like everybody else."

"More of one than the other, I do so sense."

I dropped my hands from my lap and rested them on the log. The wood was smooth and dry. When my eyes followed, I noticed the faintest of whorls etched into the driftwood, cut by tide and time, I assumed.

I was fidgeting and avoiding Merry's implication. Was my sadness so obvious? Or was it something the man said to every stranger he bumped into? The ones not sensible enough to walk straight past him anyway.

"Are you a fortune-teller, Mr Merry?" I replied, squirming under his attention. I was used to being ignored. Frank stopped noticing me years ago, after all.

"Many people have called me many things over my many years. I'm not sure any of them have quite nailed it yet."

"What would you call yourself then?" I glanced sideways, happier to meet his eye if we were talking about him.

"Me?" Merry scratched his beard, "Oh, I try to do some good, to right some wrongs. When I can. But for the most part I'm nought but flotsam. I float around, going wherever the tides and currents take me. No purpose other than those that find me might put me to."

He smiled, and the glint in his eye reminded me of the diamonds the lowering sun casts across the sea. Then he patted the driftwood log we perched on, "Just like my trusty steed..."

"I think you're someone who does not like to give a straight answer."

"That makes two of us."

I gave him my polite smile again, the one honed by years of careful practice in not giving offence.

"It is time for you to head for home," Merry pointed inland; a few clouds had risen over the marshes.

"They don't look very threatening."

"Trust me, Beatrice, a storm is coming."

I wasn't ready to return to the Castle, and the clouds didn't seem to herald rain, but I nodded all the same. I'd spent most of my adult life doing exactly what I was told. It had become ingrained deeply enough to apply as strongly to a man I'd never seen before as it did to my husband.

As I stood, Merry jumped up beside me. He was a tall man and broad with it. I wondered how old he was. It was difficult to tell beneath all the hair. Although streaks of grey cut his beard, the darkly tanned skin around his eyes bore only the faintest of creases.

"We shall meet again," he declared, "I like you, Beatrice."

His words did not sound like a proposition, yet I found myself blushing again, which was not something a woman of my years should be doing.

"I'd like that," I smiled, unsure if I did. He was peculiar but seemed harmless. Was I so starved of company I wanted to seek out a stranger on the beach? I thought of Tom again and decided it would be best if I didn't. Loneliness had become a comfortable enough companion over the years.

Merry beamed and bowed elaborately.

"Good day, Mr Merry," I said.

"Oh, is just Merry. Sometimes it is Father Merry, but only when the wind is blowing from the north," he licked his finger and held it up before him, "no, just Merry today."

"You are a priest?"

He shook his head, "The wind is currently from the southeast."

"Ah, of course..."

I managed a hesitant smile and backed away from him. Rather than pounce, Merry simply waved and went back to his log.

Returning his wave, I stared at the long coat he wore. I suspected it had once been a vivid blue but was now faded to little more than grey. Whorls cut the brocade much like the pattern upon the bleached skin of the driftwood.

Giving a final wave, I turned my back on Merry and hurried back down the beach towards the Castle, the crunch of shingle under my boots the only sound bar the sea.

The strangest certainty set in that if I looked back, Merry and his driftwood steed would have vanished. After a minute or so, I forced myself to glance over my shoulder to dispel the feeling.

Merry was as he'd been when I'd first seen him, astride the bleached log and staring intently out to sea.

When I turned back, I was smiling.

Foolish old woman!

I traipsed along the beach, aware the clouds inland thickened with every stride. An hour later, as I approached the Castle's door, the first fat raindrops started to fall. By the time I was inside, rain smeared the windows, blurring the world into a kaleidoscope of greys.

It poured for the rest of that day, the steady staccato of rain drumming over the deeper throb of the sea. I paced the Castle. I considered reading. I thought of Tom Dupree, I thought of my boys, I thought of my long-lost Owen and dreamed of Camelot.

Mostly, however, I thought of Merry without knowing why. The memory of his voice becoming whispered echoes above the hiss and kiss of the rain and sea beyond the confines of the Castle.

Have you had a happy life, Beatrice?

The following day the rain passed, leaving a smeary silvered sky in its wake. Later, I walked down the beach again, but I found neither Merry nor the driftwood log he'd sat upon.

1943

I met Tom Dupree much as I would later meet Merry.

I can't be sure, but I believe it was almost the same spot. Perhaps the very one. Although, in 1943, barbed wire, tank traps and landmines covered the beach, making me feel even more imprisoned than I had before the war.

I still walked every day, save when the weather was too foul. However, the enhancements made by the Ministry for War limited my excursions to the marshes and dunes fringing the shingle.

There was more company too. Aside from the ever-present gulls, Home Guard soldiers patrolled the beaches, bored-looking men with binoculars peered at the horizon from squat concrete lookouts, and gangs of workmen appeared from time to time to repair and re-enforce what the sea continually tried to rinse from its domain.

I spotted Tom a long way off. As I'd become accustomed to men in uniform intruding upon my solitude, I didn't think too much of it. The path between the marshes and the beach was narrow. To my left, dark water, reed banks and spongy untrustworthy ground discouraged any discreet detour; to the right, I risked barbed wire shredding me to pieces and landmines blowing whatever remained to smithereens.

I could have turned around. But as the servicemen I'd seen on the beach had never caused me more inconvenience than a smile, a nod and a "Good day," I decided that was silly.

The day was fine, the Castle was empty, and my legs wanted to walk.

So, I let them.

He sat on a fold-up canvas chair. At first, I thought he was scribbling in a notebook, but as I grew closer, I realised he was painting. A set of watercolours, brushes and a jar of murky water clustered on an equally fold-up little table next to him.

He was so intent on his painting he didn't notice me until my shadow fell across him. He looked up with a start, the expression on his face not unlike Francis on the rare occasions I'd caught him doing something he knew he shouldn't be (which had usually involved biscuits, jam, or both).

The memory came so hard that my throat tightened and stomach clenched. For a moment, all I could hear was the screaming gulls. When I got hold of myself again, I found my hand was over my mouth, and the man was on his feet. Concern replacing the look of childlike guilty surprise.

"Ma'am?" he asked, "Are you ok?"

I noticed several things.

Firstly, he was American. Since the war took Frank away, I'd become a regular at the *Regal Picture House* in Creethorpe, so I well knew what Americans sounded like. Secondly, he had a nice smile. Not just in terms of what it did to his face, but he also looked like he meant it. Twenty-three years of marriage had given me little of value beyond my children, but if it'd taught me anything, it was to know a false smile when I saw one.

The final thing I noticed was that when he'd jumped up, he'd knocked his box of paints and jar of water over, redecorating his rather swanky uniform.

"Damn it!" he said when he noticed too.

"Here," I offered him my hanky.

His smile returned, and he shook his head, "I wouldn't want to make as much of a mess of it as I have with my pants."

He found his own handkerchief and started to rub himself down. Which was probably a good time to leave. Instead, I said, "I'm so sorry. I didn't mean to startle you."

Another shake of the head, another grin, this one more boyish than rueful, "Nothing to apologise for, Ma'am; I've always been as clumsy as they come. It's a wonder they let me fly a plane."

"These are desperate times..."

He laughed; he'd a nice laugh too. It made me want to smile. I tried not to. Though smiling probably wasn't as unseemly as watching a man rub his damp crotch with a hanky.

"They sure are, Ma'am. Still, I haven't made as much of a mess of any of Uncle Sam's fine flying machines as I have of these pants," he stopped rubbing, pulled a face and straightened up, "this is going to be my first black mark when it comes to air force property."

"I wouldn't call it a *black* mark," I said, attention flicking between his eyes and his discoloured trousers, "more purplish, green and yellow. With a few splashes of blue."

That won me a laugh *and* a grin.

The paint had indeed made a colourful mess of his uniform, though it still looked much better than anything Frank had ever come up with.

"It's only watercolour... it'll wash out easy enough. No permanent damage, Ma'am."

"It's lucky you don't paint in oils," thinking of Frank made me want to scurry back to the Castle. Regardless of the condition of his trousers, talking to a strange man would earn me a taste of Frank's belt if he got wind of it.

But Frank was away, and there was no one here to tell tales but the gulls, so I added, "...and my name's Beatrice, not Ma'am..."

19

Another smile. They came easily to him, "Tom," he stuck out a hand before realising he still had a paint-stained hanky in it. Once he'd swapped it and wiped his fingers on an as yet unsoiled part of his trousers, he offered it to me again.

It seemed odd to shake a man's hand, but I was prepared to overlook the peculiarity as he was American. He gave my hand only the gentlest squeeze, but it was enough to set butterflies dancing.

How strange.

"Nice to meet you, Tom," my eye held his before flitting away with the butterflies as our fingers parted.

Was I *flirting?*

I didn't know. I'd never done it, though I'd read about it in some of the racier romances I borrowed from the Creethorpe Municipal Library.

"And you, Beatrice..." he smiled again, but no more words followed.

I was being silly. He was much younger than me. I was just some frumpy woman of a type the USAF had no doubt warned him to be pleasant too and do nothing to startle for fear of upsetting the locals.

I also had a husband who had told me on numerous occasions he would kill me if I slept with another man.

In Frank's book, there was probably little distinction between flirting and fucking, to use the vulgar word he was so fond of banding about whenever his blood was up.

"Well, best I don't keep you..." I noticed the notebook on the ground and crouched to retrieve it without thinking... and met his eyes again as he descended in time with me. His hand found the book, which was A4 and leather bound, before mine.

"No need," he pressed the book to his chest. We remained on our hunches for somewhat longer than the situation probably required.

He had rather lovely eyes too.

I was intent on being silly, it seemed.

"I hope you haven't been sketching our impressive coastal defences for the Nazis?" I asked.

Tom grinned. He really did do a lot of that. He had good teeth as well. Perhaps he liked to show them off.

Slowly he straightened up and held out a hand.

I took it and let him pull me gently to my feet.

"I have heard old Adolf does like all his spies to work with watercolours, due to their versatility, you understand, but no... I was more interested in the sea, clouds, and light."

"Show me," I said, still not doing much in the way of thinking. I held out a hand.

When I think back on meeting Tom, I don't know where my boldness came from. Perhaps I was sick enough of being scared and lonely not to care anymore. As I met so few people, it was difficult to know if I was behaving differently. All I knew was that I was out of Frank's long shadow for a while, and there was something about this Tom fellow I liked.

He fidgeted with the book and looked at me like I was a teacher demanding to see homework he hadn't finished, "They're only rough preliminaries; I'm just trying to capture the colours and the light. I'm from Kansas, I haven't seen much of the sea, I-"

When he didn't hand over the book, I waggled my fingers and raised an eyebrow.

"They're not very good."

"I'll be the judge of that," when the book still wasn't forthcoming, I said, "my husband is an artist, so I know a thing or two about painting."

"Really? Is he... like... famous?"

"No," I laughed, "he's terrible."

"Gee, you don't hold back, do you?" he looked between me and the sketchbook.

I added a wiggle to my waggling fingers.

He passed me the book, his grin becoming decidedly uncertain.

The sketch he'd been painting hadn't dried when the book shut, so I didn't take it as the best example of his work. I carefully peeled back the pages to look at his earlier paintings. They were of the sea, sky and shoreline. Without the barbed wire and tank traps, I was glad to see.

"What do you think...?"

I raised my eyes from the sketchbook, looked at him for a heartbeat, noted the way the wind pleasingly teased a lick of straw-coloured hair across his forehead, then flicked over to the next watercolour and returned my attention to his painting without comment.

When I'd, impudently, asked to see Tom's sketchbook, I assumed no one could produce anything as ghastly as the canvases Frank churned out in his draughty studio.

And I was right.

Tom's work was rather lovely. Simple washes of colour, blending and bleeding into each other, depicting the shingle beach, restless sea and a cloud-strewn sky that dappled sunlight across the world below with subtle shifts of tone and hue. They had a soft, dream-like quality coupled with a warmth the insistent wind stripped from the reality.

My eyes found his again.

"They are beautiful."

I carried on staring at him and told myself I *was* only talking about the watercolours.

He laughed awkwardly. The American military must have given their men stationed here briefings to familiarise themselves with local customs. No doubt he'd been warned several times about our chronic politeness and how far most British people would bend to avoid causing offence.

"If I was just being polite, I would say they're *nice* or maybe, *oh, this is good*, I handed the sketchbook back to him, "I wouldn't say *beautiful*. I think you have some talent, Tom."

And as I lived with a man who had none whatsoever, I knew what I was talking about.

"Thank you..." he smiled. It was hard to tell, but I think he blushed a little. I had a terrible urge to give him a hug.

"Do you paint here often?"

"When I can get away. I've always thought the sea magical..." he shrugged and let his gaze flit away to the shoreline "...growing up in Kansas, I guess."

"I walk here most days. Bring some of your finished work next time; I'd love to see it."

"Well, it's not really-"

"Tom..." I leaned in slightly, "...you're American. You're supposed to be brash and over-confident. Please don't shatter all my illusions."

"Sorry, Ma'am," he touched a finger to his forehead, "I'll try to do better."

"Splendid!"

With that, I bid him a good day and wheeled away towards the Castle without a backward glance.

I managed a dozen yards before my hands started shaking uncontrollably, I had to grip one with the other. My legs wobbled and no longer appeared entirely attached to the rest of my body, while my stomach wanted to reacquaint me with my breakfast.

For a few strides I was in very real danger of keeling headfirst onto the shingle, grass and sand of the rudimentary path skirting the marsh's edge.

I sucked in salty air and concentrated on putting one foot in front of the other.

What am I doing? What would Frank say? What am I doing? What would Frank do? What am I doing? What would Frank say? What am I doing? What would Frank do?

The words in my head mixed with the gull shrieks into a single mocking carousel.

Frank would kill me. Literally, he would kill me. He'd once taken the belt to me after a man in Creethorpe walked past us and said good morning to me in a manner he took exception to.

Frank might be in London, but if I started flirting with men, he would find out, somehow, and then... and then... and then...

I stopped, half turned towards the sea and watched the wind ruffle its grey pelt.

If I looked back, I'd probably still be able to see Tom.

Would he be watching me?

No, of course, he wouldn't. Nor did I want him to be.

This was foolish. Stupid. I wasn't a girl anymore; I wasn't a young woman with a soft head filled with daft romantic notions. That Beatrice - Beatrice Clay - was as long dead as poor Owen. I was Beatrice Harryman now, for better and, for the most part, very much worse.

I wasn't going to risk my life to flirt with some young man who was probably already laughing to himself about the silly woman he'd met on the beach.

Calming myself with the sea's restlessness, I carried on towards the Castle, back to the empty, lonely life I shared with a man who teetered on the brink of lunacy and could only express a feeling with the snap of a leather belt on my flesh.

I decided I would not walk this way for a while.

And tried not to listen to myself whispering back that the life I didn't want to risk in return for a kind man's smile wasn't worth one damn thing.

.

1930

According to the crackling voice of the BBC man on our unreliable radio, unemployment had reached two million. That was 7th August 1930. So much for the land fit for heroes Mr Lloyd-George promised after the war.

I often felt removed from the rest of humanity on our lonely stretch of coast. Disconnected. We had the radio and newspaper, but the world they described beyond the shingle banks, grey water and wind-tossed reed beds surrounding the Castle was ever more unfamiliar and alien to me.

1930 was my tenth year in Grey Gull.

Ten years that brought me the joy of Francis and Simon. Ten years that brought me the despair of Frank's tempers, whims and torments. And the anguish of Tilly.

But it wasn't just the world beyond the sea and marshes that were becoming increasingly alien.

Even when Frank was at home, our paths crossed little. The kitchen table and my bedroom were the only places our lives regularly intersected. In the kitchen, he could be whatever kind of man his moods made of him that day, from sullenly quiet to jovially verbose and everything in between. Sometimes, all within the space of a single meal. In my bedroom, however, he was only one kind of man.

Most days, and many nights, he never ventured from his studio. Which was the grand term he used for the wooden shack where he did his painting. It was a dilapidated wreck of weathered planks and broken, mismatched tiles when we'd arrived in 1920, and, despite Frank's occasional efforts, it was still much the same in 1930.

Each winter, I expected the storms to blow it to matchsticks. Each spring, it remained; sagging, discoloured, peeling paint, rusting hinges. Forlorn and yet defiant, refusing to accept the inevitability of its own imminent demise.

Considering the relevant importance to him, I sometimes wondered why he hadn't put me in the outhouse and used my bedroom as a studio.

He'd stopped showing me his work years ago. As I was too afraid to say anything that might provoke one of his rages, I'd never given him an honest opinion. Even Frank, however, was sensitive enough to read through my pinched smiles, shallow nods and thin praise to guess what I actually thought of the ghastly things.

They never changed. In the years of churning them out, you'd have thought he might have come up with something different at least once or twice. But no, they were always the same twisted mess of dark, angry, discordant colours.

Sometimes suggestions of a gaping maw, disproportioned limb, bleeding eye or deformed figure whispered from the chaos, but, back then, I could mostly make out nothing but splatters and slashes hacked across the canvas.

They always made me think of pain and suffering, loss and misery. Like Frank was trying to visualise the eternal agonies of damnation.

I really should have paid more attention to them...

Still, he was nothing if not persistent. Despite the years of rejection, constant fruitless trips to galleries and dealers, unanswered letters and returned submissions, he continued to lock himself in the studio for hour after hour, day after day, week after week of relentless assaults on canvas.

Much to my surprise, in the latter years of the 1920s Frank did start to sell a few pieces. Just occasionally he found someone prepared to give him actual real money for one of his creations. Quite who would want such hideous things on their wall, I couldn't imagine. People with acute mental problems were the best I could come up with.

Still, it made Frank happy, and that was something. In fact, I don't think I ever saw him happier, even after the children he wanted so badly were born. He wasn't continually morose, but there never seemed to be any joy behind his laughter. His humour never had any depth, any roots, anything at all but barren soil hiding hard rock.

It took me a long time to realise he was the kind of man who only ever laughed at his own jokes.

But when he sold a painting, there was actually *something* behind the smile. It touched him in a way nothing else did and if not dispelling whatever demons resided inside him, it made them retreat far enough for something else to reside in his soul. For a little while, at least.

Then the economy, which stagnated throughout the twenties, sank into the Great Depression.

In a lot of ways, it affected us less than most people.

Frank had inherited money along with Grey Gull. I don't know how much and never asked; money was one of the many things Frank told me I *didn't need to get myself lathered about.* And, of course, he'd stolen all my money, somehow, from my bank account as well.

I didn't know where he kept it, or what he did with it. But there was always enough. We lived a modest life, but we never had to scrimp or go without. Every week Frank gave me housekeeping money. If I ever needed more, for the boys or the house or for special, he never once complained, queried, or refused. He just put it in my hand.

Even the Devil has a good side, I suppose.

Selling his art was never about money; it was about... validation, acceptance, recognition, a purpose to his existence on God's Earth... I don't know. Frank seldom talked about what went on behind his intense, burnt-hazel eyes.

But for most people, money *was* a problem. Even the rich people, many of whom had lost a lot when the stock market crashed. And rich people tended to be the ones who bought paintings. Especially the bad ones.

By the summer of 1930, when unemployment reached two million, Frank's sales and commissions slumped back to the big fat nothing they had always been.

And his spirits plunged lower than his sales. After tasting the sweet nectar of "success," the return to the more familiar territory of abject failure was far harder for him to bear.

Curiously, he bothered me less.

His visits to my bedroom became more infrequent. He barely said a word to me and only a begrudging one here and there to the boys. His mood was generally sullen and becalmed.

Instead, he spent more time in the studio, as if he thought disfiguring enough canvas with enough paint would eventually make the fools of the art world see beyond the petty inconvenience of a global recession.

By the time summer faded and the autumn gales started lashing the shingle into new troughs and peaks, the recession, which had been nibbling around the edges of the Creethorpe for years, became more noticeable. Shops with white-painted windows spread along the High Street, businesses closed, unemployment, which had been high since we'd moved into Grey Gull ten years earlier, became much worse. Desperate men walked door to door looking for work. It made you wonder where it would all end.

It didn't stop Frank from trying to sell his paintings, though.

That autumn he got Harvey Liston – whose battered old Great War truck was the nearest thing to a taxi in those days - to take him and a selection of new canvases to the train station at Creethorpe.

I waved him off with Francis and Simon. He grinned back and leaned out the window as the truck trundled off to blow kisses at us. He looked happy, full to the brim with hope and excitement as he always was when he went to London.

His black moods were getting blacker, and his blackest moods always followed him home as he returned with all his canvases under his arms, seemingly weighing twice as much as when he'd left.

I watched the truck cough clouds of blue-grey smoke, as it trundled away from the Castle. A strange mix of relief and dread washed over me.

The relief of being alone with the boys and the dread of knowing Frank would inevitably return.

And when he came back, I knew things would be bad.

Which they were, but just not in the way I expected.

1943

I didn't leave the Castle for the next few days. I told myself this was due only to the incessant banks of rain washing in from the sea on a malicious wind. I also told myself I was not relieved or disappointed there was no opportunity to see Tom again, despite the fact I felt both simultaneously.

For some absurd reason, I half expected Tom to come knocking on Grey Gull's front door with a stack of watercolour canvases wedged under his armpit for my consideration.

He didn't.

More relief. More disappointment.

On Sunday, the weather improved. Or at least dried sufficiently to allow me to navigate the muddy track through the marshes to church in Creethorpe without getting soaked to the skin.

When I spied a couple of American airmen parked outside the Post Office my heart actually raced. They were too engrossed in pouring over a map to look at me, but neither was Tom. My heart rate subsided.

This was ridiculous!

I took my usual pew at the back of *St Luke's*, listened attentively to Reverend Vaughn's sermon, sang the hymns heartily and tried not to think too much about why I was behaving like a lovestruck schoolgirl.

Afterwards, I chatted with the Reverend Vaughn. He was one of the few men Frank tolerated me talking to without complaint or recourse to the back of his hand. Even he didn't think it likely I would jump into bed with an octogenarian vicar.

We tutted about the weather, discussed the summer fete, Mrs Vaughn's delicate feet, shared a hope the awful war would soon be over and the wicked Mr Hitler would get his just desserts. I said nothing about having improper thoughts about a man I'd met on the beach.

You should, of course, be able to talk to your vicar about anything, but as I had known the Reverend for many years and had never once mentioned any of the things Frank did to me, I dismissed that as a very minor sin.

Later, as I walked back across the marshes, the throbbing drone of aircraft overhead interrupted the birdsong. The clouds, a uniform gauze from horizon to horizon, hung low, ensuring nothing was visible, but they were definitely American bombers. The British and Germans only flew at night.

Wave after wave of them. Young men going to a foreign land to kill and destroy. Young men going to a foreign land to die. I prayed for them to all return safely and then another that their bombs killed no one. Save the wicked Mr Hitler, of course.

I started walking again, unable to stop wondering if Tom was in one of those planes. It was another reason, amongst all the other excellent ones, not to see him again.

Why gain a friend only to have him ripped away by this war?

I didn't think too deeply about exactly what I meant by *friend*.

Back in the Castle, I kept busy. Things were better with Frank gone. Peace lived in the silence. Even the sea's constant whispers brought some comfort; if you listened hard, you could almost fool yourselves there were voices caught within it, the voices of those you'd loved, the voices of those you'd lost. Sometimes the voices scared me. Sometimes, I tried to work out what they were saying. Sometimes, I heard things I didn't want to hear.

Mostly, I told myself to stop being so bloody stupid.

Enough voices existed inside Grey Gull already. I didn't need to invent more...

Monday broke bright and warm. Dazzling, deep endless blue replaced the sullen grey beyond the Castle's small windows. It was like waking to find oneself transported to another place entirely. It's strange how sunshine, or, rather, the absence of clouds, can suddenly make the world seem full of possibilities,

The sun always shines, after all. It is just that sometimes we cannot see it.

My mood lifted somewhat and I found myself whistling as I did the morning chores.

Later, I went for my walk. The fact I chose the same time and same direction as the day I met Tom was purely coincidental.

My years in the Castle with Frank had taught me you can believe whatever you want if you put enough of your mind behind it.

And if I took a little more care over my appearance, putting on my better coat, less worn shoes, most flattering hat, and a faint dusting of makeup... well, that had nothing to do with anything either, thank you very much.

It was a lovely day. My spirits were high. That was all.

I ignored the slow queasy roll my stomach gave as I neared the spot I'd met Tom. Equally, I ignored how it dropped when it became apparent no one was there.

"Silly old woman..." I said, watching the gulls scavenging along the wrack line, pecking at clumps of seaweed and whatever else the tide had washed ashore.

I walked a little further before turning and retracing my route. I could circle back through the wetlands but preferred the beach, even with the wire and tank traps added in recent years.

There was still no sign of Tom. No doubt, most days, he had more important things to do than paint or meet women old enough to be his mother.

Almost old enough, I corrected, after a little thought.

Although it sometimes felt otherwise, I wasn't dead yet.

I recalled the sound of the bombers over the marsh the previous day and looked up. There was nothing to see but a blue sky burning to silver-white around the sun.

I'd listened for them returning late into the night. A few distant thrums disturbed the silence, but they were so faint I couldn't be sure. I hoped most of those boys got back. The Nazis couldn't have shot them all down, but it chilled me to think the handsome young man with the quietly beautiful paintings might now be nought bar charred meat entombed within the twisted metal carcass of his warplane.

By the time I returned to the Castle, my mood had lowered and darkened. I did no more whistling that evening.

My days stretched out, one after the other, each much the same. I took my ration book to Creethorpe twice a week for shopping. The *Regal Picture House* showed an afternoon matinee on Wednesdays. Without Frank around to disapprove, I regularly went, sitting in the same seat next to the aisle, three rows from the back. That week I saw *The Dancing Masters* with Laurel and Hardy, which made me laugh.

I heard nothing from Frank and didn't expect to until he came home, or I got a telegram to say the Nazis had bombed his anti-aircraft emplacement in east London.

By Friday, I stopped expecting to see Tom again. He'd probably found some other bit of coast to paint. Where he was less likely to be bothered by silly women with even sillier ideas they would never do anything about.

Of course, life has a habit of teasing and toying with our expectations.

A painter's sky blessed the day. Clouds from pure white through every variation of grey to the occasional bubble and twist of bible black adorned the sky around slashes of pale blue. Sunbeams sheared through like searchlights over the sea to the south.

It was what I thought of as a Possibility Sky.

Kitted out with my raincoat, scarf, sturdiest umbrella and crossed fingers, I left Grey Gull's shadows and memories to walk the familiar path along the beach.

The wind was fitful but not unkind, tugging at the licks of hair escaping my scarf. It was warm whenever the sun escaped its shackles but cool the moment it returned behind cloudy bars. I was continually buttoning and unbuttoning my coat. Over the sea, the balance between blue, white, grey and black forever shifted.

It was probably wise not to venture too far. If the black won out, it might turn nasty. Bad-tempered squalls out here often arrived quickly, full of spite for anyone it could vent fury upon. Regardless, my feet insisted on walking.

Perhaps they knew more than I did.

Every other day I'd walked this way since meeting Tom, butterflies had put my nerves on edge and my stomach hanging over it. Today, however, a sense of calm descended as soon as I saw him. Which I found both curious and peculiar.

He smiled as I approached, "Hello again."

I smiled back. I don't *think* I blushed.

"Not painting?"

He shook his head, "Thought I'd just..." his eyes drifted from the sea back to me, "...take in the view."

"It's quite some sky..."

"Yes, it is," he agreed, still looking at me.

He had a bolder regard this time.

"How are your trousers?"

"It was touch and go for a while, but they're making a good recovery. I'm told they should be fit for service again soon."

"I'm very glad to hear it."

He ran a hand through his hair. It was greased back, but the breeze took a liking to it all the same.

"Are you going anywhere?" he asked.

"Just... a stroll..."

"I don't get to stretch my legs as much as I'd like. May I... stroll with you?"

My absent nerves and sleeping butterflies decided this was an opportune moment to take note of the latest happenings.

"I'd like that," I said, regardless of their alarmed clamouring.

We walked.

Later, we did other things.

It was one of the better days of my life.

1915

Owen's parents never really approved of me; they thought me rather *hoity-toity*, as I overheard Grace tell Mrs Popkin at the back of *Larke's Greengrocer's* once.

I was a vicar's daughter and had far too many airs and graces for Mr and Mrs James' liking. In their opinion, I thought myself too good to be a farmer's wife and would whisk Owen off to the city as soon as we were married, where all kinds of foolish modern thinking would corrupt him.

However, they approved of him going to war even less than they approved of me, and so, in that respect, at least, we were united. It was possibly the only thing we ever agreed on.

Of course, they were too polite to say anything to my face. The fact it was evident to anyone that Owen and I were blissfully happy together also staunched their misgivings about me and my modern ways.

I saw them from time to time during Owen's training, dropping in for somewhat painful afternoons of tea and stilted conversation with Grace while Ken busied himself on the farm, "More work to do with Owen away soldiering," he'd say, pointedly, whenever he breezed through the kitchen without stopping.

Owen had no desire to take on the farm, but as neither Grace nor Ken could blame their only son for anything, they blamed me instead. As the months passed, I visited them less, which I think was a relief to all of us. Particularly after I enrolled in secretarial college, which they took as more compelling evidence of my hoity-toitiness.

Owen hadn't been best pleased either.

"Why do you want to take yourself off to Birmingham?" he demanded on one of his visits home.

"Why do you want to take yourself off to France?"

"That's not the same thing!"

"No. I doubt anyone in Birmingham will be trying to kill me."

Owen hadn't replied. Christmas had come and gone, and the war still ground on. The casualty figures were horrific; the regular army had been all but destroyed at Ypres. More men were desperately needed to take their place, and Owen would be sailing across the channel soon.

He had a proper uniform now, and his training was all but finished. He didn't talk about it a lot, but I took it to mean he knew how to kill people. He didn't look much of a killer to me. Even in his proper uniform, he had the same soft eyes and infectious smile. If anything, his hands felt softer. They'd lost the callouses he'd always had from working on his Dad's farm since he'd been old enough to carry a bucket.

"I can't just sit here and wait. I need to do something or I'll worry myself half to death."

"You don't have to worry; no German's going to stop me coming home to you."

He'd said it with such conviction. He was scared, I knew, but he didn't doubt he'd be coming home eventually. I wished I shared his faith. But the more I read Dad's newspaper, the more the worry swelled in me. So many young men were dying over there. And even more came back horribly wounded. Why would my Owen be any luckier than those poor souls? As much as I loved him and prayed for him, I didn't think either would offer enough armour to protect him from the bullets and shells of the Western Front.

We were sitting at a window table in the *Mimosa Tea Rooms*, which were definitely *hoity-toity*, garnering more approving looks and smiles than Owen's parents ever managed. Several men had come over to shake Owen's hand and wish him luck. He'd blushed each time and mumbled a thank you. Women clucked over us, gushing that we made such a bonny young couple.

"Isn't there enough to do at church?" he ventured.

"Dad doesn't like idle hands," I admitted, "but being in a new place, learning something different…"

"Are… are you going to wait for me?" Owen's eyes fell to the barely touched tea and slice of marble cake.

"Of course!" I said, loudly enough to solicit a few glances, "I just cannot hang around with nothing to keep me from thinking of you over there and… what might happen. I'll lose my mind." Owen didn't look convinced, so I reached over and rested my hand on his, "I love you…"

"Bea…" he said, "…let's get married."

"We are getting married. You already proposed, remember?" I raised my left hand and wiggled my fingers.

"No. Let's get married *now*. I don't want to wait any longer."

"Owen, we agreed to wait. We don't have the money yet, for the wedding, for a house and-"

"I'm going to Dover next Friday, then on to France and the front," he looked at me with hard earnest eyes I hardly recognised, "I'm going to war. I don't want to wait anymore."

That was 2nd March 1915. That was the day I knew Owen was going to die, and that was the day I broke his heart for the first time.

1930

Frank was gone for a week.

I didn't worry about what he was up to or what might have happened to him. I just worried about him coming home.

Francis and Simon kept me busy and happy, rocketing and bouncing around the Castle whenever the weather was too bad to keep them indoors. Francis loved the sea, the beach, the surrounding marshes and fields. He would spend every minute outdoors if he could, while Simon was at the age where his older brother was a God to follow wherever he went.

It was when they were at school or during the long hours of the night, when the only sound was the hiss and rumble of the waves on the shingle, that the dread swelled.

What would Frank do this time?

His belt? A cigarette end? The back of his hand? Some sudden act I wouldn't see till I was on the floor, laid out at his feet. Or something slow, something he'd take his time over.

Whatever it was, it would be *something*.

It was *always* something when he returned weighed down by disappointment and infuriated by failure, ready to take it out on his wife because he couldn't take it out on the world.

That's what I thought. Before I knew better. By the time I did, it was far too late for this life.

By the Saturday, I'd started to wonder (and perhaps hope) whether he wouldn't come home at all. He'd never previously been away for this long. His trips to London usually lasted a couple of days. Even Frank's thick skin could handle only so much rejection in one go.

Perhaps he'd thrown himself under a train after his latest masterpieces had received the same reaction as all the other ones stacked in half-forgotten piles. Maybe the police would come, Constable Perkins on his bicycle most likely, to regretfully inform me they'd been a terrible accident.

I knew I wouldn't cry.

Outside, the wind lashed clouds of spray from the peaks of the white-tailed waves racing across the darkening sea. Francis was at the window, nose to the glass, watching. If he couldn't go out, he'd sit and stare at the world.

I had no idea what he saw that fascinated him so much, but he could be there for hours.

Simon sprawled on the floor at his brother's feet, pushing crayons around a drawing book. The multi-coloured snail trails swirling across the pages were already far better than anything his father had ever produced.

I was trying to read. Dinner was finished, washed up and put away. Outside, the light was fading to grey. When Francis could no longer make out his restless friend beyond the stone and shingle beach, I'd shoo the boys off to bed.

Contentment settled in Frank's absence. Just me and the children. I only felt lonely when my husband darkened the Castle's door.

What if he doesn't come back this time? What if...

The thought kept interrupting the words on the page. Each hour passing without Frank's return swelled my dark hope. It also made me ask, yet again, why I was still here. However, I knew the answer whenever my eyes bounced from book to window. The boys were happy. Frank ignored them as often as not, but he never hurt them.

Perhaps that was his nature. Maybe something in me raised his ire, provoked his anger, stoked his demons. The boys never did. Or perhaps he just knew that was the one thing that would finally make me flee the Castle. If he laid a finger on them, if he ever treated them the way he treated me, then I would go. He had damaged me in ways I did not fully understand, but if he ever did the same to my children, I would take them and go.

I didn't know where and how, but anything would be better than seeing him crush them as he had crushed me.

That's what I told myself, anyway.

I didn't know if that was another lie. I never got to find out.

I didn't discover the things Frank did to our children until it was far too late to protect them.

The sky thickened towards night, the cloud too heavy for any sunset. I was about to commence the rigmarole of chasing the boys off to clean their teeth when Francis' head snapped around.

"A car!" he shouted. Simon's head shot up too. He liked cars almost as much as his brother liked the sea.

I heard nothing.

The boys both barrelled out of the kitchen - we did most of our living in the Castle during the colder months between the enormous black iron range and the fireplace.

I hurried after them, the thrum of an engine reverberating down the narrow hallway. Sharp electric light rushed inside as soon as Francis tugged open the front door.

I didn't know much about motor vehicles, but it wasn't coughing and spluttering like Harvey's old truck. And Harvey was the only person likely to drive up to Grey Gull this late (after Frank offered him enough to vacate his stool in the *Horse & Hounds* for a lift home anyway).

What if Constable Perkins now had a car?

I walked faster.

The bite of exhaust fumes tainted the familiar smell of the sea, and excited noises young boys reserve for things of particular wonder filled the air.

On the patchy mix of grass, shingle and sand that made up the Castle's "drive" sat a motor car. I didn't know what kind; other than it was a very fancy one. Long, sleek, dripping with chrome. Its headlamps pushed back the coming night to illuminate the Castle's stained and pitted wall.

"Daddy!" Simon bellowed, dancing from one foot to the other as Frank, rather improbably, jumped out of the car. Almost as improbably, Frank scooped Simon up and whirled him around, much to his son's screeching delight.

I stood on the doorstep, unsure what to make of it. I made even less of it when the headlamps died, the driver's side door swung open, and a woman, every bit as fancy as the car, climbed out. With a slightly bemused look, she adjusted the white fur stole draped over her shoulders whilst ensuring the wind didn't whip off her cloche hat.

On seeing the woman, Frank dropped Simon (he didn't *quite* throw him to one side), scurried around to close the car door and usher her towards the house.

Francis and Simon were far more interested in the car than the woman, who Frank presented to me with the air of a smug cat dropping a dead bird at my feet.

"Izzy, this is my wife, Beatrice," Frank said, beaming between us.

The woman, Izzy, clutched my arms and air kissed both my cheeks. She smelt of something... well, *fancy*. Fancy and expensive. It wasn't strong enough to be pungent, nor discreet enough that you had any chance of missing it. Whenever this woman walked through a room, you'd know about it for a good few minutes afterwards.

"Darling!" she said in my ear, pulling back. I'd have guessed she was somewhere betwixt thirty and forty, but there was so much powder and make up it was hard to be sure in the colourless autumn twilight.

"Hello," I said. I thought about asking who she was but decided it didn't matter, "Please, come in..."

"What a darling place..." Izzy floated by. Frank brushed past me in her wake, eyes and smile wide.

It took a couple of goes to get Francis and Simon to stop gawping at the fancy woman's fancy car.

"It's an Austin 20!" Francis said, which didn't really mean much to me.

"That's nice," I muttered, hurrying them along the hallway.

"Get the kettle on, eh, Sweetness? We're parched. It's a long drive from London," Frank said as I reached the kitchen. Izzy sat at the big table, peeling off white leather gloves. She looked around as if she'd just awoken in a world populated by elves and unicorns.

"These fine young men must be your sons?" Izzy purred.

"Yes," Frank said, adding, after only the briefest of pauses, "Francis and Simon. Come and say hello to Mrs St. Clair."

He arranged the boys to his liking in front of Izzy, and they took her hand like proper little gentlemen.

"What delightful children," Izzy bestowed a smile on each of them, then produced a packet of cigarettes from her bag.

"Your car is a beauty," Francis announced.

"It is!" Izzy agreed, letting Frank light her cigarette, "Would you like to go for a ride in it tomorrow?"

"Yes!" the boys shouted in unison. Simon looked like he might combust.

"Then you'd better get off to bed now," I said.

"Aw, mum," Simon protested.

"Do as your mother says," Frank jumped in, sitting next to Izzy. Which made my internal eyebrow twitch. He was normally so happy to leave the boys' care to me, whole days could go by without him even acknowledging their existence.

After some cajoling and hand clapping, I hurried them off to prepare for bed. I dangled the additional bribe of a bedtime story to get them on their way, even though that was thin fayre compared to the prospect of trundling around in Izzy's car or getting a toot on her horn.

I wondered if Frank had already tooted her horn.

However, Izzy St Clair, whoever she might be, was clearly a woman of money and style. Any attraction to an overweight artist who struggled to tuck his own shirt in seemed far-fetched.

Still, once I'd settled the boys and dispatched their story, I returned with no little curiosity and quite some hesitation.

The Castle did not receive guests. No one had ever stayed in the ten years we'd lived here. I had no family, and nor did Frank. I had no friends and, as far as I knew, neither did my husband beyond the old goats he occasionally got drunk with down at the *Horse & Hounds.*

"Are the darlings asleep?" Izzy asked when I got back to the kitchen. Frank sat by her side, a fug of smoke around their heads.

"Soon, hopefully. They're rather excitable," I found a towel to wipe my hands despite them not being either wet or dirty, "they're not used to... cars."

"Oh, it is a thing, isn't it? I'm quite smitten, couldn't be without one now. Such independence! Such freedom! Everyone should have one, really, they should!"

I smiled thinly and kept turning the towel over in my hands. I hadn't thought much about my appearance in years, but Izzy's immaculate, fashionable attire made me feel as dowdy as a washerwoman.

"Any chance of a bit of supper, Sweetness?" Frank asked, grinding out his cigarette in the ashtray between him and Izzy.

When your husband unexpectedly brought another woman home with him, particularly a slim, attractive, ridiculously stylish and evidently wealthy one, at what point did it become polite to ask who the hell she was?

For most wives, I expect that point had whizzed past some time ago. But I wasn't most wives. And Frank certainly wasn't most husbands.

So, instead, I served them the remainder of the pie I'd cooked for the boys, accompanied by some mashed potato and peas I'd kept back for tomorrow's dinner. I listened to low voices interrupted by occasional laughter behind me as I worked, without learning much about Izzy St Clair or why she was sitting at the kitchen table with my husband.

"How delightfully... rustic..." Izzy said, leaning over the plate after I put it in front of her.

"Gravy?" I asked.

"Of course, one simply must have a little sauce with one's meat, don't you think, Frankie?"

Frankie chuckled so hard I thought he might choke. I fetched them *sauce* from the pan warming on the stove.

"Is there wine?" Izzy asked, fork poised above my lumpy mash.

"Wine...?"

"I'm afraid not," Frank answered, "We live a simple life out here."

"Yes..." Izzy's eyes flicked around the room before settling back on me, "...I suppose you do."

"It helps with my creations," Frank explained as my cheeks reddened.

"Of course, the artist!" Lacking wine, Izzy saluted him with a fork full of mash.

Frank's own cheeks appeared to redden a little. Had I ever seen him blush? Embarrassment was not something that came readily to my husband.

After emptying her fork and pulling only the slightest of faces, Izzy's attention returned to me, "Please sit down, darling," she said, nodding at one of the free chairs around the battered old kitchen table, "there's no need to wait on me."

For a few minutes, I watched them pick over their food. Frank had never been an enthusiastic eater; at times, the whole business seemed a burden to him. Quite how he'd put on so much weight in our ten years together remained a mystery to me. Izzy ate enough to be polite before sliding her plate away and lighting another cigarette.

"You are very lucky," she said after blowing smoke towards the ceiling.

"I am?"

"To have so talented a husband," her eyes found Frank, a hint of a smile twisting the corner of her dark red lips, "such a wonderful man. I am rather jealous."

I assumed there was a joke there but was blown if I could see it.

"Oh, Bea isn't really interested in my work," Frank said.

"But why should she be?" Izzy laughed, "She is the mother of your children. That is where her interest should and does lie. It's for others to be interested in your art."

"You... like Frank's paintings?" I asked as evenly as I could.

"Darling, they're exceptional..."

"Izzy has a gallery in London. She wants to hold an exhibition of my work!" Frank grinned. I seldom saw much of my husband in our sons, but the bright, cheery expression of wonder made him look like Simon.

What my own expression of astonishment looked like however, I can only imagine.

1943

I politely declined when Tom asked, with a nervous casualness, whether I would care to go for a drink with him.

"Because you're a respectable married lady?"

"No," I shook my head, "because you're American. I would never be able to walk down Creethorpe High Street again for the shame of it."

"Oh," he looked puzzled.

I managed to keep a straight face for a few seconds, then burst out laughing. Which, I think, surprised both of us.

We were standing by his jeep. Across the bonnet, which Tom kept referring to as the "hood," were a selection of his paintings.

They were larger and more detailed than the sketches I'd seen when we met, but otherwise, much the same. Each was a land or seascape, and all had a dreamy quality. Soft-edged and blurred, colour and mood taking precedence over form and structure. I loved them.

He fidgeted at my shoulder while I examined the six canvases spread over the *hood*. It struck me that Tom appeared to paint dreams, while Frank painted nightmares. I wondered if that meant anything.

Earlier, as we'd walked on the beach, Tom told me he had brought some of his paintings for me to see.

"You remembered?" I asked, looking out the corner of my eye.

"Of course, why wouldn't I?"

I wondered if that meant anything as well.

He'd parked the jeep on the other side of the marshes. We retraced our steps along the beach, then over the grass-fringed ridge of low dunes disfigured by concrete tank traps, like a giant child's discarded set of building blocks. We then cut across the marsh on one of the earth dykes.

The wetlands had been progressively drained and turned into farmland since medieval times. Before the war, only a narrow strip behind the shoreline remained, filled with ponds and meres haloed by thick reed banks that attracted flocks of redshanks, ruffs and bitterns in the summer. Dragonflies and damselflies danced over still waters, and wet earthy smells scented the air. In 1940 some of the pastures had been flooded and returned to nature to act as a further barrier to any Nazi invaders who broke through the concrete crust of defences along the beach.

The thought I was going off into an empty expanse of ponds, reed banks and spots well secluded from the rest of humanity with a man I didn't know crossed my mind.

He could rape me, kill me, and dump my body in one of the black still meres, never to be seen again.

I ignored the thought. For the first time in years, I felt alive. I'd take the risk. I'd survived decades living with the strange tempers of a violent man. I sensed nothing threatening about Tom Dupree. Unless you counted how he made my heart beat faster.

We picked our way along the footpath. Even in summer, patches of cloying mud lingered. In places, the path was no more than part memory, part aspiration.

He took my hand at one point to help me around a particularly challenging spot. Only a ribbon of grass stretched between the mud on one side and a drop into black water on the other.

If he's thinking of kissing or killing me, this is where...

He did neither, and my neck, lips and shoes all survived unsullied.

His jeep waited in a rutted farm lane where the marsh gave way to woodland. It was a twenty-minute yomp, far enough for the wind to have reduced to a gentle breeze and the air to warm in the shade of the alders edging the lane. Wrens sang in the overhanging branches.

We'd talked a lot, mostly about Tom. Growing up in Kansas, his family, learning to fly crop dusters, the war, his friends on the airbase. He skirted around questions about what it was like flying over Germany dropping bombs; whether that was due to keeping military secrets or not, I didn't know.

After seeing his work, I told him I thought they were beautiful, and he simultaneously managed to look happy and embarrassed.

"I don't show them to most people, the guys at the base..."

"I'm glad you showed them to me," I wanted to ask him if this was how he tried to impress women but held it back. I didn't know if he *was* trying to impress me. I wasn't at all sure what he wanted. When he asked if I'd like to go for a drink with him, I was... torn.

"Are you married?" I asked, turning to rest my back against the side of the jeep. No ring adorned his finger, but not all men wore them.

"I was..."

I kept looking at him.

"She died. Three years ago, since then..." his shoulders moved up and down "...I got a bit lost. Started drinking too much, getting into fights. Stupid stuff. In the end, I signed up for Uncle Sam to... I dunno... find... something..."

41

My hand was on his arm; I didn't remember putting it there, "I'm so sorry."

He pinched a smile back at me, and I let my hand slide away.

"And your husband?"

"Oh, he's still alive," I stopped myself adding *sadly* just in time. My tongue seemed far more inclined to misbehave than usual. I suspected the rest of my body was much the same.

"If I wasn't American, would you come for a drink with me?"

I laughed, flicked at my hair and kept his eye without replying.

"Did you know Kansas was in Canada?"

I shook my head.

"A little-known fact... if it helps."

"Tom... I'm married."

"Happily?"

I guess the look on my face was akin to the one on his when I'd asked him about dropping bombs on Germany.

"It's just a drink... it's nice to spend time with someone who isn't..." I thought he was going to say airman or soldier; instead, he said, "...an asshole."

"That's quite the compliment, I must say."

"I was once renowned for my silver tongue when it came to the girls, but... I'm a little out of practice."

"Regardless of my marital status, I'm also old enough to be your mother."

"I'm not a child. I'm thirty-five!"

"*Almost* your mother, I meant to say."

"How old are you?"

"Don't be impertinent."

"I like you."

"You have peculiar tastes."

"Come and have a drink with me. Please. Just one."

I wanted to say yes. I wanted to say no.

I'd spent the last week and a half unable to stop thinking about a man I'd spoken to for ten minutes. How would spending an afternoon with him leave me feeling?

What would spending a-

I clamped down hard on *that* thought.

What was happening to me? I didn't behave like this!

Desire was something I hadn't known for a long time. Intimacy with Frank always left me hollow, dirty and used. It was just a bodily function to be endured and, if possible, avoided. It brought me no pleasure beyond the children who were the consequence of Frank's lust.

I still remember what it felt like when Owen touched me and how it made me yearn for more. I remembered the one night we shared, and it is impossible to count the times I wished the world and the choices I made had allowed me to have known more than that beautiful, unfulfilled moment. But I never expected or wanted, or craved to try again with anybody else.

I didn't want to kiss Mr Wakefield, the greengrocer, or unbutton the shirt of Mr Hodges, the chief librarian. I didn't want Mr Lawrence, who ran the Regal Picture House to put his arms around me, and I certainly didn't want to jump into bed with Mr Coker from the ironmongers, despite his cheery disposition and admirable collection of rather dapper hats.

So, why Tom Dupree?

Admittedly, he was good-looking, but even with my lonely, isolated life in the Castle, the occasional good-looking man crossed my path over the years. I hadn't suffered the faintest desire to... engage in that kind of business.

Had I suddenly become a wanton harlot?

While all this flicked, bounced, crashed and reverberated around my mind, Tom carried on staring at me. A smile, half hopeful, half encouraging, dusted his lips. He had a good smile. The eyes weren't bad, either. Not intense like Frank's, not the sort of eyes that made you both wonder what was going on behind them, and, if you ever figured it out, would you wish you didn't know again, but soft.

Like his paintings, they were rather dreamy...

Oh, for goodness sake, woman! Get a grip.

"Tom..." I eventually managed to say, "...I'm married, and if I wasn't, well... I'm a little bit too old for you, really... and I don't know you anyway... I can't... it's not that, well, I don't know, really. Why would you... I mean... erm... you're... well..."

I was doing a singularly bad job of getting a grip on anything.

Tom obviously thought the same.

So, he kissed me.

This took me back somewhat.

Owen had kissed me at every opportunity. The first time beneath an oak tree in the corner of Mellow's Field, where we'd shared a picnic consisting of bottles of lemonade, jam sandwiches and the largest pork pie ever made. I'd been fifteen and discovered, after the initial surprise and uncertainty, that kissing was very much to my liking.

Frank rarely kissed me, other than a peck on the cheek or the back of my head. Usually, as a thank you for dinner or when he'd finished his business with me. On the odd occasion he did kiss me on the lips, it felt like having something wet, squishy and quite possibly dead pressed against them.

Tom's kiss was gentle, soft, fleeting. I was kissing him back before he had a chance to pull away.

I decided, as his hands fell to rest upon my hips and my arms went around his neck, I would probably go for that drink with him after all.

1926

Tilly was born on 30th September 1926.

Frank nodded when I told him I was pregnant, in much the same way he would have if I'd announced I'd bought a leg of lamb for Sunday dinner.

"Good," he enthused before heading off to the studio.

For a man who was so often angry when I wasn't pregnant, he never displayed one jot of happiness when I was.

The pregnancy went smoothly, far easier than with Francis and Simon. Which made me suspect I was carrying a girl all along.

The birth was without drama too. Perhaps my body had grown accustomed to childbirth; maybe I simply knew what to expect. Regardless, when the midwife put Tilly into my arms, all my woes and sadness shrivelled away. My failings and mistakes paled into insignificance when held against that small pink bundle.

Later, when her eyes opened to stare back at me, it was like looking into my eyes in the mirror. I saw little of Frank in Francis or Simon, which was a blessing, but there was nothing of him in Tilly.

Frank came and stared into her cot a few times in the days after her birth. His face remained blank. My knowledge of men is limited. Aside from Dad, I only ever became close to Owen, Frank and Tom. But I found my husband's behaviour almost unnatural.

He wanted children. His mood blackened every time I failed to catch with child, to the point he accused me of somehow deliberately failing to conceive. As the years passed, those accusations moved beyond words to violence. Yet, whenever he looked at our children, I saw no happiness, no love, no anything. Or almost anything.

With Francis and Simon there'd been a blankness I'd put down to awkwardness around children, an unfamiliarity, an uncertainty of what to do with what he had created and the enormity of the responsibility that came with it.

With Tilly, however, there was an edginess I could not explain. Something akin to a child finding the birthday present they had spent months yearning for turned out to be something else entirely. A ragdoll instead of a rocking horse.

I thought perhaps it was because he only wanted sons; some men are like that, I believe.

Sometimes, as I nursed Tilly, he would stand in the doorway and stare at us. I would tell him what a bonny daughter he had, how hungry she was, how feisty, how beautiful. All the things mothers say about the precious little soul in their care they pour their love into.

Frank never said a word. He just stared. Those burnt hazel eyes, intense but unreadable, no expression on his face. It was as if he were watching something so far beyond his comprehension, he could make no sense of it.

Sometimes Tilly would cry, whether picking up my unease or her father's presence, I cannot say.

Then Frank would snap something like, "Keep her quiet, can't you?" and storm off. Taking all the warmth in both the room and my heart with it.

I did my best to ignore him. Looking after three young children is a blessing that leaves little opportunity for much else. Frank spent even more time than usual in his studio or took himself away from the Castle altogether. Sometimes he'd be gone all night. I hoped he had a lover, then he would not bother me in the bedroom, and perhaps she could make him happy in a way I clearly couldn't.

Occasionally, booze soured his breath when he returned, but usually not. I never smelt perfume on him or found any makeup on his shirts when I washed them. If he had a lover, he was careful not to bring home any trace of her, which made me think he didn't. I couldn't imagine Frank would give a jot if I did know.

A couple of months after Tilly was born, I noticed Frank had lost a little weight. He hadn't been eating any less, but he never ate a lot. Still, he'd only put on weight over the years. Slowly blurring and softening the sharp lines of the looks that had once put me in mind of a Hollywood film star.

Several times I nearly asked him, but I always stayed my tongue in the end. Frank didn't like questions.

He'd been big when I met him, not fat, nor muscular, just... big. A burly, heavy frame that dwarfed me. I once, very, very briefly found that attractive; it made me feel safe, protected.

I am not, I suspect, a good judge of character.

Outside the Castle, winter claimed the world. Short grey days fading into long, bleak nights. The same bitter wind whipped in off the sea during both to rattle windows and cut you to the bone whenever you ventured outdoors.

When I was strong enough again, I'd make the trek into Creethorpe to shop, leaving the children in Frank's begrudging care for a few hours. It was too cold to bring Simon and Tilly with me down the rutted excuse for a road cutting through the marshes, though Francis often came. He'd be starting school soon and would have to get used to making the journey.

Leaving the children with Frank made me uneasy for reasons I could not express. He rarely seemed to enjoy being with them, but he'd never done anything to harm them either. He reserved all his cruelties for me. Of course, neglect is another form of cruelty, but there was nothing to make me fear for them. Yet, whenever the Castle came into view above reeds turned brown and brittle on the winter's breath, I picked up my feet, not wanting them to be alone with Frank for a moment more than necessary.

He started coming to my room again leading up to Christmas when the long night's silence enveloped the Castle.

The first time, I'd finished checking Tilly had settled in her cot for the night and was readying myself for bed. I was exhausted; Tilly had kept me awake for most of the previous two nights.

"You're ready for more children," he told me, closing the door behind him. At least he didn't slam it. He nodded towards the bed.

"Tilly's asleep..." I whispered.

"Then take your clothes off quietly."

The last thing I wanted, besides waking Tilly up, was Frank inside me. There was never any pleasure, comfort or love in the act at the best of times. But I knew better than to refuse my husband.

When I moved toward the bed, Frank shook his head.

Sometimes he liked to look at me, sometimes he didn't. That night, he did.

I undressed for him. Without tease, playfulness or foreplay. This wasn't a lover's game.

He said nothing until I finished stripping. Goosebumps pimpled my skin. I didn't want to shiver, didn't want him to think I was afraid, though we both knew I was.

"You're letting yourself go," his eyes flicked up and down me, noting the inevitable consequences of three pregnancies.

I didn't know what to say, so I said nothing.

He crossed the room and stood before me, close enough to make me look up at him, close enough to see the lamp glinting in his eyes, to see the blackheads clustered around his nose and hairs sprouting from his nostrils.

"You belong to me..."

He ran his fingers down my cheek, neck, shoulder. Then squeezed my breasts, heavy and swollen with milk. His touch made me gasp. It was so cold it felt like he must have had his hands in icy water before he came to my room. Perhaps he had.

"...to me and nobody else. Ever again. Understand?"

"Yes..." I dropped my eyes, feeling shame without knowing why.

"Good."

He jerked his head towards the bed and started undoing his belt.

I did as I was told, but when I began pulling back the covers, he said, "No. On top."

He followed me as I lay myself out for him, the winter seeping into my bones.

He shook his head again, spinning a finger in the air, "I don't need to see any more of your face today."

Before I could roll onto my tummy, Tilly stirred, just a little squeak. Frank's head snapped in her direction. The light was poor, but the way he glowered at our daughter made me pray she would quickly settle herself.

Tilly moved under her blanket and gurgled. I half climbed from the bed to go to her, but Frank's head shot back to me.

"Stay where you are."

"But-"

"If she starts crying, you can deal with her when I'm done."

I hesitated, torn between the urge to care for my baby and the fear of what might happen if I didn't do what my husband wanted.

"Don't make me, Sweetness," Frank said; the words were soft. The implication behind them wasn't.

I eased back onto the bed and rolled over, legs spread for Frank.

Tilly settled back down, which was the important thing. I closed my eyes and shivered. The kitchen was the only warm room in the Castle this time of year. No matter how many fires you lit in the other rooms, the chill never lifted till the world warmed in the spring.

Frank got on the bed. He hadn't even taken his boots off, which at least promised my ordeal would be brief.

After spitting on his hand, he gave my private place a cursory rub. His belt buckle, hanging from his unbuttoned trousers, pressed against the back of my leg, the metal cold enough to make me wince.

It wasn't the only thing to make me wince, either.

I was in no way ready for Frank, in any sense of the word, but he forced himself inside anyway. In the early days of our marriage, I put it down to thoughtlessness and eagerness. By 1926, however, I knew he just enjoyed hurting me.

I didn't cry out. I didn't move. I screwed my eyes shut and buried my face in the pillow.

It won't take long, it won't take long, it never takes long...

Although this was true, when something lasts most of your life, it adds up to a very long time.

The words echoed around my mind as the bed creaked. Frank snorted in rhythm with the springs. He had one hand on my right shoulder, the other on the back of my head, grasping a fistful of hair. His weight pushed me into the mattress, fingernails digging into the soft meat below my collarbone. He slammed himself in and out of me with fast, hard, almost hateful thrusts.

I thought of my Owen then. Poor Owen, ten years dead in the mud of some French field. All the times we'd spent together; kissing, holding, touching, exploring, loving.

But not this.

I had refused him this for fear of catching with child. And here I was, letting this man do what he liked to me, letting him hurt me, letting him use me. Because I wore his ring on my finger. Because I had stood before God and promised to love, honour and obey him.

Owen would *never* have done this to me. Owen would have cut off his own hand rather than hurt me. I loved him so much and I sent him to his death never to know what it would feel like for us to be joined together as one.

Frank's snorts became louder, his thrusts harder, the discomfort sharper.

Tears wetted my pillow. Not from the pain but from the memories. The possibilities of what might have been, the life I might have had. I should have married Owen as he wanted. And even if I hadn't, I should still have let him have me, love me, and give me his child. The shame of bringing a dead man's bastard into the world would have been nothing compared to this. Would it?

Even then I knew that was not true. Owen would have married me the next day, certainly before he returned to France to die. A wedding would not have been difficult to arrange in the few days we had, particularly when your father was a vicar.

But I'd said no. I'd turned him away. Denied him. Denied myself. Through fear. And now... and now... and now...

I have this.

Frank gave a final thrust, a final grunt, a final snort.

Self-loathing consumed me, dragging me down to a place with no name. Where I was nothing and no one, where a faceless figure laughed at me for squandering my life.

Frank didn't pull out as soon as he finished, instead letting himself shrivel inside me. One hand on my shoulder, the other still gripping my hair, pressing me down so I bore his considerable weight. More discomfort. More pain. It was all I deserved.

I kept my face in the pillows. I didn't want him to see my tears.

Behind me, he was trembling. Perhaps with the cold. But it didn't quite feel like shivering. He was holding his bulk above me. His belly moved against my bottom as he breathed, long, slow inhalations, slightly faster exhalations as if he was enjoying some exquisite scent.

Gradually, he shifted. Slipping out of me, he lowered himself till his face was in my hair. His full bulk pressed on my back, making it a struggle to breathe.

"I've missed you, Sweetness, but now you're back..." he said, "...we must have more of this..."

With that, he pushed back onto his knees, cleaned himself on my sheet and left, still buckling his belt as he went.

I contained my sobs only till the door closed. Tears flowed down my cheeks, and I hugged my pillow to stifle the noise, so I didn't wake Tilly.

All I could think of was my Owen, cold and alone in the mud all these years and me here, in this place, cold and alone too. I missed him so much and the life I might have had in our little Camelot.

I burrowed under the blankets, my teeth chattering, disgusted by the wetness between my legs, the ghosts of Frank's fingers still pressing into my flesh.

I calmed myself, sucking in air, wiping away my tears. I was being selfish and stupid. I lifted myself onto my elbows and listened for Tilly, but thankfully she slept soundly.

Before I could ease back down or find the strength to get up, put on my nightgown and douse the lamp, I did hear something. Not Tilly, but from the corridor. The scuffle and squeak of boots.

Frank had been standing on the other side of the door, listening to me cry.

I shivered again, but not from the cold this time.

1943

"Jeez..."

It probably wasn't the most eloquent piece of art criticism ever made, but it said everything needed all the same.

"Your husband makes a living selling these?" Tom scratched his head.

"Surprisingly, he *has* sold some over the years; mostly, however..." I waved a hand at the crates inside, "...they earn nothing but dust."

We stood in the doorway of "The Repository," which was the grand name I'd given the shed next to Frank's studio. He'd laid the majority of his work to rest here in packing crates until the art world awoke to his genius.

They now filled the outhouse from floor to ceiling. If the art world didn't wake up soon, we would need another shed.

"They're all the same," I said when Tom reached to pull another canvas from the crate. He'd looked at half a dozen already.

"All?" Tom gazed into The Repository's shadowy depths.

"More or less," I said, a sense of relief washing over me when he dropped his hand. Staring at Frank's work too long gave me a headache.

"Make sure they all go back as you found them," I smiled, running my fingers down Tom's arm. He nodded, then grazed my lips with his before turning back to re-wrap the paintings he'd looked at. Frankly, the creased brown paper was a significant improvement.

I stepped outside while Tom worked, glad for the fresh air. The Repository was gloomy and oppressive. It was only a shed, but something of the paintings, the anger and pain Frank poured into them, leached out to foul the atmosphere in there.

Melodramatic of me, probably.

My eyes turned to the Castle, squatting, stained and scoured, before the sea. Its black windows stared back disapprovingly at me.

I lit a cigarette and put my back against The Repository's splintered wall. Frank didn't think women should smoke - *It's not appropriate, Sweetness* - so I only did when he wasn't around. It was one of the petty rebellions that kept me sane.

I listened to Tom whistling as he reinterred Frank's work. Of course, some of my recent rebellions were less petty than others.

I was glad for the wall at my back; my knees had been wobbly for most of the day. In fact, much of my body had been behaving peculiarly since I'd invited Tom to spend the night.

"Jeez..." Tom said again when he emerged, blinking into the sunlight.

"I told you they were terrible."

He scrunched up his face, "Dunno if they're terrible or... inspired."

"Careful," I said, grinding out the cigarette beneath my toe, "you're in danger of lowering my opinion of you."

"They've got *something* about them."

"They give me the creeps," I said, with more vehemence than intended. I don't think I'd ever expressed it like that before. I'd never liked Frank's paintings, but saying it aloud made me realise just how unsettling I found them.

It was one of the small mercies of my life that Frank never hung any of his creations on the walls of our home. The violence, mood swings, cruelties and abuse I learned to live with over my years here. However, having to stare at those evil monstrosities every day would have driven me completely over the edge.

"Thank you," he said, taking a place against the wall next to me.

"For what?"

"For showing me."

Ever since I told him my husband was an artist, he'd been interested in Frank's work.

I'd never planned to show him Frank's paintings, but I'd never planned to bring him to Grey Gull either. Or planned to...

I narrowed my eyes and looked out to sea; a warm and gentle breeze kissed my face. It was calm and benevolent today. If not approving, at least not disapproving.

I wanted another cigarette but stopped myself. It was just nerves.

Since Owen died twenty-seven years earlier, I'd only known my husband. You'd have thought that experience would have burned away all desire.

Tom held my eyes and smiled.

But it seemed not.

He had a way of smiling that washed away all my doubts and reservations. That made me want things I'd thought little more real than unicorns. That made me think of Owen and the very different life I might have lived.

You don't get second chances in life, only choices you get to make once.

One of Mrs Hollister's little pearls that came back to me from time to time. Most of mine had been bad, I thought it likely this one would work out the same.

I was married. I'd taken vows before God. I was forty-seven years old, an age at which people should know better. My husband was disturbed and sometimes violent. He'd told me he'd kill me if I ever slept with another man, and I had no doubt whatsoever he was talking literally.

Many things tied me to Grey Gull. Fear of what he would do if I left was one of them. Yet here I was.

Feeling another man's eyes upon me and wanting his hands to follow.

There had to be more to this than how he smiled at me. Didn't there?

I wasn't sure. In fact, wasn't sure about anything.

Was it rebellion? Was it lust? Was it loneliness? Was it the simple yearning to feel loved and wanted? Was it reaching an age where I didn't care anymore? Where I was too old and too tired to be scared. Probably it was a mixture of all. Or maybe I'd lost my mind.

Tom took my hand and gave it a little squeeze.

He didn't say anything. Just another little grin. Just another little flutter of my heart.

I pulled my eyes from the sea to flash a smile that might have been thought of as coy on another woman, before my gaze shot back to my oldest friend, my oldest enemy, my only companion.

Tom carried on not saying anything. Giving me time, giving me space, giving me a chance to change my mind.

Which made me like him even more.

I squeezed his hand back.

We'd met whenever we could since I'd kissed him for the first time and gone for a drink with him.

The first time had been at a pub in a place I'd never heard of, despite being only fifteen minutes from Creethorpe. I'd sat terrified someone in a village I didn't know would spot me drinking with an American airman.

We'd garnered a few looks, but no one said anything. Eventually, I'd relaxed and found myself entranced by Tom, his smile, his eyes, his soft way of speaking and the warmth of his laughter. He made me feel good. He made me feel alive.

Afterwards, with the sky starting to darken to a deep blue, he drove me home, or as close to the Castle as I let him. I made him park halfway across the marshes, afraid Frank would be waiting for me.

That didn't stop us from sharing a sweet and exceedingly long goodnight kiss before I climbed out of the jeep and found that, after all, my legs did still work.

Needless to say, the Castle had no telephone, Frank liked us as cut off from the rest of humanity as possible, and Tom just "dropping by" to knock on the front door wasn't an attractive option either. At some point, Frank was going to come home.

So, we agreed to meet at the same place on the beach at the same time. He would be there when he could, which wasn't going to be always, or even usually. He had a war to fight, after all.

Every day I walked down the beach. If I saw Tom, the same light-headed sizzle always sparked through me. I blushed, smiled, played with my hair and waited expectantly for the touch of his lips on mine. I never had to wait long.

When he wasn't, I would sit and stare at the sea, whose smile was never half so enticing. Sometimes the drone of aircraft broke the wave's refrain, making me ask if he was up there. Then I would think of Owen and wonder if I was going to lose another good man to the idiocies of war.

He never said when he was going to fly, "I'd have to kill you if I told you..." he'd grin and shrug, "...and that'd be a damn shame."

Still, I quickly began to spot the little signs and knew when I wouldn't see him for a few days. A slight tightness around the eyes, a little hollowness in his laugh. The way his gaze sometimes drifted off to some place a thousand miles away.

And it always made me fear I'd never see him again.

I read the papers more avidly after meeting Tom; I paid more attention to the chatter as I stood in the queues with my ration book in hand as well. I knew how many airmen weren't coming back. Some ended up in German prison camps. A lot didn't.

It wasn't like Owen. I wasn't in love with Tom; he was only a distraction. A little fun. Some happiness. That's what I said to the woman in the mirror every day. The one I kept catching with a smile on her face.

Whether I ever convinced myself, I really can't say.

After seeing each other for a few weeks, Tom told me, somewhat sheepishly, that he'd heard of a particular hotel in Lowestoft that didn't ask questions about couples spending the night. Even when the men wore American uniforms and the women spoke with British accents.

"Doing their bit for the war effort?" I asked, remembering another hotel, with another lover, during another war.

"I'm sorry?"

"Keeping up morale..." I shook my head, "...it doesn't matter."

"We don't have to," he said, perhaps misunderstanding me.

The sea was a sheet of quicksilver that afternoon, almost painful to look at. We sat atop one of the low dunes on a blanket we'd spread over the sand. Tom's arm was around my waist. It made me feel safe. It made me feel loved.

"I don't want to go to a hotel," I said, turning my head from the sea's glare to find Tom's eyes.

"Oh, that's ok..." he sounded disappointed.

He wanted to make love with me. He thought there was a fair chance he would soon be dead. Owen had felt the same things, and I'd said no when he wanted us to marry immediately so we could. Tom wasn't asking me to marry him, but it was the same in all other respects.

Life never gives you second chances. Only choices you only get to make once.

"Spend the night at my house," I smiled, then kissed him before he could say anything stupid.

"What about your husband?" he asked later.

"He won't come home yet."

I knew no such thing. It was a bold, reckless and probably ridiculous risk to take, especially when certain hotels in Lowestoft, apparently, didn't ask questions.

But I wanted to be bold and reckless. My entire history of bold recklessness pretty much amounted to getting drunk and letting Frank have what I'd refused Owen.

And we've seen where that got me.

This time I wanted it to take me somewhere else, somewhere better, somewhere beautiful. Even if it was only for a few hours. I wanted to glimpse the distant towers of Camelot again.

So, there I was. Standing outside the Repository with a man I was going to be unfaithful to my husband with. The Castle in front of us. The place didn't approve of me and never had. Or at least whatever it was we shared that place with didn't.

Perhaps I should not have been so dismissive of Lowestoft.

I'd never been, after all.

Since Frank had been away, I'd heard and seen nothing inside the Castle that I couldn't explain (beyond why I was still there, of course). I had begun to suspect nothing was there; the things I'd experienced were no more than projections of my own fear and unhappiness. With Frank gone, the cause of that fear and unhappiness was absent, and I no longer needed to see and hear those manifestations around me.

That's what I'd told myself. And it had seemed entirely plausible, entirely believable, entirely sane.

But standing with Tom, looking at the house, the nagging suspicion it had simply been biding its time, seeing what the dog would do when its master was away, wouldn't leave me.

"You look... uncertain?"

I didn't look uncertain; I looked scared.

"Hold me," I said.

He did.

And that made me feel much better. Solid and whole, flesh, muscle and bone. Not a phantom I'd conjured out of shadow and silence. Something good, something that could stop me being frightened, for a little while at least.

Over his shoulder, the Castle's windows fixed on me, black but not sightless. Waiting. Watching.

"Take me to bed," I whispered.

A gull shrieked beyond the Castle. A manic cry of derision.

Tom let me slide from his embrace, and we walked together hand in hand towards the house.

And I tried to ignore the distant drone of aircraft, low and ominous, all but lost between the wind and the waves.

1925

There was Frank. There were the children. There was me.

But we were not the only ones in Grey Gull.

And whatever else resided in that house did not care for me.

I wasn't sure how old the house was, but my guess was late eighteenth century, with a couple of additions over the years. Frank didn't talk about it a lot. As he usually found talking to me a tiresome chore best avoided, his reticence never seemed odd.

He didn't say much more about the man he'd inherited it from. "My uncle," was all I ever got out of him. There was never anything about boyhood visits to Grey Gull, who his uncle was or what he did out here in this lonely, forsaken place.

After I first met Frank and we were corresponding as I looked after my Dad when he was ill, he told me he'd cared for the old man during his last days, which was something that warmed me to him. But subsequently, on the few occasions I did ask, Frank just said, "I never really knew him."

Perhaps he didn't, but I always harboured a suspicion there was more to *Uncle* than Frank let on.

I once asked old Mutt Harris, who was as close as we had to a neighbour. I'd been doing the walk into Creethorpe one blustery day. It was in the autumn of 1925, I think.

Mutt didn't have any time for new-fangled motor vehicles and regularly made the trip into Creethorpe behind the swaying rump of his saggy-backed mare. Whenever he saw me, he'd pull Mildred to a halt, tip his hat and ask, "How yew a' diddl'n, Mrs H?"

I'd always reply I was diddl'n just fine, regardless of the actual status of my diddl'n.

He'd always offer me a ride, but I tended to refuse unless I had the children with me. The boys would never forgive me for passing up the opportunity to get that close to a horse's backside.

Frank didn't approve of me talking to anyone, particularly men. But I was tired, and the wind was ripping in from the sea, so I gratefully clambered alongside Mutt.

After bemoaning the lamentable state of the world, the road and the weather, he'd fallen into silence, and I'd asked him about Frank's uncle.

Mutt removed the roll-up from the corner of his mouth, which turned downwards as he replied, "Right miserable boi, nah friend to nah man."

"He lived in Grey Gull a long time?"

"Almost as long as oi lived on moi farm," Mutt's puffy eyes glanced sideways at me beneath the peak of his flat cap as he chuckled, "And that's a bleedin' long time, excusing moi French."

"Was he born there?"

"Nah, moved in when oi wer' a boi, 1860 summit oi'll wager."

"And he never married?"

"He married roight enough. Her name was..." Mutt screwed up his face, which had more than its fair share of crumples to start with, "...Jane. Plain name fah a plain as lass. Pale and sad-faced thing she wer'. Naht tha' oi saw much of her. She got out even less than yew!"

I offered a thin smile at that.

"No children?"

"Oh, had nippers," Mutt's face crumpled again, then dropped with a shrug, "dunno how many. All died. Don't think many of em lived tha' long."

"No...?" I pulled my coat tighter about me.

"Hard life out here. Hard now, harder then. Especially fah nippers."

"And Jane?"

"Same. All gone long 'fore the owd century wenna bed. Then wer' just him on his own. Never much talked to nah one. Kept himself to himself and gave anyone who went near him as sour a look as yew'll ever care to see."

I nodded. We were past the marshes now and I stared out across the fields towards the distant cluster of buildings making up Fandle's Farm. The greyness of the light bleached most of the colour from the world.

"What was his name?"

For some reason, I was sure he was going to say Frank, but Mutt scratched his ear and said, "Mr Shackle."

"No first name?"

Mutt laughed, "Tha' owd boi weren't on first name terms with nah one. Guess oi must of heard it once or twice, but damned if oi can remember it. Moi owd bonce getting roight soft these days."

We rattled along a bit further before I asked, "Have you heard... anything else about that place?"

"Like what?"

"Stories?"

Mutt half turned to me, peering through the smoke rising from the smouldering remnant of the latest roll-up, "Somethin' on yewr mind, girl?"

I wanted to ask him if Grey Gull was haunted. But the prospect of saying it out loud seemed even more foolish than the thought, so I shook my head.

Mutt carried on peering at me, he took a last drag on the roll-up before flicking it away with a nicotine-stained finger.

"Don't like th' place," he said, twisting back to stare at Mildred's backside, "somethin' sad 'bout it, like it ain't ever heard nah laughter."

"It's a desolate spot," I admitted, keeping my attention on the twitches of the horse's tail.

"Nah place fah a girl and her nippers..." Mutt sighed "...some places in th' world just got bad air."

"Bad air?"

"Ain't right. It's sloightly on th' huh."

Which was the local slang for when something was not quite straight.

"More than sloightly..." Mutt added, putting the reins between his knees to commence work on the next roll-up.

"What makes you say that?"

Mutt didn't answer until he'd got a match to take in the wind, and blue-grey smoke was again sharpening the damp air.

"We had sheeps back in th' day. Buggers are sheeps, excusing moi French. Always wanting to be someplace other than where yew want em to be. Stupid animals they is, save for when it comes to gitting some place other than the one yew want them to be. Then they be as sly as Old Scratch.

Sometimes they wandered here..." Mutt waved a hand towards the stubbled fields to our right, "...sometimes they wandered ther'..." he jerked a thumb back towards Fandle's Farm "...and, if th' buggers felt especially bothersome, they wandered out to Grey Gull."

Mutt shook his head, "Never much worried me going to round em up anywhere else. Like being outdoors, even now when this damp aches moi joints. But up at Grey Gull..." he glanced at me, "...never liked going near ther'."

"Why?"

"Usually nuttin'. Just a feeling. Sadness. Something... sloightly on th' huh. You know what oi mean?"

I wanted to laugh; he was probably teasing me. But his eyes, whenever they flicked sideways at me, didn't hold anything that looked like a tease.

"Yes, I think I know..."

I never mentioned the things I saw and heard in the Castle to Frank. He would only have laughed and told me to stop being so stupid. And, in truth, there wasn't much to tell. Most of what I experienced back then was fleeting and easily dismissed, especially when the children permanently distracted and exhausted me.

What I could feel was more intangible, but I doubted my feelings less than my senses. There *was* something malevolent about Grey Gull, something cold that tolerated my presence within its damp, stained, salt-scoured walls begrudgingly.

There were times when I was certain someone was standing behind me, watching me with resentful eyes, reaching out to pull me around by my shoulder and slap my face the way Frank did when I'd done something wrong. But whenever I whirled around, the room was always empty.

Sounds like nerves and imagination, doesn't it? Perhaps.

Save, now and then, I *did* see something.

Just for a heartbeat. Something my eyes never quite managed to focus on. A figure, a shadow, a blur of movement, never enough to be certain, but more than enough to scare me.

"Did you ever *see* anything there? Anything you shouldn't?"

Mutt was quiet for long enough to make me think he wasn't going to answer, then he let out a sigh along with his cigarette smoke.

"Seen? Naht really. But heard a few things when oi wer' up there chasing them damn sheeps."

"Heard?"

"Crying sometimes. Laughing sometimes. Whispering more often, though never clear enough to make out proper. Other times nuttin' save the wind and the gulls, but all the hairs stood up on moi arms and oi felt this weight on moi shoulders. Like all the troubles of moi whole life, those been and those yet to come, wer' suddenly on moi shoulders, pushing me down, making me wanna sit in th' grass and ball moi eyes like oi wer' a nipper again. Thas a rum owd dew, oi can tell yew."

Mutt laughed, but it was a hesitant fleeting chuckle that fled into the wind.

A rum owd dew indeed. A strange old situation and one that sounded terribly familiar. An overwhelming and inexplicable feeling of melancholy. I'd thought it simply the consequence of my life with Frank, the loneliness, the occasional violence and cruelties I endured for the children's sake. But here was Mutt Harris, an old man I'd never considered fanciful, expressing the same thing, albeit in his colourful native dialect.

"You said you'd not really seen anything," I turned to stare at him, "that's not the same as not seeing anything."

"Nope. Ain't," he agreed.

"Then, what *have* you seen?"

"Nothing. Thas th' truth. But oi *almost* seen a few things…"

Mutt pulled Mildred to a halt; we'd reached the edge of Creethorpe, where he dropped me on the odd occasion I accepted his offer of a ride.

"Mutt...?"

He smiled, showing me the numerous gaps between the wonky remnants of his teeth. The smile faded when I made no move to clamber off his cart.

"Why yew so interested, girl?"

"Because I want to know if you've almost seen the same things I've almost seen."

He nodded and worried his bottom lip a little, "Just things out th' corner of moi eye. Just sometimes. Now and then. But only ever up around Grey Gull. Never nahwhere else. So, it ain't moi marbles. And when oi first started almost seeing things, oi wer' still a young un with me bag chocker with marbles."

"I think you've still got all your marbles, Mutt."

"Dunno 'bout tha'," his throaty chuckle turned into a phlegmy cough. He ground out the butt of his roll-up on the side of the cart before flicking it away and wiping the back of his hand over his mouth.

"Weren't ever anything oi was ever sure of. Something moving, something watching, something tha' weren't ever ther' when oi get moi eyes straight on the bugger, excusing moi French..."

Mutt held up a gnarled and knotted hand peppered with liver spots; he extended a finger.

"Three things oi'm sure of, though. First, it happened too many times fah it to be moi imagination. Weren't every time mind, but often enough. Something. Something like a figure, but not quite. Like its bits weren't arranged quite roight. Something a bit like grey smoke, but not quite tha'. Something... sloightly on th' huh..."

I swallowed and nodded.

"Second thing," another finger joined the first, "It never once happened outta soight of Grey Gull. Not a once. It happened in th' morning, it happened in th' afternoon, it happened in th' evening. Can't say if it happened at night as oi never been up tha' way after dark in all moi years. And I ain't got nah intentions of starting now."

Mutt dropped his hand.

"You be careful in that place, Mrs H. Yew believe wha' yewr senses tell yew. Dunno if whas ther' is dangerous or just maudlin'... but something's up ther' roight enough.

"What was the third thing, Mutt? You said there were three things?"

He nodded. Head down, he started rolling up another cigarette. His hand was shaking slightly. I'd never noticed him doing that before. After he'd sprinkled tobacco on the paper, his eyes moved back to me.

"Whatever tha something is. It's hungry. Thas th' only other thing I ever felt up ther' beyond sadness. Hunger..."

He finished rolling his cigarette and lit it. After he'd blown smoke into the damp air, he added, "Reckon its nuttin' tha' can really hurt anyone. Mr Shackle lived to a ripe owd age, after all, but tha' place gives moi th' roight collywobbles..."

He fixed the roll-up into the corner of his mouth and pointed a nicotine finger at the lane leading off towards the hamlet of Westerbury.

"Best oi git gorn, gal."

I climbed down.

"Anything ever happens yew need to wag yewr chin about, girl," Mutt tapped his thumb against his chest, "Oi'm always round. And if oi ain't round, oi'm abouts."

I nodded and said I would. Both absurdly grateful I now had someone to talk to and unsettled that Mutt's experiences at Grey Gull mirrored my own.

Mutt winked at me behind his pall of smoke, clicked his tongue and got Mildred moving again.

I watched his cart clatter off down towards Westerbury till it was out of sight before heading into Creethorpe to do my shopping. The thought I had someone I could talk to lifting my spirits despite the damp, grey weather and what Mutt had told me.

It was a feeling that did not last long.

The next time I came into Creethorpe, I learned Mutt Harris had died peacefully in his sleep.

1930

"Don't do anything to mess this up for me," Frank said, sitting on the edge of the bed. His eyes narrowed to hollow slits as he pulled on a cigarette.

"I won't."

I wanted to say things like, *How could I mess it up? Don't be so daft*, or any of a dozen other replies that might spring to mind when someone says something remarkably stupid to you. But I didn't.

I knew better.

"I want you to be a success," I added.

"You do?" Frank reached over and ground out his cigarette with a savage twist. At least he used the ashtray.

I was sitting up in bed, knees drawn to my chest, though I felt I was perched on something much thinner and more precarious. With a long, long drop beneath my dangling feet.

Frank rocketed up to begin pacing again. My eyes followed. I thought about warning him he'd wear more holes in the rug. But I didn't.

I knew better.

Izzy was in Frank's room as we didn't have a spare one. The boys shared the Castle's third bedroom.

What would we have done with Tilly...

I twisted out that thought as hard as Frank had extinguished his cigarette. It still hurt too much.

Frank stopped. He stared at me and seemed to shiver.

"I won't mess it up for you..."

"Make sure you don't," he said, lips pressed to white lines above the double chins he'd grown since we moved into Grey Gull ten years before, "This is important. This is *vital*. Life doesn't give you too many opportunities, no matter your talent."

My husband had no talent that I could see whatsoever, but Izzy St. Clair disagreed. I suppose she knew a lot more about art than I did.

We had retired an hour ago. The novel prospect of spending an entire night in bed with my husband left me queasy and edgy.

Restless energy crackled off him. When he wasn't pacing, he was smoking. When he wasn't smoking, he was pacing. Reciting every detail of his trip to London, at least the parts after he walked into Izzy St Clair's gallery on Grosvenor Street.

"Whatever she wants, she gets. You understand?" Frank wagged a finger at me.

"Yes, Frank."

"*Anything.* If she wants the clothes off the boys' backs, she can fucking well have them," he took a couple of paces then stopped again, "actually, if she wants the boys, she can have them too."

I eyed Frank. I *thought* that was a joke...

It was late. I assumed he would quit pacing soon. The room was so thick with smoke I wanted to open the window despite the rattling wind outside, but I stayed where I was.

I knew better.

"This is what I've worked for, what I've waited for. To be recognised," He was talking to himself more than me. I kept quiet, which was how he liked it.

"Anything she wants ..." Frank prowled back and forth across the room. It wasn't a large room, and he stalked from one end to the other like a caged beast.

"Perhaps... you should come to bed, get some sleep. It's late."

The clock next to me said it was nearly midnight. It felt later.

"Won't sleep," he said, pausing to light another cigarette.

I wanted to tell him to go somewhere else to pace and smoke so that I could.

But, of course, I knew better.

"You don't want to be tired tomorrow. It's a big day, showing Mrs St. Clair all your work..."

"I know... I know. Very big day. Big... big..."

Frank took constant sharp drags on the cigarette as he muttered. Flicking the ash on the floor. I'd sweep it up in the morning. And open the windows. I was starting to get a headache.

"So... come to bed."

He stopped in his tracks.

"You think I want to fuck you tonight?"

"That's-"

"I've got more important things on my mind than you."

"I know, I-"

Frank loomed over me, nostrils flaring, eyes suddenly wide. I wanted to shy away from him.

But I knew better than that too.

I was sure he was going to hit me. Instead, he crouched by the bed and cupped my face in his hand.

"This is important to me, you understand, don't you, Sweetness?"

"Yes, Frank..."

"I'm sorry if I'm being a bit tetchy. I know I can be difficult. Angry. But... I do love you."

Anger I understood, lashing out in a moment; we've all done that, though my rare outbursts involved no more than slapping the table or using a word Dad would never have approved of. Whatever drove Frank to do what he did wasn't anger.

But I just smiled and nodded. Because I knew better.

"Good," he kissed me softly and suddenly on the lips. The way you might if you meant it.

I'd been here before. I didn't fall for it so easily, but hope is sometimes hard to kill.

"I'm going to go the studio for a while, get my work in order for Izzy. I'll only keep you awake here."

"Don't stay up all night, Frank."

"I won't," he grinned, straightening up and looking boyish.

He ground out the cigarette and headed for the door, "Can you make some breakfast for eight. We've got enough, haven't we?"

I nodded.

"Great! Get some sleep, Sweetness," he blew me a kiss before leaving.

I let out a long shuddering breath.

Sometimes I thought it would be easier if he was nasty all the time. The way he could change in a heartbeat always unsettled me. Each time some part of me, some foolish part, pricked up its ears and thought, Maybe, just maybe, this time...

It's strange that as the years passed, that foolish voice became ever fainter while the binds tying me to Frank became stronger.

I didn't expect to sleep, and if I did, Frank would wake me when he came to bed. As it happened, I slept well, and Frank didn't come to bed at all.

I tend to rise early, and I tend to rise first. But that morning, I rose last and rose to the sound of a honking car horn.

I found Izzy in the kitchen, wearing a black silk robe across which Chinese dragons chased each other's tails. She could have tied it with more diligence. She wore a full set of flawless makeup and looked as bright, shiny and beautiful as I felt dull, dowdy and ugly.

"Good morning, Beatrice," she beamed; black hair, cut to a short bob, framed her face without so much as a single disobedient strand.

I distractedly shoved my unruly mop to one side and reminded myself I was overdue a trip to the drawer where I kept my scissors. I peered out of the window.

"The boys are all over your car!" I said with some alarm. God, as I well knew, had created boys with a particular calling to break most anything they could get their grubby hands on.

"Oh, I told them to," Izzy smiled, lighting a cigarette.

"You…" Simon was bouncing up and down in the passenger seat like he was on a trampoline while Francis was wrenching the steering wheel one way and then the other, "…did?"

"They're such darling boys! The way their eyes lit up when I said they could go and play. What a joy! You're so lucky!"

I thought it best to turn my back on the window. Frank would have to sell a lot of his awful paintings to buy Izzy a new car.

"Do you have children?"

The smile withered on Izzy's face, "No…"

The awkwardness stretched between us until I asked about her husband. Which stretched it further.

"He died in the war."

"Oh, God, I'm so sorry…"

"It was a long time ago."

I thought of Owen. A long time ago could just as easily seem like yesterday.

"Still… I know how you feel. My fiancé died in the war too."

Izzy nodded and blew some more smoke towards the ceiling, "Terrible business. Such a waste. Still, life goes on. I inherited loads of money, and you met Frank, so things turned out for us both in the end, really…"

The temptation to ask if she wanted to swap teased my tongue, but I clamped down on it. There was no funny side.

I started getting things together for breakfast in the hope busy hands would keep me from saying anything too stupid. It was a strategy that worked reasonably well around Frank.

"You didn't remarry?" I asked over my shoulder, feeling Izzy's eyes following me.

"No. That's the problem with being an independently rich woman; men see you as a sack of pound notes with a pair of tits. As opposed to just a pair of tits."

She tapped ash into the ashtray, "The money makes you suspicious of everyone's intentions. Lust is one thing; avarice is quite another. No, I rather enjoy the role of the merry widow…" she emphasised the point with a shrill laugh.

It seemed Izzy didn't want a husband, but did she want other peoples?

If she wanted to take Frank back to London with her in that fancy car Francis and Simon were now using as a climbing frame, she was welcome, but if she did, why come here to see the little woman and children? And, if she was only interested in Frank's ghastly paintings, what had they been doing for a whole week? Frank's account skated over what he'd been up to all the nights he'd been away.

The boys interrupted my ponderings over the bacon, hurtling breathlessly into the kitchen.

"Mum! Mum!" Francis bellowed, tugging at the sleeve of the shapeless cardy I wore over my housecoat, "Auntie Izzy said she'd drive us to school tomorrow!"

"Isn't that nice," I managed to say, turning from the range to the table where Izzy was ensuring nothing a young boy shouldn't see was hanging out of her silk robe.

She smiled at me. All perfect, pretty and sparkly.

And looking pleased with herself.

I smiled back. And clamped a hand on Francis' shoulder.

Auntie Izzy...

1943

It was very different with Tom Dupree.

I loved Owen about as much as a human heart could bear, but neither of us knew a lot about anything. Our unfulfilled fumblings should have been the beginning of a long and wonderful journey. But the war stole that from us and that was all I knew for so many lonely years.

Frank never cared. Sex was a bodily function to him. Where it sat on the spectrum compared, to say, going to the toilet or sneezing I can only guess, but it certainly wasn't something he did for my pleasure.

But, as I said, it was very different with Tom.

He wasn't a boy. And he wasn't a monster, either.

In all honesty, I knew what to expect no more than I knew why I wanted to take him to my bed in the first place. Intimacy with Frank was a brutal, hateful thing. Perhaps if I'd never known Owen, I wouldn't have considered the possibility it could be anything else.

But I had, and as much as I hated it whenever Frank came to my room to do his business, part of me never stopped wondering.

And when I met Tom Dupree, that part of me curled open an eye and pricked up its ears. Not long after, it began howling.

And once that started, there was only ever going to be one way to stop it.

Every step I took to the bedroom, leading Tom by the hand, I expected Frank to burst through the front door, screaming at me that I would get worse than his belt this time.

My heart skipped and lurched in time with the Castle's creaks and groans. But my husband did not appear.

Sunlight raked the window, illuminating a slow-motion ballet of dust motes. A warped square of light fell on the spot Tilly's cot once sat so many years before. Reminding me of all the sorrows I'd known in this house, echoing its whispers and shadows.

"Would you like me to close the curtain?" Tom asked, which I thought was a odd thing to say. Perhaps something had crossed my face as my eyes lingered on that barren space against the wall, or maybe he didn't want to see my slightly creased, slightly flabby, quite frumpy and much-abused body lit so starkly.

I shook my head, "No, I like the light…"

It always seemed to me daylight fell far less brightly than it should upon the melancholy interior of Grey Gull.

"Beatrice, are-"

I stepped in and put a finger on his lips. Their touch on my skin didn't quieten the howling within me. In fact, it had the reverse effect.

"No more words..." I replaced the finger with my lips.

And for a long while, there wasn't any more need for them.

Later, when such things as speech became possible again, we lay in a tangled mess. Only gentle evening light fell through the window, making the room gently glow. Much like me.

Not that I knew what to say. Or think. Or feel.

So, I did nothing but continue to return the soft kisses and caresses, pretending nothing existed beyond the four walls of that room, including the life I had endured.

At some point, I slipped into a doze. Anticipation, second thoughts, fears and longings had conspired to keep me awake for days.

When I awoke, the light had softened, starting to steal the colour from the world. Tom breathed next to me, sleeping too. I blinked a few times and stared at the ceiling. Then at Tom, his back was to me, and I was pressed against him. I wanted to press harder.

Instead, I tried to make sense of how I felt.

Happy.

That was the word that came quickest to mind.

I closed my eyes.

Other words came.

Contented. Blissful. Peaceful. Joy.

Aroused.

Again.

I moved closer to Tom, mirroring the contours of his body with my own.

He continued to sleep, his breathing more of a purr than a snore. I revelled in the sound of it.

The war would end one day. If Tom survived it, he would go home. I played the fantasy of going with him. Leaving Frank, leaving his spite, anger, violence and strangeness, leaving Grey Gull, leaving those awful paintings and the unsettling things I sometimes thought I heard and saw here, leaving the memories and the ghosts and the never quite knowing.

Even in the glow of everything, the likelihood Tom would want to whisk a frumpy, older, married, middle-aged woman back to America with him seemed unlikely.

I have done stupid things in my life, with my life, but that didn't make me stupid. It was a release, a diversion for a man who knew there was a very good chance he would die every time he climbed into his big silver plane and flew to Germany.

I would give myself no expectation or hope other than the comfort and pleasure we could take from each other.

But still, it was a lovely dream.

Kansas was, after all, an awfully long way from the sea.

Tom finally stirred, interrupting my daydream by rolling around to face me.

"Beatrice-"

I put my finger against his lips again.

"No more words..."

He showed me his amazing smile, and then we made love again.

It's a peculiar business, really. The mechanics of the things I'd done with Frank and Tom in that bed were not any different, yet one was awful and the other simply beautiful.

Later, I went down to the kitchen to make us something to eat. I fried my weekly egg ration to have on toast. Outside, darkness pressed against the windows. As the eggs sizzled, I looked up with a frown when I heard a curious noise above the spitting fat. It took me longer than it should have to realise I was whistling.

As I was dishing up, another sound came. A squeaking floorboard. I looked behind me, expecting to see nothing save maybe a fleeting shadow move for no good reason. Instead, I found a rather handsome man looking at me.

He'd put his trousers back on but had neglected to button up his shirt; there was more fat in my frying pan than on Tom's body.

"Something looks good," he said, coming up behind me to peer over my shoulder at my rudimentary cooking.

"Sorry, I haven't got more fancy, with the rationing and everything..."

"Oh, yeah." he pecked my cheek, "the food looks good too."

I shot him a grin over my shoulder, feeling both the blush warm my cheeks and absurdly pleased with his silly flattery.

We ate and talked of nothings and everythings. When done, I apologised a few more times about dinner. There was only fruit for pudding if he wanted it.

"I brought something," he said, shooting out of the kitchen. He came back with three bars of chocolate.

"You do know the way to a girl's heart, don't you?" I told him as he slid them across the table. To be fair, Tom Dupree knew the way to various other parts of a girl too, but I didn't tell him that.

I don't like to encourage big-headedness.

After dumping the plates in the sink, we took the chocolate, two bottles of beer and a blanket and went to sit on the beach. It was a mild and still night; a quarter moon had risen high enough to cast a silvery wake upon the still water. Stars washed the sky with ancient light.

Tom drank the beer, I nibbled the chocolate, we shared cigarettes and kisses, sitting shoulder to shoulder.

"Beautiful sky tonight," I whispered, looking up.

"More stars in Kansas."

"Really?"

"Uh-huh."

"Everything's bigger and better in Kansas, huh?"

"Damn right it is!" Tom lifted his beer in salute, accompanied by, I strongly suspected, a salacious wink.

I giggled.

When I stopped, I tried to remember the last time I'd done that. I couldn't.

"I've had the most wonderful day, Tom."

"Night's still young, sweetheart."

Another lift of the bottle. Another wink. Another giggle.

I could get used to this.

The giggle faded, and I distracted myself with chocolate.

But I knew I couldn't.

"I'm flying tomorrow," Tom said as if sensing my thought.

"I thought you weren't allowed to tell me things like that?"

"After an extensive analysis, I've decided you're not a Nazi spy..." he lowered his beer, "...still, best not to mention it to anyone."

"Military secrets are safe with me. I only talk to the seagulls."

Tom chuckled, thinking I was joking.

I found his hand, "What's it like?"

"Cold, noisy and boring, mostly. Till the Luftwaffe turn up, gets a bit more interesting then..."

"Don't you get scared?"

"Scared..." he took a swig from the bottle before shaking his head, "...man, I'm fucking terrified. All the time. Even when its just cold, noisy and boring. You try not to be... but... I reckon its pretty scary for the people we drop bombs on as well."

"Nazis."

"Most are just regular folk, like everyone else."

"Hopefully, it'll be over soon..." I was twisting chocolate foil into a little ball between the thumb and fingers of my free hand. How often did I say that to Owen?

71

"I signed up because I thought I'd nothing left to live for after Claire died. I thought getting blown out of the sky was better than trying to exist day after day with this... empty, hollow pain inside me. It's surprising how many ways a guy can find to be an asshole in his life."

"And now?"

He was quiet for a while, staring out at the dark black expanse of the sea, before he said, "I wish I'd met you back home. Would have been a lot easier way of proving I was wrong."

I squeezed his hand.

"Not likely you would have met me back home. The closest I've been to Kansas is Weston-Super-Mare."

"Where's that?"

"A long way from Kansas."

Tom nodded, "Guess maybe coming here wasn't a completely bad idea then."

"You're not having a totally terrible time, are you?"

"It has its moments."

"Do you think you could stay over again?"

"Luftwaffe permitting..." he laughed darkly.

I pulled his hand into my lap and held it tight with both of mine.

"I'd like that. Are they okay with you... not going back to base?"

"Aircrew get some... perks. Given how..."

"Oh."

"Still, they'd be pissed at me if I didn't bring the jeep back."

I raised his hand and kissed it.

He was going to die. Just like Owen. Maybe I'm a natural pessimist, but it felt as certain as the sun rising in a few hours.

"Won't your husband come home eventually?"

"I don't give a damn about my husband."

Tom's face turned towards me, features ghostly in the starlight. I'd spat those words out and the vehemence was heartfelt. Nothing was keeping me here in this empty house other than the fear of what Frank might do to me if I tried. But with Tom next to me, Frank seemed a lot less frightening.

"Why don't you leave him then?"

"I don't want to talk about him, not tonight, not now," I leaned in and touched my forehead against Tom's face.

His hand found my hair and stroked it.

"I just want one perfect night..."

"Seems to be going pretty well so far."

We kissed. He was right. It was.

When we finished, he asked if I wanted to go back to bed.

I glanced behind us. Grey Gull was a black presence, cutting out an oblong of stars from the sky, darkening the light of the universe.

"No, I'm happy here."

Tom twisted to stare back at the Castle too.

"If you don't mind me saying, there's something strange about that place."

"How so?" I asked carefully.

"Dunno how to say it."

"It's the isolation."

"I come from Kansas. Few places in the world have more nothing than Kansas," he shook his head, "it's just..."

Sloightly on th' huh.

I didn't say it. I didn't want to have to explain that saying meant something that wasn't straight, something wonky, something that didn't hang the way it should. Better to dismiss it than have to tell him about some of the things I'd seen or heard over the years, how it made me feel. About what happened to Tilly. Even after all those years, some locals still gave me funny looks and wide berths, and I liked how Tom looked at me too much to want to risk changing that.

Still, the fact he sensed some wrongness about Grey Gull sent a chill through me.

I pushed myself closer to Tom. Only one way of dispelling a chill came immediately to mind. I'd had a blissful day, and I hadn't had many in my life, not since Owen took himself to the Milford Conservative Club to volunteer anyway.

"You're gonna put your finger on my lips again and say something about no more words, aren't you?"

I nodded. Then kissed him. And kept on kissing him as we both slid all the way down.

I rolled onto my back. The stars above us shone bright and I wished upon every single one of them that this day would never end.

1916

I always replied the same day when one of Owen's letters landed on my doormat. He talked about the war and his pals in the trenches, but not a lot. Every now and then, I noticed he hadn't mentioned one lad or another for a while. He never said why and I never asked. It was easy enough to work out. Mainly he wrote about us. About how much he missed me and how much he loved me.

I cried every day. At first.

As the months drifted by, I suppose I became used to him not being around. More so when I went to Birmingham and started at *St Andrew's Secretarial College*. It's not that I forgot about him or stopped loving him or anything like that. It was more a kind of grief. No matter how heartbroken you are, you find a way to go on. You learn how to harden your heart, or it'll never mend.

That's what I told myself.

Maybe it would have been better if I'd learnt how to harden my heart a bit more.

I gave him gossip from home, how everyone was doing, and about the girls at college after I went to Birmingham. All the trivial things, you know, the ones I thought he'd be missing.

What he wrote about most, however, was marriage. The wedding, the honeymoon, living together, children. The simple stuff of life. It was almost like a mantra, a prayer, something for him to hold on to, something for him at the end of the tunnel he found himself in.

Years after I'd moved into the Castle with Frank, I spread Owen's letters over the table and counted how many times he asked me to marry him.

Forty-three.

We were already engaged, of course, but he wanted a date. One before the war ended.

And each time, I gave him the same answer.

Once you're home for good. Once the fighting is done. Once the world returns to normal.

I never forgot the look on his face when I'd told him that for the first time, sitting in the *Mimosa Tea Rooms*.

It wasn't hurt, it wasn't disappointment, it wasn't incomprehension, and it certainly wasn't anger. I've never been quite sure what it was, but I imagined it on his face each time he hunkered down in the trenches as I repeated the same answer in my letters.

I did want to marry him. I wanted it more than anything I ever wanted in my life. Owen was not only the love of my life but also a good, kind and honest man. He would be a wonderful husband and beautiful father.

If he got the chance.

It was prudent to wait. When the war finished, we would have our life. But for now, Owen didn't need distractions. He needed to stay alive, and that should be enough for anyone. And I didn't want the distraction either. Marriage meant opening my heart to the future when all I wanted to do was live from one day to the next.

That is what I told myself. Beatrice Clay, after all, had always been a sensible girl. And it was true too.

It just wasn't the whole truth.

The thing I never said to Owen, could never say to him, was that I knew he was going to die. When I'd waved him off at the train station that last visit home before shipping out to the war, I never expected to see him again.

So, each time he asked. I said no. We would wait. As we agreed.

He would die over there. We had no future. I didn't want to be a war widow. I didn't want to bring up a child conjured on a snatched honeymoon night on my own. The possibility scared me. Terrified me. Being alone! A widow! A mother! I was barely twenty, for God's sake! I still felt like a child myself.

Every night, I prayed I was wrong and Owen would come home. That waiting was the right thing to do.

I often wonder if my life is a punishment for that choice.

That selfishness.

I should have married Owen. I should have had his child.

And whatever life I had after his death would have been far better than the one I endured.

And part of Owen might still be alive too.

It turned out I was wrong. I did see Owen again. He came home once before he died.

As it was thought the conflict wouldn't last long, no one initially anticipated men returning until the war ended. As the fighting dragged on through 1915, however, it became increasingly apparent that this wasn't going to be a short war after all.

The Secretary of State for War eventually decided enlisted men should have at least one period of home leave every fifteen months. Owen got his ten days in April 1916, and the first I knew of it was when I got a telegram he'd sent from Chocques before getting the train to Boulogne and a boat to Folkstone.

He wanted me to meet him in London, and we'd travel home together.

Mrs Brickly (simply "the Brick" to the girls in her class at *St Andrews*) was a woman of no known expression or emotion. I'd expected a lecture on the importance of a career to the modern young woman when I asked for a leave of absence that morning.

Instead, she'd reached over, patted my hand and told me to take all the time I needed. I think it was the only time I ever saw the woman smile.

I rushed to get the London train and then took a taxi from Euston to Victoria. I didn't know which train Owen would be on, so I waited on the platform as each Folkstone train rattled in on billowing sighs of steam alongside all the other anxious mothers, wives and sweethearts.

Every hour a train disgorged its load of young men dressed in khaki and mud. Some wore bandages, too, and a few came off on stretchers after the crowds dispersed. I stared at each one in case it was Owen.

Four trains came and went, and I stood alone as men and women hugged around me. Some smiled like it was the best day of their lives, others looked confused, some were just hollow-eyed and vacant.

What expression would Owen have?

Each time I found myself alone on the platform, I went off to get a cup of tea while waiting for the next one.

"I'm sure he'll be here soon, luv," the woman serving the tea said when I came back empty-handed again.

"He didn't say which one he'd be on," I confessed.

"Oh, it's always a palaver with all the comings and goings from the front, he wouldn't have known. See plenty spend all day in here. But their boys all turn up in the end, you mark me words," she offered a smile as she sorted out my change before adding, "My youngest is in Mesopotamia of all places. I won't see him again till it's all done and dusted. So, make the most of your time together."

Owen was on the 7pm train, which, thanks to a points problem, didn't arrive until after 8pm.

I'd resigned myself to the fact Owen wouldn't be on it. Something had gone wrong with his crossing, or he'd arrived early and not waited, or, somehow, we'd walked straight past each other. How much could we have changed in a year? I seemed the same to me, but Owen...

I looked at some of the boys coming off those trains and wondered what they'd looked like a year earlier.

When I finally picked Owen out from the khaki wave sweeping down the platform, I recognised him immediately. He was thinner, gaunt enough in the face to sharpen his cheekbones and his head was severely shaved. He also had a nasty scar over his right eye.

I didn't know whether to cry, laugh, scream, punch him or kiss him.

He didn't appear as different as I feared, and when he smiled at me, he looked like he always had.

The most beautiful man in the world.

I don't recall too much about those few minutes. I think I may have behaved... with some abandon.

He smelt of sweat, must, tobacco smoke, something vaguely stale and an over-generous helping of cheap cologne. The latter presumably applied liberally to disguise all the former.

"I was worried you wouldn't recognise me," he said, echoing my own fears when I pulled back an inch or two.

"Well, I have to confess, you are *slightly* more handsome than I remember," I ran a thumb across the scar over his eye and winced, "A close shave with a German bullet?"

He shook his head. And looked sheepish, "I fell off a ladder."

"A ladder?"

"It was a very tall ladder. A rung snapped, and... it was a long way down. Luckily, I hit the ground headfirst, so, less chance of breaking something important."

I giggled. Then laughed. Then burst into tears. He hugged me again, burying my face in his stinky, overly perfumed chest.

I didn't want him to say anything. I didn't want to say anything. I just wanted him to hold me, if not forever, then at least until one of the station porters came over and told us to start behaving ourselves.

He eased me back, kissed me, and found a grubby hanky to dry my eyes. Once done, he hoisted his kit bag over one shoulder, took my little suitcase, and held my hand like he was in a fast, icy river, and it was the only thing that might keep him from being swept away towards the sea.

Then we were walking down the platform, both grinning like idiots. Just like we were heading off for some adventure as we had in the golden days before the war when we saved up enough pennies to catch the bus to Gloucester or the train down to Weston-Super-Mare.

The lady from the station tea shop was outside smoking. She waved and flashed an *I-told-you-he'd-turn-up* grin.

I smiled, still wiping my eyes and hoping my mascara hadn't run too much.

And for a little while, I was truly happy again.

For almost the last time in my life.

After that, the sorrows came.

1929

I had no inkling of what was to come.

Frank had been bright and cheerful for days, even taking time from his studio to read to Francis and play with Simon. I should have known something bad was coming. With Frank, the calm always heralded the storm, but each morning he greeted me with a kiss and a smile. I tried to kid myself that perhaps, this time, he had changed.

The fool in our hearts is always the most gullible one of all.

I never loved Frank. I was broken, lonely and vulnerable when I met him. All it took was a little charm and far too much gin.

By such small measures, can we ruin our lives.

I had long since given up on so frivolous a notion as love by 1929, but I still hoped some kindness existed within him and it might one day overcome whatever demons tormented him. Then I might at least have a husband who didn't raise his hand and voice to me.

I had no expectation or desire for anything to mark our ninth wedding anniversary. It was just another day. And, for once, it had been rather a good one. I'd made a picnic, and we'd walked along the beach with the children. Frank had laughed heartily, held my hand several times and played with the boys, skimming stones across the flat sea and hunting for shells. Simon adored his father, chasing after him on not quite reliable legs at every opportunity, Francis was old enough to sometimes look quizzically at Frank when one of those dark expressions haunted his father's face, but I never saw Frank harm the children. He rarely even raised his voice to them.

If they misbehaved, I was always the one who had to take the punishment.

Later, after the boys went to bed, I'd read alone in the parlour while Frank retreated to his studio, a happy but tuneless whistle on his lips. My mind kept wandering from the words to recall the boys laughter. I loved them both dearly, but I wished they were Owen's sons. It had been thirteen years since he'd died, and I still thought of him every day.

When Frank was out, I would retrieve Owen's letters, my old engagement ring, and my photographs. I still wept over them. All the hopes, dreams and promises Owen filled those letters with. All those things that never came to pass; marriage, children and the happy life we would have together.

I should have got rid of them. Frank would be furious, but I couldn't; the only parts of Owen I had were my memories, a band of gold, those letters and photographs of a boy wearing a man's uniform staring glacially towards a future he would never have.

I supposed my memories would fade, and so would the photographs, but his words would last as long as I kept those letters from Frank.

I put down my book and went to bed at my usual time, pushing thoughts of Owen away for fear they would keep me awake for hours. On nights when those memories would not be put aside, I often ended up lying in the darkness, listening for my lost love's voice in the murmurs and mutterings of the waves until I cried myself to sleep.

However, it was not memories of Owen awaiting me that night. It was my husband.

Frank was waiting for me in my room, sitting on the edge of the bed, brows furrowed. His dark eyes raising to meet mine as I opened the door.

My heart sank. Like the sea upon the shingle bank outside, Frank's moods always swelled and broke upon the hard shore.

"Three years. It's been three years. What are you not telling me?"

"Three years since what, Frank?" I made sure I closed the door behind me. The boys were asleep, and a storm was about to break.

"Since you were last pregnant. Why haven't we had more children?"

It was a subject he returned to every so often. As if the lack of further babies were as much my fault as a pot boiling over or a creased shirt.

"I don't know, Frank, we've been trying..."

"Yes, we have. And yet no more babies. Are you doing something to stop yourself catching?"

If I could, I would have, but that was beside the point, "Of course not; how could I?"

"Women have ways of getting what they want..." his lip twisted into a sneer. The soft light of the bedside oil lamp gave his face a feral, inhuman cast.

"I do not, even if that was what I wanted. Which it isn't; I love the boys..."

"Don't make this about what you want! What you want isn't important. This is my house; you are my wife, and I want more children!"

I edged back against the door.

Frank sprang from the bed and seized my wrist. He twisted it till I yelped.

"Don't try to get away from me! I asked you a fucking question!"

His eyes bulged, and nostrils flared, lips curling back far enough to expose a couple of blackened molars. The whole set of his face contorted, deformed by this sudden rage so drastically he was unrecognisable from the happy man on the beach holding my hand as we'd watched the boys jumping over the waves.

"I'm sorry, Frank, I-"

His fist shut me up.

He punched me.

It was all I could think as I found myself sprawled at his feet. In the hierarchy of violence, a punch is so much more symbolic than a slap. A slap at least shows some restraint, a punch was a thing a man reserved for someone he wanted to hurt.

He'd caught me on the side of the head. It probably hadn't been a clean blow, but it wasn't for the want of trying. Whatever he'd intended, he'd stunned me and knocked me to the floor.

Frank stood, panting like a beast, though one little punch shouldn't have overly exerted a big man like him. I thought he would apologise, crouch down and kiss me like he sometimes did when he slapped me and regretted it. Or simply walk away like he did when I'd made him angry, and he considered his point made.

This time he did neither.

Instead, he bent over, grabbed a fistful of hair, and yanked me to my feet.

"No more fucking around, Sweetness! I'm your husband. You obey me. I own you. That's my ring on your fucking finger. You're *my* wife. It's your fucking job to give me children. So why aren't you getting pregnant?"

"I don't know, Frank... please!"

"Stop whining!"

This time he did slap me. A cold hard crack, before he pushed me back onto the bed.

"I've been too lax with you," he wiped the back of his hand across his nose, "you get things wrong in future, I'm going to punish you properly. And the first thing you gonna get right is giving me another child".

"I'll try Frank, I promise..." I had no idea what I could do to give Frank more children, but I would have promised him the moon in that moment, anything to calm him down. Fury burned in his eyes. But it wasn't the anger that scared me the most. It was what I saw beneath.

Frank was enjoying himself.

He started undoing his trousers, and I thought he wanted to have his way, which he did, later. But first, there was something else he needed to do.

Introduce me to his belt.

1943

I'd been smiling again, unable to focus on my book as I drifted between lovely memories and wild fancies.

However, the smile died instantly when a metallic rattle echoed down the corridor. A key was sliding into the lock on the front door, but it might as well have been fixing manacles to my ankles and chaining them to the wall of Grey Gull.

Frank was home.

I put the book down.

Would I have gone rushing to greet my husband if I hadn't been having an affair?

No, I wouldn't.

I picked the book up again.

Act naturally. I'd told myself that since the first time I kissed Tom. Just act naturally, and he'll never know. How could he?

Not that much was natural about my relationship with Frank.

I'd known that for a long time but being with a decent man had reinforced the wrongness of my life here.

"Frank?"

"Who else, Sweetness?"

The front door clicked shut, and my heart skipped a beat for all the wrong reasons.

He knows!

Bags hit the floor, boots wiped on the mat, then the squeaky floorboards.

"Cup of tea?"

I was in the drawing room, which was chilly for most of the year, but the window had the best light in the house, so I curled up in the battered old armchair in the summer to read.

Frank poked his head around the door, "Any biscuits?"

"Some digestives."

"They'll do," he disappeared, footsteps heading towards the toilet.

I had chocolate too, but there was no way I was letting on about that.

In the kitchen, I got busy making tea, trying as hard as possible not to think about Tom and failing miserably.

He'll see it on my face!!!

I shrieked at myself.

You've got nothing to feel guilty about.

I reassured myself straight back.

By the time Frank returned, tea and biscuits were on the table. I didn't know what he could see on my face, but I was surprised by what I could see on his.

"You've lost weight."

He nodded, eased himself onto a chair and commenced spooning most of my sugar ration into his tea.

"Haven't been eating right."

He didn't exactly look gaunt, but it was the first time in all the years I'd known him that his weight had done anything but go up. Perhaps he was sick.

I turned the possibility over in my head before shoving it aside, uncomfortable with how it made me feel.

He started on the biscuits while I hovered at his shoulder. There was no kiss, no hug, no welcome. Nothing, despite not seeing me for months. Not that I expected anything. Or wanted it.

"How long are you home?" I asked when he took a break from cramming biscuits into his mouth.

"Week's leave, then back to the guns."

A week wasn't too bad, I supposed...

"Well, let's pray this business will all be over soon."

Frank shrugged and slurped. He looked like he hadn't been sleeping, older too. Perhaps he really was ill.

"Are you feeling alright?"

"Fine, why?"

"You don't look yourself."

He drained the last of his tea and stood, "Bit tired, that's all. You'll fix me up, though, won't you, Sweetness?"

I tried to keep his eye but found my gaze slipping away. He ran his fingers down my cheek.

"Maybe we'll have an early night, like old times, eh?"

My eyes shot up at that. My stomach rolled too. I wanted to squirm away from his touch but knew he wouldn't stand for that.

"Whatever you want, Frank."

His visits to my room had became ever more infrequent as I got older and the likelihood of pregnancy receded further.

"Yes, that's it, Sweetness," he smiled, but it wasn't a pleasant one. Dropping his hand he turned away, "Dinner for seven, eh?"

"Yes, Frank."

With that, he turned for the door, already stripping off his khaki tunic. It hung far more baggily from his frame than it did the last time I saw him.

"I'll be painting till then. If I can remember how!" he barked a laugh as he went upstairs to change.

I curled my shaking hand into a fist and pressed it against my lips.

I'd ensured no trace of Tom remained in the house each time he left, but I scooted around again, convinced I must have missed something.

What on Earth had I been thinking, bringing Tom here! Having an affair! Being so stupid! He was going to find out! And then...

Frank's feet creaking on the stairs brought me crashing back to my senses. I sucked in air to calm myself.

When he went directly to the studio, I released a long shaky breath. In spite of the decades of turning out his turgid paintings, his enthusiasm remained unchecked. Which was something. With any luck, he'd spend the whole week defacing canvases and leave me in peace.

I had to get a grip. If I kept having panic attacks, he would find out!

And then...

I spent the rest of the afternoon tidying up a house that didn't need any and making a Woolton pie (slices of corned beef baked between layers of beetroot, carrot and mashed potato).

"No fresh meat?" Frank sniffed at it later as I dished up.

"Used the ration," I said, "If I'd known you were coming..."

I'd finished the bacon earlier when Tom stayed over. He'd given me some extra, plus a few other goodies. I shuddered to think what would have happened had Frank come home then.

"Didn't know myself until the last minute," he said before shovelling pie into his mouth.

That might have been true, or it might not. Either way, I doubt he would have sent word.

I sat down, and we ate together for the first time in months. The chink of spoons on china was the only sound.

When I'd forced down my small serving, I looked up. Frank was staring at me, "You look different?"

"Just forgotten what I look like."

Frank's eyes swept me up and down. Little looked the same as the man I'd met twenty-three years before, but his burnt hazel eyes had never changed.

He gave a twitch of the shoulders.

I look different because I'm happy...

Another thought I threw into the box with all the others I shouldn't have.

"How the boys?"

"They write when they can. Don't say much. Can't, I suppose..."

More thoughts I didn't want bubbled up. Worry for the most part. I tried not to think about them, young men fighting in a war like Owen had done all those years ago. I prayed every night they would, unlike my Owen, have the chance to grow old.

So far, God had answered my prayers.

Would being an adulteress change that?

My box of unwanted thoughts was filling rapidly.

As I washed up, Frank sat smoking and drinking tea at the table. I felt eyes between my shoulder blades.

The distant throbbing hum of aircraft cut through the incessant squawks of the gulls scavenging along the shore outside.

"Yanks," Frank said.

"Sorry?" my hands paused; my heart did much the same.

"Yank bombers. Coming back. Only sods daft enough to go on raids in daylight."

"All sound alike to me."

"You can tell the difference when you have to listen to the kraut ones over London."

"Oh..."

I listened to the planes and tried hard not to wonder if Tom was on one of them.

"Daft fuckers, getting blown to bits every time they go over. Too arrogant to admit they were wrong and make night-time raids like the krauts and us."

My hands hovered in the sink.

"Are they?"

"So I heard..." Frank's chair screeched as he got up, "...keep it hush-hush and out of the papers; bad for morale and all that. But be lucky if any of those buggers get through the war the rate Fritz is shooting them down."

Frank came and stood behind him; I glanced over my shoulder. He was craning his neck to look out the window looking for the American bombers.

"Just like the Great War. Brass don't care how many die, throw us in front of the guns, watch us cut to bloody ribbons, then send some more. Over and over."

"Hopefully, it'll end soon."

"Everyone says that, but it'll never be over. The killing will never stop; it's the way the world is."

The drone of aircraft faded below the gulls squabbling. I concentrated on washing up. Frank lingered at my shoulder, close enough to smell the turpentine he cleaned his brushes with. The stink of it was always on him, like over-used cologne.

"The wives and sweethearts of those airmen ain't gonna see them boys again..." Frank's tobacco-soured breath caressed my ear, "...they're all gonna burn..."

His heels squeaked as he turned away, "Go to bed early tonight, Sweetness; we got some catching up to do."

He started singing as he headed back out to the studio, like the bombers before him, the drone of his voice faded slowly into the distance.

It had to be you, it had to be you
I wandered around, and finally found
The somebody who
Could make me be true,
And could make me be blue
And even be glad, just to be sad
Thinking of you...

1927

Tilly fell ill in the New Year.

"It's probably nothing," Frank said when I told him she was refusing to take my breast.

"Her colour doesn't look right."

Frank shrugged and finished his tea, "Babies..."

Standing at the other end of the table, I twisted my apron. Francis watched us as he played with his porridge. Simon was more interested in the sounds made by tapping things with his spoon.

"Perhaps we should get the doctor..."

Frank's head turned towards the window over the sink. The world outside reduced to a smeary grey blur by the rain lashing against it.

"She'll be fine by tonight, Sweetness. A spot of the colic, most likely."

It wasn't colic. It probably *wasn't* anything serious, but it worried me. We were a long way from help here. Tilly enjoyed a ferocious appetite, her eyes were always bright, and she gurgled happily. But since yesterday, she'd refused to be nursed, wailing and squirming whenever I picked her up.

"But if she isn't...?"

"Then we'll get Doctor O'Conner to come and see her tomorrow..."

When he said "we," he meant me. And that would mean leaving Tilly while I walked into Creethorpe to fetch the doctor. Something knotted and twisted my insides. Otherwise, I'd have to carry her through this cold, wet, unforgiving January squall into town.

I nodded and went back to washing up. I couldn't eat a thing.

All day I attempted to feed Tilly, walking around the house with her in my arms, trying to settle and quieten her, but she continued whimpering. If she was sickening, she still had plenty of energy for bawling. Was that good? I didn't know.

Despite already having two children, I felt I knew nothing about raising them. Most women have a mother, sisters, relatives, friends or neighbours they could talk to and get advice from.

I had no one.

Instead, I watched the endless rain slash across either the sea or the marshes depending on which window I stared through, Tilly in my arms. I tried singing, I tried cooing, I tried soft words, I tried rocking her.

She carried on crying and refusing my milk.

The boys were fidgety, trapped inside by the weather, scampering about, getting under my feet, shouting and hollering. Between them and the worry, my head began pounding.

I snapped at them several times, which I didn't often do. Francis and Simon looked at me with big blank eyes, not quite fathoming what they were doing wrong.

In the end, I told Francis to take his little brother to their room, and play quietly, or there'd be no bread and jam for them.

Guilt speared me as they trudged off, but I needed some space and time with Tilly. I certainly wasn't going to get any help from Frank. He'd retreated to his studio as soon as he'd eaten breakfast. I didn't expect to see him again till he was hungry enough to venture out.

As the rain sheeted down against my bedroom window, I put Tilly back down in her cot to give my arms a rest. She was snivelling but at least quieter. When I had her comfy, I watched the sea for a few minutes, its mood as restless and troubled as Tilly's, as sombre and melancholy as mine.

Drab waves crackled along the shore, spitting froth and spray at the shingle as they broke.

I spent a lot of my life watching waves, from the gentlest ripples caressing the land to the monsters hurled with the fury of God during howling winter storms. Over the years, I developed something of a dread fascination, losing myself to them, watching, listening, feeling, smelling, tasting. As if I could discover some message, some words, something arcane and timeless hidden within their never-ending refrain.

Hypnotic, I think, is the word.

Sometimes it soothed me, sometimes frightened me, and sometimes it left me yearning for something I could not name. Eventually, I'd blink and find I'd lost time, usually minutes, occasionally hours, a few times most of a morning or afternoon.

I didn't stand there for long. Blurred by the rain-smeared glass, the sea was a malevolent thing that day, its waves nought bar manic whispers full of doom and foreboding. The alchemy of my anxiety for Tilly turning the base rhythmic thump of water on stone into the black metal of some evil prophecy.

...she is...going...to die...she is...going...to die...

The familiar feeling someone was in the room making me check over my shoulder, but I was alone. Tilly had stopped crying, the boys were silent, there was no sound but the sea, distant, constant, spiteful.

Hearing voices in the Castle was not a new experience for me. Like the things I saw out of the corner of my eye that were never there when I turned to look properly.

Sometimes, I convinced myself the place was haunted, and sometimes I thought I was going insane. By 1927, seven years into my incarceration, I'd told myself I had an overactive imagination frequently enough to almost believe it.

And forget what Mutt Harris had told me.

...she is...going...to die...she is...going...to die...

The sea was not talking to me. It *was* just my imagination. I made the best I could of that thin reassurance, as I tended to when things slipped too far from what they should be.

When things became *sloightly on th' huh.*

Still, I hurried over to Tilly's cot, terrified the voice in the waves was right. When I found her sleeping, I let out a strangled little sigh.

I tried to calm myself and pray, but the weight of my fears were too great to concentrate on anything.

I thought of Owen and Dad and how I'd felt when they died. How would it feel to lose my daughter?

The children were all I had, the possibility of losing one of them made me want to curl up on the floor.

...she is...going...to die...she is...going...to die...

With slow, forced steps, I returned to the window. A couple of tears escaped my eyes, and I rubbed them away with the back of a hand, hating myself for being so weak, hating myself for being such a coward, hating myself for not knowing what to do.

...she is...going...to die...she is...going...to die...

The mad voice kept telling me, hissing beneath the rain spilling from a wounded sky.

I dragged my eyes from the never-ending ribbons of white charging the beach. The studio was to the left of Grey Gull, behind it and closer to the sea. A corrugated iron roof, flecked with rust and lichen, sloped over the door to make a rudimentary porch. Frank had an old rocking chair by the door, where he could sit, smoke and think his deep thoughts when he took a break from releasing whatever was inside him onto canvas.

Regardless of the vicious, numbing wind whipping off the water, he sat there, rocking himself as the rain poured from the corrugated iron in a curtain of waterfalls before him.

He'd twisted the chair around to face the house, his eyes fixed on the Castle. Fixed on my bedroom window, fixed on me. So it seemed.

He only had a light jacket over the paint-splattered overalls he worked in. He must have been half frozen.

Yet he rocked slowly, like he was enjoying the shade on a sweltering summer's day. He only needed a cold beer to complete the picture.

Back and forth, hands curled around the rocker's arms. Eyes not moving from the house as the wind flung strands of dark hair one way and then the other. It was hard to be sure, given the rain blurring the glass, but he looked for the world like he wore the smile of a contented man.

...she is...going...to die...she is...going...to die...

As the sea's voice taunted me in the rhythm of its crashing waves, Frank kept on rocking in that battered, squeaky old chair, the movement perfectly in time with the breaking surf upon the beach.

And the longer he stared up at my bedroom window, despite the wind that must have been ripping his face red raw with its claws, the wider his smile grew...

1943

"My husband's home."

Tom, bless him, pulled a theatrical face and glanced over my shoulder.

"He's back at the house, don't worry; he never strays this far from his easel."

"Just as well. I wouldn't want to have to fight a duel with him," this time he conjured a mock earnest face, "That's what you guys do, right?"

I found a smile I doubt touched my eyes and ran fingers down his sleeve. Some men, I'm led to believe, are not particularly attuned to the needs of their women.

Tom wasn't one of them.

He hugged me and kept on hugging me. I didn't want to cry. With Frank home, I hadn't used any of my dwindling stash of makeup, so I wouldn't make a mess of Tom's jacket if I did. But women in their forties should not be bursting into tears at the drop of anyone's hat.

He leaned back, "What's wrong?"

"It's..." I nearly told him, but Frank had always been my problem, "...just difficult."

"Difficult?"

"Frank being back..." I let my eyes drift off to my faithful companion lapping on the other side of the tank traps, "...I almost forgot how much I hate him."

"Bea..."

"I can't stay too long," I said, reluctantly stepping away, "but he'll be going back to London after the weekend."

"I'm flying again Friday... so, after that-"

"Yes, after that."

I started walking along the path, away from the Castle. Tom was at my shoulder after a couple of strides.

"Why don't you leave him?"

"Who would have me? Where would I go? I have nothing! A few pounds squirrelled away," I didn't look at him as we walked, "besides, I made a vow before God."

Tom didn't say anything for a second or two. Perhaps he was fumbling for a gallant way of pointing out I'd already played fast and loose with those vows.

In the end, he simply said, "Come back to the States with me."

That stopped me.

"Tom, don't say things like that!"

"Why not?"

"Because you don't really mean it."

"I know exactly what I mean."

"Which is?"

"I want you to leave your husband and be with me. I love you."

I peered at him; he didn't pull the mock earnest face he used when he teased me. This time he appeared serious.

Despite talking nonsense.

"Don't be so ridiculous!"

"Why not?"

"I'm ten years older than you!"

"So?"

"And I'm married."

"Divorce him. Then you won't be."

"I can't."

"You know you're using the exact same excuses you did when I first tried to kiss you," the easy grin made another appearance, "and see how well that ended up."

"Tom, we hardly know each other, I-"

"More excuses!"

He kissed me. He was very good at kissing; I have to confess. For a few heartbeats, nothing troubled me at all. When he eased his lips away, however, everything came rushing in again, like a storm depositing the remnants of a shipwreck to rot upon the shore.

"You don't love me," I said.

"Yes, I do. And you feel the same about me."

"You're quite a confident young man, aren't you?"

The grin bloomed again.

"Tom..."

"Just think about it! What have you got to keep you here?"

"Two sons."

"You still have to wipe their asses?"

"No... but-"

Stopped by another kiss. There are worse ways of being interrupted.

"Don't say anything more," his finger replaced his lips against mine, "Think about it. Please."

The truth was I'd been thinking about little else almost since I'd met him. Well, daydreaming might have been a more accurate description.

"Yes..." I nodded, "...I'll think about it."

We moved on, listening to the sea rattle the shingle on the ebb and hiss back through it on the flow.

"I can't stay too long today," he said after we'd walked for a bit, fingers brushing and entwining.

"I'm still thinking about it."

"I wasn't chasing you up for an answer. Take your time. Nothing we can do until..."

"This is all over?"

He squinted at the sky, a bright grey dome of nothingness.

"...until my tour is done. Twenty-five missions."

"How many more have you got?"

"Ten."

...they're all gonna burn...

Frank's words echoed around me. As he'd been standing behind me, I hadn't seen his face, but the longer they stayed in my head, the more it seemed like they would have been spat through his yellowing teeth with a gleeful, manic grin on his face.

"I heard..." my eyes flicked to his "...that you're losing a lot of planes. The daytime raids...?"

He nodded.

"What are your chances of surviving another ten missions?"

"A lot better than surviving twenty-five."

I kept staring at him.

"I can't promise you I won't die, Bea. Wish I could. Ever since the first mission I've been wishing I never signed up for this madness. But, if I had, I'd never have met you. So, I see it as a coin toss."

I raised an eyebrow.

"Comes down one side and my life is over, comes down the other... and my life begins again."

His hand found mine. I wanted to squeeze it because I was scared. I wanted to jerk it away because today might be the one day Frank decided to leave his paintings alone in twenty-three years and come for a stroll down the beach.

Tom made the decision for me by covering my hand with his.

"I loved a man... a long time ago..." I said, unable to meet his eye, "...he died in the last war. I don't want it to happen again."

"I'm doing my best to stay alive. Think I'll be ok. I've got my lucky charm, after all."

"Some rabbit's foot you've had since childhood?"

"No," he kissed me, "you're my lucky charm. Having you to come back to will keep me alive."

Owen said something like that once...

I kept those words from my lips and let him hold me until my mind returned to Frank.

I'll kill you if you fuck another man...

That's what Frank always said. I believed him the first time he said it. I believed him the last time he'd said it, too.

Which had been the previous night when he'd come to my room to do his business with me.

I wore a scarf to conceal the bruises blooming around my throat. The wind kept tugging it, as if wanting to reveal my shame to Tom.

It had been a long time since Frank came to my room. I'd frozen when I heard his footsteps creaking down the hall, accompanied by his breezily whistled rendition of *It Had to be You*. Like a mouse with nowhere to run, knowing a predator was close, all it could do was stay still, hoping its trembling body wasn't noticed by the prowling, hungry beast.

Have you been a good girl while I've been away, Sweetness?

A gull shrieked. The wind picked up, pulling at my scarf more insistently.

Well, Sweetness, have you?

I fidgeted with the scarf, making sure it stayed in place. The ones on my neck weren't my only bruises; the others were just easier to hide.

"Bea?" Tom ran his hands down my cheek, "Are you ok?"

I nodded, then turned to face towards Grey Gull and the gradually stiffening breeze.

"My husband... it's hard being with him. Odd how quickly we can forget, isn't it? Even after half a lifetime."

I don't think you've been good at all. And that's disappointing, Sweetness.

How could men be so different? All made of the same stuff. Flesh, muscle, bone, blood, stitched together and stuffed with all manner of things, some wonderful, most mundane, a few terrifying. Maybe more than a few in Frank's case.

I hadn't seen the belt at first. It had been a long while since I'd tasted it. I thought Frank had got bored of it, become so engrossed in his painting sex and violence had lost whatever lustre they'd once held. I've never known if he actually liked sex that much, but the violence, I think something inside him always enjoyed that.

Perhaps it was the artist in him; perhaps he wanted to see what he could paint upon my skin.

Have you been a good girl, Sweetness?"

At first, he'd spoken those words evenly, latter they became breathless as he worked first the belt and then himself.

With Tom, it had been beautiful; with Frank, it was hideous. The same act, but as with men, it could be twisted into something else entirely.

Tom stared at me, eyes full of concern. Did he love me? How could he, really?

Owen had, but I had been a different person then. Now... now I was this pathetic thing. A useless woman who'd let a useless man break her and reduce her until she was something she no longer recognised, that Owen and Dad wouldn't recognise either.

"Leave him, Bea. When I'm done here, come back to Kansas with me..."

I'll kill you if you fuck another man...

"I'll think about it, I promise."

I pecked his cheek and started back towards the Castle.

It was too far away to see, but its gravity pulled me regardless.

1934

I spend most nights alone.

Frank never stays long after finishing his business, which is for the best. He still comes to me, he still hurts me, he still cleans himself on my sheet when he's finished.

Occasionally, he kissed my forehead or back of my head and breathed, "Goodnight, Sweetness," in my ear, but mostly, he says nothing.

Each night I wait for an hour before trying to sleep. I hated it even more when Frank woke me up.

That momentary disorientation, that unpreparedness, that sense of panic as his hands invade me. Sometimes he slaps my face to wake me up if I have fallen asleep; sometimes, he doesn't.

I prefer to be awake; to steel myself with the promise that it won't take long.

I always hear his tread on the stairs. The boards are old and warped throughout the Castle, but they're particularly bad on the stairs, protesting any intrusion with outraged squeaks. When he turns towards his room, I sigh with relief and turn out the lamp.

Sometimes there's a pause as if he's deciding just how he wants to finish his day. Straight to sleep or hurting and using his wife first. He can linger for quite a while making his mind up. I wouldn't have thought there was much to think about, but there you go.

If he whistles, I know what is coming. Frank has several tunes in his repertoire, but most commonly, it's *It Had to Be You*. I've learned to hate that song over the years. Now and then, he sings it as he comes to my room.

"It had to be you, it had to be you,
I wandered around, and finally found..."

He can sing surprisingly well, a lot better than he can whistle. A deep bass voice that would work well in the music hall. It always chilled me. Things were worse when he sang. I don't know why.

"The somebody who,
Could make me be true..."

I always wanted to hide when I heard those words. I never did, though. I just sat up and waited for my husband with a rictus smile stretched over my face as the door rattled and swung open.

And could make me be blue,
And even be glad, just to be sad...

Then he'd stand against the wall, staring at me, something smack halfway between a grin and a sneer on his increasingly flabby face.

"*...Thinking of you...*"

Afterwards, when he'd cleaned himself and said goodnight with a kiss or a slap or a warning about what would happen if I didn't get pregnant this time, I would listen to his footsteps, the floorboards marking their progress, until his bedroom door shuts.

Then I would out the lamp, curl up and hope my dreams would take me some place better. Would take me back to Camelot. During my early years in the Castle, I often cried myself to sleep, but by 1934, it took a lot more than Frank's nocturnal visits to make me cry.

Sleep was my only friend. It took me away from my life. Sometimes I wished I would never wake up.

I usually sleep till dawn. I've always been sensitive to light and rise with the day. Every so often, restless nights kept me awake, but those weren't too bad. My thoughts turned to my sorrows and losses, but if not friends, they were at least familiar companions.

It was waking in the middle of the night I didn't like.

I know it's something a child would say, but I didn't like the dark inside Grey Gull. I'd never been afraid of the dark before, not back home in the vicarage with Dad, not at *St Andrew's* in Birmingham, not in London with Mrs Hollister.

Only here.

Because here, darkness is different.

Not when I first out the light and it comes rushing in. Then it is only what it should be, and nothing lives in it bar the furniture. But when I wake in the night, it has changed.

It feels alive.

It feels wrong.

It feels melancholy.

It feels hungry.

It feels *sloightly on th' huh.*

I often managed to convince myself that was nonsense. Frank always told me I talked nonsense, alongside everything else I messed up.

But sometimes I didn't.

Sometimes it was more than imagination.

I heard things. Those warped boards complaining as they do when feet pass over them, a crackling sound, like old papers being scrunched into a ball, the raspy pant of a breathless old man.

Sometimes a smell arose, like something the tide washed onto the beach to rot in the sun. Only faintly, but always the same.

Sometimes words. The voice of the house whispering to me. Once in a while so clearly it was like someone at my shoulder; other times so faint it was almost nothing. Almost, but not quite.

Sometimes I talked back. Sometimes I didn't. Sometimes I thought I was mad. Sometimes I didn't.

I didn't scream. I didn't rise from my bed to peer into the shadows. I didn't light the bedside oil lamp. There was no point; there was nothing to see. The same as the things in the corner of my eye during daylight, it would never be there when I tried to look directly at it.

By 1934 I'd become used to it. Almost.

If I had to list my fears, Frank would come a lot higher than something nameless I glimpsed out of the corner of my eye that left a bad stink once in awhile.

Frank was much more than *sloightly* on th' huh.

But, if I could survive with Frank, I could live with whatever else resided in Grey Gull. If it was going to do me any harm, it would have done so by then.

Or so I thought.

That night, Frank worked late and went to bed without bothering me. I was thirty-nine, and the likelihood of another child, while not impossible, was receding rapidly. Frank still became irritable when I dutifully told him my time of the month had come again, like a schoolmaster inspecting the sloppy homework of a dim-witted and exasperating pupil.

He still gave me the belt when I brought him the bad news, but that was starting to wane. Perhaps it was dawning on him he couldn't beat me into pregnancy, or maybe he just wasn't enjoying hurting me as much as he used to. He'd piled a lot of weight on and smoked almost constantly. A breathless wheeze accompanied any exertion. Perhaps beating his wife was more effort than he cared for these days.

When Frank's door clicked shut, I put aside my book, turned off the oil lamp and went to sleep after a few minutes listening to the sea's lullaby.

I don't know how long I slept, but no hint of dawn teased the window when I opened my eyes.

"Frank...?"

No reply came, save a rapid, rasping pant.

Although I'd heard it before, it's still an alarming sound to wake up to.

"Is... someone there?"

The breathing grew clearer, as if coming closer. There was no other response.

This was the point I tended to screw my eyes shut, bury myself under the sheets and pillows and pretend nothing was untoward. That was pretty much the metaphor for how I'd lived my life since Owen died, after all.

Instead, this time, I sat up and stared into the darkness.

The sounds, smells, sights, feelings always faded when I responded to them, flitting away fast enough to make me doubt they'd ever been anything at all. But this time, it became louder.

"Who are you?"

The room was dark with the curtains drawn, but I saw nothing in the deep shadow to make me think someone was in the room. But the wheezy, harsh, phlegmy panting continued. It reminded me of how Frank breathed when he was doing his business atop me, but faster, harder, and more excited.

"Go away," I said, "I'm not scared of you."

That wasn't true, but the words made for something more substantial to hide behind than my pillows.

The sound swelled out of the night. As if some sicky animal were crawling up the bed, though neither the mattress nor frame suggested anything was.

I pulled my legs up, grasping my knees.

The breathing came closer still and with it a smell. Dry, dusty, stale, old. Something on the very cusp of rotting away to nothing. Again, it was something I'd experienced before.

But not this closely.

Despite knowing there would be nothing to see, I twisted around towards the oil lamp, slapping my hand on the table till I found the matches next to it.

All the time, the breathing got louder, like an approaching train. By the time a match hissed and sparked, I could feel the movement of air against my ear, as cold as anything that cut across the North Sea.

The first match died before it took. In the transitory flash of light, I thought I saw something out of the corner of my eye, something the shadows did not retreat from, something misshapen and wrong, a figure, but not quite. Something, as Mutt Harris had once told me, *sloightly on th' huh.*

I swallowed my scream. I'd only wake the children or, worse, Frank.

Instead, I concentrated on getting another match out of the box. I dragged it across the sandpaper before my shaking hand lost it.

The breathing became a dark roar. I expected hands to follow it. Long, bitter fingers wrapping around my throat to squeeze and squeeze the way I sometimes thought Frank wanted to do while he was at his business with me.

The match took with a fizz, and the breath came in one final cutting rush.

I thrust the match forward, narrowing my eyes against the tiny sun.

The room was empty, the breathing gone and that musty stink with it.

I cowered behind the match until it burnt my fingers, and I had to shake it out with a curse.

Only silence returned with the darkness.

I could have lit the oil lamp, but that was what children did. I was not afraid of the dark.

Slowly, I eased myself back down. There was nothing to hear but the familiar turn and hum of the sea. No more breathing.

But in that final panted breath before the match ignited, had a word accompanied the frigid air hissing into my ear?

I wasn't sure, but it sounded like it had.

I whispered what I thought I'd heard back into the night.

"Mine…"

Nothing in the darkness answered me.

1943

It was a long week.

Frank painted by day and came to my room every night. Sometimes he brought his belt. Sometimes, he didn't. Every night he whistled, *It Had to be You,* so I knew he was heading for my door. Each night he asked me the same question.

Have you been a good girl, Sweetness?

Each night I promised him I had. Each night he slapped my face and told me I was a lying bitch.

Each night I tried not to think of Tom till after he'd wiped himself clean on my sheet and gone to his room as if those thoughts and feelings might leach out and betray me.

Each night after he'd left me alone with my tears and bruises, the house whispered to me.

Useless woman. Useless mother. Useless wife.

The house hadn't talked to me for a long time. But now Frank was back, so was the voice. And the creaks and whatever moved in the shadows, in the corner of my eye.

The house was *sloightly on th' huh* once more.

I didn't ponder it too deeply. I didn't listen. I didn't look.

I'd become very good at such things over the previous twenty-three years.

Tom, on the other hand, was something else. I'd had no practice at pushing *good* things from my mind.

I wanted to run away with Tom. There was nothing for me here. Nothing other than what I'd endured every day since I'd rolled up to the Castle's door on Mutt Harris' cart all those years ago.

Why was I even *thinking* about it? There was no decision to make. I would leave with Tom and be happy. And if that happiness turned out to be an illusion or a transitory thing, if Tom tired of me or decided he wanted a younger woman when the difference between us became more pronounced as time took its dues with me. Wherever I ended up, could it possibly be worse than here?

I just couldn't let myself believe it.

The burdens of any life are harder to bear once you know something better is possible.

Ten missions.

That was what was keeping me tethered to the Castle and to Frank. Nothing else.

The boys were off pursuing their own lives. I worried about them daily, but I had sacrificed so much for them. I couldn't use them as an excuse anymore. Nor the vows I made before God. I couldn't be punished for breaking those vows any more than I'd already been punished for making them.

Ten missions.

And then I would be free.

He's going to die...

The voice breathlessly hissed that to me one night after Frank had cleaned himself and left.

I had to clamp my hands over my ears to adequately ignore that one.

The next time I went to our meeting place, I was sure Tom would not be there. He was dead, like the thing I shared the Castle with told me. It seemed inevitable.

I almost cried when I found him sitting on the beach's edge, staring out to sea.

"Nine to go," he grinned.

I did cry then.

"I want to go with you," I said later as we sat together, his arm around my waist.

"Really?"

"You were serious about that... weren't you?"

He hugged me so fiercely I winced. Though that was more to do with the bruises than the hug.

"Never been more serious," he said, stroking my hair.

That was the only time I ever believed I would be free of Frank. I couldn't do it on my own; whatever Frank did, I was too cowered, too scared to walk away from him. But Tom lent me his strength, and for one heady, beautiful moment, I did think anything was possible.

Nine more missions.

Just nine.

We sat, and I listened to him talk about Kansas and buying a little farm somewhere.

"Couldn't we live in a city?" I asked.

"Why?"

"I've been removed from the rest of humanity for a long time. A bit of hustle and bustle appeals."

Tom mulled it over for a second before grinning that grin again, "Sure, why not? Whatever makes you happy."

Whatever makes you happy.

Whatever makes *me* happy.

What a strange, alien, intoxicating phrase that sounded as the grey sea lapped the fragile shore.

When it was time to go, Tom jumped up and helped me to my feet. My sleeve slipped up my forearm as I took his hand.

"What's that?" he stared at my wrist before I could tug it down again.

"Nothing. I fell over. I'm clumsy."

"You've never seemed clumsy to me."

"You'd be surprised," I flashed a smile and turned away.

Tom's hand pulled me back.

"Bea... did he do that?"

Yes, when he held me down and did his business. But it's nothing. I have had far worse. He's made the most of his leave. He really has.

For a second, I swore the wind sounded like it was whistling *It Had to be You.*

"No," I insisted, "it was an accident. Like I said."

Tom was still holding my hand; he looked like he wanted to roll my sleeve up and take a better look. I yanked it away. That wouldn't be a good idea. He might notice the bruises looked a lot like fingers squeezing as hard as they could. Fingers that liked to hurt me.

"Let's not wait," Tom said, "leave him now. Today."

"Don't be silly," I laughed.

"Why not?"

"I can come and live with you on the airbase then, can I?"

"I've got some money; I can rent a place for you till we can go back home. Wherever, Lowestoft, Great Yarmouth, Norwich, maybe... Timbuktu, anywhere you're not with him!"

There was anger in Tom's voice. I'd never heard it before. I don't think he believed those bruises were an accident. I'm not much of a liar.

The idea rushed through me. Like I'd poured half a bottle of gin straight down my neck. My knees went weak, I wanted to giggle, I wanted to kiss him, I wanted to hit him, I wanted to scream, cry, laugh... anything, something!

Instead, I groped for reasons to say no, because saying yes frightened me far more than whatever whispered to me in the Castle.

"And what would happen to me if you don't make it back from one of those nine missions, eh, Tom? What happens then?"

It was the same argument I'd made with Owen. What happens to me if you don't come back?

"You won't have any more *accidents.* And maybe you won't get that look in your eye whenever you mention his name."

"What look in my eye?"

"My Uncle Earl was a mean sonofabitch. Treated the whole world like it was his personal latrine. Beat my aunt, beat my cousins, beat anyone who so much as caught his eye in a way he didn't like. He scared everyone. Had this dog, Barney. For some reason, he hated that dog more than anything else. Beat it, starved it, locked in an outhouse on hot days without water. Treated that dog as bad as you could without ever getting around to killing it. Got to the point Barney would hide whenever he saw Uncle Earl. He'd tremble, he'd whimper, he'd paw at the floor like he was trying to dig himself a lil' old hole to hide in. Got this look in its big brown eyes, more than just fear. A look like it wished it didn't exist because at least if you didn't exist, nothing could hurt you anymore."

Tom stared at me hard before adding.

"*That* look, Bea."

I stood rooted to the spot. Like a child caught doing something they knew they shouldn't be, while thinking they'd been awfully clever at hiding it.

Was it so obvious?

Competing emotions surged through me; anger, shame, fear, confusion, hope, despair. Others, too, the things we don't have names for. The primal, bestial remnants of what we once were.

I could see why Barney had wanted to dig a hole for himself.

I span away from Tom and started back along the beach towards the Castle. Escaping to my prison.

Tom caught up in a couple of strides, grabbed my wrist and pulled me back.

I tried to hit him. I think. Or maybe I just wanted to. It was hard to remember for certain, even thirty seconds later. My mind wasn't doing the things it should.

At some point, I stopped hitting him, or trying to, or wanting to, and he just held me.

And that made me feel safer than any hole in the ground ever could.

"Come with me, now. Don't go back. Please, Bea, never go back there. You never have to see him again."

I didn't say anything. I let his words fall upon me like fine, warm rain.

"I've got the jeep; I can take you wherever you want. I can..."

I closed my eyes and stopped listening, letting his voice, his Kansas drawl, wash me and bathe me. It was all impossible, but the sentiment was beautiful.

For the first time since Dad and Owen died, someone other than my children loved me.

"Bea?"

He pulled away to gaze down at me.

"I must look a frightful mess..." I said, dabbing my eyes.

"No more than usual."

"Careful."

That won me one of his grins.

I basked in it before saying, "He will be gone again soon."

"When?"

"Monday."

"You can leave him on Tuesday. Pack your things, and I'll take you away."

"Tom, I-"

His hands took my forearms, not tight enough to hurt but tight enough to bring my eyes back to his.

"Bea, I love you. But that doesn't matter none. You deserve better, and you ain't ever gonna know better if you stay in that house. With or without him. That place ain't good for you. Ain't good for no one."

"What do you mean?"

He shrugged, looked away as if groping for the right words before settling for, "It just feels wrong. It ain't a happy place."

No. It wasn't a happy place. It was *sloightly on th' huh*, after all.

"Tuesday," he said when I said nothing.

"I'll think about it," was all I trusted my tongue to say.

"Please..."

I nodded. And saw myself in some little room in some little town, alone and penniless. Nine, eight, seven, six... it didn't matter how many missions Tom had left. He wasn't going to complete them all. He wasn't going to come home, he wasn't going to see the trees lose their leaves, he wasn't going to see snow, he wasn't going to see Christmas. He wasn't coming home.

I knew.

As I'd known with Owen.

And though I knew what had happened because I hadn't married Owen, I couldn't stop myself from making the same mistake again. Perhaps some of us never can.

"I'll think about it," I said again.

"Bea..." he squeezed my arms.

"There's no hurry; he'll be gone on Monday. Then I'll have time. We'll have time. Act in haste, repent in leisure..."

He nodded and looked unconvinced.

And he was right.

Frank didn't go back to London on Monday.

The telegram came instead.

1930

The boys liked Auntie Izzy.

Partly it was the fancy car, partly the novelty of having someone different around, but, mainly, I think it was because she was happy to spend time with them. She talked to them in a way they understood. She always laughed and made them laugh in return. She played games with them; she let them take her off to show her all the wonders of their little world.

The inexhaustible supply of chocolate she kept conjuring for them probably didn't do her much harm either.

Having no children of her own, I suppose it gave her a chance to embrace her maternal instincts.

She was the perfect mother.

Which was easy when you didn't have to do any of the cooking, cleaning, washing, ironing, shopping and sundry other chores that being an actual mother involved.

I watched them playing together on the beach from the window. The boys were laughing, Izzy, too. More strangely, even Frank was smiling. He'd managed to drag himself away from his painting to be with his sons. And Izzy.

The perfect mother with her perfect family.

Jealousy wasn't something I was familiar with.

I didn't care about Frank. If Izzy wanted him, she was welcome. Given she thought his paintings were wonderful, it wasn't impossible her lack of taste might run to having some attraction for the fat, cruel, violent, emotionally stunted man I'd somehow conspired to share my life with.

But the boys were mine. They were all I had. The only thing.

However, if Izzy *was* attracted to Frank and wanted this ready-made family for herself...

I span away from the window, collected the sheets I'd ironed and folded in the kitchen and took them upstairs.

I was being silly. Foolish. I had more important things to worry about.

After I put the sheets away, I made the beds.

Izzy's perfume haunted Frank's.

He was supposed to be sleeping with me while Izzy stayed, but each night he'd left after an hour or two, claiming not to be able to sleep.

Had he come here instead of going out to the studio as he claimed?

If Izzy enjoyed what Frank liked to do in bed, then good luck to her. But...

The sound of the boys' laughter filtered through the window. It was unseasonably sunny and mild. A bonfire of autumn colours dressed the distant trees beyond the marshes. There wouldn't be many more days to enjoy being outdoors this year.

But my children were outside with Auntie Izzy. Who'd spent all week driving them to school in her fancy car, no doubt much to the amazement of their pals.

How long was she staying anyway?

I'd nearly asked Frank several times. He was keeping the worst of his temper in check, but it was still inside him. Taking notes and waiting. Simmering.

I thought she'd only be with us the one night. It didn't take long to rummage through Frank's paintings, even if he did have hundreds of the bloody things.

She'd now been here a week and showed no sign of going home.

It seemed a funny way to run an art gallery to me.

I made my bed last.

When done, I drifted to the window again. They were all still on the beach, throwing a ball to each other. All enjoying a merry old time.

I can't lose them. I can't.

My eyes slid to the cot, which had once been Francis' and then Simon's before it was Tilly's. It still sat in the corner, as bare as salt-dead trees in flooded pasture, without mattress, sheets, or blankets.

I'd pleaded with Frank to move it for the time being. He'd always shook his head, "No point," he'd say, eyes fixing on me, his words more accusation than ham-fisted reassurance, "They'll be another one along soon, won't there, Sweetness?"

I put my back to the wall next to the window and sucked back the tears. It still hit me, a wave of sorrow as sharp, bleak and cold as any of those breaking on the shore.

Like those waves, it always receded, ebbing back into the grey, leaving me shivering and torn from my battered senses. I feared one day, a wave too powerful to resist would carry me out into that vast nothingness, and I would be lost forever to grief and misery.

I curled shaking arms around myself. The shivers came. A coldness so deep and profound I wanted to crawl into the bed I'd just made and pile every blanket we had on top of me.

The shaking took a long time to subside. I screwed my eyes shut so I couldn't see that barren, empty cot. So I couldn't see the floorboard in the corner under which I'd hid the canvas bag containing Owen's letters, his ring and my photographs of him. So I couldn't see the walls of the Castle, which, without the children, was just a prison slowly tumbling back into the surf.

In time, the tears dried, the shivers passed. Only the melancholy remained, like the drying foam on a wrack-line marked the memory of the sea.

Another sound came, harsher and stranger than the gulls but just as mad.

Frank was not just laughing but braying. Uncontrollable, gushing, side-splitting almost lunatic merriment. It pulled me back to the window.

I almost expected to see him standing over Francis and Simon, poised with a bloody axe, maniacal grin stretching and contorting the fat of his face into something grotesque and inhuman. That Izzy, good old Auntie Izzy, would be hooting away, hands on hips, blood-red nails stark against her cream trousers, asking Frank to be an absolute *darling* and chop another bit off one of the *darling* boys for her.

Of course, there was nothing of the sort.

The four of them were at the sea's edge. The tide was high, hissing and rattling back and forth over the shingle. They all had their shoes off, standing in a line, wobbling on the uncertain footing and screaming as the numbing water frothed around their ankles.

Izzy held Simon's hand. She was looking at him, mouth open, eyes wide as my son bounced excitedly up and down. Frank held his other hand. Francis splashed a few feet further in the sea, trousers rolled up to his knees. He was looking back over his shoulder, giggling.

And Frank, head thrown back, laughing louder than the swirling gulls and incessant surf.

I put my hands on the windowsill, trying to steady myself.

Stop being silly. Stop it now!

The thought, the possibility, the darkest fantasy of losing my boys, ripped me deeply.

What if he threw me out? What if he moved Izzy in to take my place? What could I do? Go to the police? Would they give a hoot about a man not wanting his wife anymore? I could go to court, but I had no money save a few shillings and pennies squirrelled into my derisorily named running away fund.

He always told me what a bad mother I was; perhaps he'd decided enough was enough. I knew I had never made him happy. I'd tried to convince myself that was his nature rather than anything I could do. But what if I was wrong? Maybe it wasn't Frank, maybe it *was* me? Perhaps I was a bad mother. And a bad wife. His anger and tempers didn't happen because that was the kind of man Frank Harryman was, but because I *was* a useless woman. A disappointment, a failure. Too broken by Owen's death to ever be a woman capable of making any man happy.

Outside, Frank's laughter, so unfamiliar it sounded more like a discomforted beast than a man playing with his children, grew louder.

When I raised my eyes again, the four of them were walking back to the house. Francis talking animatedly to Frank, basking in the rare light of his father's attention. Simon clutched Izzy's hand, chatting with a machine gun's speed while pointing at something overhead with the hand holding his shoes. He was probably warning her about getting bombed by a seagull. He was at the age where things like a seagull pooing on your head was both the funniest and most fascinatingly terrible thing imaginable.

I watched them pass under the window. Something tried to claw its way out of my stomach.

Frank was listening with rare interest to whatever Francis was talking about, but, just before they disappeared from view, my husband's eyes shot up towards me.

He was still smiling, but in that instant, something cold and predatory turned beneath it. My imagination, of course. Imagination coupled with the sun choosing that moment to disappear behind a cloud, bringing a shadow racing from the sea, up the beach and onto the Castle in the beat of my heart.

Still being silly.

A few seconds later, boots and voices echoed from downstairs as they piled into the kitchen to warm and dry themselves.

Frank called up the stairs.

"How about a spot of lunch, Sweetness? Dunno about everybody else, but I'm absolutely starving…"

1916

We found a pub on one of the streets around the back of Victoria Station, filled with men in uniform supping their first beers back in Blighty. Though, from the look of it, some of them had got off much earlier trains than Owen.

Owen bought a stout for himself and a port and lemon for me, the barman wished us both all the luck in the world, and we took the drinks and best wishes, along with our bags, to a little table in the corner.

I sat and stared at him. Owen sat and stared back.

"What are we going to do?" I asked.

Owen sipped his pint, and the sip didn't stop till it was a gulp. He reduced half the glass to white foam.

He reached over and took my hand.

"If it means being with you, I'm happy to sit here for a week until I get the train back."

"Happy to sit with your pint, more like."

He winked, and the remainder of the stout chased the rest down his throat.

"Thirsty?"

"Only for you."

"Go on, get another for yourself," I laughed.

He stood up, bent over and kissed me softly on the lips. Which was a bit forward, even for a pub, in 1916. However, no one paid us any heed. The war was changing a lot of things. Didn't stop me from blushing as Owen returned to the bar, though. A couple of old goats in flat caps slapped Owen's back as he waited. I assumed for his military service rather than the public display of affection.

When he came back with a fresh stout, I repeated my unanswered question, "What are we going to do?"

Owen went at his new pint before answering; when he did, his eyes held mine for only a second, then skipped away, "We'll have to get a hotel for the night."

As we'd missed the last train home, the only alternative was a night on a bench in Victoria or Paddington Stations, so that made sense. Although, of course, it presented problems, too, given my refusal to marry Owen before the war was over.

He took another gulp. I realised what I'd first taken as reckless drinking brought on by what Owen had endured in France was nothing of the sort. It was nerves. He wanted to ask me something. And this time, it wasn't going to be to marry him.

"Bea, why..." he put the already half-empty glass down and twisted it in a beer puddle on the table, "...why... why don't we get a room together...?"

"Because we're not married," I said evenly enough.

"But... if the war hadn't happened, we would be!"

"I don't think God sees it quite like that."

"Sod God," Owen muttered, lifting his pint.

"Owen James!"

The drink froze halfway to his lips; he looked like he was going to say something, then shook his head and sipped a little. When he put the glass down, he looked at me.

"If you'd seen half the things I have, you'd know God doesn't give a stuff about any of us..."

I bit down on my tongue. Such talk didn't sit easily with me, but the truth was I *hadn't* seen any of the things Owen had, and a lecture from me about blasphemy wasn't what he wanted as a welcome-home-glad-to-see-you-after-a-year-apart present.

However, I did have a pretty good idea what he did want.

"We said we'd wait..."

It was my turn to reach for my drink. I didn't exactly throw it down my neck with Owen's gusto, but the sudden fluttering in my tummy needed something to calm it.

"I just want... I just want to be with you. For one night. We don't have to do things. Well, not *everything*. I wanted to get married first, but you want to wait. And wait. And wait..."

His gaze flitted between me and the glass as if something in the foam was prompting his hesitant words.

I stared into my own drink but found nothing offering any advice.

"Most of the time," he said, suddenly sitting back, "it's like some big lark. An adventure. If the war hadn't happened, we'd all be working in the fields, factories, shops, offices. We'd be in the shipyards, the foundries, the mills. Down the mines. But the war did come, and we all got packed off to France. They gave us a rifle and a uniform and told us to kill Germans before they killed us, for king and country and all that.

Didn't tell us about the mud and the rain and the cold. Didn't tell us about living in a hole in the ground, didn't tell us about the rats and the flies. But you know what, Bea? There's times when it ain't so bad. We're just a group of lads having the biggest adventure of our lives. We sing, we laugh, we joke about, we talk about our girls and our families, our mates back home, we play cards, and we make the best friends we'll ever know, because you'll never be closer to another man than the one fighting at your shoulder..."

Owen scooped up his pint again. His hands, I noticed, were shaking slightly.

"But sometimes.... Sometimes it ain't alright. Sometimes it's like waking up and finding yourself in Hell. When the guns roar for hours and the shells fall about you, you have to listen to men dying, begging, crying, pleading and there ain't... ain't a damn thing..." he drained the glass, then put it carefully back on the table.

"There's this one lad, Pete, though everyone called him Geordie on account of him being... a Geordie..." he snorted, "...we aren't always the most original bunch at times. Anyway, Geordie bunked with me. Over there, a bunk's not a bed, just a couple of planks high enough off the ground so you won't drown in the mud.

Big, tall, gangly. You know the sort? All arms and legs. Talked faster than Fritz's machine guns, and with the way they speak up there, could hardly understand him half the time. Always larking about..."

Owen reached for his beer, remembering he'd already finished it, his hand slumped to the table beside it.

"One day, Geordie got a bit careless with his head. He was goofing about; the next, a kraut sniper got him. One minute alive, the next..." Owen ran a over his chest, "...and his brains were splattered all over my coat..."

"Owen..."

"Thing was, most of the snipers miss. Them German lads, they're the same as us. Don't want to be there any more than we do, but their Kaiser says the same as King George. Don't really see em. Hear em sometimes, laughing, singing, whatever. Just like us. Only in German. Our snipers tended to give em a warning shot if someone sticks their head out of the trench. They do the same. Sometimes they'll shout a warning, "Get your head down, Tommy!" then stick one in a sandbag."

Owen sat back up, his eyes glazed and distant, "Maybe the bastard who did for Geordie was having a bad day, or was new, or... or..."

I reached across the table and put both of my hands over his.

His eyes eventually focused.

"Thing is, what I'm trying to say..." he lapsed into silence, then took a deep breath "...I've loved you since we were in school. When Mrs Rabbit were trying to get us to memorise all the kings and queens of England, I kept getting it wrong because I was too busy stealing looks at you."

"And I thought it was just because you weren't very bright," I found a grin from somewhere.

"Well... and that..." he found one too, but it faded quickly, "...I don't want to go back, Bea. One heartbeat, I'll be thinking about you, and the next, some other bugger might be scraping my brains off his coat. And I live with that every second of every day. I just want to be here, at home, with you. But I can't. Not till the job's done. If I don't go back, they'll find me, put me up against a wall and shoot me. And that'll be a terrible waste of all Mrs Rabbit's shouting."

I wanted to say something. Anything. But I didn't know what, so I said nothing and just kept holding his hand. Sometimes, that's all you can ever do.

"They keep saying there's going to be a big push soon. Lots of boys are being allowed home. Might mean nothing. We have a lot of time on our hands to make somethings out of nothings. But Fritz and the Frenchies are knocking lumps out of each other along the front at Verdun. If we can throw enough at Fritz while he's got so many men committed at Verdun... we could break through. We could end it all. We could come home."

"That'd be something... wouldn't it?"

He nodded, "But that means going over the top. That means facing the guns and the shells, getting through the wire, getting past the mines, clearing out their trenches. They won't be warning us to keep our heads down then. No matter how many we send..." he swallowed and looked at his empty glass "...a lot of boys won't be coming home..."

But sometimes, holding a hand wasn't enough.

I picked up his glass, squeezed his shoulder and headed for the bar. I ordered a stout and another port and lemon. I wasn't much of a drinker, but I felt my hand shaking like Owen's.

I frowned when the barman put two pints in front of me to go with the port and lemon.

"I only asked for one," I said.

"I know, luv," he nodded at Owen, who sat hunched forward, head down, hands clasped together on the table, "but he looks like he needs more than one. Poor buggers, I'd buy them all a pint if I could..."

"You'd buy them all a pint if you weren't such an old skinflint, Stan," one of the men in caps propping up the bar said.

Stan the barman ignored him, "The second one's on the house."

"Thank you," I said, putting coins in his palm.

When Stan returned with my change, he pulled a face and lent across the beer-slickened bar, "Look after him, eh, luv. I lost my boy at Ypres. Trust me, he needs all the sunshine he can get."

"I will," I promised, taking a pint glass in each hand, "I will..."

1943

Grey Gull was a place of sadness.

And not just because of the life I lived within its walls. There's something about its very fabric. The scoured stone, lichen-flecked slate. The warped, floorboards anguished protest at every intrusion. The way the old glass ever so subtly distorts the light falling through it.

And outside, too, beneath the tranquil veneer that fools the eye and heart. The way the sea never rests from its agitation, the sky stretches, the gulls wheel and weep. How the grass and reeds forever sigh, the shingle crackles and clicks. It's as if this spot upon the Earth connects with something else, something deeper. Something that remains out of sight but still seeps into this world to stain and soil it.

There *were* moments of happiness. Every single one of them involved my children. But even then, the sadness always remained close. On the other side of a door, beyond a window, at my shoulder. Waiting in the wings. Watching. Eternally jealous and resentful of any interruption to its all-consuming melancholy.

The worst moments involved my children too.

Giving birth to Francis, terrified and alone. What happened to Tilly. Convincing myself Izzy was going to snatch them away from me. Listening to the whispers in the dark of the night and believing my children were in danger here, knowing my own weakness and fear jeopardised them by not taking them to safety. The knowledge that Frank tied me to this place throughout their childhoods.

Then there was the telegram.

Just a piece of paper.

I never expected it, yet always had. Ever since my boys went off to war, just like Owen had before them.

Frank rested a hand on my shoulder. An uncommonly gentle touch. I wanted to shake it off but didn't. Couldn't. Simply breathing was difficult enough. He was trembling. So was I.

I sat at the kitchen table. I don't remember sitting down. I don't remember much about those hours immediately after the telegram arrived.

When I opened the door to find a pale-faced telegram boy on the other side, I knew what the envelope in his hand contained. They called those boys the Angels of Death for a reason.

I just did not know which of my sons I had lost.

I will never forget the twenty-one words on the telegram he handed me.

The Ministry for War regrets to announce that your son Pte Simon Harryman has been killed in action. Letter to follow.

Gone. Just like that.

Later I found out he died in the allied landings on the Italian mainland.

I drank tea, watching the ripples slosh from side to side in time to my shaking hand; I cried. I stared at the sea through the window and thought of Francis out there somewhere.

Would I lose him too?

Thoughts, fears, and memories echoed and ricocheted around my mind.

I found myself at the backdoor, seeing my boys playing on the beach as they had so many times. Francis, quiet and serious, studying some shell or stone that'd caught his eye, Simon a whirl of limbs in perpetual motion as he tore about.

He'd never liked to be still.

Perhaps he'd always known he wouldn't have a long life and had tried to cram as much in as he could.

That didn't seem likely, but it was enough to bring more tears.

Not just tears but a wailing screech that forced itself out of my soul, until I couldn't help but vomit it into the otherwise silent house.

Frank put his arms about me. I would have collapsed to the floor if he hadn't.

He held me tight as I screamed at a world I could only see through tears and refracted memories.

In time, the fit passed. I found myself on my bed. Frank must have brought me upstairs, but I don't remember it.

He stretched out beside and behind me, one arm wrapped over my hip, face pressed into my hair.

"Could it be a mistake?" I may have asked Frank that before.

"No," he said, the slightest shake in his voice.

"Can you leave me on my own for a little bit, please," I said sometime later.

"We should be together."

I didn't argue.

Instead, I looked out of the window and watched the daylight soften with glassy eyes. Or at the bare, unfurnished corner of my room where the cot Francis, Simon and Tilly had all slept in had once rested.

At some point, I drifted off into nightmare-tossed sleep. When I awoke, both the light and Frank were gone.

I should do something.

Anything was better than this. Cook, clean, wash, iron. It didn't matter. Just something to dislodge the numb, all-consuming emptiness the angel of death had brought to my door.

Or run away with Tom.

That thought sent something else spearing through my grief and pain.

Guilt.

Was this, somehow, my fault?

Was God punishing me for my infidelity, for breaking the vows I'd made before Him?

I told myself God is neither cruel nor pernicious. But the idea He would take my son's life as punishment for me finding a little happiness in another man's arms refused to go away. It buzzed around my head like an agitated bluebottle.

In the end, I sat on the bed, hugging my knees, squeezing my eyes shut to keep in the latest tearful wave threatening to break upon my cheeks.

Useless woman...

I physically jerked away from the words spat into my ear.

The voice was always only a whisper, something, in the cold light of the next day, I could just about convince myself had been the wind, the sea, the groan of old timbers or the cry of a forlorn bird.

But this had been as clear as if Frank had still been beside me.

My eyes snapped open. Between tears and shadows, the world was a dark blur. But something moved across the room; I was sure of it.

Something with too-long limbs. It balanced upon its toes rather than the soles of its feet, like a cartoon villain sneaking about. A hunched back, a misshapen head. All its proportions a little askew, all its angles a bit wrong, all its features a fraction distorted.

Something *sloightly on th' huh...*

I blinked.

The room was empty; only the night kept me company.

The curtains hung open, allowing moon and starlight to dust the bedroom. I rubbed my eyes and stared into each of the darkest places in case someone – something – lurked within, but I could see nothing.

"Who are you?" I demanded.

Nothing.

"My son is... dead. Can't you leave me alone this one night?

Nothing.

I'd leant to ignore the voices, the sounds, the things I caught in the corner of my eye. Whatever it was, although it felt malign, it had done me no harm in my years in the Castle. If I convinced myself there was a rational explanation for what happened to Tilly. Which was something else I'd always just about managed in the cold light of the next day. Usually, I ignored it.

But I sat and lit an oil lamp, letting its light push the shadows back.

No figures lurked or prowled or sneaked about its periphery.

I was alone.

Slumping back onto the bed, I closed my eyes again.

'tis your doing...

Once more, I sat up. My heart should have been pounding, but I felt too tired for fear. That's the thing about intense grief; it leaves no room for anything else.

The room remained empty, though, again, the voice had been clearer and more distinct than ever before. Perhaps grief left no room for even scepticism.

"I'm not scared of you..."

Whatever it was, it wasn't much of a conversationalist.

It might not frighten me, but I kept my eyes open. After a few minutes, I kicked off the covers and crawled under them. Lacking the energy to undress or clean my teeth, I stared upwards, waiting for the thing to speak and painting Simon's face upon the ceiling while I could still remember it.

Would I forget him? If enough years passed, would I lose even that?

The tears welled again, the pressure growing on my chest as if something squatted atop me.

I sobbed. I don't how long for. Enough to feel drained of everything but breath by the time it abated.

Grief passes.

Eventually.

I knew that. The awful, clawing, racking pain of it, in time. It subsides, it fades, it reduces until it is something you can lock away inside yourself. You'll carry it always, but it stops eating you. At least it had with Owen and Dad.

That first night, such a possibility seemed a remote one. If I possessed the strength, I might have just walked into the sea and let it take me. Eat me, consume, destroy me and eventually discard what was left upon the wrack line with the other debris it did not care to keep.

He died because you are a whore...

The voice jerked me back.

This time I said nothing and kept my eyes on the ceiling. There would be nothing to see.

Bad, useless woman...

The words were a hiss. Clearer than usual, but there was something serpentine about them. If I could see the thing's mouth, I'd expect a forked tongue to flicker between its lips.

Another sound came. A creak. Like a foot on a floorboard. I still didn't look. Why bother? It didn't matter. There'd be nothing there. Perhaps it had always just been inside me. Perhaps life had finally cracked and broken me open, allowing this thing to slither out.

Maybe it was me that was *sloightly on th' huh.*

Frank will kill thee if he ever gets to see...

Another creak, louder, closer. Like something trying to sneak across the room on long, pointed tippy-toes.

Crush thee, break thee, chop thee up and throw thee away like an unwanted pup...

A shadow drifted over the ceiling. Elongated, gnarled, hesitant but restless.

Shoulds I tell him, Beatrice? Shoulds I? Maybe I really shoulds..."

A snicker, wet and throaty, accompanied the hiss this time. I kept my eyes on the shadow. Did it look like a hand reaching towards me? A hand with fingers bent and twisted in all manner of wrong angles? Or just a trick of the light, a trick of my imagination. A trick of guilt and grief, loneliness and heartbreak.

Useless woman, bad mother, whore... no one loves thee, no one wants thee... everyone close to thee dies in the end... don't they?

"No..." the word squirmed away from my lips before I could stop it.

Laughter came in reply.

Did I feel my hair move? Did something cold and old play across my face, fetid air expelled from somewhere rank? Was there a sound like a hand would make creeping over a pillow. Creeping like some giant, deformed, five-legged spider?

They all die in the end. And all Beatrice has left is sorrows. Francis is going to die. Tom is going to die. Thee knows that. Doesn't thee?

More laughter. The shadow on the ceiling was darkening like a coming storm, purple-black clouds preparing to weep upon the world.

Mummy, Daddy, Owen, Tilly, Simon. All gones. All gones. All gones...

My throat tightened. Loss. Sorrow. Anguish. A misshapen hand around my neck. Squeezing. My breath came in hard, harsh gasps.

Only Beatrice will be left. The useless woman. The bad mother. The whore.

I tried to speak, to protest. But nothing could escape my mouth.

The light was fading. Maybe the oil was running out. Or something was blocking it. Maybe the light was being sucked out of the world by a thing that only lived in the shadows, or in grief, or in the things that are cracked and broken.

But don't worry thy old bone. Thee won't ever be totally alone.

Something moved over my forehead. Something like a hand, but not quite. Something both cold and fetid. Something that had sharp bristles that made me think again of a giant deformed five-legged spider.

Thee still haves Frank, whistling It Had to be You, bringing his belt to thy room and doing his dirty businesses on thee...

Another snigger, another stroke of my forehead. Bristles scratched my skin. All the warmth of my flesh drained away. The touch was beyond freezing. The ceiling was black now, the room dark, my throat tight shut, a weight on my chest crushing me, pushing me down into the mattress, pushing me down into oblivion.

...but bests of all...

Something snapped next to my ear. Teeth. Hard, sharp and more than any mouth should hold.

...thee will always haves me!

I cried out, sat up and twisted around towards the lamp.

The room was empty. The lamp burned brightly. Nothing darkened the ceiling.

I was alone.

1927

Dr O'Conner could find nothing wrong with Tilly.

"Babies are hardy little things, tougher than we give them credit for," he said, lighting a cigarette in the kitchen after we'd come downstairs, then coughing hard enough to go even redder in the face than he already was.

"But she won't eat properly," I insisted.

"Her weight is good, her colour is fine, her lungs are clear, her heart is strong. She has no temperature. There is no swelling or tautness in her stomach," Dr O'Conner said, cigarette wedged in the corner of his mouth as he put his stethoscope back into the brown leather bag he'd brought with him, "Tilly's development is as it should be. She's lifting her head and looking around; she is not in discernible pain. You said her poo is normal?"

I nodded.

"And her pee is not dark?"

I shook my head.

"After three months, babies eat less. It's quite normal, Mrs Harryman. Please, do try not to worry yourself," Dr O'Conner's tone, as he pulled on his overcoat, was one of mild annoyance rather than reassurance. I was just a silly woman wasting his valuable time.

I knew full well babies needed less regular feeding after three months; I'd been through it twice before, after all.

"But she's hardly eaten at all for days!"

Dr O'Conner patted down the few long strands of hair he was valiantly trying to hide his baldness under, "And yet her poo and pee are normal, yes?"

After three babies, I considered myself well-versed in the fundamentals of poo and pee and had to agree they were.

"Well then," Dr O'Conner flashed me his yellowing teeth. I thought he would pat me on the head and tell me to run along now.

Instead, he turned his back on me, shook Frank's hand, repeated nothing was wrong and he'd have his bill sent in due course.

Frank saw him out. Their voices retreated down the corridor. I couldn't make out the exact words but guessed things like "overreaction" and "hysterical" were bandied about before concluding with an apology and a "you know how women can be," from Frank, accompanied with a roll of the eyes or a shake of the head.

Frank returned to the kitchen as O'Conner's car coughed and spluttered into life (it didn't sound any healthier than the doctor).

"Told you," he said.

"He's wrong."

"He's a doctor. Seen more babies than you ever will," Frank snapped. He sounded tetchy, a sign it was best to keep quiet and out of his way. For once, I was too worried and tired to pay it due heed.

"How many has he fed from his breast?" I snapped back.

Frank took a couple of casual paces across the kitchen and slapped me hard enough to make me stagger backwards.

"Baby's probably just bored sucking on your saggy tit. Fuck knows, I am."

I thought he would hit me again, but Simon chose that moment to rush in. He was past the age when he was falling down all the time and into the one where he wanted to run around exploring every corner of the world he found himself in.

And, if possible, either cover it with jam or break it.

He skidded to a halt and looked back and forth between us with big, unblinking eyes. They were the same colour as his father's but without the burning intensity. Or subtle hints of lunacy.

As I straightened up, still holding my smarting cheek, Frank shot me a look that said he'd be back to conclude our discussion at a later date before turning and sauntering out.

He patted Simon on the head as he went by, "Why don't you see if Mummy's got some biscuits, kiddo..." then his footsteps faded down the corridor along with an airily whistled rendition of *It Had to Be You*.

"Biscuit?" Simon asked, hopefully.

I handed him a digestive from the tin, then crouched down and hugged him because I needed one. Simon squirmed and giggled, far more interested in the biscuit than the hug.

"You be a good boy," I said, pecking his cheek.

He ran off, leaving a trail of crumbs in his wake.

I went upstairs to check on Tilly. Whatever Dr O'Conner's opinions on poo and pee, I knew she wasn't eating as she should. I had got her to take a little milk, but nowhere near enough. The painfully swollen state of my breasts told me that if nothing else did, and, frankly, my tits talked a lot more sense than Dr bloody O'Conner!

I was angry, though not with Frank. My husband slapping me was such a regular occurrence it counted as "normal." A familiar part of any day, like making the tea, washing the children or bickering over some mundane chore. I no longer cared what Frank did to me; I was too exhausted from looking after three young children and keeping on top of the Castle.

I was angry with Dr O'Conner. I had trudged through ice-skimmed mud and eviscerating wind to fetch him, and he'd treated me like a fool. But mostly, I was angry because I was scared.

"How are you, baby girl?" I asked, lifting Tilly gently from her cot.

In return, she made some gurgling noises, and her little hand reached for a stray lock of my hair.

A rocker was in the corner, and I sat by the window, trying to get Tilly to take my breast. She suckled a little, but not enough for my liking.

"What's the matter, beautiful? Why don't you want to eat? What's wrong? Is something upsetting you?" I held her up and bounced her, "And don't tell me nothing's wrong, like silly Dr O'Conner!"

Tilly babbled back at me.

In the window light, her colour was better. And then there was the serious matter of her poo and pee that Dr O'Conner put such trust in. Which, as I'd confessed to the Doctor did look (and smell!) entirely normal.

I settled Tilly back down in my arms and rocked her.

Perhaps I *was* being foolish.

Unnecessarily worrying over nothing but worry. Frank was always telling me what a bad mother I was. Maybe he was right. I wasn't bothered about everything else he said I was bad at, but I wanted to be a good mother, to fill my children's lives with love and happiness, even if, beyond those three little souls in my care, I was bereft of such things.

Good mothers worried, didn't they?

Mum died when I was little, Dad and Gran brought me up between them, but they were both long gone by the time I was sitting with Tilly, listening to the sea and my baby's breathing. I had no one to talk to about babies.

Or anything else.

Tilly seemed to return to normal over the next few days, still eating less than I (and my breasts) thought she should, but more than before. The incessant crying stopped, she slept better, her colour improved and she became more aware of her surroundings.

Maybe just a little bug then. Something trivial. Perhaps Dr O'Conner had been right after all. Silly me!

Three weeks later, my beautiful baby was gone.

1943

We held a memorial at *St Luke's* for Simon. Perhaps his body would come home one day, but we assumed he would rest in Italy for now, maybe forever.

Reverend Vaughn gave a lovely sermon and reading. Simon's friends, those who weren't off with the war, came. Francis was at sea, I wrote to tell him the awful news, but how long it would be before he received word, I did not know. Diane came, managing to get a 48-hour pass from the WRNS. She stood beside me, pale, thin and pretty in her uniform, and held my hand. We both cried. Frank was on the other side of me. He didn't.

As we trooped blinking into the churchyard, the drone of bombers greeted us. I paused, not wanting to look up, feeling guilty, feeling numb.

Diane slipped her arm into mine.

After thanking Reverend Vaughn, who clucked and tutted and squeezed my hand between his bony, liver-spotted ones, we walked to the *Horse & Hounds*. We'd arranged a wake in the upstairs room. Tea and sandwiches. Beer from downstairs for those who wanted it.

All the time, aircraft passed overhead. I tried to ignore them, but they kept drawing my eye skyward.

Was Tom up there?

Diane hurried me on, presuming the bombers were just an unwanted reminder of the wretched war that had taken my son's life.

Inside, Diane pressed a cup of tea into my hands. At least they weren't shaking as they had done throughout the memorial.

I was supposed to be doing something, I was sure. Thanking people for coming, accepting their commiserations, their sympathies.

All I could do was sit in the corner, drink tea and wish I were elsewhere.

I let Frank do the talking. He was better at it than me. He drifted around the well-wishers. Pressing flesh, nodding his head, pulling the right faces, saying the expected words.

He seems quite normal when he tries...

The thought almost made me smile.

Instead, I cried.

Diane gave me a handkerchief. She appeared well-supplied.

There must come a point when the human body can muster no more tears. You become too emotionally dehydrated. I had yet to reach that point, though I quickly regained control of myself. Crying in public was not very British. And I was not the only person in the room who'd lost loved ones to the war.

When I finished my tea, Diane went and fetched me another one. And a cucumber sandwich to go with it.

I didn't eat the sandwich, but I did ask Diane if she'd set a date with Francis for the wedding. It was a question she was probably expecting.

"When the war is over. We both think that's best..."

I wanted to put my fresh tea and cucumber sandwich aside, seize her hand and beg Diane to marry my son as soon as possible. Never delay doing the things you want. Waiting is fine if you have endless tomorrows to fill with dreams and possibilities. But that's the thing. None of us do.

Few people get to live their whole lives in Camelot.

Diane and Francis had been sweethearts since they were fifteen. Just like Owen and me. They were engaged to be married, but Francis went away to war. Just like Owen and me.

Diane hadn't wanted to wait at home, neither had I. She'd joined the Women's Royal Naval Service rather than attending secretarial college like I had. But there were too many similarities.

I didn't want to see life repeating itself, though I feared it would.

They all die in the end. And all Beatrice has left is sorrows. Francis is going to die. Tom is going to die. Thee knows that? Doesn't thee?

Yes, I knew that. But I couldn't tell Diane, with her dark, intelligent eyes and quick mind. Not rational, smart Diane who considered life something solvable by calculus and slide rules.

I didn't know exactly what she did in the WRNS, "cypher officer" was as much as she'd ever say. From the significant look she gave me the few times I'd asked more, I thought it was something hush-hush. She was clever and a bit of a whizz at languages. Her contribution to the war involved a lot more than keeping the boys morale up.

What would she say if I told her something was whispering in my bedroom at night?

Grief puts terrible stress upon the mind, or some such, most likely.

What would she say if I told her I was having an affair with a younger man who wanted me to run off to America with him?

Good for you, I suspected.

Diane was far too polite a young woman to say so, but she'd never been much taken with Frank. His enthusiasm for Herr Hitler, Mr Mosley and antisemitism when she'd started coming to visit probably had something to do with that. Though maybe she also noticed just how odd Frank was.

She saw a lot with those dark eyes of hers.

As soon as it was polite, we walked back to the Castle together. Frank opted to stay in the pub and get drunk. His compassionate leave would be over soon. And I would be alone with whatever I shared Grey Gull with again.

Frankly, my husband was by far the more unpleasant and unnerving of my two night visitors.

Most of the way we talked about Francis and Simon. More accurately, I talked while Diane listened to my well-worn anecdotes from their childhoods.

By the time we reached the path across the marshes, and the reed buntings and warblers flitted about us, the conversation had dried up. My throat was sore from talking and tears.

"I'll stay till Frank gets back," Diane said as the Castle came into view, immediately adding to the weight around my heart.

I shook my head, "That might not be till the pub closes. When he gets a thirst..."

Diane shrugged.

I liked her; I always had. I would have even if I'd never noticed how Francis looked at her.

Once inside, Diane took off her Wren's hat and unbuttoned the tunic, then set about making tea while I fidgeted about the kitchen table. I wanted to get out of my funeral blacks but found no desire to go upstairs. It was still bright outside, but the weight of Grey Gull's shadows pressed particularly keenly upon my shoulders.

And these were shadows that sometimes moved, sometimes talked, sometimes told truths I had no wish to hear.

"Let's go outside," I said when the tea was ready, "it's too nice to be cooped up in here."

There were some deck chairs I'd left facing the beach. We sat, sipped and stared. Sunlight speared a becalmed sea through the broken clouds, turning it a dark blueish grey where shadow fell, aquamarine dusted with sea-sparkles where it reached.

My eyes darted back to the house. We were far enough away to be out of earshot.

"I'm having an affair," I blurted without warning.

Diane put her tea aside. Was this the kind of conversation you should have with your son's fiancée? I wasn't sure. I couldn't remember the last time I'd shared a confidence with anyone.

"Does he make you happy?"

"Yes, he does."

"We all deserve to be happy once in a while."

"I made a vow before God."

"We all make mistakes; they're usually in front of someone or other," she smiled, "divine or otherwise."

"He's asked me to leave Frank. To run away with him. To Kansas. Of all places."

"Go," Diane said without hesitation.

"Just like that?"

"I love Francis very much. More than I can ever find the words for. And I know a lot of words. French ones, Hebrew ones, German ones. Latin ones, even a few Arabic ones. But sometimes... sometimes I worry."

"Worry?"

She turned her hands, then pulled a packet of cigarettes from her pocket. I took one when she offered, and after we'd battled the breeze to light them, she blew a stream of smoke towards the sky before replying.

"I worry how much of Frank he has inside him. His Dad always has... unsettled me."

"He has Frank's eyes. He has Frank's hair. Everything else is me."

Diane nodded, "That's what I think. That's what I hope..."

"But-"

"That doesn't matter. What I am saying is..." she glanced back at the Castle, "...I don't know how you've stayed here so long. It's such a sad place. Don't you think, or is it me?"

"It's not you."

Diane wrapped her arm across her chest to rub her other shoulder as if the air carried a chill. "Francis has told me things. Not everything. And I'm sure there is more he doesn't know. About his Dad, the way he treats you."

Those dark bright eyes fixed on me. I drew on my cigarette before hurriedly looking away. Diane was twenty-three, roughly the same age I was when I first came to Grey Gull.

"Frank..." I didn't have the strength to make excuses for him, so I let his name fade away in another stream of smoke.

"He has a shadow," Diane said.

"A shadow?"

Diane paused, as if struggling to find exactly the right ones of all those many words she knew.

"A darkness. Something follows him. You've seen his paintings?"

"I didn't know you had?"

"Francis showed me some when his Dad was away," she shuddered, "Just the once. I don't think I slept for a week."

I thought she was joking, but the way she stared into the middle-distance, cigarette poised on her lips, hinted she was serious. Her eyes snapped back to me, "But it goes a lot further than bad – disturbing – paintings, doesn't it?"

I suddenly wished I'd said nothing. I'd spent twenty-three years saying nothing. I'd become very good at saying nothing. Opening your mouth can often take you to places you don't want to go.

"He's a difficult man," was all I conceded.

"If Francis... if Francis turns out to have more of his Dad in him than his eyes and his hair. I would leave him..."

"Francis is the love of your life, Diane," I said.

She pursed her lips, flicking away the ash accumulating on her cigarette.

"Was Frank the love of yours?"

I smiled. Thin and forced, "No, he wasn't. The love of my life died in France twenty-seven years ago."

"I didn't know."

"I don't talk about him much."

In fact, I didn't talk about him at all. Frank didn't approve of me talking about Owen. I stubbed out my cigarette.

"His name was Owen. We were sweethearts from the age of fifteen, like you and Francis. He went to war, and we decided not to marry until the war ended. Like you and Francis. He didn't come home."

"I'm so sorry."

"My life has had more than its fair share of sorrows. Owen, Frank, Tilly, now Simon."

"But now you have a chance to be happy? Away from this place."

Away from this place.

I could barely imagine such a thing.

Even less so whilst I was still trying to comprehend losing another man I loved to the madness of war.

Diane leaned over and took my hand. She was as serious looking as Francis. Her face had too many angles to be classically beautiful, but she had something about her. Something sharp, bright and intense. Something that shone through. My son saw it, and so did I.

She might be young, but she was smart and wise. Anything she said was always worth listening to.

"Go. With this man. If you love him and are sure he feels the same. You've done more than anyone could ever have asked of you when you stood before God and made those promises. You've been a wonderful mother. Francis is a good man. Simon was too. What happened with Tilly wasn't your fault, whatever some idiots say behind your back. What's left to do? There's nothing for you here. *Nothing.* We get but one life; please make the most of what remains of yours."

She was right about some of those things but wrong about others.

And I would never have the chance to leave this place.

1952

It was a year before I saw Merry again.

It wasn't until later I realised it was *exactly* a year. To the day. Probably to the hour. Maybe the minute.

I hadn't quite forgotten Merry. Despite only talking to him for a few minutes, something about him stayed with me, but I'd long since stopped expecting to see him again.

In the days and weeks following our first meeting, I walked that stretch of beach more often and for longer. I didn't know why. It wasn't any foolish notions of romance, as well as being far too old for such silliness, I wasn't attracted to him. Maybe it was just loneliness. Despite spending the majority of my adult life alone, Frank and Grey Gull hadn't fully extinguished the yearning for friendship that most of us have somewhere in our souls.

Or was it something else? Curiosity? Perhaps. But I couldn't shake the feeling there was some connection between us, not romantic, physical, or emotional. Just... *something*.

Still, that day I drifted down the beach, I was not thinking of Merry, nor that the day was very much like the first time we met. Blue skies, a kiss of breeze lacking its seasonal bite and a sea troubled by only the softest of ripples.

I don't recall what was on my mind. Nothing of significance. Those long walks along the shingle often emptied my head, the crunching beat of my feet the only accompaniment to the ever-present melodies of sea, wind, and birdlife. I could lose hours here. Sometimes, I suspected, days and weeks might evaporate on the breeze if I wasn't paying attention.

When my mind did come back into focus, a man sat on a large piece of bone-white driftwood ahead of me.

Merry waved.

I stopped and stared at him.

The same as with our previous meeting, I couldn't understand how I hadn't noticed him earlier.

After a second or two, I raised my hand and crossed the bank of broken shells and sea-smoothed stones towards him.

"Lady Beatrice!" he jumped up, whipping out a handkerchief as I approached to dust down the driftwood. He ushered me to sit beside him.

"Merry," I said, not knowing what else to say.

He licked his forefinger and stuck it in the air, "Yes, still just Merry today... come, rest your weary feet."

Merry sat aside the driftwood again. Likewise, I daintily lowered myself, facing the beach I had walked along and the distant out-of-sight Castle. Just as I had last time.

"I trust you made it home before the rain?" Merry asked.

"Yes, thanks. I'm surprised you remember?"

"Why shouldn't I?"

"It must be the best part of a year ago."

"Really?" Merry's eyebrows, which were bushy and as threaded with grey as his beard, shot up.

"Time flies..." I smiled.

"Oh, that's just one of his tricks! Flies, skates, leaps, twists, turns, wobbles, dawdles, swings about a bit, wiggles its hips and hides behind the bushes. It can stop completely if you take your eye off the sneaky chap," he leaned forward a fraction towards me and added in a conspiratorial whisper, "sometimes it even goes backwards. Funny old fellow is Mr Time."

"I can't say I've noticed it doing most of those things."

Merry was clearly as mad as any hatter, but he made me smile. And I could forgive someone a lot of faults in return for that gift.

"The trick," Merry tapped his nose, "is to know which way to look. If you stick to staring at it head on, you'll only ever see it do the one thing. However..." he leaned to his left as if peering towards the grass-fringed marshes "...if you peek at the sides you can catch Mr Time up to all manner of mischief. And if you manage to snatch a peep around the back..." Merry rubbed his hands together and chuckled as he straightened himself up.

Merry was dressed exactly as he had been before, faded leather brocade coat with silver buttons, once-white linen trousers and sandals. The fact a man might wear the same clothes a year apart is not remarkable. It was the driftwood we sat on that nagged at me.

It obviously couldn't be the same piece of wood. I had not seen anything like it since that day; fifteen feet long and so bleached it was almost painful to look at in the sunshine. Yet, here it was, with an identical faint patina of whorls vaguely mirroring the nearly imperceptible pattern on Merry's coat.

The more it tugged at my attention, the more I didn't like it. So, I did what I'd learned to do with things I didn't like.

I ignored it.

Instead, I concentrated on Merry's sea-grey eyes, staring out at me through half-closed slits in his tanned skin.

"Where have you been?" I asked.

"Been?"

"For the last year. I haven't seen you on the beach and I walk here almost every day, weather permitting. So, where have you been? If you don't mind me asking?"

"Mind? Oh, I mind very little in life. Even less so when it is a question from a beautiful woman."

I laughed at that.

It'd been a long time since anyone had called me beautiful.

A long time I happened to know precisely.

1943. Not so very far from this spot.

That memory twisted inside me. Guilt and pain. As always. I looked away and found a marsh harrier to fix my attention on.

Merry's attention, however, remained on me.

"Beauty is not absolute; it is subjective. No one is completely devoid of beauty any more than they are free of ugliness. Beauty is never anything more than a gift bestowed upon you by another..."

That pulled my eyes back to him.

"So, my Lady Beatrice, as I believe you are beautiful, sitting here with me on this fine sun-blessed day, then you *are* beautiful..." his smile split his beard, "...'tis a very simple kind of magic, really."

"Are you trying to seduce me?"

The idea any man would want to seduce a dowdy woman slipping frumpily towards old age like me seemed utterly ridiculous. Merry, however, didn't laugh. Instead, he shook his head.

"Rest easy; I am not a man pulled in such directions anymore."

"I'm glad to hear it," I said, moving to cross my legs, before deciding it might be interpreted as flirtatious in some quarters. I ensured my knees remained clamped together.

"Tell me about your life?" Merry asked, gaze drifting from my knees to my eyes.

"What do you wish to know about it?"

"Everything."

"Everything might take a rather long time."

Merry's eyes flicked heavenwards. When they returned to me, he said, "It is not going to rain today."

"That is very reassuring, but-"

"Or tomorrow."

"I'm not sure my life has that much in it to tell."

"Then start now and come back tomorrow if we do not finish today. I shall be here."

"You will?"

"Oh, yes, Beatrice Clay, I will be here for you."

The slightly pinched smile on my face wavered. Something ran along my spine that had nothing to do with the mild air of a pleasant day.

I was going to ask him how he knew my full name, but the question never reached my lips.

He would say I told him, which would be the only reasonable explanation. But I hadn't. I knew I hadn't. I told him my name was Beatrice, and that was all. And even if I had told him my surname, I would have used my married name, *Harryman.* Not the name of a long-dead girl who'd once loved a wonderful young man who'd gone off to war and never came back.

Instead, I stared into eyes the same shade of blue-grey as the sea behind him.

And for the second time I did what I usually did when confronted by something that scared me.

I ignored it too.

After a brief hesitation, I started talking.

"I fell in love with Owen James in the autumn of 1911. I should be able to recall the exact day. Such things are important, after all, but I must confess I don't..."

1943

I thought of Tom regularly but briefly.

Every time my mind wandered to him, it recoiled, pursued by the knowledge I should not be thinking of happiness at this time. It was guilt coupled with the deep, illogical suspicion Simon's death was divine punishment for abandoning my marriage vows.

I didn't leave Grey Gull much. When I did, I went no further than the shoreline behind the house to stand amongst the dry, blackened twists of seaweed marking the wrack line. I often ventured close enough to the sea for water and foam to bubble around my shoes. Sometimes I slipped them off and took a pace or two into it.

Even in summer, the water numbed my toes. I wondered what it would be like to keep walking and let it consume me. Only thoughts of Francis, out there serving somewhere on a grey ship upon the grey sea, stopped me.

If the war claimed him too, I decided, I would give myself to my old companion. My keeper, my guardian, who'd serenaded me from the margins of my life for so many years.

I would take the sea as my lover and walk into its bitter, endless embrace.

Despite the melancholy weight of the Castle pressing at me whenever I was inside, I had no desire to escape its confines and never once walked to our meeting spot.

How long would Tom keep going there?

As far as he knew, Frank was back manning his anti-aircraft battery in East London.

Would he come to Grey Gull to find me?

To get an answer to his last question?

To take me away from this place, away from Frank, away from whatever whispered to me in the night.

Unless what whispered to me in the dark was me, of course.

I stared at myself in the mirror one morning. A pale, drawn creature, bloodless as any ghost, stared back.

Downstairs, Frank was singing. Not *It Had to be You*, for once. Something new he'd heard in London, I supposed. I didn't know it.

People demonstrated grief in unusual ways, though I hadn't expected appearing happy to be one of them.

Frank looked better, too; colour had returned to his cheeks where it had faded from mine. The bags under his eyes had receded where they had grown under mine. He had put weight on again, too, whereas the grey-faced wraith in the mirror looked gaunt, frail, old.

Why would Tom want to wake up next to this unsightly thing every morning?

Would Tom give up on me? Would he eventually stop going to our meeting place, believing my failure to be there was my answer? Or would he ride up to the Castle upon a white stallion to whisk me away from my imprisonment?

That seemed unlikely. But he was American, so who knew?

I left the sallow creature in the mirror and went downstairs. Frank would be back in London tomorrow, his compassionate leave over. Then I would go and see Tom.

Maybe.

Frank tended to ensconce himself in his studio by this time of day, but he was still in the kitchen reading the local paper, whistling something tuneless through his teeth.

He looked up as I came in and flashed me a smile. Which was odd in itself.

"You look tired," he said, folding the paper and putting it on the table.

"Bad night," I replied. Every night was a bad night these last few weeks.

Frank had come for his business last night, which hadn't helped. At least he hadn't brought his belt with him.

"Sit down," he said as I made for the stove, "I'll make some tea."

Frank, being nice. This was a novelty.

"You feeling alright?" I asked.

He looked over his shoulder as he filled the kettle, "Life goes on."

I was too tired to argue, be annoyed or even stand. I slumped into the chair he'd vacated.

"You're looking peaky. Why don't you put your feet up today? Have a bit of a rest before I go back to London, eh?"

This wasn't like Frank, whose idea of consideration didn't go much beyond not peeing on the toilet seat.

"Life goes on," I echoed, staring blankly towards the window.

"Yes, Sweetness, of course it does."

Frank resumed his whistling and clattering as he went about the simple act of tea-making as if he were preparing a banquet.

Grey, cold water, lapping about me. Each swell, ripple and wave climbing higher up my body as I stride away from the land. Away from this life, away from life itself...

I shook the thought away.

A cup of tea steamed before me.

I looked up. Frank appeared pleased with himself. Did he expect a pat on the head?

He got a mumbled thank you as I stirred the tea.

He shuffled from one foot to the other, then hurried around the table to sit opposite. Burnt hazel eyes, above a twitching smile, stayed on me.

At least the tea was decent.

I fingered the corner of his discarded newspaper to avoid Frank's gaze.

"Are you going to be alright on your own, Sweetness?"

I carried on burying myself in the newspaper. I wasn't reading anything, but Frank's regard was particularly unsettling for some reason.

"Of course," I managed to say, "you have to do your bit, like everyone else."

"That's right. Like everyone else. We all chip in... don't we, Sweetness?"

I glanced up at him. His gaze remained nailed to me. The smile, however, was gone.

"Yes," I said, not knowing what we were discussing.

I dropped my eyes back to the paper.

I didn't want to know either.

Frank sat back, one hand resting on the table, fingers drumming.

I reached for my tea. The sooner I finished it, the sooner I could find an excuse to be somewhere else. Frank was acting strangely. And when Frank did that, it usually meant something unpleasant was in the wind.

My eyes flicked over the paper; nothing held my attention for more than a second or two. The usual collection of stories about jamborees, road closures, prize horses, farming, acts of kindness, petty crime, and the bloody war, of course. Would there be a story about Simon? Local hero killed in Italy?

I seldom read the papers and turned the radio off when the BBC news came on. As far as I could see, nothing good was happening in the world, so, like everything else that was not good, I did my best to ignore it.

I flicked the page over. There was nothing about Simon.

But there was something.

My hand froze, my heart lurched. For a moment, I felt I was falling away from the light. Distantly, I heard the screech of chair legs scraping the floor. It sounded like a scream. Like the one inside my head.

American Airman Killed in Motor Accident.

I blinked.

The name in the piece, half a column next to a larger story about the contribution of beetroot cultivation to the war effort, did not change.

Captain Thomas Oliver Dupree.

The story didn't make any sense. Or at least the words didn't. They shifted and blurred, squirming from my grasp like a greased pig every time I tried to catch hold of them.

"Is everything alright, Sweetness?"

Frank's voice. Far away. Beyond that, the circling gulls. And, quieter still, the sea, calling to me.

Lost control. Too fast. Reckless. Tuesday evening. Left the road. Tree.

The words swam. The words swirled. The words lied. The words mocked.

Died instantly.

Kansas.

Bomber pilot.

Tree.

Too fast.

Reckless.

Thirty-Five years old.

"Sweetness?"

Lost control.

Reasons unknown.

Died instantly.

Died instantly.

Died. Died. Died.

"Sweetness?"

I looked up. Frank was leaning across the table, balanced upon his elbows, those eyes I knew so well, burnt hazel and intense, bore into me.

"Frank..." I heard myself say, my voice as quiet as the sea outside the window. But so much further away.

"There's no need to worry, Sweetness; you'll be fine on your own. Just like always."

Then he smiled.

Bright, wide and from ear to ear...

1930

Useless woman...

I stared at the ceiling, listening to the wind and the waves. I'd heard worse storms shriek off the North Sea, enough to roll over and sleep through most of them. Grey Gull had stood here for centuries, surviving the worst nature threw at its way. It was unlikely this one would blow it away.

Useless wife...

Of course, it wasn't the storm keeping me awake.

No matter how hard the wind howled or how fiercely the waves crashed. No matter the windows and doors rattled like a legion of lunatics were trying to break in. That wasn't it.

Useless mother...

It was the voice. The voice of the house, the voice of the thing we shared the house with, the voice of my own insecurities and inadequacies, the voice of my sadness and fear.

Maybe the voice of my madness.

A dry insistent rasp, both malevolent and gleeful. Always a whisper and never a shout, never loud enough for me to be sure it was really there, never quiet enough to convince myself it wasn't.

Sometimes it was silent for months. I heard nothing, saw nothing, felt nothing. But it always came back, no matter how often I thought it wouldn't.

My rational mind insisted it was just the sea and the wind accompanying the never-ending creaks of the Castle. But in the end, I propelled myself up into a sitting position with an anguished cry of frustration.

The sea, the wind, and the never-ending creaks of the Castle continued, but that taunting voice immediately fell to silence.

I rubbed my eyes. I couldn't feel further from sleep despite being exhausted. Izzy moving in made for more work. I'd stopped thinking of her presence as a visit some time ago.

Climbing out of bed, I found my dressing gown in the darkness before fumbling into my slippers. It was a chilly night, autumn fading fast towards winter.

I let my eyes sweep the room, but none of the night-cloaked shapes looked out of place.

It wasn't always like that.

Sometimes the shadows moved as well as whispered.

I made my way out onto the landing. I didn't need to light anything; I'd been here long enough to know the way.

The boys' room was next to mine, Frank's, the largest of Grey Gull's three bedrooms, was on the other side of the stairs.

A new sound came beneath the storm as I found the banister and curled my fingers around the handrail. Not a voice, though it taunted me too. And this was undeniably real.

The rhythmic squeak of bed springs.

My husband fucking another woman.

Fucking good old Auntie Izzy.

I bit my lip and lingered on the top step.

It was not a surprise. What did surprise me was that it hurt.

I didn't love Frank. I didn't even like him. He was a mistake I'd failed miserably to extricate myself from. When I'd first started to suspect they were lovers, about thirty seconds after Izzy's fancy car pulled up outside the Castle, I told myself I didn't care. I told myself she was welcome to him.

But the sound of the springs cut in ways I hadn't expected.

She's taking my place...

Given how unpleasant a business enduring Frank's cold, detached lust was, it should have been a relief. But it was what it signified that hurt me.

Useless woman, useless wife, useless mother...

A stifled cry escaped the room. It seemed Izzy was enjoying herself far more than I ever had.

Useless...

I hurried downstairs, heedless of the dark.

I couldn't escape the voice of the shadows any more than I could the storm lashing the house, but getting away from the noise of my husband fucking Izzy would be easier. So I thought.

After lighting one of the kitchen oil lamps, I made a cup of tea, which meant bringing the glowing coals in the heavy black iron range back to life. It gave me something to do.

The windows rattled with the wind, the Castle creaking about me like a restless old man. Other sounds came too, but I did my best to ignore them while waiting for the kettle to boil.

The clock said it was two-thirty.

I pulled back the curtain over the sink. There was nothing to see bar the reflection of a woman I barely recognised in the rainwater bejewelled black glass.

"Beatrice Clay..." I whispered, "...whatever *did* become of you?"

The woman in the window didn't reply, though the rain running down the glass looked a lot like tears.

I spent so long studying that distorted, haunted face, both so familiar and so alien, that the kettle's whistle made me jump.

Strange that I had almost become accustomed to the disembodied voice that floated around Grey Gull, but something as mundane as steam from a kettle could startle me.

I laughed. It sounded as unnatural as anything I'd ever heard in the Castle.

After making tea, I sat at the big family table dominating the kitchen. Old, scored, pitted and scratched. I suspected its sturdy legs would still keep it upright long after mine had given up the ghost. Francis and Simon had added their own marks to the tabletop in ink and crayon over recent years, another layer laid down upon the history of the old thing. My eyes rolled over them as I held the steaming mug in both hands, remembering their laughter and trying to imagine how worse my life would be without it.

Useless mother...

The mug jerked in my hands, hot tea splashing the table. Another stain, a little more history.

I looked around. The kitchen was empty. Of course.

The voice was only in the wind... or my mind.

As much as it sounded like it'd been in my ear.

I looked for the woman in the window, but there was no one to see from this angle, just night against glass and beads of rainwater catching the oil lamp's glow.

Frank had left a packet of cigarettes on the dresser. He didn't like me smoking, though it seemed he had no such reservations when it came to Izzy. Good old Auntie Izzy could do whatever she liked.

I lit one and retreated to the sink, putting my back to the cold stone, so the whole kitchen was in front of me.

Useless wife...

Not that watching the shadows always stopped them from whispering.

I drew on the cigarette in short furtive puffs. More concerned about whether my husband would catch me smoking than the fact he had so little regard for me he was fucking another woman under our roof.

Useless... stupid... ugly... good for nothing...

The rain drummed on the glass behind me. The thick shadows beyond the reach of the oil lamp moving whenever my eye wandered from them, the voice in the house continued to spit bile at me.

Was I losing my mind?

I blew smoke at the ceiling between sips of tea.

Insanity seemed the sanest explanation.

He's fucking someone else... because thee are... so very useless... at everything...

I screwed my eyes shut, mug shaking in one hand, cigarette shaking in the other.

Could I still hear the rhythmic squeak of bedsprings down here? It didn't seem likely over the storm. But then it didn't seem likely the house spoke to me either.

"She can have him," I hissed back through my teeth.

The wind howled louder as if the storm was suffering a sudden fit of laughter.

Something creaked; a foot on one of the Castle's many squeaky boards.

I didn't want to open my eyes, not because I feared what I might see, but because I would see nothing.

Can she have thou children too?

"No!"

She wants them... she wants them... she wants them...

Another sound, like hands being clapped together to rub in glee.

"They're mine."

All thee haves, haves, haves... poor little Bea... poor little Bea...

Air moved against my face. Old air, stale air. Grave's breath.

Izzy has everything, and Bea has nothing, but Izzy wants what Bea has got...

The wind rattled the window behind me like a madman was trying to break in. Which seemed unlikely. All the lunatics were already inside.

...is the world fair, or is it not?

"She's not taking them!" My eyes snapped open. There was nothing to see other than the cigarette had all but burnt out between my fingers.

I ground it out in the ashtray with a vicious twist. Half the butts in it bore the ghost of Izzy's lipstick.

Whatever Izzy wants... Izzy gets...

Something breathed in my ear. I swatted it away and whirled around. Nobody was there but the woman in the window. She still reminded me a little of Beatrice Clay, who was someone I once knew.

Frost-pale skin, lips pressed tight to stop them trembling, night-ruffled hair, eyes just black suggestions in the hollows of her face.

I turned my back on her. I liked looking at her even less than the pitiful, frightened thing I sometimes glimpsed in the mirror.

My tea had somehow grown cold. I finished it anyway.

It tasted better than walking past Frank's bedroom again.

1943

It wasn't difficult to find the spot Tom died.

It was a couple of miles from where he usually parked to walk to our meeting place on the beach, on the road leading back to his base. The tarmac still bore the rubber from his jeep's tyres, the tree he'd hit the scorch marks, the grass and vegetation around it blackened.

The jeep had caught fire after hitting the gnarled old oak.

...they're all gonna burn...

I heard Frank's voice in the breeze. And if I listened hard enough, I was sure I'd hear the birds whistling *It Had to be You...*

It was a hot day. I wore a wide-brimmed sun hat and a loose dress. In my hand, I held a bunch of rosemary. I placed it against the foot of the scorched oak.

Rosemary for remembrance...

From my bag, I pulled a single red rose and placed it amongst the tree's thick, twisted roots too.

Roses for love...

Did I love him?

I sucked in a breath; the faint odours of burnt wood and oil tainted the summer air.

Had I loved him?

Tom was in the past tense now. Just like Simon. Just like Owen. Just like Dad.

I stared at the base of the tree.

Just like Tilly.

Something swelled in my throat.

He'd come to see me on Tuesday. I wasn't there. Perhaps he'd come every day since I last saw him hoping for an answer to his question. Hoping I would walk away from my husband to be with him.

But I hadn't been there. Again. Maybe he'd been angry and hurt. Or confused, sad, disappointed. There were plenty of possibilities to choose from. Any of them capable of distracting and occupying the mind.

Enough that he'd driven too fast.

Reckless.

Lost control.

Tree.

Died instantly.

An animal could have darted into the road, and he'd swerved and...

I swallowed. My tears, as familiar as the sea, gathered into another wave about to break upon my eyes.

The road was reasonably straight; he hadn't lost control on a bend. The weather had been fine, no rain, and no ice in early September. It had been dusk but still light enough to see clearly. And yet...

I turned and followed the black rubber streaks along the tarmac. They went back a couple of hundred yards, some veering to the left, some to the right, before the final ones arrowing towards the trunk of that ancient oak. The oldest, biggest, most imposing tree in sight.

Could a tyre have blown?

The jeep must have swerved several times as Tom fought for control. That didn't sound like he'd simply been trying to avoid hitting something. Did it?

I'd never driven a motor car in my life. I had no idea about such things. The report in the *Eastern Gazette* was sketchy on detail. With so many young men dying in the war, this was a small tragedy hardly worth noting.

Save to those whose hearts it broke.

I closed my eyes. Standing in the middle of the road, I listened to the wind in the trees, the chatter of finches, thrushes and sparrows, the buzz of insects. I hoped someone else might come barrelling down the lane far too quickly and put an end to me. Simon was gone, Tom was gone.

"It had to be you, wonderful you... It had to be you..."

Frank had sung that as he'd walked away and left me at the kitchen table, the news of Tom's death spread before me.

Prior to that, he had come around and stood behind me to place a hand on my shoulder. He'd been trembling. So had I.

"Sweetness..." he'd said slowly, drawn out like an old man's last breath. Then he'd shuddered. They'd been a few seconds of silence, then laughter. A good-humoured chuckle. His hand had slipped away and he'd disappeared off to his studio, that damn song upon his lips.

He couldn't have known a story in the *Gazette* about an airman dying in a motor accident had any connection to me.

And yet...

There'd been something in his eyes, something in his smile, something knowing and smug.

It was my imagination. Nothing more.

If Frank had somehow discovered I'd been unfaithful, it wouldn't just be Tom who would be dead.

I wanted to fold my legs and sink to the tarmac. I'd lost my son and the man I loved in a week. The weight of my sorrow was something I could not begin to express.

If I did sit down, I thought there was a very good chance I would never stand up again. So, instead, I walked down the road, seeing nothing and seeing everything. Imagining Tom coming the other way…

Driving too fast.

…unaware these were the last things he would ever see,

Died instantly.

I could still smell burnt oil; it clung to me, an errant ghost taunting and chiding.

…they're all gonna burn…

Five minutes from the oak tree was a pub, *The Green Man*. Thatched roof, small doors and windows. It smelt of smoke, beer and time. A huge radio in a walnut case squatted in one corner; Bing Crosby was singing *Moonlight Becomes You*.

A few old men hung about inside; they cast glances my way.

The woman behind the bar - rosy-cheeked, big-chested, blonde hair halfway faded to grey - smiled at me as I approached.

When I asked if she had gin, she said she did.

"A gin, then, please."

"Anything with that, lovely?"

"More gin."

She nodded, lips pursed, "One of them kinda days?"

"One of them kind of lives."

Her laugh reminded me of a small dog getting over-excited about something.

I didn't drink much. I partly blamed gin for letting Frank get me pregnant. It had proved a fool's friend in the bleak months after Dad's death, and I'd largely avoided it since. Now? What was left to lose? Maybe I should try drinking myself into oblivion.

The landlady watched me as I threw half my drink down my neck at the bar. She didn't move away. I probably had the air of someone who'd be ordering another sooner rather than later.

"I heard there was an accident down the road from here last week?" I asked.

"Aye, a yank. Driving like the clappers. They all do. Flash buggers. Wonder more of them don't end up splattered over the countryside."

I finished the rest of my drink.

And nodded when she asked if I wanted another.

"Had he been in here?" I asked as the next gin arrived, and I put my coins in her palm.

"We get a few. Like I said, flash buggers, but no harm in most of them. Just boys. But no, Wally and Burt here saw him whizz by, going too fast. But don't think he was one of our yanks."

Wally and Bert, white-haired and red-faced beneath their flat caps, propped up the other end of the bar, following our conversation with pricked ears.

"Nah, not one of ours. Oi'd recognise one of ours." Bert, or Wally, said, pint poised in mid-air.

"Even though he flashed by so quick, looked like Old Nick were chasing him, so it did," Wally, or Bert, added.

"Was... anyone chasing him?" I asked.

Bert and Wally shook heads and jowls in unison.

"You know what young uns are like these days..." one of them said.

"...always in a bloody hurry," the other finished.

Both the old men nodded at the other before downing their pints together.

"Time for another, Wally?" Bert asked.

"Don't mind if oi do, Bert, don't mind if oi do," Wally replied.

I fingered my own drink, suddenly wishing I hadn't bought the first one, let alone the second.

"Two pints of mild, if you please, Angie..."

"You know the young fellah?" Wally asked while Angie started pulling beer.

I shook my head, "No..."

Wally raised a sceptical and wiry eyebrow at that. Probably didn't get too many middle-aged women knocking back gin and asking about American airmen without a by your leave in *The Green Man*.

"Just heard about it..." I downed more gin, eager to be anywhere else "...such a waste."

"Tragic, survived the Germans trying to blow him out of the sky, then wraps himself around a tree," Angie agreed, working on the pump, "but accidents happen. Even in wartime."

Everyone nodded at the latest piece of wisdom.

I drained my glass as Wally said, "If it was an accident, of course..."

Bert made a snorting noise, and Angie rolled her eyes.

"What... do you mean?" I put my empty glass on the counter.

"Don't listen to him, lovely," Angie glanced at the second gin I'd knocked back in the space of a few minutes, "he talks a lot of baloney, does Wally."

"Not what oi says, is old Davey Acorns. Oi know what oi saw, after all."

"Who's Davey Acorns?"

"An old fool who thinks he saw different," Angie took Bert's money, "Police talked to him, the yank MPs too, and they didn't believe him, so no cause for anyone else to either."

She looked at me, turning Bert's coins over in her hand.

"Is there, lovely?"

1927

Tilly was much better.

I would have said that made me sleep easier at night if it wasn't for the fact I hardly slept at all anyway. The baby and the boys left little time for rest. I never seemed to be able to catch more than a couple of hours of fitful dozing.

Frank busied himself in his studio, which was something at least. It would have been a lot harder to avoid him if he spent more time in the main house. Particularly as the weather, incessant bands of rain sweeping in over the churning sea upon a cruel wind, discouraged leaving the house for anything other than necessity.

By 1927 I had a bicycle for the journey to Creethorpe. A cumbersome squeaky thing that made the trip only marginally easier than walking. With the potted lane through the marshes choked with mud, I had to push it most of the way to the proper road at Fandle's Farm anyway.

Trips to the shops were my only escape from the Castle, something I usually relished. Even in the winter, the chance to be free of Frank and the damp, scowling stones of Grey Gull was a pleasure.

With Tilly seemingly recovered from whatever malaise that had so unnerved me, I was grateful to get out. Francis was at school, and Frank would, begrudgingly, watch Simon and Tilly while I was gone.

"Don't be long," Frank peered over his newspaper, one nicotine-stained finger flicking the corner back and forth.

I concentrated on fastening coat buttons. Frank hated anything that kept him from his painting, even if the imposition was the children he'd been so keen to have.

"I won't," I said. And meant it. As much as I liked to get out of the Castle, my concern for Tilly had not evaporated.

Her eating seemed normal again; she was behaving as I expected a baby to behave and her poo and pee – those ever-reliable signs of health, according to Dr O'Conner – were as you'd want them to be.

And yet...

I didn't want to be away from her. It was hardly unnatural for a mother not to want to part with her baby, but it went deeper. A persistent unease dripping from the very pores of the house. Something nagged, like the voices I sometimes heard, that Grey Gull was not a place of safety for anyone.

I'd have taken her with me if it wasn't so cold, damp and windy. The pram was even older, heavier and more unwieldy than the bicycle Frank bought me, but I'd have happily pushed it through the mud to Creethorpe rather than leaving her here.

The wind shook the windows, reminding me that was not a sensible thought.

I checked on Tilly again. I'd fed her earlier, and she was sleeping peacefully. I found Simon, ensured he wasn't destroying anything, kissed his forehead and told him to be a good boy.

"I'm always good!" he declared, somewhat inaccurately, with a gap-toothed smile, before returning to his toy soldiers.

Frank, I didn't bother with.

Outside, the wind assaulted me. Riding a bicycle was probably impossible, even if muddy potholes didn't litter the track. Still, it often dropped considerably inland, so I stuffed my shopping bags into the basket on the handlebars and put my back into pushing the creaky old thing towards the higher farmland on the other side of the marsh.

At least it wasn't raining. Broken clouds raced across the sky, but patches of blue gave me hope I could get to market and back without a soaking.

By the time I reached ground dry enough to make riding the bicycle possible, I was panting. The wind still tugged my coat but wasn't trying to rip it from me anymore.

I stopped to catch my breath. Beneath my heavy coat, I was sweating despite the bitter air. Behind me, Grey Gull was out of sight; on either side, the reed beds were dying back for winter. The barns of Fandle's Farm peaked over the lime trees ahead.

Every time I walked away from the Castle, I wondered what it would be like to never return. To never have to see Frank again. It was a fantasy that never took long to fade. Three young children I adored bound me to that place. I couldn't leave them and I couldn't take them.

All I could do was endure.

Carefully, I climbed atop the bicycle and risked riding it.

I managed only a few squeaky turns before realising I had a puncture.

"Shit..."

I'm not much of a one for swearing, but I have to acknowledge the need now and then.

After unsuccessfully attempting to stare the rear tyre into reinflating, I hauled the bloomin' thing around, and started pushing it back towards the Castle.

Repairing the tyre would take me the best part of an hour. I trudged back to Grey Gull, trying to decide if it was worth the bother. I'd spent years walking to Creethorpe and was still more than capable.

A pair of barnacle geese, coming into land on one of the black meres beyond the reed banks, honked overhead.

I was puffing again by the time I got back to the Castle. I wheeled the bicycle to the rear of the house and leant it by the backdoor. There was a puncture repair kit in the kitchen. Somewhere.

I'd always been very organised, but three young children made it hard to be sure where I'd even put my head at times.

I glanced at Frank's studio. Had he snuck off to paint rather than watch over Simon and Tilly? The closed door didn't mean much; he only left it open in summer when his glorified shed became a sweat box.

The kitchen was empty, the house silent.

Simon only had two gears when awake, playing quietly or tearing around like a maniac. Given the deep silence, I assumed he was still in first gear. As for Frank...

I shook my head and started rummaging through drawers that had once been neatly and logically ordered, but now, inexplicably, were stuffed to the point of jamming with all manner of bric-a-brac I had no recollection whatsoever of owning.

I was about to force open the fourth over-filled drawer of the big Welsh dresser occupying most of one wall when the plates atop the dresser rattled together. I looked up.

The wind makes all kinds of noises out here. I'd turned many of them into the taunts of some kind of disembodied, malevolent adversary, but I'd never quite heard it make this sound; like the sigh of a breathless old man experiencing something between contentment and excitement.

But the it hadn't come from outside the Castle; I was sure of it.

I whirled around, certain someone was behind me. The kitchen was empty.

The sigh faded, only the gentle rattle of chinaware continued to break the silence.

I put a hand on the dresser, solid oak worn smooth by countless years and hands. It vibrated under my fingers.

"Frank? Simon?"

No answer came, not that anything my husband or little boy could do would make that huge piece of wood hum like a tuning fork.

I stepped away, staring up at the plates till they stilled. I touched the dresser again, tentatively, like it was a beast that might roar in my face, but it was now still.

An earthquake?

Not something very likely in this part of the world, and, if it was, why hadn't anything else in the kitchen moved?

I turned in a slow circle, looking for things that shouldn't be there. Nothing was out of place beside some of Simon's toys, which were never where they should be.

I moved from the kitchen to the corridor running to the front door and the stairs. Even on the brightest days, it was a gloomy space, full of deep shadow. It always smelt of dust and old-time, however often and thoroughly I cleaned it.

The doors to all the downstairs rooms remained closed.

I opened the first, its protesting creak the familiar voice of an unloved relative.

It was the parlour, little used during the colder months (which amounted to most of the year here). Simon sprawled on the floor amidst a semi-circle of coloured bricks and little metal soldiers mown down in boyhood slaughter. My throat caught for a second till I saw his chest rising and falling. He was asleep, which was unusual for the time of day, though he often suddenly dozed in the midst of playing.

I took a step into the room, meaning to wake him, the urge to scoop him into my arms almost overwhelming, but I managed to stop myself. Simon was fine. But my sense of unease persisted.

The chinaware on the dresser was not the only thing that had been rattled.

I shut the door on Simon and checked the rest of the downstairs rooms. There was no sign of Frank, but the familiar feeling I was not alone refused to leave me.

An inhuman shriek startled me as I returned to the corridor.

No matter how many years I lived in the Castle, I doubted I would ever get used to the seagulls.

My skittishness made me laugh, the sound hollow and almost as unsettling as the birds' demented squawks.

I should repair the puncture and get to Creethorpe while it was dry. Instead, I hurried upstairs to check on Tilly. Once I'd reassured myself she was fine, I'd get to market.

I stood on the landing for a few breaths.

Had it got darker? It seemed gloomier than usual downstairs, but up here was worse, as if some of the world's light had leached away with each step I'd climbed.

Thicker cloud must have swept in off the sea; the weather could change in a couple of heartbeats out here. That was all.

I hurried to my room, a sense of unease thickening in my chest till I almost struggled to breathe. I was being silly, I knew, but I wanted Tilly in my arms again, wanted to be sure she was still well.

The floorboards screeched like the circling gull as my feet pounded over them. I burst into the bedroom and crossed to Tilly's cot.

It was empty.

My beautiful little girl was gone.

1943

Old Davey Acorns apparently lived in a cottage deep in Dirkley Wood.

Though shed was a more accurate description, according to Angie.

Bert, Wally and Angie, whose collective curiosity I'd clearly piqued with my interest in Tom's accident and ambitious gin consumption, appeared stumped as to why I wanted to go trekking through the woods to find an old reprobate. One, who, in Bert's considered opinion, was hauling way less than a full load of kippers.

"I just do," was the best I could offer on the hoof.

"You with the press?" Wally asked, eyes narrowing.

"Something like that."

Bert shrugged and rattled off a lengthy list of instructions involving at least three right turns at significant trees, crossing a stream that might or might not be dry, given the weather, swinging behind Mrs Clobber's dairy yard and then keeping on going till I got there.

"Maybe I should write that down..."

"Or you can wait here till six, lovely," Angie bounced a disparaging look between Wally and Bert, "Davey comes in most nights for a couple before he goes off to work.

"Oh..." I smiled as Bert and Wally laughed, "...what does he do?"

"Davey Acorns? Well..." Wally managed through his chortling, "...let's say that owd boy been living off the land for years."

Which I took to mean he was a poacher.

Joe Loss and his Orchestra started playing *Only You*, a song I liked, though I could barely make it out above the crackles and hiss of the radio.

"I'll have another gin then," I told Angie, "better have a tonic with this one, though."

I took my drink outside. The afternoon was warm, and the little garden at the back of *The Green Man* had no prying eyes. I sat at a table and left the glass in front of me. It was just gone four, and my head was already buzzing from the two neat gins I'd knocked back.

I listened to the birdsong, which was crackle-free as ever, and watched the clouds. Every now and then, I heard something rattle by. Trucks, for the most part. Once, what sounded like a motorbike. I couldn't see the road from the garden, which was a blessing. If I could, I would've been drunk as a Lord long before Old Davey Acorns showed up.

After thirty minutes, two cigarettes and no gin, Angie came out, turning a towel between her hands.

She smiled, "Some of them yanks can be right charmers, can't they?"

I was going to say I wouldn't know, but my throat tightened too much to trust it to words. I nodded quickly instead.

Angie gave the towel a couple more turns around her hands, then sat next to me.

"Cigarette break," she explained.

When I offered her one of mine, she shook her head, "Never really cared for them."

I let my gaze slip back to the garden; a pair of finches hopped about the next table, squabbling over crumbs.

"You look like you done some crying, lovely?"

I bit my lip, still not trusting myself to say anything.

"Seen a lot of that these last few years. Sometimes it helps to talk. Sometimes it don't," Angie put the towel aside, "I don't make no judgements, lovely, but I reckons you knew that yank, didn't you?"

"His name was Tom..."

Angie patted my hand, then wrapped coarse, plump fingers about it.

"I'm sorry."

"He was... I..." a tear, fat and warm, rolled down my cheek.

Angie conjured a handkerchief for me to dab it away. She squeezed my hand and smiled. A miasma of beer and lavender hung around her, reminding me of a hard-drinking granny.

"Dunno what you're looking for here, lovely, but best you be gone before Old Davey gets here. He's a harmless bugger, but..." she put a finger to her temple and made a circular motion, "...spends too much time alone in the woods at night. Reckons he's seen almost everything out there at one time or another: fairies, unicorns, demons, devils, funny lights in the sky, ghosts and sprites. He even reckoned he once ran into a vampire with a long pale face and a mouthful of fangs. Can you imagine? The silly old sod!"

"I just-"

She squeezed my hand again.

"People want answers, reasons, explanations when bad things happen so they can make sense of things that don't make no sense. Don't you go listening to Davey Acorns, lovely. Sometimes bad things happen. Your yank – your Tom – he was driving too fast..."

I sipped my drink; my throat felt raw.

"Bad things happen..." I repeated, "...I lost my youngest son too, in Taranto harbour... his transport ship hit a mine. The Italians all laid down their weapons when we landed. Only casualties were from the sinking of *HMS Abdiel.* Bad things... happen..."

I almost told her I'd lost my fiancé in the last war and my baby girl, but I held my tongue. I wasn't looking for sympathy. Besides, I was close enough to home that she might have heard about Tilly. To many, I was still the mother who'd lost her baby.

Actually,   I   was the mother who'd *lost* her baby.   Something   usually   said accompanied by a knowing look.

"I'm so sorry, lovely. Lost my little brother in Norway and my eldest boy at Dunkirk... I know..."

Angie stopped herself. Nobody knows how you feel. Every bereaved mother hates being told someone knows how you feel. Doesn't matter a jot if they've been through the same thing. Every life is unique, every memory, every relationship. Every word. Every love.

"All I'm saying is you're suffering enough. No need to dig for answers. Old Davey ain't gonna tell you anything that'll make you feel better. He's off with the fairies that one. Literally, if you'd believe some of the things he says."

Angie pushed herself to her feet.

She was right. Tom was gone. Just like most of the other people I'd loved in my life. Nothing was going to change a thing.

Still...

"What did he say?"

Angie chewed it over, then said, "Wally and Bert saw the jeep go racing by as they left here. They ain't the most reliable, especially after a few pints, but they hadn't had that many. I was serving em, and I always keep a count so I knows when to show a fellow the way to the door. Driving too fast, but nothing else of note.

Davey Acorns said he saw the jeep whizz past by Gallows Field, in which case it would have been right after Wally and Bert saw him. And I remember him rolling up that day as he was a bit later than usual, so that fits."

"And what did he see?"

"Said there was someone else in the jeep with him."

My eyebrow shot up, "Maybe he-"

"No, lovely. It's just Old Davey Acorns seeing things."

"But why do you think that?"

"Because he said the man with him..." she shrugged, "...was more than sloightly on th' huh..."

1930

"You're not going to make a fuss about this, are you, Sweetness?"

I was at the big stone sink by the window, washing up. I hadn't heard Frank come up behind me.

"Fuss?" I looked sharply over my shoulder.

"About Izzy."

"Izzy...?"

"You know I'm not painting all night, every night, don't you?" his nostrils flared with his snort, "You're not *that* stupid."

"Do what you like," I said, returning to the washing up.

Frank spun me around. The plate I'd been holding slipped from my wet hands to shatter against the sink's rim.

"When I'm talking to you..." his fingers dug deep into the soft flesh of my arms, "...you bloody well pay attention!"

Izzy – *Auntie* Izzy – had taken the boys to school in her fancy car again, leaving the house quiet save for the ticking of the battered grandfather clock in the hall and the occasional demented screech from one of the gulls outside.

And Frank's breathing.

There was a slight, phlegmy wheeze to it, so faint you only heard it if he was close.

Like he was now.

"Yes, Frank..." I said, holding his eye for only a heartbeat before dropping mine.

The pressure on my arms eased. He ran hands up and down the sleeves of my housecoat as if trying to smooth out creases.

"I heard you last night, sneaking about while..." he let the words drift off, "...there's no need to spy on us, Sweetness. Listening at the door. Really? That's a bit beneath you, don't you think?"

My eyes shot up, looking for a sign Frank was making some kind of twisted joke. There wasn't.

"I wasn't snea-"

He cut me off with a slap. Not the hardest he'd ever given me, but it still caught me by surprise. I rarely saw them coming, even after ten years with Frank.

"Don't argue, please, Sweetness..." he patted my arms and then retreated to the kitchen table to light a cigarette.

I wanted to touch my stinging face but kept my hands at my side. Frank was talking, and he liked to see me paying attention.

"I'm not fucking her because I want to! You understand that don't you?"

I assumed the question was rhetorical; they tended to be with Frank. When I said nothing, he added, "It's for my art."

I would have laughed, but my smarting face told me that wouldn't go down well.

"It's what Izzy wants, and she's my big chance..." Frank gave a roll of the shoulders, suggesting that was very much that.

Several responses fizzed through my mind, but none reached my mouth. I didn't want him to slap me again, or take the belt to me, so I nodded, "Yes, Frank... I understand..."

He beamed, "I knew you would! But don't worry; once my work's out there, things will go back to normal. I promise."

I swallowed, "Yes, Frank."

"You're my wife, after all, for better or worse."

He picked tobacco off his tongue and flicked it on the floor, before adding, "Obviously, she's prettier than you, smarter, has money and is so, so much better in bed. But marriage vows do mean something, don't they?"

Frank stared at me through the cigarette smoke curling around him, perhaps looking for a reaction. He didn't get one.

"Even when made to such a useless woman as you."

Useless woman...

He'd said those words with the same spite and venom as the shadows spat them at me the previous evening.

Frank tapped ash into the ashtray, eyes not leaving me.

"She is very good with the boys, though, isn't she?"

My lips twitched but did not betray me.

"I don't think she sees herself as a full-time mother; why would she? She's beautiful and clever. But..." he shrugged, "...I'm sure she'd do a much better job if she wanted to..."

I took a step forward. I don't know why or what I intended to do.

Frank tilted his head and raised an eyebrow. It was enough to ensure I didn't take a second.

I pushed back against the sink.

Frank's eyes dropped to his cigarette, which he began twisting between his fingers, "Though, who knows, perhaps she will give me more children? That would be a bonus, wouldn't it, Sweetness? Now you seem to have dried up..."

That stung as much as his slap. A tear welled up, making me hate my own weakness.

Why did I put up with this?

I didn't need to look at the boys' scattered things around the room to know the answer.

Frank stepped away from the table to stand close enough for his growing belly to squeeze against me.

"I'm glad we've had this little chat, Sweetness. Cleared the air. I won't need to fuck you while Izzy is here, which will give you a chance to think about what you're missing, what you're doing wrong. I still want more children, you know that... don't you?"

He stilled my nod with his hand, thumb under my chin, fingers along my jawbone.

"What happened with Tilly was hard, I know. And it wasn't your fault. Well, not really. But you have to stop wallowing. And start getting pregnant again. If you don't, maybe I'll give Izzy a baby, though she's a bit old for it. So, if that doesn't happen, I could get another girl to move in. A younger one. Who can do the job..."

He leaned so close I could taste the smoke on his breath.

"...then I won't need you anymore. And neither will the boys."

He lifted his cigarette so close to my face, I feared he would burn me with it.

Instead, he kissed my cheek and dropped the cigarette into the sink with the broken plate and the washing up.

Then he spun away.

"I'll be working," he said, not looking back, "have dinner ready for six; Izzy and I want an early night..."

As he headed down the corridor, the chuckle he left hanging in the air faded into a whistle, his usual breezy rendition of *It Had to Be You*.

I wrapped arms around myself and held in the sobs till the front door closed behind Frank.

The house creaked in the wind while I cried. Like Frank, it was laughing at me in its familiar dry sibilant voice. Too quiet to be certain, too loud to ignore.

Useless woman... useless, useless woman...

1943

Davey Acorns chose that day not to visit *The Green Man*.

I considered asking for those directions again, but it would already be dark by the time I got home, even if I went directly back to the Castle. If I started blundering around Dirkley Woods, God alone knew where I'd end up.

When I said to Angie I was going; she broke off from singing along to *You Are My Sunshine* to nod and smile. It was a smile that said, *I'll see you tomorrow then.*

Did I have the look of the desperate and broken-hearted about me? Probably. I suppose it was common enough in 1943.

I told myself I wasn't going to come back, that I wasn't going to go looking for Davey Acorns, and there was nothing to gain from the ramblings of a man *not hauling a full load of kippers*.

I carried on telling myself the same thing all night as I lay in the dark, listening to the murmurings of the sea as it licked the shingle. At least no one else spoke to me and, with Frank back in London, it was only my own mind keeping me awake that night.

My thoughts flicked from Tom's smile that I would never see again to wondering exactly how Simon had died on *HMS Abdiel*. Had it been quick? Had he been killed in the initial blast or after the black water rushed into the ship? Had there been time for him to know his life would end?

Had he... had he... had he...

I got up, took up the loose floorboard in my bedroom, spread Owen's letters around me and talked to the three photographs I had of him. So young, so handsome, so long lost to me.

My kind, sweet, gentle Owen.

I told him everything that had happened since I'd last talked to him. Which had been before Frank came home and Simon and Tom died. I asked him if he could find Tom and Simon and take care of them for me. They were brave men, but they might be scared in the dark...

I cried again, but when the tears dried, I felt a little better, a little calmer.

Silly how three photographs of a man twenty-seven years dead could give me strength. Not a lot, but a little. Enough to make taking another breath bearable, at least.

And I stopped believing the lies I was telling myself about not going to find Davey Acorns.

I didn't return to *The Green Man* the next day, though. Maybe Davey would turn up, maybe he wouldn't, but I didn't want to be sitting there for another day sipping gin and eliciting Angie's sympathy.

Instead, I checked the map we had in one of the kitchen drawers. It was decades out of date, but I doubted Dirkley Wood had moved much in that time. It didn't look big. Even if I couldn't remember Bert's directions, I thought it wouldn't be too hard to find any cottage – or shed – within its boundary.

Despite my life, part of me still managed to be an optimist.

The next day was cooler, the sky overcast, the breeze fresh. Summer was drawing to a close. No more walks in the sun holding Tom's hand, no more waiting for Simon's letters home. The future only held the prospect of the coming winter and the cold, biting wind I'd become so familiar with whipping in off the North Sea.

The future held only the prospect of being alone. Again.

But still, I wanted to know what had happened to Tom.

It wouldn't have hurt any less if he'd died over Germany, but I would have accepted it. From the moment we'd first kissed, I'd understood there was a fair chance that was how it would end. But driving into a tree...

And had he done it because of me, because he thought I'd jilted him or because... because something was *sloightly on th' huh?*

The dawn chill still freshened the air as I left the Castle, the faintest hint of mist hung around the low folds of land beyond the marsh.

I took a cheese sandwich and some water, my twenty years out of date map, and one of my three precious photographs of Owen in my pocket.

Just in case I needed someone to talk to.

The walk to Dirkley Woods was straightforward, but once there, I couldn't find any trace of Mrs Clobber's dairy, never mind the three significant trees Bert had told me to turn right at. Perhaps he'd pulled my leg more vigorously than I'd suspected.

I met one portly woman waddling an even more portly dog along a bramble-fringed path skirting the edge of the trees. When I asked her if she knew Davey Acorns, she shook her head and hurried her fat dog as if I were the one not hauling a full load of kippers.

After crossing the woods several times without encountering anything bigger than a squirrel, I sat on a fallen tree and ate my sandwich serenaded by birdsong and my own swirling sorrows. I tried not to think about the life Simon might have had as hard as I tried not to think about the life I might have had in Kansas or the one I might have had if Owen had come home.

What ifs, maybes and might have beens.

Nightmares can haunt you. And so can daydreams.

If you let them.

I brushed away the crumbs from my sandwich and climbed to my feet.

The trees were thick here, subduing the light. This was an old wood, oak, ash, and alder towered over ferns. Thickets of blackberry briars choked any spot where the canopy allowed enough daylight to kiss the ground. It smelt of slow time and the passing of years, the rich, musky scents of life that got on with living away from the eyes of man.

I didn't know which way to go. If it were a larger place, one might get hopelessly lost, but fields hedged the woods on all sides and striking out in any direction would return me to civilisation before long.

Turning towards where the undergrowth was thinnest, I found a man standing amongst a huge oak's gnarled, moss-flecked roots.

"Oi heard yew looking fah me?" the man said, hitching thumbs into his belt. Which was a length of rope knotted around his trousers. At least, I assumed some trousers remained beneath the stains, mud and patches.

"What makes you think that?" I asked, recovering. He had a large knife hanging from his makeshift belt, I couldn't help but notice.

It might only be a small wood, but it felt a long way from the rest of the world.

"Angie says thas a girl looking fah me. Don't git a lot of girls here. Yew're a girl. Oi see. So, oi reckons..." he shrugged.

"Davey Acorns?"

"Thas wha' people call me latterly. Been called other things. Been called worse. Suits me well enough, reckons."

"Nice to meet you, Mr Acorns."

That made him laugh. He didn't have many teeth left.

"My name's-"

"Don't matter wha' yewr name is, girl. Yew ain't come a courting, 'as yew?"

"No."

"You come 'bout tha' yank, reckons..."

I nodded.

"Nah one else believes moi, so why yew wanna know?"

"Does it matter why?"

Davey chewed it over, hooded eyes peering at me from beneath the shade of a beaten flat cap before nodding, "Reckons..."

"I want to know because... I think my life is slightly on th' huh."

Davey sucked in a breath and turned away, "Best come with me then. We'll 'ave a brew and a dicker..."

He didn't look back, and I didn't hesitate to follow. I wasn't going to run from an old man I'd come to find just because he had a big knife.

"Have you lived here long?" I asked, following him down a path that barely existed between towering blackberry briars.

"A whiles…"

I didn't ask anything else, instead concentrating on picking my steps so my legs didn't get shredded by thorns or my eye put out but the low-hanging branches.

Davey stopped and pushed some vegetation back to allow me through a couple of times. He didn't appear overly perturbed by thorns or branches.

It only took a few minutes to make our way to a clearing where, presumably, Davey lived.

Neither cottage nor shed accurately described his home. Shack was, I thought, a better word.

Roughly constructed out of mismatched wood planks and an angled roof made from doors, a metal funnel stuck out of the top from which a faint wisp of woodsmoke curled.

"Take a pew…" Davey indicated bits of tree trunk cut into two-foot chunks and arranged in a rough semi-circle to one side of the shack.

"Do most of me entertaining out 'ere if th' weather's good…" he looked up at the bright but grey sky above the trees and nodded, "…weather's good."

I plonked myself down on the nearest. It didn't wobble as much as I expected.

"Tea, girl?"

"Erm… thank you," I smiled. Davey disappeared inside, clanking and rattling duly followed. The smoke from the chimney thickened.

Various bric-a-brac filled the clearing. A tin bath, a log pile, a bicycle missing its back wheel, a mound of rusting cans, a couple of buckets, a blackened oil lamp sat on a crude shelf nailed to the side of Davey's shack. A washing line run between two trees from which a single shirt of no particular colour hung limply. A rough wooden frame had rabbit skins stretched out on it.

One of the "stools" had several bleached animal skulls sitting on it, staring back at me. I started trying to identify them but found it was a game I didn't much care for.

I raised my eyes to the trees and blackberry thickets. If Davey hadn't found me, I think I could have spent an awfully long time bumbling about Dirkly Woods before finding this place.

Davey emerged blinking through the door, a steaming enamel mug in each hand. He handed one to me then lowered himself onto the next log along.

"Thas nettle tea, girl," he explained as I peered into the mug, "suffen good, tha' is."

Davey flashed a mostly toothless smile and braved a swig of tea despite it being so hot I struggled to hold it.

"You live on your own?" I asked, using the next trunk as a table until my nettle tea cooled enough not to scald my tongue.

"Just me."

"Don't you get lonely?"

"Oh, Oi git all sorts of company, girl. Never gits lonely," he chuckled, sipping more tea, "See. 'ere comes tha' cheeky owd bugger Roger roight now!"

I followed his gaze but saw no one.

An old man with a big knife and imaginary friends...

Davey stuck a liver-spotted hand into his jacket pocket and pulled out a handful of acorns. He tossed a couple beyond the semi-circle of tree trunk stools, then put a finger to his lips and winked.

A squirrel emerged and, after carefully sniffing the air, bounded over towards the acorns.

"Thas Roger," he explained, "trees full o' acorns, but he likes owd Davey to git them fah him. Lazy bugger is tha' bor!"

Roger kept one eye on me and one on the acorn. It started nibbling.

Davey he didn't seem bothered by.

"Still, best to keep in with th' neighbours, eh, girl?"

"My neighbours are mainly seagulls. There's no keeping in with them."

"Seagulls? Rum owd buggers!" Davey chuckled, tossing Roger another acorn.

Davey watched Roger until he scampered off to add his latest booty to some nearby hoard he was stashing for the coming winter. As the fluffy tail disappeared into the trees, Davey straightened up; faint smile fading as he turned to me.

"Oi guess yew ain't 'ere to dicker 'bout squirrels though, are yew, girl?"

"No," I agreed.

"Yew wanna know 'bout th' yank?"

I nodded.

"And you wanna know who killed him?"

"Killed him?" I moved on the trunk sharply enough for it to rock back and forth a little, "Someone killed him?"

Davey worked his lips, sucking on the remnants of a tooth before shaking his head.

"Nah, girl. Naht someone. *Something...*"

1930

I feared Izzy would never leave.

What you can put up with is amazing when you think about it. Generally, however, I tried not to think about it. By 1930 I'd become very adept at not thinking about things; Frank, Tilly, the choices I'd made and the ones I continued to refuse to make. All shoved to one side, locked behind doors, keys out of sight.

I kept busy with the house, with the boys, with chores stretching from when I climbed out of bed until I slumped back into it. I had moments to myself, shopping in Creethorpe, going to church, taking long walks along the shore, but mostly I didn't. My life was Frank, the boys, the Castle. One thing I hated, one I loved and one... one I couldn't find a word for. Unsettled is probably the best I could come up with back then.

My walks grew longer while Izzy was with us; she was easier not to think about when I couldn't see her. When the boys were at school, that wasn't difficult. When they were home, it became much harder. They circled her incessantly. A brighter star pulling them out of my orbit and into hers.

I didn't know what to do; the gnawing fear she would steal them from me was something that refused to be locked behind a door and forgotten.

Before she came, the one pleasure of my life was being with them, playing games, reading stories, caring for them, listening to their chatter and sharing their boyish laughter. But when Izzy was around, they went to her for those things. All I did was cook their food, wash their clothes and make their beds.

I wanted to do something, anything to get rid of her, but my inspiration stayed in bed with its head under the pillows. If I gave Frank any kind of ultimatum, he would choose her, and he would rip away the one thing in my life that had meaning. I couldn't lose the boys, not after what happened with Tilly. I simply couldn't.

Izzy never said a word about sleeping with my husband.

Occasionally, I caught her looking at me with equal parts pity and amusement, but otherwise, she was just good old Aunty Izzy – playing with all the boys. One way or another.

Sometimes I'd come across her sitting in a chair, eyes closed. Or outside, as still as a statue, staring at the cottage. Once in a while, I came across her muttering, lips moving silently. When she saw me, her face changed, the familiar, easy smile reappeared, and a cheery greeting followed. Like I was an old friend. She didn't spend much time looking at Frank's paintings.

No doubt there are people able to dream up calculated, cunning schemes to eject the unwanted from their life, but I am not one of them. Everything I thought of brought me back to the fear Frank would choose her over me and I would lose the boys.

One night I stumbled across her in the Castle's drawing-room. The boys had gone to bed; I assumed Izzy and Frank had, too, while I'd found things to pretend to do in the kitchen.

"You work so late, Beatrice, what a busy, busy *Bea* you are!" she laughed.

She was sitting in the corner of the room, smoking. A single oil lamp burned; the wick turned down as low as it was possible to go.

"No rest for the wicked," I muttered, turning on my heels.

"Please! Come, sit with me," Izzy offered me a vacant chair with her upturned hand.

"I'm quite tired."

She indicated the chair again when I made no move to join her.

I sighed, inwardly at least, and did as she asked.

Once I'd settled myself, her dark red lips curled into a half smile.

"How does your gallery work with you not there?" I blurted. It was as close as I was likely to get to telling her to go home.

"Oh, I have people. They're very capable. I take little sojourns now and then; things can tick along nicely without me.

I wondered how many of her sojourns involved other women's husbands, but the question never got near my tongue.

After another painful silence, she stubbed out her cigarette and rearranged herself before saying, "This house is peculiar."

"It is?"

"I'm quite sensitive. I have a friend, Gladys, who is a gifted clairvoyant. She often tells me how attuned I am. If I ever wished to embark on a new career..."

"I don't really believe in that sort of thing."

"Ah, a sceptic! You should be more open-minded. There are more things in heaven and earth, Horatio, than are dreamt of in your philosophy..."

"I suppose."

"That's Shakespeare."

"I know," I said, perhaps a little piqued, "Hamlet, the first act."

That earnt me a fleeting smile, then, "Still... peculiar."

"How so?"

"Energies. I'm sensitive to them."

I said nothing, not wanting to encourage her.

"There's a presence here; have you not sensed it?"

"No," I said smoothly.

Izzy stared at me. Perhaps I'd said it too smoothly.

"You've never seen... anything then? Anything... odd?"

Disembodied voices and malign giggles, things moving out of the corner of my eye, rattling and shaking.

Tilly.

"No," I said.

"How strange," Izzy reached for another cigarette.

It didn't seem she was in a hurry to go and fuck my husband tonight.

"Have you?"

"Nearly," she said after lighting the cigarette and blowing out the match.

"Nearly?"

"But not quite. I've almost seen something several times, but whenever I turn around... nothing's there."

"The boys are always getting up to mischief."

"It's not those *darlings*. This is more something...

Sloightly on th' huh.

"...wrong."

"Perhaps you've read too much Hamlet; there's a ghost in that, as I recall."

"It's not a ghost."

"You can tell?"

"Oh, I've encountered spirits many times. Ever since I was a child. And at the seances I attend."

"Your friend, Gladys?"

"Among others. The dead are fascinating. Harmless for the most part, usually just waiting to pass on. No, what's here is... different."

"If it's not a ghost you *sense*, what is it?"

"Have you ever considered leaving your husband?"

Her words made me blink as if my face had been slapped. A sensation I was familiar with.

I'd lied about never experiencing anything in the Castle without hesitation, but some lies are sharper on the lips than others.

"That's none of your business."

"Don't you get lonely..." Izzy cast her eyes around the room; it was sparsely furnished and little used, "...here?"

"I'm going to bed," I shot to my feet, spitting over my shoulder as I headed for the door, "say goodnight to my husband for me."

"You should leave; this place is not healthy for the soul."

"Best you get back to London then," I snapped, tugging the door open.

"Ah, but it is not my soul in peril, Beatrice, is it?"

I wanted to slam the door shut and stomp up the stairs; instead, something about the tone of her voice speared me, making me turn back.

Izzy sat watching me, the only movement from the smoke curling away from the cigarette poised at the side of her face between two red-nailed fingers.

"Peril?"

"The sea erodes the shore, in slow, incessant increments, reducing stone and rock to sand so fine the wind can carry it away. The same thing can happen to the soul."

"Has anyone mentioned you talk an awful lot of shit?"

"Funnily enough, quite a few, actually.

"Perhaps they wouldn't if you said what you want to say more directly."

"Directly?" Izzy wrinkled her perfectly powdered nose, "Oh, where's the fun in that?"

I found a smile.

And then I did slam the door.

1927

I kept the cuttings from the *Eastern Gazette*, folded neatly and pressed inside a copy of Rudyard Kipling's *Stalky & Co*. I don't know why I cut them out and preserved them within the pages of that book.

But, in hindsight, there is so much of my life I do not understand.

Baby Disappears in Mysterious Circumstances declared the first cutting, a single column from page seven, dated 12 February 1927.

Would a baby disappear in any other kind of circumstance?

I remember Mr Shaw, an earnest young man with slick hair and crumpled suits. He covered the story and appeared on our doorstep at regular intervals despite the long journey from the *Gazette's* offices in Cambridge. I should have asked him, though, in truth, I was in no condition to answer anyone's questions, let alone ask them.

Mr Shaw had a particularly implacable face for a young man. I could never tell what was going on behind his little round spectacles. He asked his questions; I tried my best to answer them even when all I wanted to do was crawl into a deep black hole.

Frank usually just told him to piss off.

Whatever response he got, Mr Shaw scribbled it in his pocketbook, no expression troubling him, before moving onto the next question. Unless Frank slammed the door in his face.

Detective Inspector Breaker, on the other hand, was as easy to read as *Stalky & Co*. He thought either Frank, I or both of us murdered Tilly. He just couldn't prove it, which I think annoyed him immensely. Whether he was the kind of man who suspected the worst of everybody, I couldn't say. Given his profession, I suppose it was entirely possible.

He seemed a joyless man, though there was little to laugh about by the time he darkened our door.

Tilly had been missing for three days when he arrived from Ipswich. The local police had arranged searches of the shoreline and surrounding marshes, but no one thought Tilly had wandered off on her own. Nothing had been found and no one had seen anything.

We sat around the kitchen table while Breaker questioned us. Like Mr Shaw, he had a little pocketbook, but his notetaking was far more methodical. A painful silence followed each question as he wrote our answers down. He had a sidekick, Detective Sergeant Collins, who stood by the dresser drinking tea and smoking. He never spoke, he never took a note. He just stared at us in turn. I avoided his eye, Frank glowered back.

Constable Perkins, the local bobby, was there too. He shuffled from foot to foot, offering the occasional apologetic smile. He did make the tea, though.

Frank wanted to do most of the talking, Breaker wanted to ask me most of the questions.

"Please, Mr Harryman, let your wife speak," Breaker said several times in his nasally London accent.

Frank didn't take to Breaker, which was no great surprise. He didn't take to anyone much.

I told Breaker the same things I did Perkins the day Tilly vanished. I assumed Perkins had briefed the CID officers accordingly when they arrived to take over the case, but he made me go over the story again. And again.

A meticulous fellow was Det. Insp. Breaker.

"And you saw no one, Mrs Harryman?" Breaker asked, pen poised over his notebook, sharp, narrow eyes fixed on me.

"She's already told you that!" Frank snapped.

Those sharp, narrow eyes moved from to my husband.

"Please, Mr Harryman, let your wife answer the question," he said again.

"No one..."

"You're sure?"

I turned the damp handkerchief in my hands.

"Very few people come out here; I'd remember if I saw anyone."

Breaker nodded and scratched out another note. A further long silence accompanied it before his attention returned to me.

"And what did you do when you found your daughter was missing?"

Frank opened his mouth, no doubt to make the same protest, but Breaker silenced him with a warning look. He had that kind of regard. He was a big man, not the soft, flabby kind of big Frank had grown into over our marriage, but the hard, broad, intimidating kind. Not that he needed to flex any muscle. He had an air about him that brooked no argument. He would have made a good headmaster.

"I went and found Frank. I knew he would be in his studio," I kept my voice even. Frank wasn't supposed to have been in his bloody studio, he should have been watching the children, but I knew where I'd find him.

"And was he?"

"Yes."

Breaker wrote something else with his slow, careful hand. I wondered what kind of handwriting he had. Copper-bottomed and faultless, I imagined. Once he'd finished, with a perfectly executed full stop no doubt, he asked his next question. It was a good one.

"So, the children were left unsupervised?"

"I only popped out for five minutes!" Frank protested before I could say yes.

"And your daughter happened to vanish in this particular five-minute window?" Breaker's eyes, as grey and cold as wet slate, fixed on Frank.

"It might have been ten..." Frank reached for his cigarettes.

"Was it five minutes? Ten minutes? More?"

"I wasn't watching the clock."

"Or your children."

Frank's cigarette hovered over the match he'd struck, his own eyes narrowing. I thought he was going to swear, instead, he lit it, shook the match out and blew smoke at the Detective Inspector.

Breaker watched him. Then wrote some more when it was clear Frank wasn't going to give him anything other than a dirty look.

"Are your children often left unsupervised?"

"No," I said quickly.

"How often do you go to Creethorpe, Mrs Harryman?"

"Several times a week, for shopping."

"The same days? The same times?"

"Wednesday is market day, but otherwise, no. It depends on what we need."

"And the weather," Frank added, "the weather can be bad here."

"Much like the rest of the country, then."

No one smiled.

"So, if someone were watching you, there would be no discernible pattern for them to learn."

"I'm sorry?" I asked.

Breaker gave me a patient, if cold, smile, "A pattern someone who wished to steal a baby could learn, so they would know the best time to enter your house. When the children were unsupervised."

"They're not usually unsupervised," I said.

Breaker nodded and wrote some more. Behind me, Constable Perkins started making tea again.

"Have you seen anyone watching the house or lurking in the area?"

"No."

When Frank said nothing, Breaker and I looked at him. Collins, I noticed, continued to watch me.

He shook his head.

More questions followed. Almost all of them already asked at least once. Perhaps he was seeing if we gave the same answers. It wasn't hard to work out what he was thinking, and it was the same as most anybody else would be.

Collins slid the mugs of tea he'd taken from Constable Perkins in front of us. Breaker stirred in sugar as slowly and meticulously as he did everything else before asking me, "Mrs Harryman, is there anything you are not telling me?"

"Why wouldn't she tell you everything?" Frank demanded.

Breaker ignored him.

"Mrs Harryman?"

"No. Nothing I can think of."

"Are you sure?"

Breaker had a way of looking at you that made you think not only you were lying but he knew you were lying, and it was only a matter of time before he proved you were lying and got his Sergeant to slap on the handcuffs.

Perhaps it was something they taught at policeman school.

Of course, he was right; there were things I wasn't telling him. The voices I thought I heard in the house, the malign presence I suspected we shared the Castle with, the way things had rattled and shaken when I'd returned home. How I knew something bad had happened before I'd found Tilly's cot empty.

But if I said any of that, he'd think me mad. And, frankly, I wasn't convinced about my sanity either.

"Yes... I'm sure."

Breaker nodded and slid his I know you're lying look over to Frank, "And you, Mr Harryman. Is there anything else you'd like to tell me?"

I looked at Frank too.

Was he lying?

His demeanour was as you'd expect of a man who always liked to be in control and suddenly found he wasn't. He was moody, irritable, fidgety. When the policemen left, I expected he'd hit me a few times to remind us he was the master of the Castle.

Frank was not a good man, not by any twisted stretch of my imagination, but I did not believe he would have done anything to Tilly. He was negligent with the children but never cruel. I'd never seen him hurt any of them; he reserved his rage for me.

So I told myself.

"The only thing I've got to say," Frank said, after drawing heavily on his cigarette, "Is why are you wasting time interrogating us when you should be looking for my daughter?"

"We are looking for your daughter, Mr Harryman," Breaker sipped his tea, eyes never leaving Frank, "we've been looking for her since she was reported missing."

And they carried on looking for her.

In the reed banks, in the ponds and meres, in the dunes, along the beach. Men walked the hedgerows and drainage ditches, the fields, barns and outhouses of the farms beyond the marshes.

Anywhere someone might dispose of a very small body.

There really were only two explanations. We killed Tilly for reasons unknown, or some stranger sneaked into the Castle and snatched her away. Detective Inspector Breaker was of a mind one of those explanations was a lot more plausible than the other. From the way people looked at me whenever I ventured into Creethorpe over the following years, most everybody else thought much the same.

But they were all wrong.

Something else entirely had happened.

1943

Frank called the accent locals like Davey sported *deep yokel.*

He always said it in such a patronising way you might think he had a particular dislike for these country folk, but the reality was Frank didn't really like anyone, regardless of where they came from and how they spoke.

It could sometimes be hard to follow, despite twenty-three years living out here.

"I don't understand."

"Yew won't believe neither, reckons. Owd Davey Acorns lost too many a screw over th' years. Thas wha' they says roundabouts. Hear em right enough, even tho' oi mostly keep to moiself and have done fah many of these good long years."

Davey sipped his tea.

I tried mine; it had cooled sufficiently not to take the skin from my lips. It tasted like something you might give a child when you thought they were pretending to be ill to avoid going to school.

"Davey-"

"This is an owd place, see? Whole world used to be like this. Now it's filling up with machines and smoke, cities, factory mills and motoring cars, war and madness. But naht 'ere. This is still an owd place and oi walk the owd ways and see th' owd things. Yew still can when it's quiet if yew got a nose fah it..."

Davey gave me a long hard stare, his eyes dark beads in the shadow of his hat. His face was thin, pinched, weaselly, even, if I wanted to be unkind, cut by deep lines around his eyes and mouth. Loose flaps of skin made it look a little like he wore the face of a much bigger man upon his bones.

I thought he was looking for a reaction. So, I held his eye, sipped tea and refused to give him one.

He nodded at the tree line.

"Things live 'ere. Oi seen em. Oi know."

I got the impression he wasn't talking about Roger the squirrel this time.

I kept sipping the tea.

"Most of em are 'armless, leave em be and yew'll be alroight, even when one comes a walking down the path roight in front of yew in the moonlit."

Perhaps I should have listened to Angie.

"Don't see em so much in the daylit. Maybe they don't like to be seen, maybe they don't like wha' ther' be left to see under th' sun nowadays, maybe... summit else. Dunno. Just is."

He paused again, eyes holding mine.

"Yew think oi'm a mad un, but yew too polite to says...?"

"Davey... someone I cared about deeply died. He drove into a tree. Everyone says it was an accident. It probably was. Almost certainly was. But I've been told you saw something else. I'd like to know what. I..." the words hung on my lips, reluctant to cross the threshold into the world.

An eyebrow disappeared under the rim of his flat cap as he took another sip of nettle tea.

"...I see things too. Sometimes. I tell myself I've imagined them. That I'm going mad. Even more so when I hear them. But sometimes I think they're real too. So, maybe we're both... not hauling a full load. I just want you to tell me what you saw."

Davey mulled that over, drained his mug and put it on the ground amongst the grass and woodchips.

"Oi wer' walking to *Th' Green Man*, cos oi sometimes take a pint or two fah me thirst. Don't care so much for the company of people, but drinking on yew'r own is a maudlin business," he shrugged, "oi don't like walking on the road, moi owd feet prefer th' feel of the earth, the crunch of leaves, of twigs, of natural things. So, oi does moi best to avoid the buggers. Don't like them motoring cars neither. Smell of the Devil's cack and thas a fact.

Anyways, moi path takes me close to the motoring cars road as it goes by Gallows Field, where it's spoken highwaymen got strung up. Always been a sad place, Gallows Field, but thas by th' by. Oi 'eard a motoring car a ways off. Knew it wer' a yank. Sound different, their motoring cars. Loud, like they is," a look of distaste soured Davey's face, whether at the thought of motoring cars or Americans, I couldn't tell.

"Mostly, I puts moi 'ead down and whistles when one of them things comes by, but summit made me keep moi eyes on th' road. Was one of them jeep things, roight enough. Ugly, noisy bugger. Going devilish fast it wer', swinging from one side of the road to th' other, screeching, squealing, growling and howling..."

"And you saw the man driving?"

Davey nodded, "Fair-haired, well-built, wearing sunny glasses an a leather jacket. One of them flying bors..."

My stomach tightened. I gripped the cooling mug tighter between my hands, wishing it held gin rather than nettle tea.

"...th' one with him tho' wer' summit else."

"He... wasn't alone?"

Davey shook his head.

"Another American?"

"Nah... summit from further away. Reckons..."

"Further away?"

"Further and closer."

"Davey...?"

"Sorry, girl. 'ard to find words tha' don't ever wanna fit yewr mouth," Davey pulled off his cap to run a hand through thinning silver-grey hair.

"But who was it?"

"Dunno who. Dunno what. Seen a lot oi 'ave, but naht this. Wer' but a shadow, almost, but not quite. Like the sunlit didn't wanna touch it. Next to the flying bor, fighting 'im fah th' steerings wheel, turning it one way thens th' other, its arms wer' wrong. Too long, too twisted, like th' rest of th' bugger. Like some little un's crayon picture. All the roight bits, but nuttin' drawn the roight way.

Flashed by so fast, but oi know wha' oi saw. Know what oi 'eard too."

"Heard?"

"The flying bor screaming and th' other... laughing, like a mad banshee, whooping, crying, 'ollering. Like summit from a looney bin, summit tha' made you wanna cover yew'r ears and start a screaming too..."

I felt like shooting to my feet and running into the woods; I felt like slapping his face, I felt like shouting at him, I felt like weeping. It was all nonsense. Grief had sent me on a wild goose chase to find something from a man who probably should have been in a looney bin himself.

Instead, I just sat, staring at him.

"Wer' one other thing," Davey said, turning his cap over in his hands, "everything else oi heard wer' gibberish but made out one word clear enough 'fore th' motoring car shot round th' bend."

"And what was that?" I forced myself to ask.

Davey stared at me for a while, and the only noise was the chattering of birds before he spoke that one word.

My heart both sank and broke at the sound of it.

"Beatrice."

1916

"Mr and Mrs James."

I stared at my feet, my face burning, and waited for God to start hurling thunderbolts at us. At the very least, I expected to be shown the door and given a stern lecture about the dire consequences of a sinful life on the way back to the street.

As it was, the bespectacled man at the reception desk of the *Agincourt Hotel* simply said to Owen, "Right you are, sir..."

He took Owen's money and fetched a key from one of the hooks hanging behind him.

"Room 205, second floor. There's a bathroom across the landing. Do you need a hand with your bags, sir?"

"No, thank you," Owen scooped up the key while I fought conflicting urges to run for the stairs or the front door.

"Goodnight then, sir... madam... God bless you and keep you safe," the receptionist beamed at us as I took Owen's arm, and we made our way up.

"Is it always like this in London?" I asked out of the corner of my mouth, flabbergasted at the ease with which we, an unmarried couple, had found a room for the night.

"Dunno... I've only been here with my wife before."

I gave him a look.

"Ow!" he yelped when I gave him the sharp end of my elbow in his ribs as well, "Just joking!"

We went up to the room in silence. No doors swung open, no one peered curiously at us, no one demanded to know why my left hand, with its solitary engagement ring, remained so resolutely in my coat pocket.

And still no thunderbolts.

Outside the den of iniquity known to the rest of the world simply as Room 205, Owen put down our bags, took the key and slid it into the lock. It took him three goes. His hand was trembling.

I'm not sure any bits of me weren't.

The room was dark. I waited in the doorway while Owen fumbled about and found a lamp to light.

Once the orange glow pushed back the shadows, Owen grabbed his kit bag and my suitcase and ushered me inside. It was a comfortable room, though it smelt faintly of mothballs, furniture polish and old smoke. And it had a bed. A large one.

"It's alright, Bea," he smiled. I must have looked terrified.

After kicking the door shut and dropping the bags, he put his arms around me, and I folded into him without hesitation.

"I'm frightened..." I whispered. Pressed up against him I could see little splatters of mud dotted his tunic. I thought of his friend, Geordie, and closed my eyes.

"You don't have to do anything you don't want, Bea. I just want... I just want to be close to you. Just for a little while."

I wasn't really frightened of the bed or the prospect of sharing it with the man I loved, I was afraid this would be the only time it would happen. The one moment we would have. The fear I'd lived with since 1914 Owen was not going to come home from the war, curled and coiled around me, squeezing my limbs and heart as surely as it constricted my hopes and dreams.

He kissed me, which helped me forget my fears, and everything else, for more than a few heartbeats.

But kisses never last a lifetime.

Eventually, he stepped away and smiled, eyes holding mine.

When he started unbuttoning his tunic, I didn't know what to do, say, or even where to look.

I took my hat off. It seemed the least I should do.

Owen threw the tunic over the back of a chair. Then rummaged in his kit bag. I stood in the middle of the room, fiddling with my hat.

"I'm going to take a bath," he said, straightening up, with soap and shaving gear.

"A bath?"

"There's one across the landing..." he said, rattling around the cupboard to discover a dressing gown. before helping himself to one of the off-white towels waiting on the bed, "...haven't had many baths lately."

"I had noticed."

"Thought... I should..."

I wasn't quite sure whether to feel touched or put off. After all, I didn't have much experience to draw on.

I nodded and looked for somewhere to hang my hat.

Owen interrupted my search with another kiss.

"I won't be long," he said when our lips parted, then found a hand to squeeze before hurrying off. When I couldn't hear his footsteps anymore, I hung up my coat in the cupboard, the home of the mothballs, and looked around the room, unsure what to do.

I hoisted my little suitcase onto the bed and opened it. My nightgown sat folded on the top. It looked back at me disapprovingly. It was the kind of austere flannelette garment my grandmother would have worn to ensure an undisturbed night's sleep.

I snapped the case shut and stepped back.

What was I supposed to do?

I had left Birmingham in something of a hurry that morning. Did I need to have a bath too? I sniffed an armpit. Nothing particularly unpleasant. Still... maybe I should?

Or perhaps dousing my bits with perfume before draping myself decorously over the bed to await Owen was what was expected of a woman here?

A couple of the flightier students back in Secretarial College often regaled the rest of us with quite ribald tales of assignations they'd enjoyed with gentleman friends. I'd been both shocked and fascinated. But I hadn't taken notes. I'd never thought I was *that* type of girl.

In the end, I'd sat by the dresser and smoked one of Owen's cigarettes, continually flicking it at the ashtray. I thought it might have calmed me down, but it just made me feel a bit lightheaded and a little sick. I rarely smoked. It wasn't something nice girls, especially ones who happened to be a vicar's daughter, did. But then, neither was spending the night with a man they weren't married to.

Not married to *yet*, I corrected.

I told myself to stop being silly. I wasn't a hussy. I would be Owen's wife by now if it wasn't for the war. I loved him. He loved me. But the war had come and kept us apart for over a year. If not now, when? I was the one pushing back the wedding, not Owen.

After stubbing the cigarette out with a decisive twist, I faced up to the challenge of my nightgown again. I'd only added it at the last minute; I'd thought I'd be sleeping in my own bed back at the vicarage that night and had plenty of clothes there. But something made me throw it in before I rushed to New Street to catch the London train.

A practical girl. That was me. Always prepared for every situation.

I unpacked the nightgown and held it out. It very nearly reached my ankles.

Well, almost every situation.

I bit my bottom lip.

It was this or nothing.

Under the circumstances, nothing was probably the more practical choice for a truly practical girl. But...

I undressed quickly.

I didn't know how long Owen would be, but from what I knew of men's bathing habits, I expected him back sooner rather than later. I didn't want to lock the door, but somehow being caught half-undressed seemed far more scandalous than the decorous draping of myself over the bed.

In the end, I was more tucked up than draped. I didn't quite have the sheets pulled to my chin, but the nightgown did pretty much leave everything to the imagination. I had sprayed a little toilet water around and let down my hair, balancing that brazenness by keeping my bloomers on under the flannelette armour of my nightgown.

Then I remembered I hadn't taken my makeup off.

Should I?

Was it better to keep it on whilst... *being* with a man?

I didn't know. I wasn't the kind of girl (you know, that kind) who used lots of makeup, but I was always meticulous about taking it off. I didn't want spots.

I sat up.

Were spots the biggest issue currently?

Probably not.

I laid back down again.

Owen's return waylaid further dithering.

He wore the dressing gown, soiled clothes hung over his arm, army issue short back and sides hair wet and combed back.

"You're in bed?" he said, closing the door behind him.

Wasn't I supposed to be?

"Are we going dancing?"

"Do you want to?"

"Probably a little late now."

He nodded and fiddled with the clothes he was holding. He looked as nervous as I did.

"Come to bed..." I said, smiling at him in what I hoped was an alluring, but not too shameless, way. Then I rolled on my side and stared at the wall to ensure I didn't see anything alarming.

I'd known Owen since childhood. We'd been in love for a long time and had done things. Just not everything. I'd seen him in partial states of undress. We'd gone to the beach at Weston-Super-Mare, and the swimming pool in Cheltenham, and even paddled and splashed about in the Windrush on fondly remembered summer days when we'd picnicked and grappled with our yearning in the grass.

My hand had strayed under his shirt, and his under mine. I had felt his excitement through his trousers, and he had brushed against mine. But we had agreed to wait until we were married for more.

Now we were going to bed together for the first time.

And I feared the last.

1930

The wind whipped in off the sea. A good day for both waves and washing lines.

I'd laundered all the sheets, including the ones from Frank's bed smelling of perfume and sex, and hung them out. They billowed like sails on the line.

I watched them snap and flutter, the empty basket at my feet, imagining I was on a great sailing ship heading for some exotic shore. A land where the sun always kissed your skin and Owen would be waiting for me on the quayside, with roses, kisses and arms that would hold me forever.

I'd had that dream the night before. When I awoke, it'd been the happiest I had felt in years. Then sleep fell away, and realisation dawned that only laundry to wash, dry and iron awaited me.

Still, I remembered with rare clarity. In those wind-ripped sheets, I heard the distant echo of what I'd experienced in both the world of dreams and in those long-lost pre-war days when love had been more than a dream and I lived in Camelot.

When I turned and looked back at the Castle, the echo faded to nothing.

Squat, ugly, scoured by salt-sharpened wind and peppered with seagull poo. No roses waited for me here. No Lancelot either.

The squawk of a black-headed gull sweeping overhead towards the sea pulled my eyes upwards. Hopefully, the sheets would survive, but gulls were much like life. Both rarely passed up an opportunity to shit on your laundry.

Shaking the thought away, I went back inside. I had bigger problems than whether the gulls would dirty my sheets today.

I found my biggest current problem sitting at the kitchen table, drinking my coffee and effortlessly looking glamorous well before noon.

"Darling!" Izzy beamed, "You look fraught."

Maybe if she'd spent the morning washing sheets, she'd look less glamorous and more fraught.

"Good morning, Izzy," I said instead, tossing the empty laundry basket aside, "sleep well?"

"Like a lamb, an absolute lamb."

"That's good," I took off my coat and made to get out of the room pronto.

"Coffee? Cigarette?" Izzy offered.

"Too busy."

"Oh, tosh. Everything is spic and span, come and have some coffee. I made extra..." she indicated the pot in front of her. When I stood there glaring, she poured another cup and slid it across the table, "...sit, let's be friends."

"That's a little difficult, in the circumstances."

"Circumstances, darling?"

"You. Fucking my husband."

"Well, we shouldn't let that come between us. Men! Really not worth the fuss, in my experience."

"You've got some gall..." it wasn't quite a hiss, but it came close.

Izzy sat back, a half smile upon her painted lips.

"It's strange," she said, "you're prickly with me, but around Frank, you're such a timid little thing. Mousey, one might say. Why is that do you think?"

I crossed to the table, pulled out the chair and sat opposite Izzy. How long did she spend putting on all that makeup every morning? I wondered what she looked like without it.

"Because I don't give a damn about Frank."

"I'm not sure I follow."

"But I love my children."

"Sorry, I'm still not-"

"I'm not going to let you take them off me."

Izzy threw back her head, "Oh, darling! I've no interest in your boys. Why should I? I'm not at all maternal."

"But if you take my husband-"

"I'm not taking your husband either. You're quite welcome to him."

I frowned, "Then why are you doing this?"

"Everybody needs a hobby."

"Other women's husbands are your hobby?!"

"No," Izzy said, "the spirit world is my hobby. Your husband is a... line of enquiry, shall we say."

"What..." I straightened sharply, "...on Earth are you talking about?"

Pushing the coffee aside, Izzy stood up, "Why don't we go outside for a bit? It looks delightful..."

She didn't wait for an answer. Her coat and the bits of dead animals that were its collar and cuffs hung on a peg with the others. She slipped it on and was out of the door before I'd decided if I would go with her.

Perhaps the years of doing what I was told had conditioned me, but I grabbed my coat, a far less glamorous beast, and followed Izzy.

She was already marching towards the sea. One hand on her hat, she twisted around without pause to wave me on with her free hand.

I hurried after her, not sure who I should be cursing.

Izzy waited for me on the wrack line of seaweed and other debris discarded by the surf, snarling at the bottom of the shingle slope exposed by the low tide. She wasn't dressed for the beach. I'd have likely broken my ankle trying to walk across shingle in heels, but she'd glided over it.

"Walls have ears," she explained when I caught up with her.

The wind was tugging at my coat, a baggy, shapeless thing Izzy wouldn't have used in a dog basket and throwing hair about my face. I couldn't have felt more bedraggled standing next to Izzy if I'd been washed up alongside the seaweed at her feet.

"Why-"

"Frank isn't a very nice man, is he?" Izzy flicked back a few errant licks of hair poking out from beneath her cloche hat.

"You seem to like him well enough?"

"I don't like him."

"But-"

"He intrigues me. Which is something else entirely," she turned her back on the sea, eyes narrowing as she stared at Grey Gull and the cluster of dilapidated outbuildings in its orbit.

"Do you believe in ghosts, Beatrice?"

"I told you, I'm a sceptic."

"About clairvoyants, yes. But spirits?"

"I... don't know..." I thought of the things I'd seen and heard inside the Castle, "...possibly."

"Do you think only buildings are haunted?"

I pushed back my own hair. The woolly hat I usually kept in my pocket wasn't where it should be, and the sea-breeze was having a riotous time with my lank, greasy locks.

"What has any of this got to do with-"

Izzy's eyes returned to me, narrowing further as she twisted back into the wind, "Beatrice, what do you think happened to Tilly?"

1943

I was sure I hadn't told Angie my name, and I certainly hadn't told Davey, but I guess I must have. It really was the only explanation.

The only one I wanted to countenance, anyway.

"Is this a joke?" I managed to ask.

Davey pulled a face, "Ain't much oi can see to laugh at, girl."

"My name isn't girl," I plonked the half-drunk tea on the ground and shot to my feet, "it's Beatrice!"

"Oi did wonder if tha' be th' case."

"I don't know what kind of game you-"

"Ain't nah game, girl... Beatrice..." Davey shrugged, "...just saying wha' oi saw..."

"What? That some *thing* killed Tom? That's ridiculous!"

I span away, furious at myself for being made a fool of.

"Wha' yew seen then? Wha' yew seen, Beatrice?"

I was halfway to the trees before I stopped.

"Wer' it summit tha' looked a bit like a man but weren't? Summit with only shadows fah a face? Summit th' sunlit never falls on?"

I looked over my shoulder.

"Summit sloighly on th' huh, oi'd guess?"

That kept my feet where they were.

What had I seen back in the Castle over all those years? I didn't know.

"Something I've only ever caught in the corner of my eye."

"Best way to see it. Reckons..." Davey hunched forward, cap crushed between his hands, staring at his worn-down boots, "Can't say oi done much sleeping since oi saw it."

"Just my imagination. Probably."

Davey snorted, "If yew thought tha' yew'd not come out 'ere fah owd Davey Acorns. Only two reasons folks come a looking fah tha' silly owd bugger."

"Two reasons?"

He raised eyes that looked both tired and sad in the soft light of a cloudy day, "They either wanna laugh at me or they seen summit to scare em. Oi don't think yew'r much of a one fah laughing, girl..."

"What do you think it was you saw?"

"Nuttin oi seen before. And oi've seen a lot. Nuttin oi wanna see again, neither. Wer' like madness'd become a man."

"What did you do after?"

"Do?" Davey coughed up a dark chuckle, "Oi went and downed more pints than oi done in many a year, thas wha' oi did, girl."

"You didn't go to the crash?"

Davey shook his head, "Didn't know th' motoring car crashed till next day. Being a stupid owd bugger, oi'd already told the fools in the *Th' Green Man* wha' oi saw. They laughed royally at me, like oi'm th' local plum fool. Still, th' coppers got wind of wha' oi'd seen and came to dicker 'bout it. Then th' yank coppers came. Th' coppers been wanting to lock me up fah years. Wanna lock me up more now. The yanks didn't know wha' to make of me. Not sure they even understood moi way of talking. None of em believed me either ways. Should learn to keep moi lips sewed, so oi should. Beer fah yew. Loosens moi tongue too much, always has. Should pack it in. Reckons..."

"Did the Americans find anything suspicious about the crash?"

"Said nuttin' to me."

Davey pushed himself to his feet, grimacing in the process. He walked slowly over to me. He wasn't a tall man, and he didn't use the tin bath outside his shack much either.

"Where'd yew see what yew see?"

"At home."

"Nahwhere else?"

I shook my head.

"Dunno wha' yew hoping to find 'ere, girl. But oi can give yew one truth."

"Really?"

"Oh, aye," Davey nodded, "high time yew looked fah somewhere else to live."

I had to smile, despite myself.

Part of me wanted to believe him, a lot of me didn't.

"How long yew lived there?"

"Twenty-three years."

Davey sniffed, "Almost as long as oi lived 'ere."

"And you've never seen anything like... *this* before?"

"Wouldn't still be here if oi 'ad, girl. Seen plenty. Yew do when yew walk the owd ways like oi do. Some strange, some beautiful, lot tha' just make yew scratch yewr 'ead. Probably wher' most of moi 'air's gone. Reckons... but nuttin' like this."

He leaned over and patted the piece of trunk I'd vacated, "Why don't yew tell me it all. And then oi'll tell yew wha' oi think. Tha' ain't worth tuppence, mind, but it won't cost yew nuttin' neither."

I hesitated. The part of me that thought he was a mad old coot spouting nonsense wanted me to walk away. All the way back to the Castle and whatever I shared it with. Back to what remained of my life.

Instead, I did as he bid.

Davey looked at me with interested eyes. They didn't appear to be the eyes of a mad old coot. They were sharp and bright. They were eyes that had seen a thing or two. Reckons...

So, I sat down and told him things I'd told no one else.

But mostly, I told him about Tilly...

1927

I don't remember much about the rest of 1927.

Perhaps that is why I kept those clippings of Mr Shaw's work from the *Eastern Gazette* pressed inside *Stalky & Co.*, in case my mind somehow completely expunged Tilly from my memory.

I thought the grief I'd experienced after losing Owen and Dad was as much emotional pain as it was possible to endure. I've been wrong about so many things in my life, and I was wrong about that too.

It's said there's no feeling on Earth worse than that suffered by a parent who has to bury their child, but I descended to a realm of such soul-crushing despair I would have welcomed the opportunity to stand over my baby's grave.

It's the not knowing that kills you.

What had happened? Where was she? Was she alive? Was she dead? Was there some chance, some hope, some faint, gut-wrenching possibility she would be returned to me?

I was not dead, but I wasn't alive either. I could not sleep, I could not eat, I could not rest. There's a place inside where I'd kept the best of me safe from Frank's petty cruelties; the love for my children, my memories of Owen, Dad and my own sunlit childhood. It was where the tiny flame of hope that one day I would find some manner of happiness flickered defiantly against the cold wind of my life in the Castle.

That place became a chasm. An empty, hollow cavern where grief wailed and sorrow stalked now the last light had been extinguished.

Days stretched into weeks. Detective Inspector Breaker and Mr Shaw came, asked their questions, made notes, and left. The same questions, the same answers. There was never any news. Nothing was found, Tilly had vanished from the face of the Earth, and my heart wept without end.

I should have been able to find some solace with Francis and Simon, but their innocent faces cut me, reminded me, and whispered of my loss. Of how I had failed my daughter and how I would, inevitably, fail them too. The first duty of a parent is to protect their child, as I could not do that, what hope was there the boys wouldn't, one day, be ripped from my life too?

Frank was as he always was. As soon as Breaker, Shaw or any of the others left, he reverted to the man he always was. I didn't know if he simply lacked the capacity to care. Sometimes, I heard whistling or singing from his studio. He sounded happy, which made me hate him more than I already did. He seemed to grow fatter, bloating, face reddening and gut swelling. I told myself it was my imagination, my hatred creating an ever more grotesque caricature to loath. It didn't help.

He offered me no comfort, no compassion, no love. My tears did not move him; Tilly's disappearance did not move him. Nothing did. Only his wretched paintings interested him, same as always.

Breaker and his men searched the house twice. They found nothing. I don't know how thorough they were as they never discovered Owen's letters, my engagement ring or the pennies I had squirrelled away in the forlorn hope it would one day be enough to take me far away from Frank and this bleak shore.

I said little about the day I lost Tilly to my husband. Only once did I ask Frank why he had left the children? He had looked at me like I was a simpleton.

"To paint," was all he replied.

The day Tilly disappeared, I had burst into the studio and found him assaulting another canvas, twisting oil and pigment into some anguished, ugly, awful thing.

"Problem, Sweetness?" he'd asked, looking over his shoulder, nothing flickering on his face but the happiness he demonstrated when creating his dreary art.

The thing on the canvas looked like a scream emanating from a broken and bloody maw.

It was the thing that always made me dismiss the idea he had anything to do with Tilly's disappearance. He'd been doing what he always did, day after day, year after year. If he had anything to do with it, he would not have been there. I had not been gone long enough for him to spirit Tilly away, I thought whenever the possibility nagged at me.

Then there was the house.

It started laughing at me.

I told myself it was the wind, and when there was no wind, I told myself it was just the creak of old wood or simply my overwrought, grief-broken mind conjuring imaginary monsters.

In other words, the same excuses I'd used for all the other things I'd heard within the Castle.

It usually came when I lay alone, thinking about Tilly and turning everything that happened that day over and over. Sometimes I would be staring at the ceiling. Sometimes, I would find my eyes drawn by the terrible gravity of Tilly's empty cot. Sometimes, my eyes would be closed in the vain hope sleep my take me to another place for an hour or two.

I called it laughter, but a giggle would be more accurate, though even that is not quite right. A manic, gibbering. The sound a lunatic might make as he played in the darkness with dead, broken things.

The first time I heard it, I shot bolt upright in bed, certain someone, or something, was in my bedroom. It did not come again, as I sat straining my ears over the wild thudding of my heart.

Eventually, when nothing came but the familiar distant thrum of the sea, I sank back into the twisted sheets. Hours later, unable to sleep, I rose and opened the curtains. The moon was dazzling above the black waves. Then I knelt on the floor by Tilly's cot, fingers pushed through the wooden bars to caress the blanket forlornly awaiting my daughter's return.

Shivering in my nightgown, I pressed my head against the cot and watched my breath frost silver in the moonlight.

The giggle came again, wet, throaty, almost retching with glee.

"Who are you?" I asked.

The sound eased back into the night.

"Did you take my daughter?"

Only the sea replied.

"Bring her back, please. Take me instead; I'll do anything! Just bring her back..."

My words dissolved into tears, my sobs drowning out the world. I don't know how long I cried, by the time they subsided, my fingers, wrapped around the wooden struts of the cot like a prisoner gripping the bars of his cell, were numb.

A different noise came, not a giggle, but a slow, shuddering exhalation. Through my hands and up my arms, I felt the cot vibrate, not as violently as the kitchen dresser shook the day Tilly vanished, but still more than noticeable, even for my cold, stiff fingers.

"Tilly...?"

The vibrations faded to nothing. The cot remained empty.

Behind me, something moved.

"What do you think you're doing?"

My head shot around. Frank stood in the doorway, as pale as any ghost in the stream of moonlight flooding the room.

"I..."

He crossed the room, looming over me before reaching down and taking my chin in his hand.

"Keep the bloody noise down. You'll wake the boys."

When I made to speak, he squeezed my chin hard.

"Quiet, Sweetness, quiet."

When I nodded, his hand fell away.

He looked down at me. I knew he wouldn't hit me as he always closed the door behind him when he thought I deserved punishment.

"Go back to bed. And pull yourself together."

Frank followed me to the foot of the bed. He was wearing only his pyjamas and must have been cold as his hand had been shaking when he held my face, a shiver that felt much like the way Tilly's cot had vibrated.

At least, I hoped it was the temperature. If it was anger, he would go and close the door.

"Stay under the blankets, keep warm. You'll catch your death, otherwise..."

I pulled the blankets up, not realising how cold I was until they were over me. I curled arms around myself to try and contain my own shivers.

Frank went to the window. The moon lit his face as he stood there, breath clouding the glass before he snapped the curtains shut.

I listened to his feet return, surefooted and unhesitant despite the darkness. He paused again, and I feared he would climb in with me.

"Where's our baby?"

"Gone."

He moved around the bed, and his hand found my face again. Still shaking, his fingers smelt of cigarettes and turpentine.

He sighed, deeply. It sounded similar enough to the noise I'd heard as I sat by Tilly's cot to make a shiver run through me far deeper than any cold could manage.

"Things happen," he said, dropping his hand and turning away as if that explained everything.

I wanted to scream, hurl something, hurt him, kick, scratch, and break. Instead, I lifted the blankets to my chin.

"Is there something here?" I blurted out.

He stopped.

"Something?"

"In this house. Something... evil?"

A long silence, then laughter. In its way, as unsettling as the disembodied manic giggling.

"Don't be stupid, Sweetness. There's nothing here but us."

"Sometimes, I hear things."

"Of course you do; it's an old house."

I didn't tell him I saw things too. Partly because I'd never seen enough to be sure I *had* seen anything, but mainly because I recognised the edge in his tone.

I thought of it as his one-more-thing voice.

One more thing, and I'd feel the back of his hand.

One more thing, and I'd have to go and fetch his belt.

"Yes, Frank..."

"I know you're going through a lot," he said, "and I know you're not the brightest, Sweetness, but please don't talk such shit again. That sort of shit gets people sent to the funny farm. You don't want that, do you?"

"No, Frank."

"Think of the boys. Not yourself."

"Yes, Frank."

"Good. Pull yourself together. No more crying, eh?"

He closed the door.

I listened to his creaking footsteps fade to nothing. Frank hadn't shut the curtains properly; the full moon dusted the room with cobweb light through the gap he'd left.

In the end, I rolled over and threw the covers over my head rather than getting up again to close them. Slowly I curled into a ball, tightened my hands into fists and told myself the occasional snickers coming from the parts of the room the moonlight didn't touch were the natural sounds of an old house.

Just like Frank said.

1943

I spent no more than ten minutes in the Castle before I had to get out again.

No voices disturbed the silence, no creaks where nothing should creak, nothing crept about in the corner of my eye, but still, I couldn't abide the thought of staying within those walls.

So, I brewed tea, cut a slice of bread, smothered it with jam I'd made the previous year with foraged blackberries, and went outside.

I sat on the beach, in the spot I had with Tom a few weeks and a million years earlier and stared at the sea.

I thought about Tom and Simon, but mostly I thought about Old Davey Acorns.

"Wha' yew think 'appened to tha' lil' girl?" he asked when I finally finished talking.

I shook my head. I'd had no more words.

He'd pursed his lips and went to make more nettle tea.

The second mug tasted better than the first. An acquired taste. Or my tongue was simply as numb as the rest of me.

Old Davey kept staring, an expectant expression on his face. I listened to the birdsong, which was a lot sweeter than the racket made by the gulls around the Castle. I mulled over what to say next.

"Do you think the thing you saw with Tom... could have taken my baby?" I asked, immediately wishing I hadn't. It sounded even more ridiculous when said aloud than in the quiet moments the possibility had snuck into my mind over the years.

"Dunno," Davey said.

"Do you think I'm mad for suggesting it?"

"People 'ave called me a mad owd bugger fah years, girl. Laugh in moi face they dew. Words can cut and laughs make em sharper, so oi dew neither," he shrugged, "but oi dew think ther' are a lot more possibilities in th' world than most folks imagine..."

"But... if this... thing you saw with Tom is the same... thing I've seen over the years... and it did take Tilly... why did it never hurt my boys, or me, or Frank? Why Tom? Why Tilly...?

"Seems to me, yew gotta find out th' wha' 'fore yew'll find out th' why, girl."

"How do I do that?"

"Wan' me to take a peek round?"

"A peek?"

"Oi see things. Always 'ave. Maybe yew dew too. Most people see bugger all. Maybe thas why Bert and Wally only saw yewr yank in tha' motoring car, and naht tha' other thing, cos they ain't like yew an oi. If oi come and 'ave a peek an a poke in yew'r house, oi might see summit too. Maybe then we can git th' figuring of it."

Sharp, bright eyes stared out of his old worn face.

"Wha' yew say, girl?"

What I thought was that I was mad. I'd been mad for years and I was going progressively madder.

But what I said was yes.

Davey said he'd come the next day as he had some business to attend to first. I didn't ask what kind.

I watched the horizon till it grew dark. I'd have stretched out and slept on the ground, but drizzle swept in with the dusk, forcing me back into the silent Castle.

For a while, I tried to read, but my mind was too restless. In the end, I sat, eyes fixed on the black square of the window until they started to droop. I dragged myself to bed with a heavy heart.

Only the sea whispered in my ear that night. A taunting monster, but one I understood.

Eventually, I drifted into fitful sleep where other monsters waited, though ones I did not remember well come the damp grey morning.

Overnight the drizzle hardened to steady rain, dressing the world beyond the blurry glass in ashes.

I assumed Davey wouldn't come. It was a long walk from Dirkly Woods, and he was an old man. It was probably better he didn't. All I was doing was stirring embers best left to cool to dust.

Tom's death had nothing to do with any phantom, nor did Tilly's abduction.

I tried to put it all from my mind with chores, though housework was a poor salve for my grief. Still, I'd only cried once before noon, which was something.

The knock on the door came just after one.

I froze.

The only sound louder than my heart was the rain. Davey might not come in such a downpour, but it wouldn't keep the telegram boy at home. The Angels of Death didn't pay much heed to the weather. Francis was still out there somewhere. Still in danger every day.

When a second knock came, I realised I hadn't moved an inch.

"Please... not another telegram..."

I pushed my feet towards the door. Each step was an effort of will to overcome the desire to run in the opposite direction. When I reached the door, I had to suck in a breath and force my shaking hand to open it.

"Roight bugger of a day, ain't it, girl?" Davey said, dripping on the doorstep.

I rarely have the urge to hug old men I barely know...

I helped Davey out of his coat, which looked much like the one Owen had in the trenches but not so clean. I hung it and his sodden cap by the door before ushering him to the kitchen.

"This is a sad owd place," he sniffed, standing by the table. He dried his face with a grubby handkerchief.

"Yes..."

Once the kettle was on, I turned to find him stock still, staring pointedly across the room.

"Can you... see *something?*"

"Is tha'..." his eyes flicked to me, lips quivering "...blackberry jam?"

"Erm... yes..."

"Thas roight proper jam tha' is," a broad smile filled his thin face, "moi favourite!"

"Would you like some with your tea?"

"Don't moin'd if oi dew, girl!" Davey said, smile stretching further as he settled himself at the table.

He scoffed the bread and jam with big, lip-smacking bites between mouthfuls of piping-hot tea.

"Love a blackberry, me," he beamed.

"I've made jam for years. Used to collect buckets of them from the hedgerows every autumn with... with the boys..." I looked sharply away.

Davey's hanky reappeared to wipe his lips.

"Life can be beautiful, life can be cruel, thas 'ow it works, girl."

I nodded and changed the subject.

"I thought the weather might have kept you at home?"

"Bit of water on th' bonce never done Davey nah harm."

"Thank you. I appreciate you coming all this way. I'm not sure what good it will do, but-"

"Never know nuttin' till yew try it on fah size."

"I suppose."

"Yew wanna show owd Davey round then?"

I climbed to my feet, "I didn't see anything last night."

Davey did the same, with a click of the knees and a grimace. The rain might not harm his head, but his joints were probably another matter.

He trooped behind me as I gave him the tour of the downstairs rooms. He cast an eye about, nodded a few times and made an occasional noise in the back of his throat, which I couldn't decide was an opinion on the décor or clearing phlegm.

When we returned to the hallway, he asked, "Did tha' yank ever come 'ere."

"Tom... yes..." the way I blushed at the question was likely more eloquent than my answer.

"While yewr husband wer' 'ere?"

I shook my head.

He didn't smirk or give me any kind of knowing look, which I appreciated.

He nodded upstairs, "Let's see th' rest," when I hesitated, he added, "Wher' yew seen it most?"

"My bedroom," I answered, eyes falling to my feet.

"Don't worry 'bout yewr 'onour, girl. Moi owd chap been asleep fah years. He ain't gonna wake up nah matter 'ow pretty yew is."

I didn't consider myself in the least bit pretty, even less so when I was blushing furiously.

I trotted up the stairs, and Davey followed more slowly. I showed him Frank and the boys' rooms before coming to mine.

He stood in the doorway when I went to the window. I fidgeted with the hem of my cardigan.

"This wher' yewr lil' girl went missing?"

"Yes," I jerked my head to the empty corner where the cot had once resided, "this was the last place I saw her."

Davey ventured in. He still had that big knife hanging from his belt.

What on Earth was I doing?

"Sorry business. Remember it."

"You do?"

"Wer' th' talk of all round 'ere fah a bit alroight."

"I'd hoped people had forgotten."

"Talk wer yew did fah th' girl. But oi never listen th' gossip as most of wha' comes outta people's mouths is badger shit. Reckons..."

I stared at him.

"Did you know who I was when I saw you yesterday?"

"Nah. Not till yew said yew live in th' owd Shackle Place, then th' penny dropped."

If he was lying, the whole story about hearing my name had another explanation.

But I didn't want to believe that.

"The Shackle Place?"

"Wha' this house wer' known as back in th' bygone. When I wer' a nipper."

"Frank is the previous owner's – Mr Shackle's – nephew. He inherited the house."

"Lucky him..."

"What do you know about what happened here?"

Davey pulled a face, "'eard stories."

"What stories?"

"'bout this being an unlucky place."

I raised an eyebrow and crossed my arms across my chest. Behind me, the rain fell harder, the wind picking up to throw it against the window.

"Lot of people died 'ere. Nippers mostly."

"Children?"

"Uh-huh."

"Murdered? Disappeared? What?"

"Nah, nuttin like tha'"

I remembered what Mutt Harris had told me about Grey Gull all those years ago, about Shackle's wife and children all dying, about never liking to come fetch his errant sheep when they strayed here. About it being sloightly on th' huh.

"Did you know Mutt Harris?" I asked.

"Nah. I keep moiself to moiself. Even back in th' bygone. Why?"

"Doesn't matter. Have you seen... anything?"

Davey shook his head and joined me by the window, "Whas in th' outbuildings?"

"Just storage and my husband's studio."

"Studio?"

"He's an artist."

That earnt me a twitch of an eyebrow.

"A painter."

"Painter, eh?" Davey said, not approvingly. He an eye at the prints of flowers on the wall, "He did these?"

"No... he doesn't paint flowers."

"He's stuff any good?"

I gave him a pinched smile in return.

"Let's go 'ave a look see."

"It's raining."

Davey tapped his head, "Bit of rain..."

After pulling on my coat we braved the elements.

It was more than a bit of rain now, and I squinted against the wind hurling it in my face as we hurried to Frank's studio.

"Don't touch anything," I told the old man after bringing him inside, "Frank doesn't like anyone to come in here, even me."

Davey scratched the back of his neck as he peered at the canvases crammed into every spare inch, "Keeps himself busy then?"

"Oh yes..." I laughed from the window looking out over the bad-tempered sea. Although it was large, so Frank had plenty of light, the studio remained gloomy. The stink of paint and turpentine was already making my head throb. How did he stand spending so long in here?

Davey tilted his head one way, then the other as he examined Frank's work "Maybe he should try painting flowers..."

I snorted and concentrated on the view. There was nothing in here I wanted to see. Outside, everything was shades of grey blurred into one another by the rain. It looked like one of Tom's seascapes might have if he'd decided to paint in monochrome.

I'll never see another of Tom's beautiful paintings.

The thought cut me.

Just these bloody ugly things...

"Beatrice..."

Davey's voice pulled me back from the equally melancholy thoughts and world.

The old man was standing before one of Frank's creations. He looked over his shoulder and summoned me with a jerk of the head. Reluctantly I joined him.

"Whas this one 'bout?"

"Nothing. They're all about... nothing."

"Naht sure 'bout tha', girl," he pointed at the painting. His hand, I noticed, was trembling.

It was another of Frank's twisted monstrosities. Numerous red hues, slashed, scraped and smeared over the canvas, deepening to something close to black in the centre.

"Don't tha' look like a figure to yew?"

"I suppose, if..."

Davey was right; it was a figure, an abstract one. All the angles and proportions wrong, elongated limbs, stooped back, misshapen head, featureless save for splodges of pure black that could be taken for eyes and mouth. If you looked at it in a certain way, it was a cartoonish representation of a child's nightmare.

Despite my plea for him not to touch anything, Davey ran a fingernail along the figure.

"Thas th' thing, girl..." he whispered, "...thas th' thing oi saw in tha' motoring car with yewr yank..."

1927

Gypsies.

Mr Shaw told me about the gipsies, and I have the subsequent clipping with all the others preserved within the yellowing pages of *Stalky & Co.* I didn't believe it, but I grabbed it all the same.

A group of gypsies had been camping on common ground the other side of Carlesham, some five miles west of Creethorpe, when Tilly disappeared.

"Causing mischief and commotions, as is the want of them people," Mr Shaw said in his usual earnest fashion.

Frank would be furious if he found out I'd let the young man in the house while he was out, but Mr Shaw insisted he had news.

I had not seen Det. Insp. Breaker or any other policemen for nearly a week. As far as I knew, they'd finished searching the marshes and surrounding countryside and had found absolutely nothing.

The last thing I'd heard was that "enquiries were ongoing." I didn't know if that meant they were more or less inclined to think Frank and I had done away with Tilly.

I conjured a thin smile and asked Mr Shaw what that had to do with Tilly.

"I've been told they were seen with a baby..."

The young man didn't give much away about what went on behind those little round spectacles, but the whiff of a man pleased with himself arose with those words and the tiniest nod of the head that accompanied them.

I pinched the bridge of my nose. I'd been surviving on no more than an hour or two of fitful nightmare-ridden sleep since Tilly's disappearance. It was taking its toll.

"Don't gypsies have children, Mr Shaw?"

"Of course, but they are a dark-haired, olive-skinned race. The child was fair. Like your daughter. And the gypsies left in great haste after being seen with this child."

It seemed far-fetched gypsies stole Tilly, but if they had, then she was still alive and could be returned to me, I sat forward, "And the police...?"

"Are looking for the gypsies as we speak. They don't like to talk about what they get up to, but I thought you should know."

A little flicker of hope turned inside me, which is always a dangerous thing.

"It seems a little... unlikely..."

"Oh," Mr Shaw sipped the tea I had made him, "those people are well known for it."

"They are?"

"Gypsies steal children like Jews steal money. They just can't help themselves."

It's always the hope that kills you...

I sat back and let him prattle on to see if he had something, anything, I could cling to.

Baby-stealing gypsies were the best I got.

Later, as I manoeuvred him towards the door, he took my hand and told me how much he admired my fortitude, "I am praying for you and your daughter every night," he said, face even, voice sincere, hand sweaty.

He had a vivid pimple under his chin, swollen and full of pus. It had kept drawing my eye since I'd opened the front door on him. I felt like telling him to wash his face more thoroughly with soap and water. Instead, I nodded, pulled my fingers away and edged him closer to the door. Frank didn't like me being alone with other men, even less so with ones who touched me.

I stood on the doorstep and waved him away, my hand flopping to my side the moment his little car began chugging up the rutted track inland. I hoped it wasn't going to break down.

Gypsies didn't sound likely to me, but perhaps that was why I hadn't seen Breaker for a while. He had other people to suspect.

Once satisfied Mr Shaw was safely on his way back to civilisation, I shut the door, put my back against it, listening to the sounds of the house with my eyes closed.

There weren't any. Only the occasional gull. I couldn't even hear the sea from this side of the house. It was too early in the year for open windows.

When I opened my eyes, there was nothing unexpected to see.

Since the night Frank came to my room and I confessed I'd heard things, the Castle had been silent. No wet, dirty giggles, no sighs, no rattling, nothing moving in the furthest corner of my eye.

"Where have you gotten to, eh?"

Nothing.

"Have the gypsies taken you too?"

A gull shrieked as if in fear of its noisy life, but there was nothing unusual in that.

A few days later, Mr Shaw's piece about gypsies appeared in the *Eastern Gazette*. Frank pointed it out; I hadn't told him about the young reporter's visit.

"Maybe they'll leave us be now," he said after sliding it under my nose as I was making bread.

"Do you think it could be true?" I asked him, wiping floury hands on my apron.

He shrugged.

"But if it is, we might get Tilly back," saying it aloud made me feel stupid, but *somebody* had taken my baby.

Frank, who'd retreated to the kitchen door, one shoulder on the frame, didn't reply. He looked fatter, I realised. The sharp lines of the handsome man I'd met eight years earlier had already softened and blurred by this time, but he looked so bloated I almost asked how he was.

Before I could, he said, "Best you think we won't."

"Frank..."

"My Aunt had five children. Lost them all. That's why I'm here. It's part of life. Bad things happen, saw enough of that in the war. We carry on till the end. That's life."

"Did any of those children vanish into thin air?"

"Gone is gone. Don't matter why."

Was he trying to make me cry? I'd long learnt not to expect comfort or support from my husband, but sometimes it seemed he tried especially hard to find the words that cut the deepest. Even now, at the most awful time possible.

I sucked in a breath and went back to kneading dough with my shaking, quick-bitten fingers.

"That's it, Sweetness," Frank said, his voice almost a purr, "life goes on; better to keep on keeping on with it all the way to the end."

I listened to his footsteps creak and fade. Only when the house was quiet once more did I let the tears come again.

1930

"What has Frank told you about Tilly?"

"Absolutely nothing, darling," Izzy slipped her arm inside mine and tugged gently.

I let her lead me down the beach.

"Then how do you know about Tilly?"

"After I met Frank, I made some enquiries. I have a gentleman friend in the Metropolitan Police; he made some phone calls on my behalf... gentleman friends can be very useful for any number of things. Every modern woman should have several."

I glanced at Izzy to see if she was joking. My eyes quickly returned forward. I decided I didn't have a clue about anything she ever said.

"Gentlemen are in short supply out here."

"Oh, everywhere, darling, it's simply the same *everywhere*. It was the war, you know. What a curse to be living in an age when so many men died! If that wretched war had never befallen us, we'd all have so much more choice! I remember when I was a young-"

"I don't want to talk about the bloody war," I snapped, the screams of the gulls momentarily sounding like the cries of the dying.

"There are lots of things you don't like talking about, aren't there, darling?"

I somewhat proved her point by saying nothing.

"What do you think happened to your daughter?" As Izzy repeated her original question. Her grip on my arm tightened.

"She disappeared. That's all I know."

"The police think you killed her."

I pulled up short and twisted around to face her, "I didn't."

"Well, you or Frank, or both of you. They just couldn't prove it. No body. No evidence. No anything."

"There were gypsies..."

"The police found the gypsies who'd been staying in Carlesham when Tilly went missing. They had nothing to do with it. Inspector Breaker - he was the chap in charge, wasn't he? - thought it all something stirred up by the press. Blame the gypsies, blame the Jews, blame Johnny Foreigner or some swarthy colonial type if one's conveniently around. Always useful for an unsolved crime. Unsolved crimes look bad, after all. They make people uneasy. I, on the other hand, find them fascinating."

"Breaker never told me that..."

I hadn't seen Breaker or any other policeman in over a year. They assured me they were still making enquiries, but I had long since suspected dust had been gathering on Tilly's file for quite a while.

"Best you thought they were still chasing gypsies..."

"I had nothing to do with-"

"I know that, darling, I know," Izzy patted my arm. I thought she was going to carry on walking, but after glancing back at Grey Gull, now several hundred yards behind us, she turned to the sea. Beyond the frothing waves, a fishing boat laboured through the swells.

"Neither did Frank," I said.

Her eyes fixed on me but didn't say anything.

"He isn't... he's..." I groped for the right words, "...he didn't kill Tilly."

"Have you ever looked closely at your husband's paintings?"

"I try not to. I don't like them."

"There's a lot of fury in them. A lot of pain. A lot of... sorrow."

"They're ugly. There's enough of that in the world already."

"Art should always be beautiful then?"

"Are we out here in the cold to discuss art, Izzy?"

"No..." she clamped her hand atop her hat as a spiteful gust whipped off the North Sea.

"Then tell me why we are, or I'm going back inside before my nose turns blue."

"There's something about your husband..."

"He's a bastard," I spat. It wasn't the sort of thing nice girls, particularly ones who happened to be a vicar's daughter, tended to say about their husband. Even to their husband's lover. But I was cold. And a little scared.

There was something about Izzy St. Clair, too. Something in her eyes I hadn't noticed previously, or she'd kept hidden. Something intense, something burning, something, maybe, a bit crazy.

Izzy didn't laugh or call me "darling" or pat my arm.

Instead, she nodded.

"He came to me six months ago with his paintings. We get a lot of artists on our doorstep; London's awash with them. Every one a genius. In their own eyes, anyway. I'm not always around; I have people for that. But the day Frank came in, dripping with rain and steaming with a need to be recognised, I was there..."

"And you recognised his genius."

Now Izzy did laugh, "No, there's something in his work, but it isn't genius. I wouldn't want those things hanging on my wall. I'd get the heebie-jeebies every bloody night if I did, darling."

"Then why...?"

"Because there's *something* in them..."

"I don't understand?"

"Neither do I, but that something made me curious about Frank. The spirits took an interest."

My eyebrows shot up, "The spirits?"

"They talk to me, sometimes. I told you that, didn't I?"

"Not exactly..."

"Well, they were most unnerved by Frank and his paintings. So, I made enquiries."

"With your gentleman friend?"

"Friends. I have several. Some in quite unexpected places. All very useful. Gentleman friends should always be useful. Every bow should have more than one string, after all."

"I see," I said, seeing nothing.

I looked back at Grey Gull. It was a place I tried to get out of as often as possible, but it was cold, windy, and I was with a lunatic. That all conspired to make the Castle much more hospitable than usual.

"Anyway, I made enquiries with gentleman friends and spirit friends..."

I forced a thin smile onto my face and shuffled backwards.

"...and what they told me was enough to warrant an investigation!"

"So, you're..."

"Yes, a detective, darling," she smiled, "isn't that obvious?"

"You must have a busy life," I took another discreet step away.

"We all have our callings."

"And yours is currently investigating my husband?"

Izzy's smile reappeared as she nodded.

"By *sleeping* with him?"

"Can you think of a better way of finding things out about a man? A woman must use all the tools at her disposal. It is the twentieth century, after all."

Izzy had a point. I'd found out a lot more about Frank after I took him to my bed.

"Do you think Frank killed her?"

"No. I think she's still alive."

I shoved my hands deeper into my pockets, narrowed my eyes against the wind and refused to look at Izzy. Something was turning inside me. It should have been anger, it could have been fear, but I knew the fickle thing for what it was well enough.

Hope.

"What make's you think that?"

"The spirits tell me she is not with them."

Now I did look at her.

It would be so easy to believe. To grab any straw, rope, or passing flotsam I could cling to. I told myself every day Tilly was still alive. She hadn't disappeared into thin air, and I didn't think Frank murdered her. So, someone took her. If not gypsies, then someone, and maybe they hadn't hurt her. Perhaps it was a woman who couldn't have children of her own and... and...

I turned my eyes to the sea, fixing them on the little red and white fishing boat as it rose and fell upon the back of the beast it sailed across.

"How much?"

"How much... what, darling?"

"That's how it works, isn't it? You tell me Tilly is alive, that you can find her, and then you'll ask for money to do it."

"I'm not-"

"You can fuck my husband as much as you want, but don't you dare try to break my heart all over again!"

"There is-"

I was thirty-four years old. I'd never hit anyone in my life. Nice girls didn't. Particularly ones who happened to be a vicar's daughter.

But I shut Izzy up with my palm, the slap hard and loud enough to startle a couple of herring gulls away from their scavenging.

I didn't wait to hear her nonsense. I whirled away and headed back towards the Castle, just about keeping myself from running.

If one thing is more painful than hope, it's false hope.

But I must confess, the way my palm stung felt damn fine.

1943

"Yew didn't notice it 'fore?"

Rain drummed on the corrugated iron roof. It made me think of manic fingers tapping impatiently. Not a helpful thought.

We were in The Repository surrounded by stacks of Frank's unsold work. There was little room for us both to squeeze into. The smell of paint was fainter here, the smell of Davey pressed up against me, far stronger.

"Yes... but..."

I had seen the figure before. In some of Frank's work it was prominent and unmissable; in others, many others, you had to search for it. Sometimes it wasn't there, sometimes just a suggestion, and sometimes you had to squint and almost force yourself to see it amongst the violent brushwork and agitated colours. But it was in a lot of them once you knew what to look for.

"It's been a long time since I've looked at them," I finally said.

"Don't blame yew," Davey dropped the latest one back into its crate, "Creepy, ain't they, girl?"

He brushed his hands together as if trying to get dust off them.

I didn't answer, instead moving back to the doorway to watch the rain pelting down on the Castle.

Behind me, Davey kept on rummaging. I'd seen enough.

I'd had half a lifetime of seeing enough. Or, more accurately, perhaps, not seeing.

Once I looked properly at the paintings, at that repeated image, it was so much like the thing I thought I occasionally saw creeping about in the corner of my eye it chilled me.

The thing I'd usually dismissed as imagination or, in my blackest moments, as my own madness.

"Yew got a match, girl?"

"Don't smoke in here; Frank would kill me," I said, not looking back.

"Not fah loighting a fag, fah burning th' nasty buggers, best thing fah em."

I snorted. I didn't think he was serious, but he did have a point.

After a little more clattering and shuffling, Davey joined me, resting a bony shoulder against the opposite side of the door frame.

"Squaller of a day," he peered at the rain sweeping off the sea.

"What does it mean, Davey?"

"Means oi'm gonna git a roight proper soaking on th' way home."

I turned my eyes on him, "The *paintings?*"

"Betta to put tha' question to yewr husband. Reckons..."

"I'm asking you," the thought of asking Frank anything about his precious creations unnerved me more than what we'd seen in them.

"Guess it means he's seen wha' we seen," Davey pulled a face, "sorta thing yew'd think he moight have mentioned, tho..."

Quite.

"Didn't yew ever wonder 'bout em? Where he got his... wassit from... his *inspiration.*"

"I just thought they were ugly."

Davey chuckled, "Roight 'bout tha' yew are, girl."

"What should I do, Davey?"

The old man scratched his head, "Ain't moi place to say. But oi wouldn't wanna stay 'ere."

"I should go?"

"Yew happy 'ere?"

That was hardly the point.

I crossed my arms over my chest, lent on the door frame too and went back to watching the rain.

"Yew love tha' yank of yewrs?"

I couldn't bring myself to say it, but after a sharp glance at Davey, I nodded.

"Yew think 'bout running off with 'im?"

Another quick nod.

"And now 'e's dead..."

"You really think that thing in the paintings killed him?"

"Only know wha' moi owd eyes saw. In tha' motoring car and..." he hitched a thumb over his shoulder "...and in ther'..."

"It seems ridiculous..."

"Maybe. But yew loved 'im, now 'e's gone. Yew loved yewr lil' girl too, reckons..."

I stared at him.

"Lost yewr bor too..."

That was the war."

"Suppose so. Lose anyone else yew love?"

"My fiancé, Owen, died in the last war. My Dad, but he got sick. They couldn't..."

"Tha' 'fore you come 'ere?"

I nodded. "Frank knew Owen; they fought together. That's how I met him. Dad died shortly afterwards. But..."

"And yew didn't see nuttin 'fore yew came 'ere?"

"No."

Davey chewed his lip, "Ain't likely yew gonna love me, is it, girl?"

"Not likely."

"Good. Seems to be a pattern."

"A pattern?"

"People yew love die."

That stung. And cut. I sucked in a breath. The damp, salt-tinged air thickened in my throat, "Everybody loses people they love. Haven't you?"

"Loved me owd girl, but she wer even owder than oi am now when she passed. And oi lost me lovely Clemmie, but tha' wer' different."

"How so?"

"She run off with Albie Jenkins and went to live above 'is garage in Diss. As much as oi hold a grudge 'gainst Albie fah tha', couldn't say he wer' any kinda monster," he smiled as he spoke, but it did not come close to his eyes.

"Tom wanted me to go to Kansas with him," I sighed,

"Should go anyway. Well, maybes naht Kansas, thas a long ways aways. But somewhere. Anywhere..."

"I've got no money, Davey."

"Money! Don't need nah money, girl. Oi don't and git by roight enough!"

"Angie gives you beer for free at *The Green Man,* then, does she?"

"Beer don't cost tha' much..."

I shook my head, "I can't go. Not now."

"Why naht, girl? This place gave me th' roight willies even 'fore oi saw them 'orrible paintings. An oi've seen a thing or three in moi times, so oi 'ave."

I stared into the rain towards the Castle, watching the water trickle off the roof, washing away some of the gull droppings in the process.

"Because if that thing took Tilly, maybe it still has her... maybe she's still alive... maybe I can find a way to get her back..."

I could feel Davey staring at me. The words sounded stupid, hopeless, absurd as soon as they squirmed out of my mouth. A delusional woman spouting nonsense in a pathetic attempt to cope with grief and loss. Rather than trying to come to terms with my son's and my lover's deaths, I was twisting everything into some dark fantasy where I could rescue the daughter I'd lost sixteen years ago.

There were times I hated myself so much.

Instead of telling me he thought the same, Davey patted me on the shoulder before heading out into the rain.

"C'mon, girl. Time yew got th' kettle on, we got things to dicker 'bout. Reckons..."

1930

Frank didn't like complaints. Or opinions. Gripes, thoughts, suggestions were all things I'd long since learnt to keep to myself.

Frank appreciated peace and quiet, no disturbances to the ebb and flow of his life. He wanted to be able to concentrate on important stuff like painting and fucking his mistress.

But I was steaming mad.

A lot of what I suffered over my years in Grey Gull should have left me seething, but the thought Izzy was trying to profit from my grief was the only one that ever did.

"I want that bitch gone!"

Frank rarely looked surprised. In fact, his range of facial gestures was so limited I sometimes wondered if anything was going on behind it.

He stood at his easel, brush in one hand, abused canvas in front of him, looking over his shoulder at me. All sorts of shadows played over his face. If I'd taken a breath and a moment to think about it, I would have scurried straight back out of the studio, but I didn't. My fury gave me momentum, and I was rolling.

"Sweetness-"

"She's fucking insane or fucking evil; either way, get rid of her!"

The list of things Frank didn't like me doing was a long one, but I was working my way down it with a rare and speedy recklessness.

"Don't interrupt me, Sweetness," Frank said, carefully putting his brush aside.

"I don't want her here," I snapped, ignoring his warning. Something else he didn't like.

He turned towards me as if weighed by reluctance or regret.

He's going to hit me.

That thought would usually be enough to stop me in whatever track I found myself. But not this time.

"She's not interested in your bloody paintings, Frank. She's here about Tilly; she says she's been... spirited away... and that she can get her back. She's a confidence trickster looking for money."

I didn't actually know if that was true, as I'd stopped Izzy with the palm of my hand before she could explain what she meant, but I had no doubt that was what she wanted. Dangle some hope in front of the silly little woman in return for money, jump in bed with Frank so he'd only think with what hung between his legs and then rob us blind.

Plain as daylight! I may have done some foolish things, but I wasn't a bloody fool! Frank didn't say anything or do anything. He just stared at me.

"This isn't about you and her!" I blurted, "She's not what she seems. She's here to use us. Use what happened to Tilly. Use you. Ask her if you don't believe me."

I thought he was going to tell me to stop talking rubbish. Izzy was here to sell his art. Give his genius to the world. Nothing else would convince him otherwise. Certainly not me.

But he didn't.

He sucked in a deep breath and nodded, "I'll talk to her," he said, then breezed past me without another word.

My shoulders slumped. My whole body had tensed in expectation of his fury, his denial, his contempt. Instead, I was left alone amongst his ghastly paintings. The studio was small, cramped and reeked of turpentine and paint, just like Frank.

Even through my own rage, I'd expected nothing but anger from Frank, but his reaction had been strangely hollow.

Wind rattled the window. I wrapped my arms around myself. The studio had a little log burner, but Frank seldom lit it. Half the year I'd shiver in here, the other half sizzle. I didn't know how Frank stood it but didn't much care. The more time he spent in here, the better.

I cast an eye over his current creation.

A swirl of blacks, purples and yellows, like he was trying to paint a giant bruise.

It made my skin crawl.

Perhaps it was the turpentine fumes.

I turned away and reached for the door.

The woman is wrong, your baby is gone.

The windows shook again, and I whirled around. The studio was empty, of course. Just my imagination, making words out of the wind.

I swallowed.

What if Izzy was right?

What if...

I clamped down on that thought. Hope was not my friend. Izzy was a confidence trickster after money or some twisted pleasure in tormenting me. No monsters stalked Grey Gull, but plenty of human ones did out in the wide world. People did the most despicable things. People stole babies, people took advantage of grief and loss for their own sick purposes.

Still, I had to drag my eye away Frank's abused canvas. It was difficult to look anywhere in the studio and not see one of his paintings; they hung on hooks, stood propped against the wall on the floor, sat in piles. They were everywhere. I always avoided looking too closely at them; they disturbed me. Most of the time, I couldn't say why; they just did. Ugly and angry was how I described them, but that wasn't enough to disturb me. There was no shortage of ugliness and anger in the world, after all.

But sometimes, and one of those sometimes was standing surrounded by the things on the day I slapped Izzy St. Clair's immaculately powdered cheek, I could not shake the feeling they were watching me.

And they were hungry.

If the log burner was going that day, I might have kicked it over and burnt the damn things and to hell with what Frank might do. The ire Izzy stoked in me was still running, giving me a courage I didn't normally possess.

Frank would beat me hard later for how I'd spoken to him, but so what? Standing up to him, just the once, would be worth it.

Burning his horrible paintings would be worth it too.

Gone, gone, gone...

Just words on the wind.

Nothing taunted me here, nothing crept in the corner of my eye, nothing had spirited Tilly away. The only monster here was my husband, but he only hurt me, not the children, so I bore it.

I yanked the door open and let the salt-tainted air pour in without looking back. I didn't need to see the paintings, I didn't need to look at those malevolent, carnivorous things, and I didn't need to listen to the wind that only spoke words inside Grey Gull and its outbuildings.

I scampered across the beach, trying to silence my thoughts with the crack and crunch of shingle. Hoping the breeze could wash the heady stench of turpentine from my nostrils.

There was one thing I was sure of, though. I wasn't angry anymore.

Just scared.

Again.

I walked for a couple of hours.

It wasn't my usual time to escape the house and rather than following one of my well-worn paths, I paced back and forth north of Grey Gull.

Whenever I thought of returning, I veered away and walked some more. Frank would not believe me when Izzy dangled the prospect of selling his paintings. That was all he lived for, all he dreamed of. The fact Izzy was mad, or a confidence trickster would wilt under that possibility.

Perhaps he would pack me off for good. Throw me out and let Izzy have the boys. She could protest all she liked and prattle about spirits and monsters, but I'd seen how she was with the boys.

It was all a game. That's how rich people treated life. If I was a thorn in her side, she would pull Frank's strings and be done with me. I would lose everything. The boys were all I had. I endured so much for them, but although I detested Frank, I wanted them taken from me less than I did a hand, a leg, an eye. They were my purpose, my life, my *everything*.

Those thoughts whirled around my head, cackling and screeching like the gulls circling above.

They were the siren cries of my own demons, and they drowned out everything else, including Izzy's words and warnings about Frank.

Slowly the sky darkened. Bloated cloud pressed down upon me. Drizzle dampened the air. You learn to respect the weather out here. It has teeth. So, I turned reluctant feet back to the Castle, the rain softening its bruised stonework.

As I came around the corner of the house, Izzy's car still sat outside; sharp and alien. An intrusion from another world.

Before I reached the cottage's door, it burst open and Izzy rushed out, bag, as fancy, stylish and expensive as everything else about her, swinging from her right hand.

Her eyes widened as she saw me, black jewels set in ashen skin.

"You're leavin-"

"Get out of here," she hissed, her free hand clutching mine.

I stepped back, yanking my hand away from hers.

The wind tugged at the dark hair hanging beneath her hat.

I was used to her always being poised, unruffled, and just so damn full of herself she thought she was doing the world a favour by breathing its air. She didn't look like that now, though.

She was frightened.

Looking back, I think it was more terrified, but I could feel nothing but relief in that moment.

She was going and taking her lies with her.

Good riddance.

"Beatrice, really, this-"

"Go," a voice said.

It didn't boom, it wasn't loud, but it sounded like a thunderclap all the same.

Frank stood in the doorway, thumbs hitched in the belt his gut tumbled over. He didn't look any different. Just a man sliding into middle age and doing it badly. Yet, something was different. I don't know what it was; I couldn't place it or describe it. But it frightened me too.

Izzy's eyes jumped back to mine; they had a pleading urgency.

Come with me.

I took another step away from her.

By the autumn of 1930, I'd become well acquainted with being afraid of my husband.

"You shouldn't stick your nose into things that don't concern you," I said, "best you take your claptrap back to London where it belongs. Don't come back."

She looked like she wanted to say something. She looked like she wanted to say a lot of somethings. But she was ghost-white beneath the flawless powder.

Something had upset her. Perhaps Frank had given her a glimpse of the man he really was.

Izzy shot past. She didn't look at me or back at Frank, but she muttered under her breath as she went by, "Find me if you ever need me."

I swivelled and watched as she climbed into her car, slamming the door behind her.

The car purred immediately into life, spitting shingle as it pulled away from Grey Gull. It sped off down the rutted track cutting through the marsh.

The rain was falling harder. But I made no move to get inside.

"What did you say to her?" I said, sensing Frank coming to stand next to me.

"Say? Nothing. I just listened. You were right. She's mad. Full of nonsense," he sighed, "I should have known she was too good to be true."

He put a hand on my shoulder.

"It was only because of my work," he said, "I never felt anything for her, Sweetness, you know that don't you?"

His grip tightened.

"Of course."

"Good. Still, it's taught me a thing or two."

"What?"

"Women shouldn't be trusted..."

His hand fell away, and he left me in the rain.

1943

I hadn't seen London since I left with Frank in 1920. It had changed.

Quite a bit of it no longer existed.

Like missing teeth in a child's mouth, spaces in the streets where a building had once stood paid testament to the Luftwaffe's industry over the last few years.

Sandbags, taped-up windows, air raid shelters, Ministry of Information posters everywhere. Checkpoints. Queues. There were more cars and buses, and the faint smell of oil and burning teased my throat. It felt worn down, tired, grey. An old friend seen for the first time in years you're shocked to discover hasn't aged at all well. The kind that makes you wonder how much *you've* aged when you first spot them waiting for you.

Some things were familiar. A lot of the men wore uniforms, and women were doing many of the jobs men used to. Just like the last war. Like the next one, too, I imagined.

I didn't intend to be here long, I'd brought a few bits and most of the money I had just in case, but I intended to be back in Grey Gull by evening. Still, it did feel a little like I was running away at long, long last. Maybe not to Kansas, but to somewhere.

To my own mental breakdown, perhaps?

I shook the thought away as I hurried down Davies Street. It had already been a long day getting into Liverpool Street station and then the bus to the West End. Using the Underground Railway would have been quicker, but I'd always hated it. I doubted it had improved any during my absence. Besides, I wanted to see London, and the top deck of a bus was a good way of inspecting the damage.

It wasn't pretty. That old friend not only hadn't aged well, they'd also taken a fair old beating.

Something else I was familiar with.

After a few minutes, I stopped paying attention to the window and started wishing I'd gotten the Underground after all. So many burnt-out buildings! So many piles of rubble. The areas around the docks had apparently suffered the worst of it, but the scars were all too visible here, too.

I paused on the corner of Brooke Street, opposite *Claridges* to check my map for the hundredth time. Then I looked over my shoulder for the thousandth.

No, Frank still wasn't behind me.

Why would he be? London was a big place, and he was stationed on the other side of it. I wasn't going to bump into him. I was being silly. Perhaps not as silly as thinking some faceless, shadowy apparition murdered my lover and stole my baby, but still silly.

Stuffing the map back in my bag, I crossed the road. It wasn't far now. I still had no idea what I would say, but something would pop into my head. Probably something stupid, but *something*.

The sky was as drab and grey as London itself; sooty clouds squatted over the rooftops and spires. The air carried a chill along with the city's stinks. The summer had been short and warm, but it felt long finished despite it being only early October.

When I reached Grosvenor Street, I hesitated again. To my right, I could make out the edge of Grosvenor Square, its trees already starting to brown with the season. From a distance, they might have been flecked with rust. I went left. Slowly.

Perhaps I should have called.

I'd been toying with making a phone call since I had this bright idea, but it wasn't a conversation I wanted to have over the telephone. I wasn't sure whether it was a conversation I wanted to have, period.

But I needed to do something.

To date, something had been limited to Davey Acorns regularly calling by. He'd even stayed a couple of nights – on the sofa – to see what he could see.

What he'd seen so far amounted to nothing. The most unsettling thing we'd experienced together was some really quite prodigious dollops of seagull poo splattering the kitchen window while Davey worked his way through my blackberry jam stockpile.

"Dirty buggers..." he'd growled before returning to his supper.

Strange noises had disturbed the night, but only when Davey slept with his mouth open. Which seemed to be most of the time.

I told Davey I was going to see a friend in London, so he didn't turn up at the Castle when I was away for the day.

Halfway down Grosvenor Street towards New Bond Street, I found what I was looking for. It was both smaller and grander than I'd imagined.

The St. Clair Gallery announced the swirling gold script on the plate glass door. The Luftwaffe hadn't yet managed to crack the door or blow out the windows, though, like every other piece of glass in the city, it was taped up on the oft chance Hitler was ever foolish enough to take on Izzy St. Clair.

On the pavement, I indulged in some more prevarication.

We hadn't exactly parted on good terms. However, if I could forgive her fucking my husband, I'm sure she could put aside me slapping her face, insulting her, accusing her of being deranged and telling Frank about her spiritualist detective claptrap.

Thirteen years had gone by since then, after all.

And perhaps there hadn't been as much claptrap in what she'd been trying to tell me as I'd thought.

I'd always expected her to turn up on the doorstep again one day with an exclamation of "Darling!" and an air kiss on my cheek before breezing past to resume sticking her perfectly powdered nose into my family's business.

The fact she hadn't was one I'd always been grateful for, though now I was less sure. If she had been more persistent, I might have eventually listened to her and considered the possibility that the things I'd seen and heard weren't signs of madness at all.

Still, thirteen years later, I was now very prepared to listen to what Mrs Izzy St. Clair, Spiritualist Detective, might have to tell me.

I counted to five. Then decided ten was a better number. Took a deep breath, told myself to stop being daft and do what I came here to do.

A little bell tinkled when I finally found my courage and badgered it into getting my feet to move.

Inside paintings (muted landscapes, horses, pale women and absolutely nothing that looked like it was sneaking out of a nightmare) adorned the walls. Whatever had made Frank think this kind of place would be interested in his masterpieces?

A skinny man with a shiny head looked up from a desk at the end of the gallery. He greeted me with the thinnest of smiles and a hoisted eyebrow.

"Can I help you, madam?" he asked as I approached. His tone suggested he'd already concluded I wasn't likely to be buying anything and, whatever I wanted, I should be on my way before someone more befitting the establishment came in and found me soiling the gallery.

It was probably a good decision not to bring Davey Acorns with me.

Clutching my handbag, I told myself I had as much right to be here as anyone else, "Is Mrs St. Clair here? I'd like to see her, please."

The eyebrow crawled higher up his forehead, "Mrs St. Clair?"

"The owner. Of the gallery. I'm an old friend... Beatrice Harryman. She will want to see me."

The man put his fountain pen down and cast an eye up and down. I thought he might lean over the counter to see if my bottom half was as bedraggled as the top.

"I'm afraid that won't be possible, Mrs Harryman."

"But-"

"I'm very sorry, but Mrs St. Clair passed away."

I blinked.

"Passed... away?"

The man's face softened a little, "It was quite some time ago."

"Oh... we... kind of lost touch..."

"Would you care to sit down? A cup of tea, perhaps? Some water?"

"No... it's... really..."

I put a hand on the desk; it was oily smooth mahogany. For some reason, it made me want to vomit. I didn't know Izzy well. I didn't like her, for a long time, I'd actually loathed her, but the news she was dead was like a punch in the guts. I didn't know why.

The man stood up. He was tall and moved in precise increments. He glided around the desk and ushered me onto one of the two chairs facing it, no doubt where rich people sat whilst he tried to part them from their money.

"Please..."

I nodded and plonked myself down. My knees felt weak. I thought there was a reasonable chance I would burst into tears. Crying for your son and your lover is one thing, but crying for a woman you didn't even like was plain ridiculous.

The man pulled the pristine white silk handkerchief from his jacket's breast pocket and pressed it into my hand. It looked far too expensive to honk my nose into, but I thanked him and dabbed an eye with it all the same.

He crossed the room and turned the closed sign over in the door.

"It's a slow day," he explained, pouring water from a decanter into a cutglass tumbler. My hand trembled when I took a sip and I hurriedly put it down for fear of dropping it. The man conjured a coaster and moved the tumbler to it before retreating to the other side of the desk.

"My condolences," he said.

"I'm sorry to trouble you..." I said when I'd got myself back under control, "...I hadn't heard."

"It is quite alright, Mrs Harryman."

"We weren't close..." I toyed with his hanky, then folded it and put it on the desk.

"Still, the passing of a friend is always a dreadful shock."

"I lost my youngest son recently. I think it has left me more... fragile than I once was."

He bowed his head, "Again, my very deepest condolences, Mrs Harryman. These are indeed terrible times," he sat back and entwined his long fingers together before him, "...I hoped after the Great War some lessons had been learned in return for all that blood. That we would be spared such madness again, at least in my lifetime. Alas..."

"Perhaps this time."

"Perhaps... please forgive my manners; I am Tiberius Benjamin, the current proprietor of the *St Clair Gallery*."

"Tiberius?"

The corner of his mouth twitched up, "My father had a passion for ancient Rome. My brothers are Julius, Augustus and Claudius. Rather fortunately, he stopped having sons before reaching Caligula and Nero..."

That sounded like a well-worn joke, but it made me smile, nevertheless.

"You bought the business?"

"I inherited it. Mrs St Clair and I were friends. We shared a love for art. I was very surprised to find she had left me the gallery. And most grateful. Though, of course, I would much prefer she were still with us and running it herself."

I remembered Izzy mentioning her *gentleman friends* and wondered if Tiberius Benjamin had shared more than a love of art with her.

"When did she pass away?" I asked.

"It still seems like yesterday, but it was... what... thirteen years ago now. In a car accident..." he added with a deep sigh, "...I always told her she drove that wretched thing far too fast..."

1916

A rhythmic creaking accompanied by the occasional cry of a woman's voice interrupted the night's quiet. And kept on interrupting it.

"Is that...?" I asked.

"Sounds like it."

"Do you think they're married?"

"Hard to tell from here."

This was true.

"When I asked Stan the barman about a hotel, he said they didn't ask about... you know... *that*... here..."

"Whether guests were married?"

"Uh-huh... well, if the lad is in uniform anyway. Doing their bit for the war effort."

"Is that how he put it?"

"You know, keeping morale up."

"And is that what I am then? Good for morale?"

He reached over and stroked my hair, tucking strands behind my ear. It was an old game.

"Among other things."

I kissed his hand.

We lay on our sides facing each other. I'd suggested turning the lamp off, but Owen told me he'd suffered a year not being able to see me, so we'd left it on low.

For now.

We'd just talked, kissed and held hands.

For now.

I felt a strange, warm contentment. My nerves and reservations, if not abated, faded in the warmth of Owen's company and kisses to near silence. They were certainly making less of a disturbance than the woman upstairs.

Owen's hand ran down my shoulder and arm to gently stroke the curve of my hip. If he found the flannelette off-putting, he was doing a respectable job of hiding it.

"I dream of you every night," he said.

"You do?"

He nodded, "Not that I get to sleep every night."

"I guess it gets a bit noisy?"

The cries of the woman upstairs grew in pitch and volume, the protesting springs too. We both looked up together.

214

"Yeah, sometimes the big guns keep going at it till dawn..." he said, almost keeping a straight face when our eyes returned to each other.

After a second or two, we dissolved into hopeless giggles together.

When they stopped his arms were around me, his body was hard against mine and we were kissing with a rare intensity. He was bare-chested but had kept his long johns on. Despite being an army issue, they seemed far less substantial than my nightgown.

I see no need to recount all that happened between us that night. I was still a virgin; I assume Owen was, too, though I did not ask. Looking back, I hope he was not. The thought that he was prepared to wait for me is another burden I bore heavily over the years ahead.

Before he left for the war, he told me about French girls in the towns behind the front line who were "friendly" for a few francs. He said lots of the lads went to them at one time or another. He looked at me earnestly and promised he never would.

I wished I'd told him to spend his francs however he chose. But I didn't. I just kissed him, and afterwards, we went back to talking about a future neither of us would ever know in that life.

We did things that night I had never done before. I will spare you the details, but Janice Coventry, a particularly lewd young woman in my secretarial class, had explained in considerable detail to anyone who would listen, that there were ways of making a man happy that involved no risk of pregnancy.

I had listened to Janice's furtive talks, usually held in the canteen when the Brick and the rest of the staff were safely out of earshot, with a mixture of queasiness, curiosity, disbelief, and a rather peculiar kind of fuzzy excitement. Needless to say, the things Janice chatted about were not on the curriculum of the *St Andrews Secretarial College for Young Women*.

In bed with Owen, especially after we'd dispensed with the garments provided by His Majesty's armed forces, the curiosity quickly dispatched the queasiness and disbelief. While the excitement became very focussed.

As for Owen, only excitement was apparent.

We slept a little and talked a lot that night. I didn't want to sleep, though the few dozes I slipped into with Owen's arms around me were wonderful.

The next day when we left the hotel, I enjoyed an unfamiliar glowy happiness tempered by the vague concern God would not approve of how we'd spent the night. Sin, I'd always been taught, came with a price.

I've sometimes wondered if all that later befell me was the consequence of that night. However many times I told myself God would not be so petty as to punish two people for their love when so much else in the world was being consumed by real evil, that suspicion refused to leave me.

Still, whatever God's opinion on the matter, I was pretty sure Dad would not approve. As for Owen's parents, I didn't consider being thought a harlot an improvement on being considered hoity-toity.

Whatever their thoughts on such things, when Dad and Mr and Mrs James met us at the train station the next afternoon, only hugs, smiles and love greeted us. No difficult questions about our unexpected night in London were asked.

That time we shared was possibly the most beautiful of my life. Owen and I spent every second we could together, and I swear the sun did not disappear behind a cloud for a heartbeat.

He did not ask me to marry him again. I wish he had, and I wish I'd given him the answer I should have.

Instead, we walked the hills, woods, valleys and streams, our hands rarely straying far from each other. Our lips touched at every opportunity.

We had a day out at Weston Super Mare just like before the war, paddling in the sea, eating ice cream and fish and chips, laughing at everything. We spent time with his parents and with Dad. Every person we passed smiled at us or wished us luck.

For all the joy and laughter we wrapped around ourselves that week, in the distance, beyond the birdsong, beyond the buzzing of bees and the ringing of distant church bells, beyond the rustle of leaves and the bellowing of cows, beyond the laughter and beyond the kisses, beyond the shining walls of Camelot, the clocks never stopped ticking.

Time was passing.

Before Owen had to leave, we went to a photographer in Milford. Owen in his uniform, washed, scrubbed and pressed by Mrs James, me in my Sunday best.

The photographer, a wizened slip of a fellow called Mr Cooley, kept telling us what a bonny couple we made as we posed, still as stones, me sitting, Owen at my shoulder.

We collected the photograph before Owen left. Owen spent a long time staring at it. He already had several of me, but he told me this was his favourite. He'd never seen me look more beautiful.

I tried not to cry. Somewhat unsuccessfully.

He put the photograph into his breast pocket and said he would look at it every day. It would keep him safe.

I told him keeping his head down and not trying to be a hero would likely work better.

"I will come home to you one day, Bea," he said.

"I know," I replied.

I wanted to grab his hand, march him down to the vicarage and get Dad to marry us there and then. But I didn't.

I just looked at my copy of the photograph. It was larger and I intended to buy a silver frame to put it in. Owen said I looked beautiful. I thought he looked handsome. But we didn't look real. Statues with frozen expressions. A moment of time captured and imprisoned by the magic of Mr Cooley's camera. Forever young, forever alive, forever together.

But not quite.

This will be all I have of you one day.

I kissed him and said I loved him. Not for the first time that day.

The next day we all went to the railway station, Mr and Mrs James, Dad and me to wave him off.

After his parents finished hugging him and Dad told him God was with him as he shook his hand, we held each other for a long time. Dad and the James' found other things to stare at.

He hung out the window as we waited for the train to take him away.

"I've had the best time, Bea. Just the best."

I stood there, blinking up at him.

"Me too..." I didn't know what else to say.

He patted his breast pocket, where I knew the new photograph of us rested, "We're never going to be apart, we're together. You'll always be me Bea..."

I nodded.

A whistle blew, the station master waved his flag. The locomotive hissed steam and begun to move. Taking him away from me.

I wanted to say something special, something beautiful and poetic and memorable. Something for him to remember when surrounded by the horrors of war.

"I love you," I said. It was the best I could come up with.

He reached down and took my hand, managing to plant a final kiss on it before the locomotive picked up speed and pulled our fingers apart.

"I love you!" he shouted back and blew me a kiss.

I caught it, the way you're supposed to.

Then I stood and watched the train through the steam, smoke and tears until my Owen disappeared.

The next time I saw the photograph of us Owen carried in his breast pocket, it would be creased, dog-eared and blurred by a bloody fingerprint.

As for Owen, I would never see him again.

Until long after he died.

Part Two

Love Always Wins in the End

1943

Tiberius decided I needed tea after all.

He was probably right. I hoped my hands wouldn't still be shaking when he returned.

I tried walking around the gallery, staring at the paintings. Most were 18th or 19th century from what I could tell, interspersed with a few modern pieces. Constable, Turner, Reynolds. None had anything so gauche as a price tag. My footsteps echoed after me.

So did Tiberius' voice.

Thirteen years...

1930. The year Izzy had stayed with us.

No wonder she never came back.

How soon after she left Grey Gull had she died?

That was my next question.

I glanced at the door and the people floating by outside.

I could be gone before Tiberius came back. Then I would be free to come up with whatever answer I liked.

Except, of course, I was pretty sure I already knew.

The sound of approaching footsteps prevented me making a run for it. Tiberius reappeared carrying a tray. He poured tea into two porcelain cups. There was also a plate with digestive biscuits. Did rich people have a ration book too?

"They're all reproductions," he said, nodding at the paintings I'd been examining, "all the real art is kept out of London these days. The Nazi's are philistines. They'll bomb quite anything, I'm afraid. Art and taste offer scant protection from bombs..."

Once he'd added milk and sugar and stirred, Tiberius settled himself, "How did you know Mrs St Clair, may I ask?"

"Through my husband. He's an artist. Mrs St Clair was interested in his work... for a while," I decided to be diplomatic and not mention the husband-fucking.

"Really, what's his name?"

"Oh... you wouldn't know him. He only... dabbles. Nothing came of it."

Tiberius nodded, "Yes, Mrs St Clair was a great believer in supporting new artists..." he waved a hand at the gallery walls, "...I'm far more of a traditionalist, as you can see. She was forever telling me, *Oh, do stop being such a fuddy-duddy, darling!*"

I smiled; it was a surprisingly good impression of Izzy.

"You… were fond of her?"

Tiberius twitched a smile and pushed the plate of biscuits towards me, "I miss her terribly, even after all these years. I think sometimes I should sell the gallery. It reminds me of her too much. But she did so love this place. If I keep soldiering on with it, perhaps a little piece of her will stay alive."

"We all have to keep memories alive," I said, taking a biscuit and thinking of Owen, Simon and Tom.

"Indeed."

"You knew her for a long time?"

"Oh, absolute years. Off and on. That was the thing with Izzy, she could be the best friend you ever had, always insisting we went out for lunch, or go to the theatre, an exhibition, a walk in the park. All the things… friends do. And then, all of a sudden, I wouldn't hear a peep from her for months and months. She was off with a new best friend. I didn't mind. She'd always come back. She was… a free spirit, I think you could say."

I nibbled the biscuit. It melted on my tongue. I still had to force it down. And my next question out.

"When did she have the accident?"

Tiberius took a sip of tea, returning it to the saucer before answering, "I believe I said. 1930."

"But… when, exactly?"

Another long pause. His eyes were the colour of the sky on an overcast summer's day, and they didn't waver from mine.

"Late October."

"Do you remember the exact day?"

The eyes remained, but a slight frown creased his high forehead.

"The 25th, if I recall correctly."

What day had Izzy driven away from Grey Gull? It had been late October, a Saturday. I remembered walking to church with the boys the next day, feeling both relieved she was gone and irritated when Francis and Simon kept asking me when Aunty Izzy would be back and jabbering about her fancy car.

Had the 25th of October 1930 been a Saturday?

I had a box of old calendars back in the Castle, I've always been a hoarder. I fought the urge to ask Tiberius if he also hoarded old calendars. It would be easy enough to find out.

"Why is the date of importance to you?"

I saw no point in lying.

"Mrs St Clair stayed with us for a little while. In October 1930. I was..."

"I see."

"Do you know where the accident occurred?"

Tiberius reached for his tea, again he didn't reply until it was back on its saucer, "In Essex... somewhere. I don't recall the place."

"Do you know what happened?"

He shook his head, "Not exactly. The police said she was driving too fast and lost control. The car went off the road, flipped over, rolled..." he swallowed and lowered his eyes, "...they said she didn't suffer. I'm afraid I don't remember much more. There was an inquest. Death by misadventure was the verdict. There will be public records available, if the beastly Nazis haven't blown them up, of course. And the press. *The Times* did a rather nice obituary. They glossed over a few points, though. Which was jolly decent of them, really..."

I ate more biscuit. If she'd died returning from the Castle, wouldn't the police have been in touch? The coroner? Someone connected to the inquest? Surely.

That made me feel a little better for the five seconds it took me to realise it was quite possible nobody had known where Izzy had been.

As Tiberius said, if she had a habit of disappearing with whatever new best friend caught her fancy...

"Did you know about her... spiritualist detective... thing?"

"Oh, God, yes," Tiberius rolled his eyes, "That claptrap was one of the things Gerry at *The Times* discreetly omitted from her obituary."

"Gerry?"

"A friend of Izzy's. A bit of a louche cad if one must be completely honest, but not totally a bad egg."

Another of Izzy's useful gentlemen friends, no doubt.

"Was the spiritualist thing... serious?"

Tiberius smiled, "Izzy was serious about all her interests until she wasn't. As with her best friends, she flitted from one to the next with gay abandon. In 1930 her obsession was with the spirit world, in 1928 it had been sailing, in '26 East End orphans, in '25 all she wanted to do was go to the opera, in '24..." Tiberius sighed "...it was *something*. You see the picture?"

"She said she was sensitive to the spirit world?"

"She met this woman, Gladys Candlish, who convinced Izzy of all manner of things. Nonsense for the most part. I always thought she was a complete fraud whose only gift was rinsing money from the gullible. But I've always had a deep streak of scepticism to go along with my fuddy-duddiness."

"So, you didn't have much time for her spiritual detective work?"

"I think *work* is far too strong a word. It was just Izzy's latest bright idea cum obsession. She simply adored Agatha Christie and her silly books, read a lot of Edgar Alan Poe too, which probably explains a thing or two. Izzy thought sleuthing with the aid of the spirit world a terrific wheeze. If she'd lived, basket weaving, high wire walking, stamp collecting, or some such would have replaced it sooner or later. It was something that dreadful Candlish woman turned her on to."

"You didn't like her?"

"She put all kinds of notions in Izzy's head," Tiberius sipped his tea like he had a bad taste in his mouth he wanted rid of.

"But... they were close?"

"Izzy was never really close to anyone for long, but up to her death, she spent far too much time in Miss Candlish's parlour of poppycock trying to chat with the dead. If the spirit claimed to be murdered, so much the better!"

I drank more tea. It was strong; I doubted Tiberius Benjamin reused his tea leaves often. Could Izzy have mentioned something about Frank to Gladys Candlish? At least something more than I'd been prepared to listen to thirteen years ago.

"Do you know where I might find Miss Candlish?"

"Sadly, you'd need the services of one of her associates for that," Tiberius flashed a tight smile.

"I'm sorry?"

"She died some time ago."

"Around the same time as Mrs St Clair...?"

"A few years later. She was an unfortunately corpulent woman, dropped dead from a heart attack in the middle of one of her ludicrous seances, I believe. She had quite a sense of the theatrical. I think it was several minutes before anyone realised she actually was dead and not just sojourning briefly on the *other side* for effect. Undoubtedly, one of her spirit guides was on hand to whisk her away to the hereafter with the minimum of fuss."

Tiberius' tone had turned cold, his gaze drifted off as he shook his head, "You must excuse me. It is most impolite to speak so poorly of the dead, but the woman caused quite some distress to Izzy's family and friends after her death.

"Money?"

"No. She went around shouting from the rooftops Izzy had been murdered."

"Murdered," I grew still, "by whom?"

"By *what*, might be a more accurate description of Miss Candlish's spurious claims..." Tiberius raised both hands and waggled his long fingers as his voice deepened, "...something dark took her, something bleak and black and faceless, something in the car with her when she crashed. Something sorrowful from the pit."

"And she knew this... how?"

"Well, quite..." Tiberius dropped his hands back to the desk, then plucked a biscuit from the plate, "...that was why the police and everybody else gave Miss Candlish such short shrift. The terrible fraud insisted poor Izzy visited her after her death to tell her what happened..."

1936

Frank was much taken with Mr Hitler.

He would often sit in his comfy chair, throwing around approving quotes from *The Daily Mail*.

"You never used to like the Germans," I once said.

"I don't," he shot back, "but it's the Jews who are the real problem. About time someone stood up to them."

Frank had never complained about the Jews or anyone else (apart from me, of course), but he'd gone to hear Mosley give a speech on one of his London trips and ever since had been spouting the same rhetoric. He approved of Oswald Mosley and his British Union of Fascists even more than he did Mr Hitler.

I didn't know why Frank developed an interest in politics; he'd always been as disinterested in it as most things you couldn't smear paint over. I suspected a woman might be involved, but, as I didn't care, I didn't ask. Just so long as he didn't bring her home like he had with Auntie Izzy.

One Sunday, after I'd hung out the washing and before getting dinner ready, I found Francis sitting on the back step, book in his lap, staring out to sea. He was a quiet, studious boy, nothing at all like his boisterous younger brother, who could not stay still for more than twenty seconds unless asleep.

"You look a million miles away," I said, ruffling his dark hair. When he gave me a quick and fleeting grin, I asked, "Got some troubles, young man?"

He was at that age when boys started noticing girls, which meant he was at the age you started getting troubles.

His eyes, like his hair, were much like Frank's. Thankfully, he'd inherited little else from his father.

He frowned and pursed his lips. Then his hazel eyes focused on me, "Why doesn't Dad like Jews?"

I put the empty basket aside, brushed down my skirt, eased myself onto the step next to him and sighed, wishing it was about a girl after all.

"Sometimes... sometimes people like to blame others for their troubles, for the things that aren't right. If someone is different to you, then it makes it easier to blame them than yourself for things that are hard to comprehend, like government policies, financial markets, international trade and so on."

Francis thought about this. He rarely rushed into anything, be it thought, word or deed.

"So... Dad thinks it's the Jews' fault no one buys his paintings?"

I tried not to laugh.

"There are a lot of problems in the country. People do not have jobs, money, homes... and some blame the Jews for that."

"Like Mr Mosley and Herr Hitler in Germany?"

"Yes, like them." I hadn't seen Francis reading the *Daily Mail*, but I guessed he must have been.

They grow up so fast.

"What do you think, Mum?"

"Oh, I don't know a lot about politics."

"But what do you *think?*" the intensity of his words made me suspect this was more than a random chat about politics.

"I think..." those eyes, burnt hazel, so much like his Dad's, bore into me, "...I think you judge each person on who they are and make your own mind up about them. Do they have a good heart? That's the most important question, Francis. Not how they choose to worship God, the colour of their skin, or what kind of accent they have. What's in their hearts, that's the thing."

Francis' gaze moved to the sea, grey-brown and flecked with white. Despite the sun being warm and the skies mainly blue, it still seemed in a sour mood.

His next question took me by surprise, though, perhaps it shouldn't have. My son was a bright boy.

"Does Dad have a good heart?"

"Of course," I said, probably too quickly.

I'd always thought I'd kept the worst of Frank from the boys, but it was a small house. They both must have seen and heard more than I knew. When you try to keep secrets, especially from those you love, they are seldom locked away as securely as you think.

That's what I saw in the expression on Francis' face.

The reflection of my lie.

"Why the question, sonny Jim?"

Another long silence, another weighty stare at the waves queuing up to come ashore, this time accompanied by a shuffle and a fidget.

"There's this girl..." he said, studiously avoiding my eye.

Ah...

"A girl you like?"

He didn't nod; he didn't have to.

"Diane..." he said as if that explained everything, which, when you're fifteen, it generally does.

After all, I did fall in love with Owen James, one day I no longer precisely recalled, when I was the same age.

"And Diane...?"

"She's a Jewess. Everyone... calls her names. Behind her back. Mostly."

"But you like her?"

This time he nodded, but those burnt hazel eyes, so like Frank's and yet, so different too, remained on the sea.

"Does she know you like her?"

He shrugged. And looked so miserable I wanted to scoop him up in my arms and never let go. Being fifteen, of course, I knew that wouldn't go down too well.

"Why don't you tell her?"

"Mum..." he said like I'd asked him to fly to the moon.

"Why don't you carry her books home from school then?"

I didn't remember the day I fell in love with Owen, but I vividly recall the day he offered to carry my books back to the vicarage for the first time. It was all of a three-minute walk from school, though we soon conspired to drag those three minutes out to truly infeasible lengths.

I'd only had one book that day, *Poems*, by Alfred, Lord Tennyson. I still have a copy, and whenever I read *The Lady of Shalott*, as I often do, I smell the cherry blossom that lined the street outside school and see the spring sunlight reflected in Owen's eyes.

All in the blue unclouded weather
Thick-jewell'd shone the saddle-leather,
The helmet and the helmet-feather
Burn'd like one burning flame together,
As he rode down to Camelot...

"Mum...?"

I blinked and put an arm around my beautiful boy's shoulder, whether he liked it or not.

"Ask to carry her books home. If she says yes, ask again the next day. If she says yes again, ask her to come to tea."

"Tea? What about Dad?"

"What about him?"

"But he doesn't like Jews?"

"Sod   him," I   said,   with   more   vehemence   than   I'd   intended, "and sod Mr Mosley and Herr Hitler too. And sod all those silly buggers who call her names too. If you like her, she's good enough for me."

It was Francis' turn to blink. Then he smiled. And blushed. And laughed.

And, for a moment, I was riding to Camelot again.

1943

The Holloway Road, one of the main arteries into London from the north, was dirtier, smellier and even greyer than Grosvenor Street. A bus, belching black smoke, clattered by, a dog sniffed around the rubble of what had once been someone's home, and pigeons did much the same job as the seagulls back at the Castle. People hurried by, heads down, many in threadbare make and mend clothes. After four years of war, rationing and shortages, few people managed to look as dapper as Tiberius Benjamin.

No one paid me any heed as I slowly walked on, clutching the scrap of paper Tiberius had given me. I expected the house to be another pile of broken bricks, and if it wasn't, I'd likely find it stuffed to the gunnels with the wild geese I was chasing.

Not for the first time, I thought it would have been a lot easier to have listened to Izzy all those years ago, however ridiculous it had seemed at the time.

Tiberius had thought it all ridiculous too, but he'd leafed through several pocketbooks to find what I'd asked for all the same.

"She is most definitely dead," he'd assured me, handing over a slip of paper after he'd jotted the address on it.

"I know. But the dead *can* talk, Mr Benjamin."

He'd raised an eyebrow.

"Letters, diaries, manuscripts, postcards, random scribblings."

"I very much doubt any of Miss Candlish's writings will still be there, if the woman ever leant how to write in the first place. I only met her a few times, but she did strike me as somewhat uneducated, despite possessing a base cunning. Ghastly accent too. No idea where it was from, but not anywhere I would choose to visit based on the dreadful din she made."

I plucked the slip from his fingers.

"It's worth a try."

"Why, Mrs Harryman, may I ask, are you trying at all?"

"It's difficult to explain. And you wouldn't believe me if I told you, so, you must excuse me for not. But I greatly appreciate your help."

Tiberius nodded. He was far too much of a gentleman to press the point upon a lady. A terrible snob, but a gentleman all the same.

As I counted down the numbers of the houses on the Holloway Road, I ignored the queasiness in my stomach. Knocking on the doors of strangers was not something that came easily to me.

At least the house I wanted was in one piece, more or less. Blistered paint crinkled the front door, putty crumbled from half-rotten window frames, decades of soot soured and darkened the brickwork. A cat sat on the window ledge, eying me with despotic disinterest before returning to the far more important business of licking its bum.

I had absolutely no idea what I was going to say to whoever opened the door. Maybe it would be better if nobody was in. The day was flashing by and I wouldn't be back to the Castle by nightfall as it was.

A rag and bone man's cart rattled by behind me as I stared at the peeling door. I couldn't imagine Izzy St Clair ever coming to such a run-down house.

Summoning my scant courage, I walked up the four stone steps leading to the front door, each sporting their own patina of cracks and chips, and knocked.

After the third rap on the squeaky brass knocker the sound of shuffling feet came from inside.

I still hadn't thought of what to say but took a deep breath and trusted *something* would materialise in the vacuum of my brain.

The door shuddered and then opened far enough in a couple of jerky increments for a pale, lined face to peer out, blinking like something small awakening from hibernation.

"Yes...?"

"I'm sorry to trouble you..." I conjured a smile and hoped something coherent and sane would follow, "...I'm here about Gladys Candlish... I believe she used to live here...?"

"Gladys?"

"Yes, Gladys Candlish. She-"

"Gladys went to the Other Side. She doesn't talk to me anymore."

"I heard she passed away, yes. You knew her?"

The blinking face nodded.

"I'm sorry to intrude, but would it be possible to come in? I have a few questions about Gladys?"

"Questions?" the face retreated a little into the shadows, "Are you with the police?"

"No, I-"

"You're not a debt collector, are you? I can't pay any more of Gladys' debts; I simply-"

"No, no!" I held up my hands, "I'm not with anyone. My name's Beatrice Harryman, I'm trying to find out what happened to a friend of mine who died many years ago. I believe your sister knew her."

"I don't think I can help you, the spirits never talked to me. They never liked me like they did our Gladys."

"I don't want to talk to the spirits, just you... Mrs...?"

"Miss Candlish... Gwendoline Candlish."

It took several minutes of cajoling and reassuring to persuade Gwendoline I was neither after money nor looking to speak to the dead before she yanked the door open enough for me to come in.

"It swells up in the warm weather," Gwendoline explained, "and when it rains. Pretty stiff in the cold too. It's a right bloody pain, I can tell you."

Gwendoline ushered me along a hallway smelling of cats, cigarette smoke and dust and into a drawing room. The curtains remained closed despite it being mid-afternoon, the smell of dust and cigarettes was stronger, the cats less so. Whatever colours had once graced the room, everything was nicotine brown now.

"Don't get many visitors these days. Not since Gladys passed," Gwendoline steered me down onto a sofa after smacking a cushion hard enough to add another small cloud of dust to the air.

"I'll make tea!" Gwendoline announced as if struck by sudden inspiration. She was gone before I could tell her I didn't need any.

I let my eyes take in the room while wondering how old she was. Though stooped, Gwendoline was sprightly enough. Lines creased her face, but only a few strands of grey sprinkled her dark hair.

A tortoiseshell cat padded into the room. After a cursory inspection, it decided I didn't merit the effort of getting to know and turned on its tail to head straight back out again.

Deep silence shrouded the house. Although facing a busy North London thoroughfare, little noise penetrated. Inside, there was nothing, not even the ticking of a clock. A sparsely furnished room, the carpet, worn down to threads in places, still bore the impression of vanished furniture. Sold to pay Gladys's debts? Fading photographs of blank-faced people in their Sunday bests adorned the walls. They made me think of corpses propped up for the photographer's benefit.

Gwendoline returned with a tinkling tray of chipped chinaware and placed it on the table before handing me a cup. It was a weak, washy brew. No biscuits either. It was only a couple of miles from the *St Clair Gallery* to the Holloway Road, but it very much felt like the Underground Railway had transported me to another world.

Once seated in a sagging wingback armchair, Gwendoline peered at me again, "You wanted to talk about Gladys?"

"Yes, thank you. She was...?"

"My cousin. Though we were more like sisters. My parents both passed when I was young, and I came to live with my uncle's family."

"And you've lived here a long time?"

"Since I was six years old. First with my Aunt and Uncle, then just me and Gladys," Gwendoline gave an assertive nod of her head, "I helped with Gladys' calling. The spirits never talked to me directly, however, I always sensed their presence, which was a great comfort to our Gladys."

"And neither of you married?"

"Oh, no..." Gwendoline shuddered, "...we never wanted men! They fog and confuse the thought, the heart, the soul. All must be clean and pure. It makes connecting to the Other Side much smoother."

"It does?"

Gwendoline's cup rattled against its saucer. She curled back her lip, "Our Gladys always said so. She never approved of men. Such... lost, hopeless creatures. Full of... distractions."

I smiled. That was one way of describing them.

Gwendoline put aside her tea, pulled a packet of cigarettes from the pocket of the moth-eaten shapeless cardigan she wore and lit one with a shaking hand.

"What was it you wanted?" she asked shaking out the match.

"Do you remember a woman called Izzy St Clair? She-"

Gwendoline's eyes shot up, holding mine before she let the match fall to an ash try, "Mrs St Clair? Of course. She was one of Gladys' patrons."

"I've only recently learned of her death. It was... a shock. I understand Gladys believed there was something... sinister about her accident?"

"Sinister?!" Gwendoline's laughter bordered on a cackle, "Yes, it was sinister. She touched something dark alright. Only time I ever saw our Gladys scared."

"What happened?"

Gwendoline's eyes fell as another cat came into the room. It rubbed black velvet fur against her leg before curling up at her feet. Once it settled her gaze returned to me.

"Mrs St Clair was sensitive. Like Gladys. Not as much, of course, but then no one was as favoured by the spirits as our Gladys. She had some silly notion the Other Side could help her put right wrongs done in the world of the living."

"A spiritual detective?"

Gwendoline chuckled, "Yes, Gladys warned her the spirits don't think like we do. They can be mischievous, even malicious. Never to be trusted. We leave a lot behind when we pass."

I smiled and sipped my thin tea. I was getting the idea Gwendoline might have left quite a bit behind already.

"But Mrs St Clair... she was a generous woman. She assisted us with... material things if you get my drift. So, Gladys... indulged her."

"She helped her talk to the spirits?"

Gwendoline nodded.

"To put right wrongs?"

"That's what she said. Justice for the dead, darling, justice for the dead!" Her mimicry wasn't half as good as Tiberius Benjamin's had been, but it sent a shiver down my back all the same.

The cat lifted its head to stare at me with startling green eyes.

"And did she? Find justice?"

Gwendoline snorted, "She'd only just started when she ended up passing over herself. The spirits aren't interested in justice..."

"And what made Gladys think her car crash wasn't an accident?"

Both Gwendoline's and the cat's eyes appeared to sparkle in the gloomy room.

"Because Mrs St Clair told her, my dear. Told her about the monster that came and took her..."

1918

The letter found me shortly after the armistice declaration.

Mrs Hollister presented it to me when I returned from my day at the Board of Agriculture and Fisheries. The letter bore British Forces postage and initially I thought it was Owen, that, somehow, he'd survived as a prisoner of war and was now coming home.

I'd sat on the edge of the bed, turning the letter over in my trembling hands.

"Owen…" I whispered again and again.

I knew the letter wasn't from Owen himself, I didn't recognise the neat ruler straight handwriting, but it had to be about Owen. I didn't know anyone else in the forces well enough. Plenty of other boys I'd grown up with had gone to the war, many of them consumed by the mud of Passchendaele and the Somme, but I hadn't been in touch with any of them for years.

Since Owen's death, I had work and little else, as if life could never have meaning or worth without him.

And suddenly I had this letter. I had a hope where so long I'd had nothing but aching loneliness and the ever-growing certainty part of me had died in France too.

In the end, I put it on my pillow unopened and went downstairs to have supper with Mrs Hollister. My landlady was not a great believer in talking and eating at the same time and the meal, like most I'd shared with her, was accompanied only by the ticking of the fearsome old grandfather clock the stood guard over the dining room. Irene, the other girl lodging at Mrs Hollister's, was out, so we ate alone.

Mrs Hollister noted that Irene was out a lot in the evenings.

"I suspect she has a gentleman friend," she'd confided, before asking, "Has she said anything to you?"

I'd shaken my head and concentrated on pursuing an uncooperative brussel sprout. Irene, in my opinion, was somewhat flighty and likely to have several gentlemen friends at any given time, but I kept out of her business in the same way I kept out of everybody else's.

That amounted to the extent of our repertoire of sparkling supper conversation, and it was only as Mrs Hollister was clearing away pudding that she queried the letter.

"I haven't opened it yet."

"Is it about your fiancé?" she asked, gently.

My eyes darted up, "Why would you think that, Mrs Hollister?"

"Because you've been staring at your engagement ring even more intently than usual, my dear," she placed a hand on my shoulder, "You should open it at once. Unread news offers no virtue..."

Mrs Hollister often conjured phrases that sounded vaguely profound, but when you thought about them for a bit turned out to be nonsense. I nodded and agreed I would read the letter as soon as I retired.

In fact, it was gone midnight before I finally summoned the courage, with Owen's ring pressed against my lips. That was 20th November 1918.

The day I first heard the name Frank Harryman.

1943

It was nearly midnight by the time I got back to the Castle.

The regret I hadn't stayed in London accompanied every step. Not just for the night, but forever.

Better still, Kansas.

But Tom was gone. Something had come and taken him. The same thing, I suspected, that had come and taken Izzy after she'd tried to warn me about whatever I shared my home with.

Something dark. Something sorrowful. Something faceless. Something that didn't want me to leave.

Did I believe Gwendoline Candlish? Part of me did. But part of me was an educated vicar's daughter. Dad would have been even more sceptical about such things than Tiberius Benjamin, and I did my best to keep his common sense as close to me as my other memories of him.

But as I followed the narrow moon-washed path across the marsh towards the calling sea, the educated vicar's daughter had fallen very silent.

"What did she tell Gladys?"

The conversation played in my mind. As it had done repeatedly since I'd escaped the shadowy room filled with fading photographs of blank-faced people.

"That something had crossed over into our world and taken her life. Seized the wheel as she was driving back to London and put its foot on the accelerator till she'd lost control and crashed."

"What... *something?*"

"A thing of shadow, a thing without a face but with a mouth. Something that told her meddling never ended well."

"Did-"

"The spirits seldom speak plainly. Especially so soon after death. They are confused. You must interpret what they tell you carefully. That was one of Gladys' many gifts. To unpick the noise and chatter to find the thread of sanity in the madness."

"I see... but this thing that made her crash. It was a spirit?"

"No... that was what scared Gladys. It was... something else."

"But what?"

"Something she had no name for."

"But how could she know, if all she had were Izzy's... spirit's account?"

"Because she saw it."

"Saw it? It... what... *manifested* here?"

"No. She saw through Mrs St Clair's eyes. The last moments of her life. She saw it... and it was an abomination. Something she had never seen the like of before. And few people in this world saw as much as our Gladys ever did."

"And what did she see... exactly?"

"Something that did not belong. Something the eye did not easily hold within itself. Something not meant to be seen. A man, but not a man. Something the daylight refused to fall upon, a shadow in the sun. Something black, featureless, terrible. Something not of this world, something God did not make. Something full of pain and sorrow, something full of glee and malice..."

An owl hooted, making me jump and pulling my mind back to the present. I needed to take a care. The path was narrow, the meres on either side deep.

I looked about me, but all the shadows were as they should be. No figures lurked in the corner of my eye.

I expected it would all sound like nonsense by morning. But it also sounded a lot like Davey Acorns' description of what he'd seen with Tom and what I thought I'd glimpsed so many times within the Castle.

Calming myself, I walked on.

Was it inside?

Waiting for me to come home.

Would it have more to say about the consequences of my prying?

Would it have something to say about what happened to Tilly?

"But what was it, Miss Candlish, what *was* it?"

Gwendoline had looked at me for a long while, eyes almost glazed. A small, rictus-like smile sprinkled more creases upon her ashen face before she answered.

"Why, Mrs Harryman, it is whatever you want it to be..." the cup in her hand tinkled on its saucer, the green-eyed cat at her feet started purring as she added, "...just like all the other monsters in the world."

The night carried an autumn chill as the Castle appeared out of the darkness, stark against the star-lit sky above the black sea.

I stopped and stared at it, wondering why I had returned. What kept me here now? Tilly vanished sixteen years before, Simon was dead, Francis was a grown man, who, if he survived the war, would marry Diane and live far away from here.

Only Frank tied me to this place, as he always had.

But Frank was not the only monster stalking those stained walls. And yet, here I was. A beaten cat skulking back to the only home it knew because it could find a saucer of milk there once in a while.

I have no money.

My familiar excuse. The one I had wrapped around myself ever since I walked into the Creethorpe branch of the *London & Midland Bank* and found Frank had spirited my savings away.

Eventually, my feet took me forward, the ground under them turning from hard earth to sand, pebbles and broken shells with each stride.

Grey Gull watched me come with black sightless eyes that reflected the night. But did anything else see through those darkened windows? Something that had killed my lover and stolen my child?

"Do you know what Mrs St Clair was doing before she died?"

"Hunting..."

"Hunting?"

"That's what she told Gladys. She was excited. I remember her coming here. Fizzing with it, she was. Like she'd found... a right royal wonder! They sat in the parlour for hours. Gladys preferred to converse about the spirit world in the parlour where she held her seances. The veil is thinner, there. She always told me."

"What did Izzy say?"

"Oh, I wasn't privy to all that. I made the tea, took the coats, emptied the ashtrays. The spirits don't talk to me, see? Earthly matters, that's what you're made for, Gwen... that's all you're made for..."

"But Gladys must have said something to you?"

"Oh, she always told me something. Just a little, here and there. She was a bit of a tease. She never let me in on everything, not about the Other Side. Earthly things, Gwen, Earthly things. You see, dear? We were a team, the *Spiritual* and the *Earthly*."

"Yes, I see, but-"

"Mrs St Clair thought she had found something that shouldn't be. Something that had crossed over to our world. I don't think Gladys believed her as such, but, well, Mrs St Clair had a lot of money, so we always thought it best to humour her. Gladys didn't like to trouble herself with the Earthly things, but she made an exception when it came to money. Spirits and money, they were her business. Everything else was me. I told you we were a team, didn't I? A very close team. For so many, many years..."

The door key was in my hand. Beyond the Castle, the sea teased the shore, otherwise, all was silent.

I didn't think Gwendoline Candlish was sane. An old woman surrounded by her cats, removed from a world she no longer understood. No family, no friends, no purpose. Not an uncommon thing.

But the more pertinent question, as I stood with the key poised upon the lock's lips, was whether or not I was sane.

The door unlocked with a click, a clunk and a groan.

A familiar greeting.

It opened on to a rectangle of darkness. Anything could lurk inside that chasm. Monsters, memories or madness.

"Is anyone there?"

No one answered. No thing answered.

Why would it? I'd lived here for twenty-three years. The dark might whisper in my ear, it might drip poison, it might ridicule and insult me. But it had never answered my questions.

"Did you take Tilly? Did you?"

Nothing.

"Did you kill Tom and Izzy?"

A wave slapped the beach, heavier than those that'd gone before, but I didn't take that as any kind of answer.

I rested a hand on the door frame. The paint was starting to blister. It never takes the salt long to abrade and corrode, to wear away the skin so it can rot what lies beneath. What had this place done to me in twenty-three years?

My thumb moved over the paintwork, a flake came away under my nail and tumbled to the ground.

Exhaustion hit me like the waves pounding the shore. Black and cold, sapping my strength. I sagged against the wall. It had been a long day. Too long, too hard. And what had I learned, really?

"But what did Mrs St Clair think she'd found?"

"A haunted man."

"Haunted by what?"

"That's what she wanted to find out. By getting close to him. That's what she said to Gladys, close enough to see what walked in his shadow. I think she could see Gladys didn't entirely believe her, but she said it isn't just houses that are haunted. Something like that anyway. What she must have seen to think such a thing, I can't say because Gladys never told me.

Then she went off, and we didn't hear from her again. We didn't think much of that; she was always going off, disappearing. She was good at disappearing. When we heard she'd died in a car crash, Gladys was most upset. She tried to contact Mrs St Clair on the Other Side. When she did... well... She kept telling people it wasn't an accident, but nobody wanted to listen. People don't listen to us. They think we're frauds. More fool them..."

"I see... do you remember anything else?"

"It was a long time ago. My memory isn't what it was. Like the daylight, it fades as the night draws closer."

"Well, perhaps I won't take up any more of your time, Miss Candlish."

"There was one thing more... I think..."

"Yes?"

"Something Mrs St Clair told Gladys when she asked her why she wanted to get close to this man."

"What did she say?"

"She said it was to find a child..."

1919

I had no preconceptions regarding Frank Harryman. He was just another young man looking to restart his life now the war was over, the only difference between him and all the others being he'd known Owen.

It took me a long time to decide I wanted to meet him. We corresponded for six months, we didn't meet earlier as he'd stayed in the army while they helped clear up the mess four years of fighting had made, and the big wigs negotiated the peace treaty. For all the joy the war had finally ended, the suspicion lingered it was but a false dawn, a lull, as both sides took deep breaths before throwing themselves at each other again.

The suspicion proved to be correct; the deep breaths just took a bit longer than most of us expected.

Whenever one of Frank's letters arrived on Mrs Hollister's doormat, I would snatch it up, run to my room, put it on my bedside table and leave it unopened for several days.

They made me think of Owen. Which was no great revelation as nearly everything made me think of Owen. But they weren't Owen's; they were another man's. Another man's hand, another man's pen. Another man's thoughts, memories, feelings, fears, hopes and, occasionally, rather bad puns.

I had no desire for romance or friendship or any kind of relationship with Frank Harryman. He knew Owen, had been with him at the end and could confirm he had died in the mud and thunder of the Somme. He'd reached out to me once the war finished as he said he knew Owen, how close we'd been and how much I must be missing him.

I wasn't interested in Frank in any way other than as a source of information about Owen. Any crumb, any morsel, any fragment he had, added to the memory of the only man I could imagine I would ever love.

"Another letter," Mrs Hollister commented one morning at breakfast.

"Yes," I agreed, busying myself buttering toast to avoid her eye.

"From the same soldier?"

"Yes," the marmalade followed liberally.

"Is he home yet?"

I raised my eyes; Mrs Hollister had a cup of tea poised upon her lips. In all other aspects, she carried the demeanour of an interrogator.

"Soon. I believe."

"Are you going to meet him?"

"He... has asked," I admitted before nibbling a corner of the toast I had lost interest in.

"You should."

"Our correspondence is not of a romantic nature."

"That is of no concern of mine. But it will do you good."

"I am not sure..."

"You are still far too young to become a spinster, Beatrice. But every pot becomes cold if it is ignored long enough."

I twisted Owen's ring. Mrs Hollister sipped her tea, eyes, sharp and grey, following the movement of my fingers.

I returned my hand to the toast; Mrs Hollister returned her tea to its saucer.

"You have nothing to feel guilty about."

I felt many things. I did not consider guilt one of them. I continued to nibble the toast and thought about claiming I was late for work. Except Mrs Hollister knew precisely what time I left the house each morning.

However, Irene's arrival saved me from further questioning. Mrs Hollister shot her a somewhat disapproving look, though Irene was as often late for breakfast as I was early.

Irene was in little need of lectures about accepting invitations from strange men. From what I knew of my fellow lodger, Irene was not the type to ever pass up an invitation from a strange man.

The smells of Irene's first dab of perfume and morning cigarette mixed with the congealing fry-up waiting for her.

"Morning!" Irene smiled merrily. Although I regularly heard her sneaking home at questionable hours, she always smiled so merrily at the breakfast table I wondered if she practised.

Mrs Hollister decided it was an opportune moment to clear away the plates of those of us who'd managed to get out of bed on time. Mrs Hollister was something of a stickler. Irene must have driven her to distraction.

Despite living under the same roof, I saw little of Irene away from Mrs Hollister's dining table. I worked at the Board of Agriculture and Fisheries while she was at the Home Office. Occasionally, we got the bus to Whitehall together, but, as I have intimated, Irene wasn't exactly punctilious when it came to timekeeping. I hated waiting, so never made plans to travel to work with her.

She smiled a lot, rarely had a bad word to say about anybody and spent most of her time preening in front of a mirror, presumably on the off chance she might bump into one of her gentlemen friends. Or be presented with the opportunity to acquire a new one.

"You got your lecture?" Irene asked, leaning slightly towards me.

I nodded, pushing the unwanted toast away.

"I usually get mine in the evenings. We give the old bird a full day between us, don't we?"

I found a smile. I wasn't as good at them as Irene.

Irene looked down at her cold breakfast, pulled a face and poured herself some lukewarm tea.

"I don't know why she always puts so much on my plate; I'm always telling her I'm not a big eater," Irene stirred in some sugar, "does she think I'm too skinny?"

"She's just being… motherly…" I offered a weak smile to go with my weak reply as I climbed to my feet,

Irene eyed my uneaten toast, "Was it something I said?"

"I want to get in early. Lots of typing to catch up on."

"Do what you're paid to do, but no point doing extra; we'll all be out of work soon now the boys are home."

"Not sure how many of the boys can type."

Irene didn't look convinced.

After bidding her a good day, I hurried off to get my coat, stuffing Frank's latest letter into the pocket. Irene was only trying to be friendly, but I pushed her away like everybody else who tried.

I kept my hand on the folded letter as my shoes clipped down the pavement to catch the number 12 bus from Camberwell Green. Part of me wanted to screw it up and throw it in the bin.

The handwriting on the letter was Frank's, I recognised it now, but the postmark wasn't British Forces anymore. He was back home, shortly to be demobbed out of the army.

I ignored the letter during the bus ride, instead staring at the grey streets of London or surreptitiously reading the headlines of fellow passengers' newspapers. I ignored it when I got off at Horseguards Avenue, continued to ignore it as I showed my pass to Harry, the doorman, and continued ignoring it as I sat at my desk and started typing.

Despite what I'd told Irene, I had no more work waiting for me than I did first thing any morning. Which was very little. I was tediously efficient and never left anything in my in-tray at the end of the day, even if it meant working late.

My only deadline was to be home in time for dinner, and Mrs Hollister was not a woman for eating before 7pm.

Other than the perfunctory "good mornings," I spoke to no one.

I spent my thirty-minute lunch on a bench outside the National Gallery in Trafalgar Square. I shared a few crumbs of my cheese sandwich with the pigeons, smoked a cigarette, and watched the people rushing by, wondering who they were, where they were going, were they happy or sad? Were they loved?

All the time, I felt the weight of Frank's letter and found reasons not to open it.

He was home. He wanted to meet. He'd been with Owen when he died.

Was that a story I needed to know more fully?

Would it make the pain less? Would it make my loneliness less? Would it make me miss Owen less? Would it make me regret not marrying him less?

I didn't know. I didn't think so, but I didn't know.

There was a litter bin next to the bench. I crumpled up the paper bag my sandwich came in and dropped it inside as I stood up.

Then my hand found Frank's letter.

Throw it away. Just throw the bloody thing away.

I stared at the bin.

Two greying men in bowler hats walked by, laughing. A woman, pale and plump, scurried past in the opposite direction. Head down. Somewhere to be.

So did I.

I was taking notes of a meeting in the Under Secretary's office. I would sit and scribble and say nothing, save ask how many sugars each of the men wanted in their tea. Some would smile at me, some would ignore me. Mr Grayson would likely glance at my legs whenever the chance arose. But he wouldn't speak to me either.

Frank's letter was in my hand, hovering over the litter bin.

However long the meeting lasted, afterwards I would return to my desk and type up my notes. They would be finished before the end of the day, put in a transit envelope marked for Mr Cussler's attention. I would get the Number 12 Bus from Horseguards to Camberwell Green. I would sit down with Mrs Hollister and, possibly, Irene. They would ask how my day had been. I would politely tell them it had been "fine" or "good." If I was feeling particularly ebullient, I might go as far as "very good."

After pudding, I would retire to my room and read. I might open the window at some point and smoke a cigarette. Mrs Hollister didn't approve of women smoking but turned a blind eye to it as long as Irene and I opened our windows.

Then I would wash, rub on some face cream, clean my teeth and stare at the dark ceiling. Perhaps I would hold Owen's ring to my lips and try to remember how wonderful his kisses had been.

Perhaps I would cry. Perhaps I wouldn't.

I cried less now. But still more than a young woman should. More than anyone should. Owen had been dead for three years that September.

My fingers flexed around Frank's letter. Ready to cast it aside and continue with my day, which would be the same as yesterday and the same as tomorrow.

Then I sucked in a breath and stuffed it back into my coat.

I was being silly.

I would read it. And if he wanted to meet, I would go.

It would make for a different day. If nothing else. And, really, what did I have to lose?

As it turned out, everything.

1943

The possibility I was insane had been stalking the backwaters of my mind for some time, though I'd always dismissed the suggestion. The mad never question their sanity, do they?

Do they?

Or is it just one of those beliefs we take as truth without actually knowing anything about it?

I sat at the kitchen table smoking till I felt sick. If there had been any alcohol in the house, I would have been throwing that down my neck to see if it could make me nauseous quicker than chain-smoking.

The darkness pressed against the window, the only thing to see was my own reflection, hunched, old, frightened.

Insane?

I lit another cigarette I didn't want.

If nothing else, feeling sick took the edge off the fear.

The things I'd learned from Davey and Gwendoline should have reassured me whatever I'd glimpsed from time to time wasn't my imagination, wasn't a manifestation of my descent into lunacy, but something real.

Davey had seen it. Izzy had seen it. Gladys Candlish had seen it too.

Something faceless. Something full of pain and sorrow.

Therefore, it had to be real.

Except it was absurd!

Monsters did not skulk in the corner of your eyes, let alone snatch your baby away or murder your lover. Sensible, educated women, particularly those who also happened to be a vicar's daughter, did not believe in such nonsense.

I waited for something to whisper from the shadows to confirm all this was real. Nothing stirred in the house. The clock said it was gone two after midnight. I should go to bed.

The next day I would talk with Davey. Or clean the house. Or try to make something edible from the scraps in my cupboard. Or sit and wait for an airgram from Francis. Or dread one of the Angels of Death cycling through the marsh, telegram in hand. Or cry about Simon. Or Tom. Or Owen.

Or ignore everything and stare at the sea, listen to its song, and pretend nothing had happened, nothing was wrong. I was neither losing my mind nor living with some kind of phantom.

Just grief and imagination.

I ground out the cigarette and stopped myself reaching for another one. I felt sick enough.

Later, I lay in bed, trying not to turn things in my head, but quite unable to leave anything alone.

Several times I sat up and demanded, "Where did you take my baby?"

If the phantom, the faceless something, was in residence, it was in no mood to converse. Again.

For an evil demonic entity from the Other Side capable of snatching babies and murder, it often came across as rather shy.

I stopped looking at the clock around four. Sometime after, I must have drifted off to sleep because muted daylight filled the room the next time I opened my eyes.

That, however, was not the surprise that greeted me.

"Frank?"

His head jerked up as if he'd been dozing, "Sweetness..."

"What are-"

Frank silenced me with a soft kiss on my lips before stroking my hair. A faint smile softened the usually brooding set of his face when he sat back. I found my hand within his.

"How are you feeling, Sweetness?"

Unsettled would be the truthful answer. Not just by Frank's unexpected presence but also by his even more unexpected behaviour. He was acting kind. And, of course, it was an act. I'd fallen for it when we first met and seen it wheeled out for strangers. But it was a routine I never saw when I was alone with him. Least of all, in my bedroom, which he reserved for the very worst of himself.

But I said none of that.

"Fine," I said instead, sitting up.

The expression on Frank's face, for all the world, looked like concern, "I've been worried about you."

"Worried?" I shook my head, "Why are you here, Frank? You should be in London."

"Compassionate leave, Sweetness," he laid a gentle hand upon my arm, "you remember, don't you?"

"You got it extended when you went back?"

"I haven't been back, Sweetness, not since Simon..." he swallowed and bit his lip before adding, "...you remember what happened... to Simon?"

"Of course I remember! How could I forget?"

"You haven't really been yourself again, Sweetness. Not since we got the telegram. A setback. They said there might be setbacks..."

I wanted to snap at him, ask him what on Earth he was blathering about. But I didn't. Snapping wasn't something Frank tolerated, and I didn't want to feel his palm on my cheek. Or worse.

I started to get out of bed. I had chores to do. Frank would explain how and why he'd returned in his own sweet time.

Frank put his hand on my shoulder. I expected him to squeeze it hard enough to make me gasp. For him to be snarling in my face, pushing me down. Maybe he'd want to do his business.

He did push me down, but gently.

"Easy, Sweetness," he said, "you need to rest. I made some tea. It might be a bit cold now. I'll make some more."

Frank never made tea. Anything that kept him away from his painting was a burden he was never prepared to suffer.

A cup of tea sat on the bedside table. I stared at it. I wouldn't have been *much* more surprised if a unicorn had been sitting there munching my Sunday best dress.

Frank stroked back my hair and kissed my forehead.

"I love you," he said.

A unicorn munching my Sunday best dress while riding a bicycle and juggling.

"Frank...?"

"We must get you better, Sweetness. I'll have to go back to my unit eventually, and we can't have you here on your own if you're having another one of your... episodes, can we?"

Before I could say anything, he rested a finger upon my lips, "I don't want you to have to go back to that place, Sweetness, but if you can't care for yourself... what else can we do?"

I jerked away from his finger, "What are you talking about, Frank?"

"You're confused. Disorientated. It always happens when you come out of an episode. You need to rest for a few days. Same as always. We'll get you back on my feet quick as you like."

"What... episode?" I nearly swore. Which wouldn't have been good. Frank hated me swearing even more than he did me smoking. I thought of the overflowing ashtray on the kitchen table. He wouldn't be happy about that.

And yet...

Frank eased himself back into the chair by my bed. He rubbed his eyes, when he dropped his hands, a smile creased his mouth, although it was a thin, pained one.

"We've had this conversation so many times, Bea..."

"You're frightening me."

"Ever since we lost Tilly..." he bit his lip once more, then took a deep breath, "...ever since Tilly died, you've had these episodes. These fantasies. Of this other life where some monster is tormenting you, where I... hurt you... do terrible things to you... where you are trapped..."

"Tilly didn't die, Frank; she disappeared, remember?"

He sat forward, seizing my hand, brow crumpling, "No, Sweetness. She died of a fever. Dr O'Conner came and said nothing was wrong. You insisted there was, but I listened to the Doctor and not you. And our baby died. Since then... you've kept retreating into this fantasy. This dark, horrible delusion. The doctors say you're punishing yourself. You're escaping reality, changing your past and present, making demons represent the things you're suffering inside. The guilt, grief, pain. I thought you were getting better. Finally. But losing Simon tipped you back. You've been raving for days. All kinds of things. All kinds of things, Sweetness..."

As the words fell from his mouth, each faster than the one before, a single tear rolled down Frank's cheek.

And of all I'd ever seen and suffered. Nothing had ever scared me more...

1919

"I'm worried about you, Kitten."

"Dad, you're a vicar; it's your job to worry about everyone."

"That's not quite the full job description..."

Every Saturday, I went to the Post Office on Camberwell Green to call home. And every Saturday, Dad interrogated me about my continuing adventures in the big, bad city and how it was high time I came home. Preferably permanently, but at least for a visit.

He missed me.

My throat always tightened when he said that, but it irritated me too. I didn't want to go home, not because of Dad, who was the kindest man you could ever hope to meet, but because of all the memories haunting those limestone cottages and soft green hills.

In London, Owen was only the occasional half-glimpsed face in a crowd, who always turned out to be someone without even a passing resemblance to my love. But, in Hollscombe and the surrounding hedgerow-bordered fields, he was everywhere.

As with Mrs Hollister, I would describe my life to Dad with harmless, vacuous words like *nice, good* and *fine*. I don't think he believed them much, either.

I dreaded the weekends. During the week, I had things to occupy hands and mind. But the weekend was two full days of slow, empty clock-ticking. I called Dad around noon on Saturday; I went to *St Gile's* on Sunday and tried to find some peace in the soft light pouring through the beautiful stained-glass windows designed by John Ruskin. The Reverend Hodges' earnest sermons provided little comfort, but they filled the silence, and I'd always enjoyed singing the hymns.

Sometimes Irene suggested going to the picture house. I didn't know if she felt sorry for me, Mrs Hollister bullied her into it, or she really didn't like being alone. Occasionally, I went, but usually, I didn't. When we did, she chatted incessantly. Later, I could never remember a thing she'd said.

If the weather was fair, I might go to a park, stroll about, feed the ducks, sit under a tree and read. Little distractions.

For a treat, I'd go to the *Lyons Corner House* on Peckham High Road for tea and a piece of cake on Saturday after speaking to Dad. The walk from Camberwell gave me something to do. I'd watch the world go by out of the window without too much floating through my mind.

That Saturday, a presentable young man at the next table started talking to me. Skin fair to the point of ashen, rosy-cheeked, hair the colour of burnished copper. Scottish. Kind eyes. He stirred his tea an awful lot. A little nervous, which I found curiously endearing. He was new to London, having recently obtained a clerk's position. He didn't know anyone or quite what to do with himself at the weekends. He'd been in the army. He was glad that business was all done with. The war to end all wars. Let us hope!

I smiled. I trotted out the full range of my conversational repertoire. *Yes. No. Nice, fine, good. Very good!*

He talked about the unseasonal weather and how confusing everything in London was. Had I been on the underground railway? What an infernal thing! He asked about my favourite kind of cake, where I came from, had I seen the new Douglas Fairbanks moving picture? He glanced at the unadorned fingers of my left-hand several times. He told me his name was Alan, and I said mine was Beatrice. He told me he thought that was a lovely name. I blushed. So did he.

I was polite. I smiled, I sipped my tea and tried not to let Alan lure me too far into conversation.

Once I'd finished my tea and cake, I said how nice it was to meet him and wished him a good day.

His cheeks looked rosier, and he fidgeted on his chair as he said goodbye.

Outside, I paused on the pavement, fixing my hat and steeling myself for the walk back to Camberwell Green. Part of me didn't want to go. But although Alan looked nothing like Owen, he reminded me of him enough for the empty place inside me to stretch and yawn and fill with echoes.

I only managed a few paces before Alan barrelled out of the *Lyons Corner House.*

The rosiness had spread from his cheeks to consume most of his face.

Would I be interested in going to the picture house with him? The new Douglas Fairbanks was supposed to be *very* good.

Since I'd started working at the Board for Agriculture and Fisheries, several men had asked me out. As they had all been either old, married or, more commonly, old and married, declining had taken no thought whatsoever. But Alan wasn't old or married. In fact, he seemed nice. Very nice.

But he wasn't Owen.

So, I said I couldn't.

He looked disappointed.

"I'm spoken for," I accompanied the lie with an apologetic shrug.

He didn't look at my hand again, just offered a resigned smile, "The bonny girls always are," he said, putting on the cap he'd been wringing in his hands, "tell your wee young man he's a lucky fellow."

That made me want to both smile and cry. I did neither.

"I will..."

For a second, just a second, I hesitated. Words teased my lips.

Actually, I'm not spoken for at all! My fiancée died in the trenches, and I've been too scared to do anything but miss him ever since. He wanted us to marry during the war because he was afraid he wouldn't come home. But I said no and insisted on waiting until the war was over because I was afraid he wouldn't come home as well. I was frightened of being a widow. I was frightened of having to bring up a child alone. And now all I feel is the guilt he died without having the thing he wanted most in all the world. I don't want to feel guilty anymore, I don't want to feel lonely anymore, and I'd rather like to see the new Douglas Fairbanks moving picture with you, Alan; thank you so much for asking!

But nothing came, bar a twitchy smile, and then I was walking away.

I often wonder what would have become of me if I'd gone to the picture house with Alan and his hair the colour of burnished copper, rosy cheeks, and soft Scottish accent that Saturday night.

But I didn't.

I met Frank Harryman instead.

1943

I sat on the old rocker Frank kept outside his studio. He'd carried it over to the back door, so I could enjoy the fresh air but hurry inside if my mood or the weather changed.

He'd spread a blanket over my legs. It was a mild day, but the breeze could still chill. It did little to warm me, however, as what chilled me was coming from within, not off the North Sea.

The rocker moved in rhythm with the waves. I suppose that was down to me, though I put no conscious thought into the movement. But then there were many things I had been putting little conscious thought into lately.

Not even lately. If Frank, the new, improved kindly Frank who only ever used a belt to keep his trousers up, was to be believed, this had been going on for sixteen years. Ever since Tilly went missing.

Ever since Tilly died.

Did I believe him?

Everything around me seemed as it should. The Castle, the outhouses, the stink of paint and turpentine wafting from the studio, the cackle of gulls, the wind tugging at my hair, the smell of brine and ozone. Everything except Frank.

Were all my memories the delusions of a broken mind? Had I spent long periods not here by the sea but in some ghastly asylum? And what of my life before I lost Tilly? Had I re-written that too? Made Frank a monster because he had sided with Doctor O'Conner and not thought Tilly was seriously ill?

I tried to unpick the strands of those memories but found nothing came apart.

Frank still painted, save, in this brave new world, he regularly popped out to make me tea, kiss me, stroke my hair, hold my hand, ask me how I was and if I needed anything?

And what he painted hadn't changed. The same dire, angry, ugly collisions of colour and form, in most of which, if you cared to look, you could make out the twisted, misshapen figure of... my nightmares? The one that had killed Tom and Izzy? Or just the one I'd borrowed from Frank's paintings to fulfil the role of my own personal bogeyman. Forever whispering I was a useless woman, a bad mother, a hopeless wife. Forever sneaking about the shadows at the very far corner of my eye.

I tried emptying my mind, staring at the ever-shifting contours of the sea till it became a molten grey blur.

That didn't help, either.

I hadn't said anything to Frank about Izzy's death. And certainly nothing about Tom. But were they real? Frank said he'd been here since before Simon's death. He said I hadn't left the house since the memorial at *St Luke's*. If that was right, I'd never visited London, spoken to Tiberius and Gwendoline, or learned of Izzy's death, never…

Earlier, when Frank was painting, I'd gone to my purse. Inside, I knew, were the card Tiberius gave me with his phone number and Gladys Candlish's address in the Holloway Road. He'd written it on a page torn out of his notepad. There should also be the stub of my train ticket to Liverpool Street.

Nothing sat inside save a few coins, my door key and an old library ticket. I searched my bag and coat pockets too.

Nothing.

By the time I gave up, my hands were shaking.

Perhaps I'd thrown them away. If Frank, the other Frank, had found them, he would have asked questions. And that Frank was keen for an excuse to use his belt for something other than keeping his trousers up.

Or they never were there because going to London had been part of one of my fantastical *episodes*.

And even if they had been there, what did that prove? If I could imagine traipsing down the Holloway Road looking for a dead spiritualist's house so vividly I still smelt the exhaust fumes, conjuring a business card or old train ticket should present no problem to the warped and fertile imagination of the deranged Beatrice Harryman.

In a world of uncertainties, tragedy, pain and upheaval, one of the few constants, the few sanctuaries, are our own minds. To be confronted with the possibility my own was even more fractured and damaged than the world around me was so terrifying I could barely grasp the idea.

I rocked, I sat, I stared.

"Would you like a little sandwich, Sweetness?"

Frank startled me enough to make me jump. I'd been too lost to hear him come up beside me.

"I don't think we've got any bread."

Did we have bread? We didn't yesterday. I'd used the last for the sandwiches I took to London. Except I didn't go to London. Or did I? And if I didn't, did that mean we had bread? Had I fantasised finishing the loaf? I-

Frank rested a hand on my shoulder, stilling the thoughts spinning around the inside of my head.

"I'll check, Sweetness. You rest up."

Everything was so confusing!

I stared at nothing, trying to remember the life Frank said I'd actually lived. The one with a loving husband and large chunks incarcerated within an asylum.

I couldn't, not a thing.

Tiberius Benjamin seemed real, so did Gwendoline Candlish, as did Davey Acorns, Tom Dupree and Izzy St Clair. But, if Frank was to be believed, none of them were.

Yet when I closed my eyes and thought of Tom, I could feel his lips upon mine. I could taste him, see that wicked grin and hear that Kansas drawl.

Couldn't I?

"You're right, no bread," Frank announced, sauntering back, "we've got some coupons left in the ration book; I'll cycle into Creethorpe and get some bits later."

My Frank never went to the shops. Even when I'd been heavily pregnant, I'd still had to go.

I found a smile, "I'm not hungry anyway."

"You need to eat, Sweetness. Besides, you might get hungry in a while. Will you be ok on your own? I'll be quick?"

"Of course," I nodded. Noting Frank's hesitant look of concern, I nodded more forcefully, "Thank you, that's very kind."

"Anything for you, Sweetness," he brushed back my hair and kissed my forehead, then hurried off to get the bicycle, whistling as he went.

It Had to be You...

I bit my lip and counted to ten before throwing off the blanket and trotting down the side of Grey Gull, peering around the corner for a view of the track through the marsh. I watched Frank till he disappeared.

Then I hurried inside.

We kept a stack of old newspapers for lighting the fire, stove and other sundry messy tasks. I rifled through them, looking for the copy carrying the piece about Tom's death. Tuesday, 14th September 1943. I was certain that was the day. If Tom wasn't real then the newspaper would make no mention of him.

Unless I'd read the story and created a whole fantasy from that. Was such a thing possible?

I went through the entire pile. When I couldn't find that day's paper, I went through it again. Nothing. I must have lit the stove with that issue. There'd been no need to light the fire for months. The Monday 13th and Wednesday 15th issues laid on top of the newspapers now sprayed across the kitchen floor.

I went through both. Nothing about Tom's accident.

Was it odd the papers either side were here, but that one was missing?

Something moved behind me.

I whirled around, expecting to see Frank. The kitchen was empty. Silent as always, save for the gulls, and the sea beyond the Castle.

"Hello...? Frank...?"

I bit my lip. Just my imagination. Though, in my present state, imagination took on a whole heap of new possibilities.

My attention returned to the newspapers, fanned in a haphazard arc before me. I flicked through some more but found neither the one I was looking for nor anything else about Tom.

The window rattled, making me jump. I looked up, but this time it was only a gust of wind. I hastily gathered the newspapers and piled them up by the fire again.

The library would have copies. I could also phone the airbase and ask about Tom Dupree. Would that be a military secret? Either way, it would involve a walk into Creethorpe too as we didn't have a telephone.

I pulled myself to my feet.

What was I looking for, exactly? Evidence I wasn't insane? But if my mind conjured such vivid fantasies, how could I be certain *any* evidence wasn't just another facet of my delusion.

"I am not mad," I said aloud. No one answered, and no one was convinced.

I almost ran to the shelves holding my mostly old and dog-eared books. Some had travelled with me since childhood, the others had arrived via second-hand bookshops.

Frank said Tilly's death became the catalyst for my delusions, my episodes.

But I had a collection of yellowing clippings that said otherwise, pressed together between the pages of Kipling's *Stalky & Co.*

Part of me expected the book to be gone, but it sat where it should. My doubts insisted I'd find nothing inside bar the adventures of Stalky and his school chums.

I let out a little hiss of air as I opened the book and found the clippings.

Baby Disappears in Mysterious Circumstances.

The same headline I'd read a thousand times. My fingers traced the edge of the cutting. It looked real enough to me.

I went back to the kitchen and slammed the book down on the table.

I felt angry. And sane.

What was going on? Why was Frank spouting this nonsense? Tilly had been snatched away, it said so. In black and yellowing white. And if my memory was right about that, it was right about everything else. I wasn't having *episodes* and I hadn't spent months and years locked away in some asylum, concocting the memories I had out of thin air while crushing and destroying the real ones.

Did I confront Frank or play along?

What was the most likely way of finding out what was going on?

Or maybe I should pack a bag and leave?

That sounded a damn good idea, even if I'd never get to Kansas on my own.

Maybe I didn't have much money, but I could get a job. There was a war on and, like last time, most of the men were away. My secretarial skills might be too rusty to be of use to anyone, but I could do something.

And then I'd be away from Frank.

It was almost laughable that this new caring Frank scared me more than the one who'd been beating me and making my life a misery for twenty plus years.

Still, Frank would be back soon. How far could I get before he returned?

When I looked at the clock, I was surprised to find he'd already been gone over an hour.

No. I didn't want him coming after me. Best I did what I always did. Play meek and docile. He couldn't stay here indefinitely. He had to go back to his unit at some point, and then...

My head span so much I had to sit down.

I'd go.

This time I meant it. I really did.

No more excuses.

I didn't know what he was up to, but he was trying to convince me I was a lunatic.

Something in this house had killed Tom and Izzy, and probably stolen Tilly. A dark and faceless entity lived here. It wasn't a fantasy, it wasn't an episode, it was real.

"What's your game...?" I whispered, looking around me.

Nothing answered. Nothing ever did. It only spoke when it wanted to.

But had it done something to Frank? To make him try and persuade me I was the one that was insane. Or was this something else entirely?

If I ran, was I deserting Tilly? What if the faceless thing still had her... somewhere?

What if? What if? What if?

I pressed the balls of my hands into my eyes.

When that didn't do any good, I returned to the rocker outside and went back to staring at nothing. The indecision churning like the grey sea before me.

1919

I spotted Frank straight away.

He was still in uniform, which made my tummy clench harder. At least it wasn't splattered with mud like Owen's had been the last time, the only time, he'd come home.

He was standing outside Tottenham Court Road Station on the corner of Oxford Street. We were supposed to meet at 5pm. Thanks to my bus breaking down I was twenty minutes late.

I thought he might be annoyed, I thought he might have decided I wasn't coming. Part of me wished he had. Anxiety and nerves had been acting like a vice on my stomach ever since I'd agreed to see him. By the time I caught the No 1 bus from Elephant and Castle my heart was racing, and as it ground to a halt on Waterloo Bridge, I was having to force myself to breathe. I sat, staring at the grey-brown ribbon of the Thames disappearing into the smoky haze, clutching my handbag so tightly my knuckles turned to bony white ridges.

By the time the bus trundled down Charing Cross Road I was convinced my legs wouldn't work. Surely, I would fall flat on my face if I tried to stand up!

As the conductor rang the bell for Oxford Street, I managed to prove myself wrong. Several standing passengers shuffled aside to let me pass. When I finally got my feet on the pavement, I gratefully sucked in air tainted with exhaust fumes rather than cigarette smoke.

I thought I was going to vomit.

An old woman selling matches asked if I was alright.

"You in the family way, luv?"

I shook my head.

"You look right peaky?"

My hand was on a lamp post somehow. I told the woman it must have been something I ate.

A man in a baggy cap wanted some matches. I hurried across Oxford Street toward the station before she could ask me anything else.

Frank Harryman lifted the rolled-up newspaper in his hand in greeting as soon as he saw me. I prayed my wobbly knees would not betray my anxiety.

Although I'd never met him, and had no idea as to his appearance, he was the only man in uniform in sight. He also recognised me without hesitation, which puzzled me till he later told me Owen had showed him my photograph so many times he knew my face almost better than his own.

That had made me cry.

I did quite a bit of that. And when I wasn't crying, I was nearly crying, or trying to stop myself crying or pretending I wasn't crying.

Frank was a big man, not fat, not then, but big. Tall, broad shoulders, wide chest. The kind other men probably got careful around at the bar, just in case, though nothing in his face or manner hinted at his temper or propensity for violence. His hair was sharply slicked back. He sported a thin, razored moustache that put me in mind of one of those Hollywood picture stars. He smelt of the bergamot pomade he'd used to oil his hair, distinct even with the competing stinks of Oxford Street swirling about us.

I don't remember too much of what we said above the rattle of passing omnibuses. There was nothing about him that made me think I was going to spend the rest of my life with him. I was meeting him to find out the exact circumstances of Owen's death. It wasn't something I wanted to know, but it was something I needed to know. Or thought I did.

Looking back, I can see I was still so traumatised by loss I didn't have the faintest clue about what I either wanted or needed. Despite over two and half years passing since Owen's death, I was still broken into pieces. Time had healed little, the scabs remained sore and bleeding, the bone brittle and badly knitted.

I could not comprehend the way I felt, nor the possibility I could ever be like the rest of the world. That I could find love or happiness with anyone else. Or even some kind of balanced contentment with my lot. I feared, in so many ways, my life had ended with Owen's.

I was meeting Frank Harryman not only to discover out how Owen had died, but to find out how I died as well.

Part of me yearned for this to be over, to move on, start anew. To put away my grief and mourning before it was too late and my life flashed by. I just didn't know how. Whenever that thought began to coalesce into something I could begin to express, guilt chased me ever further from the world. Retreating deeper into isolation. As if solitude could some how be a salve to the pain that was still, by increments, destroying me.

We found a pub in Charing Cross. I have no recollection how we got there. Frank could have thrown me over his shoulder and slapped my rump as he carried me for all I can recall. My memory is a blank. It was as if the trauma of meeting a man wearing the same uniform my Owen had died in, who had been with him at the end, so overloaded my senses my little brain could not cope.

The first thing I remember clearly is sitting with Frank in the pub, wrapped in a miasma of cigarette smoke and beer fumes, a port and lemon in my hand. I was staring at the glass, watching the way it shook, trying to figure out a way to stop the little waves rippling back and forth.

He had a pint of stout in front of him. The same as Owen always drunk. I looked at my own glass. Port and lemon. My usual drink. Had Frank asked me what I wanted? He must have. I couldn't remember.

We talked of inconsequential things at first. Or, rather, Frank did. I mainly nodded, pinched out crippled smiles and mumbled the occasional lonely syllable in reply.

Frank spoke softly for a big man. At the sight of him, you'd think he would have a deep, booming voice that would carry across any room, but I found I had to lean over the table to hear him clearly above the babble of conversation. The pub was one of those old Victorian gin palaces, full of mirrors, brass and discreet nooks for those not wanting to hog the bar. It was filling up for a Saturday night.

At some point I noticed I'd finished my drink. I didn't remember putting it to my lips. Frank sprang up and got us both another. The door crashed open as I sat alone. A couple came in, young, happy, laughing. Eyes only for each other.

I looked away, catching my reflection in one of the pub's many mirrors. Pale-faced, drawn, lipstick so garishly red and inappropriate I immediately wanted to wipe it off. I didn't. I just dropped my eyes.

When was the last time I'd smiled and meant it?

Yet another thing I couldn't remember.

It took a while for Frank to get served. I thought about going to the ladies. I thought about slipping out of the door and running back to Mrs Hollister's.

He reappeared with our drinks and plonked himself back down in front of me, "Sorry about that, they had to change-"

"Tell me about Owen," I blurted.

Frank pursed his lips, nodded and drained the dregs of his previous pint.

"What do you want to know?"

"How... how did he die?"

There was part of me, still, that clung to the fantasy Owen wasn't dead. There was no body. There'd been a service for him, but no funeral. Nothing to put in the ground and weep over, no soil to throw on top of him. No punctuation mark for the end of his life.

Perhaps he was still in Germany somewhere. All the prisoners were supposed to be home now, but mistakes happened. Or he was in a hospital, or he'd lost his memories and was wandering around the back lanes of France with no idea who he was.

I'd entertained every kind of fantasy possible that, somehow, my Owen was alive and one day he would come back for me. We loved each other, we were meant to be together forever. This wasn't how life worked in the books, in the moving pictures, in the theatre. Love won out. Always.

So why not for me?

I needed to hear otherwise. As much as it would hurt me and break me further apart. It was the only thing I could think of that might finally convince all of me he was gone. That might allow my wounds to heal and bones to mend. There would always be scars, there would always be aches, I would always miss him. But I couldn't live like this. Not for the rest of my life. I would go mad.

Nothing could be worse than the truth.

Could it?

1943

Frank watched me closely.

Which, after twenty-three years of him ignoring me, I found a little unsettling.

Whatever he was about, I decided I could play games too.

I just had to wait. He couldn't stay here forever. Eventually, he'd have to return to London and his anti-aircraft battery. However compassionate the Secretary of State for War was, James Grigg wasn't going to let Frank spend the rest of the war tending to his "sick" wife.

Maybe Frank would try, and the thought of the Military Police locking him up for desertion was one I found so darkly amusing it immediately speared me with guilt.

What if-

No!

I wasn't insane. Frank wasn't caring for me. I wasn't his wife, I was his prisoner and had been, one way or another, since I'd opened my legs for him in a moment of drunken, life-changing stupidity.

So, I played the damaged, meek little woman he wanted me to believe I was. It wasn't difficult given that was pretty much the role I'd filled during our marriage. Doing whatever Frank wanted me to do, even when those things involved him beating me.

And while he watched me, I watched him.

How long could he keep playing "nice" Frank, the doting husband? How long before the real Frank lost his temper, or got bored with making me tea, cooking my meals, doing the chores and going to the shops. How long before he started begrudging all the time I kept him from his precious paintings?

Whatever really churned behind the burnt hazel of his eyes, it stayed well hidden. Never a glare, never a snarl, never a sneer. Never any of the expressions I'd come to know so well.

One night he came to my room. My heart sank, expecting him to do what he always did when he came for his business. Instead, he climbed into bed, told me he loved me, and held me till he fell asleep.

I laid awake, staring at the shadows, listening to his low, throaty snores. Confusion and anger kept me from sleep. The confusion I understood. Part of me wanted to get my copy of *Stalky & Co* and throw it at him, demanding to know what he was doing? Why he was lying, why he was treating me like this?

I didn't.

I'd be patient. I would wait. Soon he would be gone. And so would I.

My eyes turned to the empty space where Tilly's cot once stood and everything churning inside me melted into guilt.

Another what if.

Should I stay and try and find out what had really happened to my daughter? Perhaps it had been gypsies. But if a faceless thing could kill my lover, why couldn't it snatch my baby away. And...

And what would some dark apparition want with a child anyway? Had it spent sixteen years nurturing and caring for her? Not likely. But I still wanted to know.

And it's always the not knowing that kills you.

Several times I thought something moved in the room. As always, I never saw it directly. Just the turn of a shadow out of the corner of my eye. The first time I half sat up sharply enough for Frank to shuffle next to me.

When I stared into the darkness, nothing stared back. I wanted to scream, wanted to know what it had done with Tilly? Why it had killed Tom? But I didn't. All that would achieve was waking Frank. Who would no doubt smooth my hair or squeeze my hand and give me his new look. The one I was starting to think of as pained sympathy.

My delusional wife is screaming at thin air now...

Poor lamb.

I eased myself back down. Waiting for it to skulk about some more.

If I could just get a proper look at it.

Several more times the shadows in the corner of my eye moved, but whenever I turned there was nothing.

How could I discover what something was and whether it'd snatched my baby when I never got more than the most fleeting of glimpses, when it would never answer my questions?

But the thing *could* be seen.

Davey had seen it. Gladys had seen it. Izzy and Tom, before they died, had seen it.

So why couldn't I?

When Frank finally stirred, I pretended to be asleep. If he wanted to do his business that wouldn't deter him, but it might save me from having to talk to him.

The new improved Frank didn't wake me. He just kissed my forehead and tiptoed out of the bedroom. When the door clicked shut, I didn't move, waiting till his footsteps creaked down the corridor before opening my eyes.

The sun wasn't up, but it couldn't be far off as the night had softened a fraction.

I let out a shaky breath.

I hated Frank.

This wasn't any kind of revelation, but it felt more visceral now. Unlike the thing creeping around Grey Gull, the hatred was no longer something I could only see out of the corner of my eye. It had come into the light and was insisting I do something. The days of swallowing it and putting up with Frank were over. They should have been over a long time ago. The children had kept me here, along with my own fear. But now, the children were gone and the anger and hatred had devoured my fear. At least enough of it to do something other than cower and make excuses anyway.

A wet, lingering snicker rolled out of the shadows.

I sat bolt upright.

"Who are you?" I hissed, "What are you?"

Only a gull squawking at the coming sun answered me.

"What did you do with my baby?"

I was shaking, but with anger rather than fear.

Crazy woman... craaazzzyyy woman...

"I'm not crazy. I know you're real. You took Tilly, you killed Tom and Izzy and..." I gulped "...I'm going to kill you!"

More laughter. This time a gleeful hoot.

My bare feet thudded across the floor as I ran to the window and ripped back the curtain. The sea, grey, formless and stretching to the brightening horizon, greeted me.

Crazy! Hazy! Lazy! Lost your own baby!

I whirled around.

Nothing.

But something was in the room. I could sense it.

I hadn't felt it for weeks. Hadn't heard it or seen it. But now it was here again. A palpable sensation of dread and wrongness. I'd become so accustomed to it over my years in Grey Gull I hadn't even been aware of it beyond the unfocused certainty something here was *sloightly on th' huh.*

"I didn't hurt my baby; you did!"

I staggered into the middle of the room, spinning around as if I could just see every corner at the same time I'd spot my phantom tormentor, but whatever way my back was turned, the sound of scampering feet came from behind me.

Crazy! Hazy! Lazy!

"Stop it!"

Lost your own baby!

I wasn't thinking. I was beyond such rationality. The desire to understand it, communicate with it, trap and destroy it submerged beneath twenty-three years of hurt, anger, pain, fear and loss.

It whirled around me like an invisible dervish, taunting and laughing, and all I could do in return was shout and scream.

Crazy! Hazy! Lazy!

I lashed out with my fist. Connecting with nothing but gales of spiteful laughter as I stumbled forward.

Lost your own baby!

The laughter grew louder, dark and gleeful. I could almost feel spittle dampen my skin as if the thing was bare inches away, howling in my face.

I was screaming, it was laughing.

Then arms were about me, engulfing me.

"Beatrice, please..."

Frank.

I hadn't seen him come into the room until he was on top of me.

Trying to stroke my hair, hold me, shush me like I was a child awaking from a nightmare.

"Sweetness," the word breathed in my ear almost lost to the sniggering of my faceless, mocking companion.

Whore! The thing spat, *Loves you, but you fucked another. Dirty, nasty, ungrateful whore!*

I squirmed away from Frank.

"Bea!" he called after me, "This must stop. You know what the doctor's said..."

"No, I don't, Frank!" I shouted back at him from the doorway, "I don't know, because there are no fucking doctors! You're making all this shit up!"

Frank's eyes widened like I'd slapped him.

So much for playing along with this charade till he went back to London.

I stormed out of the bedroom and flew down the stairs two at a time. Ignoring the gibbering that followed me.

Useless whore! Unfaithful slut! Craven harlot!

Frank's feet pounded after me. He was going to beat me hard for swearing at him. The veneer would crack and the sneering, controlling bastard I'd lived with for twenty-three years would be back. Belt in one hand, the other clenched into a fist.

I didn't care.

I was too angry to care.

Downstairs, I ripped *Stalky & Co.* from its place on the bookcase. Spinning around I found Frank bearing down on me, face crumpled with concern rather the anger. For some reason that just stoked my fire further.

I threw the book at him.

He batted it away with his forearm, and it fell to the floor, scattering newspaper cuttings like fat yellowing confetti.

"Stop playing games, Frank!" I yelled, scooping up one of the clippings as he stood dumbstruck. He wasn't used to me standing up to him, answering him back, not being his plaything, his scalded cat.

"Read this!" I screamed at him, holding up the cutting for him to see, "And tell me what happened to Tilly again?"

"Sweetness..."

"Read it."

Franks eyes moved from me to the clipping. His shoulders sagged; his mouth twitched. Quite what would happen when he had to admit this was all some stupid game, I couldn't imagine. I hadn't thought this through, but if it involved me walking out the front door of Grey Gull cottage and never coming back, maybe this wasn't a bad thing.

My faceless companion tittered.

Frank's eyes, all confused and sad – damn I'd never realised what a good actor he was – returned to me.

"Bea, please..."

"Well?" I demanded, waving the clipping as triumphantly as Neville Chamberlain returning from Munich under his nose, "What does it say, Frank, what does it fucking say?"

Frank's nostrils flared and he sucked in a breath before saying, "Prized cat disappears in mysterious circumstances..."

I laughed as manically as my faceless companion ever had.

Frank tilted his head, eyebrow inching up, "Read it for yourself, Bea."

Part of me wanted to screw it up into a ball and throw it at him. I didn't need to read the clipping. I'd read them all a thousand times in a vain, futile quest to find some clue to Tilly's whereabouts, to what had happened to her. I'd spent sixteen years tilting at that particular windmill.

"Read it," Frank said again, softly.

Almost despite myself I did. All those years of conditioning ran deep.

I blinked. My eyes taking a moment to focus and make the black letters on the yellowing paper stand out enough to make sense of them.

Prize Cat Disappears in Mysterious Circumstances.

I took a step backwards, then another till my back pressed against the bookcase.

"This has to stop, Sweetness..." Frank started saying, but I barely heard him. Partly because my eyes were too firmly fixed on the shaking slip of paper in my hand, trying to make the words say what they should say, but mainly from the hissing voice spitting gleefully in my ear.

Useless whore! Useless whore! The useless whore made up what she saw!

1919

My Owen, who I had fallen in love with on a particular day in 1911 that I could no longer recall, died on 9th October 1916 on the Ancre Heights, which, Frank told me, was a series of hills to the north-east of a place called Thiepval. It was the one hundred and first day of the Battle of the Somme.

Some of it I knew from Frank's letters, but the details had been sketchy. I wanted to know more. I wanted to know the things Frank kept from the letters. I wanted to smell the gun smoke, feel the mud, know the fear, hear the explosions. I wanted to know what my Owen had known at the end of his short life.

At least, I thought I'd wanted to know.

The more he said, however, the more I wanted him to stop.

Frank spoke slowly, eyes not wavering from me. They were a brown and dark as burnt hazel, intense, rarely blinking. In other circumstances I might have thought them captivating. The more he talked, the more he looked at me, the more difficult I found it to pull my gaze from those eyes. They had a terrible beauty to them as I sat listening to the things they had seen.

Frank and Owen's battalion formed part of the Reserve Army which had been held back from the dreadful first days of the Somme in order to push through and exploit the gains made in the initial attacks. But nearly 20,000 British soldiers died on the first day and the expected gains did not materialise.

Over the coming months their battalion fought at places called Pozieres, Mouquet, Thiepval Ridge amongst others, alongside Canadian and Anzac troops. Owen had never said where he was, all his letters went through a censor to make sure he didn't give anything away a German spy might be interested in, but the tone of his letters changed in those last months. They became shorter, the handwriting looser, his words seemingly rattled out as if he were throwing down what he could in a hurry. He started writing less about the future and more about the past. More about the things we'd done than the things we were going to do.

I'd read them so many times I'd all but memorised them word for word. Now I had the names of the places he'd been in when he wrote them. It made nothing easier or harder. But it was something.

"Plenty of our mates didn't make it through those scrapes, but Owen, me and another lad, Fred Greenwood, we stuck together and didn't get a scratch. Had lads gunned down on one side of us, blown to bits on the other, but we was charmed..." Frank's eyes dropped for a second as he swirled his beer, "...so we reckoned..."

When his eyes returned to me, he said, "All Owen used to talk about was you. He got right teased about it by the other lads, but it never stopped him. He was always reading your letters and scribbling down ones for you, looking at your photograph, talking about how good things were gonna be when the war was done."

I wiped the back of my hand over my eyes. I wanted to scream, I wanted to throw my drink against the wall, I wanted to curl up on the floor, I wanted to run out of the smoky pub and keep on running till my heart burst. But I didn't do any of those things.

I just sat. I just listened.

"Greenie and me, we didn't have girls back home. Greenie did at the start, but he got a letter calling things off as soon as we reached France. I..." he shrugged "...but Owen was so in love it was almost like it was enough for all of us. He was going to make it through just so he could marry you. Greenie and me, we reckoned if we stayed close to Owen, maybe we'd see it through too. We thought he had enough love for all of us.

We'd hear what you'd been up to as soon as Owen read your letter, I guess he kept parts back, but..." he snorted and finished his pint, "...it was almost like you were our sweetheart too..."

Those intense eyes swept over me again, he scooped up his empty glass and headed for the bar without another word.

As soon as he submerged into the crowd at the bar, I shot to my feet.

I'd been wrong. I didn't need to know how Owen died. Nothing was going to change by hearing about his death, my life was what it was and... really it wasn't so bad! Maybe I was a little lonely, maybe... maybe...

I took a step towards the door. A woman glanced at me, the man with her smiled and nodded at the table.

For a moment I was caught between their regard and the flood of emotions swirling around me, battering my soul from side to side.

Then I shook my head and dropped back down. The man gave me a rueful grin, the woman scowled at me like I'd stolen a pauper's sandwich.

Frank returned with more drinks soon after. I looked at my previous glass and found it empty. Had I drunk it? I supposed I must have.

I thanked him and took a sip. The sip went on for quite a while. My hand was shaking badly when I put it down.

"You want me to go on?" Frank asked, his tone gentle. Which was something I mistook for kindness.

I nodded.

"If this is too much...?"

"Tell me how it happened..."

My voice sounded together even if the rest of me was in pieces. I exchanged the drink for a handkerchief to dab my nose.

"We were attacking Fritz atop a hill overlooking the Ancre valley. The brass wanted it taken as it would allow us to fire artillery down on the German positions. The Germans were well dug in; they always were. There was a redoubt, a fortress cut out of the soil, tunnels connecting trenches and bunkers. It had seven machine gun emplacements, all protected by masses of barbed wire. We knew it'd be the Devil's own job."

Frank pressed his lips together hard enough to force most of the colour from them.

"We'd been trying to get them off that hill since the beginning of July. For a week and a half, we'd been attacking Fritz; us, the Canadians, Aussies and Kiwis. We'd get a foothold in a trench, they'd counter-attack and push us back, we'd go again, they'd go again. All the time hurling artillery shells at each other, all the time having to get through the barbed wire, having to get past the machine guns...

It was all bad, but Ancre Heights..." Frank sipped his stout, blurring the sharp edges of his thin moustache with white froth. I noticed his hand had started trembling. His eyes followed mine, and he curled the hand into a fist.

"On the 9th, we were to launch another attack; before dawn, this time. 4.30am it was. Nice early start, boys, Captain Boyce told us. I remember that. Must have been one of the last things he ever said..." Frank tapped a finger against his forehead, "...took one between the eyes before we'd gone twenty yards over the top. It was supposed to be a surprise attack..." Frank shook his head, "...but you had to get up a damn sight earlier than 4.30am to surprise Fritz...

Hard thing running towards people trying to kill you. To keep going forward when everything in you is screaming to go the other way. It was dark, but the Germans fired flares, these little suns. We tried to find cover every time one ignited, like some children's game. You only moved when they couldn't see you. If they saw you move..." he shrugged "...then you got knocked out of the game for good."

My hands were gripping each other to stop them shaking as I visualised what Frank was describing. The pub became a battlefield. The cigarette smoke hung about us like the smoke from exploding shells, the laughter, screams, a banging door, a rifle's retort.

"Between the flares, we sprinted from one piece of cover to the next, hoping the wire wouldn't snag us before the next one went up. One guy, Spoons we called him, dunno why, he was with us, then he screamed, the wire got him. A flare went up; he couldn't move. We threw ourselves into a crater. When I looked back, he was like an animal caught in a trap. A machine gun got him. Cut him near in half..."

I felt sick. My fingers were cold, the blood must have drained from my face. Frank looked up from his pint, I thought he was going to ask if I was alright again, if I wanted him to stop. He didn't.

"Dunno what was worse, the dark or the light. Without the flares, there was just the blinks and flashes of weapon fire, the boom of the artillery and mortars. Ours going over to try and keep Fritz's head down, theirs... theirs trying to take ours clean off.

About halfway up the hill, I thought we were gonna get stuck. I said something about staying where we were. Greenie said they'd shoot us for cowardice if we did. Didn't seem a bad deal right then, least I'd get a breakfast and a cigarette before they shot me..." Frank laughed, hollow and empty.

"Owen said something about us having a job to get done, that we'd be alright if we stayed together. Looked out for each other. Dunno if he believed that or not. We could hear lads crying, begging for help in the silences between the gunfire. One of them might have been Spoons... nothing we could do.

Not sure how long we stayed in that hole, seemed like forever, probably more like five minutes. Then Fritz's guns quietened, where we were attacking anyway. We were on the far right of the attack. Learned later the other end of the line was a slaughter, and they got nowhere near the redoubt. We did better.

Went again. It wasn't a steep hill, but it felt like a mountain when we ran up it. Going as fast as we could, hoping our artillery would keep their heads down long enough to quieten the machine guns while we cut through the next wall of wire.

Tricky business. Our artillery was trying to put down a curtain ahead of us to allow us to move forward. During daylight, we'd have aircraft up to make sure we weren't putting shells where our boys were. But in the dark, it came down more to guesswork.

We crept up that hill a few yards at a time. Machine gun teams setting up to return fire, running when the flares fizzed out, and our shells were falling on the redoubt."

Frank raised the stout to his lips, this time wiping away the froth from his moustache.

"Run, cut, shoot, throw yourself down... over and over... over and bloody over..." he shook his head, "...dunno how long it took us to get there, but it was starting to get light. A grey, sombre dawn it was, no sun to see even if smoke hadn't been shrouding the world.

Don't remember too much about getting to the first trench... I don't want to remember. Running across no man's land is terrifying, fighting in a trench..." he shook his head again, violently this time, as if irritated by a wasp "...all bayonets, grenades, rifle butts, fists. When you can't see Fritz, you think he's some monster, blood red eyes, seven foot tall, invincible. When you see him face to face... they were just boys, as scared as we were. And you had to kill him. Up close... close enough to smell, close enough to taste..."

Frank shivered and closed his eyes. He was trembling like a cat in a thunderstorm.

He stayed quiet for a long time. Eventually, he released a slow, shaky breath and opened his eyes again. I half expected there to be tears, but his eyes remained dry. The emotion that had bubbled beneath his last words was gone when he started talking again.

"Dunno how many of us made it into the trench. Enough to force Fritz out. Suddenly, there was no one left to kill. There was only silence. It was like God had paused the whole war to give us a moment to catch our breaths and think about what we'd just done. I think I even heard some birdsong. Though maybe I imagined that.

We looked at each other. Amazed we were still alive, wondering what to do next. There weren't any officers with us, just a couple of NCOs who were as young as the rest of us.

Weren't time to put a kettle on, though; we all knew that well enough. Fritz wouldn't let us get comfy in their lovely deep trench. It was only one small section of the redoubt, and they'd be looking to kick us out pronto before we could get more men in.

We sent up a flare to signal we'd secured part of the redoubt; there was nothing else to do but wait for Fritz to come and try and turf us out. It was a race, and our boys had a lot further to come than Fritz, and they were under fire from artillery and other machine gun posts. It weren't no walk in the park to reach us, but we hoped..." Frank sighed.

"Turned out we didn't have long to wait, and it weren't a close race in the end. Fritz came pouring back at us. We tried to hold our position, enough of our mates had died to take it in the first place, so we weren't gonna give it up without a fight, but... but... there were too many of them. Too bloody many. They came at us from either end and over the top from their positions behind.

In the end, there were only two choices: get out or die. And that's never really much of a choice.

Sergeant Holly started screaming at us to retreat. He was the most senior man left, and no one was inclined to argue. Owen, Greenie and me were still together. We didn't need telling twice. We scrambled out of that trench as fast as we could. Some boys were still fighting further up. Dunno if any of them got out. I don't think so.

Greenie and me went up first; Owen waited at the bottom to cover us. Once we were up, we covered him, firing back along the trench as Fritz came barrelling in.

Owen came up and over the sandbags with us, but he slipped as he got to the top. Greenie grabbed him and hauled him up, but Owen lost his grip on his rifle, and it fell back into the trench..."

Frank's eyes turned hollow, as if he couldn't see me anymore. He paused for a moment, and I wanted to scream at him. Whether to finish or to shut up, I couldn't tell you. With each word he spoke, I felt something growing, some dark bubble pushing out in every direction, filling me and cracking me.

"Thing is, if you go backwards and have your rifle, it's retreating under enemy fire. If you got back safely, they said, *Better luck next time, boys, get a brew on and take a break*. But you go backwards without your rifle, and it's discarding your weapon. That's cowardice in the face of the enemy. They put you up against a wall and shoot you for that."

I think I said something. I don't know what. I'm not sure it was anything coherent.

"Owen didn't even think about it; he just jumped straight back down after that bloody rifle. The stupid thing was there were any number of rifles he could have grabbed on the way back down that hill... but he was gone before we knew it.

He was down in a flash. He was a fast bugger was Owen. Got the rifle and was scrambling back up. Greenie was screaming at him. Most of the other lads left alive were legging it, but Owen, Greenie and me, we stuck together. That's what we always said. We'd stick together till the end..."

Frank took another long sip, his eyes staying on the glass as he carried on, "Bullet took him in the back, first one, then another. I had his hand, trying to pull him up. I'll never forget the look on his face; it was just... surprise. Like he was thinking... hey, this ain't meant to happen. Then he said, "Bugger..." and he fell backwards into the trench.

There was an explosion. I didn't realise at first, but Greenie had lobbed a grenade at Fritz and sent them packing.

I don't remember doing it, but I jumped back in. I couldn't leave Owen. Don't think I realised how bad he was hit...

He was still alive, but the blood was already bubbling out of his mouth. We'd seen enough to know when a lad wouldn't make it. I tried to get him up, but he shook his head. Then he said, "Bea..." and started clawing at his tunic pocket. I knew what he had in there. We all did.

I took out the photograph for him. The one of you and him together. He loved that bloody photograph. Said it was like looking at his future. Of how the world was gonna be after the war finished. Was forever staring at it. If you could wear something out just by looking at it..."

Frank's eyes rose back to mine.

"That was the last thing he ever saw. You and him together. Happy."

Frank undid his own tunic pocket and pulled something out. Avoiding the beer puddles on the table, he placed a photograph before me. Owen and me. Him in uniform, me and my Sunday best. Taken that final time he came home. After we'd spent our one night together. After I refused to marry him till after the war. Again.

I don't remember too much more after that. The tears came, floods of them as I stared at that photograph. It was dog-eared and stained. Dark smudges and a single bloody fingerprint.

I pressed my finger over it and kept staring till I could see nothing for crying.

Frank put his hand atop mine. He gave me a handkerchief at some point. Later, he moved his chair next to me so he could hold me.

Inside something had burst. That great black swelling, exploding to fill my mind with black stars.

I took to my bed for days, unable to eat, talk, think, do anything. I was lost, I was shattered, I was broken.

But I knew how my Owen had died at last. Which was something, or at least I thought it was.

It was the other side of a lifetime before I found out how little of what Frank had told me was true.

1943

Frank placed the tray next to the bed.

There was soup and bread.

Did Frank know how to make soup? It looked like lumpy ditch water. So, probably not.

"You need to eat, Sweetness."

I made no move to either eat or acknowledge him. It all took too much effort.

"There's an airgram from Francis. He sounds... well..."

Frank put the envelope on the tray. It was more appealing than the soup, but I didn't pick it up. There was no hurry. I had plenty of time. One of the lesser-known advantages of going mad turned out to be giving you quite the abundance of free time.

"How are you feeling, Sweetness?"

My shoulders twitched. Everything seemed so hard. Even thinking. The burden of hauling my lunacy around, I supposed.

I expected my faceless companion to howl its demented agreement. But there was nothing. It was a quiet day. Which was good.

"If we go back to the hospital, you know what will happen, don't you?"

Frank brought up what the doctors wanted to do regularly. The way a parent tried to make an errant child behave with threats of Santa Claus deciding you hadn't done enough to deserve any presents that year.

My eyes, tired, heavy and probably bloodshot, held his burnt hazel ones for a second or two before drifting away.

"Yes," I said.

I still possessed no memory of any doctors, but Frank was adamant their next treatment would be a lobotomy. It was the best hope. Cut out a piece of my malfunctioning brain, and the rest would start working as it should. It was a very promising technique. They'd had a lot of success with it.

So Frank said.

"You've got to try really hard to get better. That's the important thing. Isn't it?"

When I dutifully replied, "Yes, Frank," he bent down and kissed my forehead.

Even his breath smelt tinged with turpentine and paint. Which couldn't be right.

"That's the ticket, Sweetness," he ruffled my hair then finally left me alone.

I watched him lock the door after him and waited until his creaking footsteps faded into the silence. Then I wiped a hand back and forth over my forehead till I no longer felt the impression of his lips.

Several days had passed since I'd discovered the newspaper clippings I'd preserved within the care of *Stalky & Co*, mainly concerned a pedigree cat by the name of Mungo that had disappeared the night before a prestigious show. One his distraught owner insisted he was going to win. The story intimated foul play, though there was no mention of gypsies. The clippings continued over subsequent weeks, but Mungo and the circumstances of his disappearance remained unresolved in the final one.

I wasn't sure exactly how many days had passed. Things were a little foggy. In fact, they were so foggy I'd begun to wonder if Frank was slipping something into my tea. It didn't seem likely he'd laced my soup as there was clearly nothing in it besides water and the off cuts from a mouldy turnip.

That made me want to giggle. Then cry.

I managed to do neither and went back to staring at the ceiling.

At one point, I thought a board squeaked the way a board might under a sneaky, tiptoeing foot. Later, I thought I caught something move in the corner of my eye, something dark and *very* on th' huh.

I didn't turn my head either time. Why bother? I was imagining it. If I could imagine reading those clippings time and time again and not figure out they were about a cat rather than my daughter, I was capable of imagining just about any bloody thing.

So, I kept my eyes on the ceiling and my foggy, broken mind drifting nowhere in particular.

Sometime later, when I did look, the tray with its watery soup was gone. I must have drifted off to sleep because I hadn't heard Frank come in. Perhaps he was better at tiptoeing than my faceless companion. Or maybe I'd been too busy off being Catherine the Great or Joan of Arc or... *someone*. Someone other than Beatrice Harryman nee Clay, at any rate.

Earlier, I asked Frank when he was going back to London. He'd simply smiled, kissed my forehead and told me not to worry about. He was kissing my forehead a lot lately. Was he hoping to kiss my splintered, misfiring brain better? On the face of it, it seemed as likely to cure me as a lobotomy, and it'd be a lot less messy.

Perhaps there was no war. Maybe Churchill wasn't Prime Minister and the Nazis didn't exist. When you thought about it, the chances of one little man with a side parting and a silly moustache causing so much trouble did seem a little unlikely.

Perhaps Mr Chamberlain was still Prime Minister, and the world was ticking over very nicely. All the nasty stuff was only bubbling about inside my broken head.

Several times I did hear the drone of bombers overhead, but were they real?

It hurt to think about it. Having to turn every single thing your senses told you over and over to check how likely it was to be real. Better to watch the ceiling, not seeing anything out of the corner of my eye and not hearing anything but the sea and the gulls. I was sure the sea and the gulls existed, but I was prepared to flip a coin on pretty much everything beyond that.

The fact Frank was locking me in my room should have rankled, but as I had no interest in getting out of bed, it didn't matter.

"It's for your own good, Sweetness," Frank had told me in another sentence punctuated by his lips on my forehead.

Of course it was. Who knew what trouble I might cause if I got out of the house?

Later, I dreamt of Owen and Tom, the three of us were walking through a field choked with wildflowers; Owen held my right hand and Tom my left. Neither man troubled by the fact I was in love with them both. Birds – none of which were gulls – sang and the warm breeze carried the scent of a million flowers.

Nobody spoke. We just walked. The field went on without end, but that didn't matter. Golden light flooded the world, and the sun would never set.

When I awoke, I had a smile on my lips, though it soon melted away. Even a mind as sick as mine couldn't imagine that had been anything other than a dream.

As I tried to keep the memory from evaporating in the way dreams often do in the daylight, I heard voices in the distance. Someone was shouting.

I frowned. I could have been imagining it, but the voices seemed real. Just muffled.

Stupid as a turd, makes up everything she heard!

That voice seemed real too, and close enough to make me jump.

I sat up and looked around, despite telling myself I wouldn't let my personal phantom bother me anymore. For a second, I thought I saw something in the far corner. Something so tall it had to bend its misshapen head beneath my bedroom's low ceiling, a figure upon which the hazy afternoon light didn't fall. Something with too many angles, too many bends. Something that didn't hang the way it should. Something sloightly on th' huh.

By the time my eyes focused and settled, however, nothing was there.

Despite my heavy leaden limbs, I pulled myself to my feet and padded barefoot to the door. Even though it was locked I turned the handle anyway. The door rattled in its frame.

Crazy bitch! Mad as a witch!

This time I didn't jump or look around. Instead, I pressed my ear to the door. Could you hear anything better that way, or was that only something the hero did in a storybook? I couldn't say, but I made out the next voice clearly enough. It was Frank.

And it sounded like angry, mean Frank. The one I knew well, even if that recollection might not be any more accurate than the newspaper cuttings I'd kept in my copy of *Stalky & Co.*

"Fuck off! And if I see you again, there'll be trouble. Hear me, do you?"

There was another voice, but no matter how hard I pressed my ear to the door, I couldn't make out who it might be or what they were saying. The next thing I heard was more identifiable, though. A door slamming shut. The front door, presumably.

I frowned; who would Frank be angry with? Old Frank, make-believe Frank if I had invented so much of my past, had been angry at just about the whole world, me included. But the new, improved, loving, caring Frank? He hadn't raised his voice to me once.

Mad, mad, mad. Mad and bad and so, so sad...

"Shut up," I snapped. Probably at myself, if that was where my faceless companion actually lived.

Despite everything, a part of me insisted – insisted with red-faced indignation – I was not a lunatic. Maybe all lunatics heard that voice. Maybe believing it was part of the whole lunacy package. But that was still the voice I wanted to listen to over Frank and his forehead kissing soothery or my faceless companion's jabbering insults.

No more voices came from downstairs. No more sounds.

I moved across the room to the window. Tiptoeing like my faceless companion liked to do. I didn't want Frank to know I was out of bed. I didn't know why, I just didn't. My madness probably had something to do with it, but so what.

The bedroom window faced the shingle beach, dropping down to the sea. The front door and views of the path cutting through the marsh connecting Grey Gull so tenuously to the rest of the world were on the other side.

I didn't expect to see whoever Frank had been shouting at from this window, but it was my only shot as I didn't have any others readily available.

Nobody was about. I could see the studio and some of the other little outhouses the salt-wind was gradually reducing to split, grey kindling. Beyond them, a gunmetal sea swelled and bobbed all the way to the cloud-curtained horizon.

I pressed my nose against the glass.

For all the years I'd thought myself trapped within the confines of the Castle, I'd always had the freedom to leave it. To feel the sea-air on my face, the shingle under my feet and the great expanse of sky above me. It was an illusory kind of freedom, but at least it was beautiful. Now I really was a prisoner.

It's for your own good, Sweetness...

But was it?

I might be a lunatic, but I wasn't a dangerous one. Neither to myself nor anyone else.

Was Frank keeping me under lock and key for my own protection, or because, finally, the possibility of walking away from this place, from Frank and this life we shared, had become something more than a pipedream? Tom was gone and the promise of a new life in Kansas with him, but the door my lover opened was still ajar.

All I had to do was walk through it.

But Frank couldn't know that, could he?

If Tom was an illusion, nobody outside my mind knew about him, what I'd felt and what he'd offered.

A floorboard creaked. I didn't look, but I caught a reflection in the glass. Something was behind me, something tall and wrong. Something not quite hung together the way a man should be.

Something that was watching me.

I whirled around.

The room was empty, as it always was.

But the sense of not being alone remained, along with a faint, familiar smell of something rotten. I couldn't see it because light didn't fall on it the way it should.

But it was there all the same.

What was I thinking?

That this thing, this faceless companion, was whispering in Frank's ear? That it'd told him about Tom?

It seemed unlikely, not least because Frank would have killed me if he knew I'd been unfaithful. The Frank of my memories anyway. But was he the real Frank?

I closed my eyes and turned back to the window, trying to calm myself and find something to cling to that would tell me I was not mad. Since seeing those clippings, I'd been prepared to accept everything Frank said was true.

But was it?

I opened my eyes.

A figure stood on the beach, watching the cottage. Not a nightmarish figure, but one that, in its own way, was slightly on th' huh too.

Davey Acorns.

A man who, if Frank was right, didn't exist.

The day was overcast but bright, I wasn't mistaking him for anyone else. He stood at an angle to Grey Gull. Would he be able to see me? I waved frantically but Davey just stood, hands thrust deep into his pockets, the peak of his flat cap pulled low over his eyes.

Slowly, Davey turned away and started ambling up the beach, head lowered as if in thought, hands still in his pockets.

He didn't fade away like some apparition; he just walked along the shoreline till his feet took him out of my eye line.

Like any real man would…

1919

The days after I first met Frank passed in a blur, though the man I would spend the rest of my life with featured little in them.

His words, given breath by my imagination, swirled constantly about me. Seeing that rifle slip from Owen's hands, screaming at him to leave it, begging him to run, pleading with him not to jump back into the trench. All as if I could just summon enough belief, he might somehow hear me and change his fate.

Frank had been kind, gentle, compassionate and absolutely nothing like the man he really was, but thoughts of Owen and his death raced around my mind like a howling storm, deafening and dumbing my senses.

Perhaps if I had kept my wits about me, I would have noticed things that would have benefited me greatly. Maybe I would have spotted his compassion was hollow, his gentleness affected, the kindness a mask. But I didn't.

I have little recollection of leaving him; he walked me to the bus stop and waited with me. He asked me several times if I was alright, he told me to keep his handkerchief which was now well soiled with tears, snot and makeup from my excessive crying. He hugged me. I recall thinking it felt nice and that his hands never wandered anywhere untoward. I remember him trembling as he held me for quite some time. Naturally, I cried again. I thought perhaps he needed the comfort as much as I did after recounting the death of his friend so vividly.

One more thing to add to my list of wrong assumptions.

He said something about seeing me again. I said yes. I had not considered it a romantic invitation. I didn't consider it as anything; I was too numb. My wounds, which had never fully healed since I'd received the telephone call from Owen's Dad in 1916, had split open again.

I did not sleep for days. Mrs Hollister floated around me with endless cups of tea and slices of cake; even Irene noticed my slack-faced staring and puffy eyes.

I went to work, somehow. If I achieved anything productive, I really cannot say. I just kept imagining my Owen on the edge of that trench, the rifle slipping from his hands... the whole scene as Frank described it on a never-ending carousel. I was trapped in some satanic picture house, forced to watch the love of my life die over and over and over again.

Several times I thought I could actually hear the crump of artillery shells, the rattle of machine guns, the cries of the dying. The smoke of battle obscuring my vision, the stink of war assaulting my nose.

Like the apparitions to later come in Grey Gull, they were too fleeting and uncertain to completely convince me anything uncanny was occurring, but they rattled me badly all the same.

Like most people, I had always suffered the occasional nightmare, but I'd never experienced them awake.

This continued deep into the week following my meeting with Frank. I was starting to believe it would never end; perhaps it wouldn't have if things had happened differently. But life has a way of intervening sometimes, though, if it was God's way of saving my sanity, it was at a price I never would have agreed to.

When I returned to Mrs Hollister's on the Thursday after another glassy-eyed day at work, I found a telegram waiting for me.

It was from Mrs Wright, Dad's housekeeper.

"Is it something... serious?" Mrs Hollister asked, hovering.

Few people sent telegrams enquiring if you were having a good day. During the war, their arrival often heralded the very worst news, but even in peacetime, being handed one was still a considerable worry.

It was. Dad, who I'd spoken to the Saturday I met Frank and had sounded his normal self, was seriously ill, and I should come home immediately.

I didn't answer Mrs Hollister's question; I couldn't. I thought I was going to be sick; I couldn't catch my breath, the world span around me. I'd never been punched in the stomach before (that came much later, care of my loving husband) but that's what it felt like.

The next I knew, I was sitting in Mrs Hollister's best armchair, having a cup of tea pressed into my shaking hands.

"My Dad..." I managed to say over the rattle of cup and saucer.

From how Mrs Hollister looked at me, I think I might already have said that a few times.

"You must go first thing in the morning. I will send a telegram so they know you're coming. Just leave me the details and I will arrange things. We shall get a taxicab to take you directly to Paddington for the first train, and I will inform your employer you have to take a leave of absence."

I didn't know what to say, so I tried sipping the tea. It was hot enough to scald my tongue and sweet enough to strip the enamel from my teeth. It helped to bring my wits back.

Mrs Hollister was as good as her word and got me to Paddington in one piece to catch the first train. I suppose I could have managed it anyway, but my mind, already off-kilter from my meeting with Frank Harryman, was in danger of collapsing.

I loved Dad to bits. He was as kind and gentle a man as you could ever hope to meet. He never got angry, never had a cross word to say about anyone, saw the best in every soul he met and left everyone's life better for knowing him. None more so than mine.

Mum passed away when I was little, so young I hardly remember her. Dad, who brought me up with some help from my Gran, never remarried. He filled my childhood with love and happiness despite losing Mum. The thought he might die was an incomprehensible one. Surely the world couldn't keep turning without the Reverend Arthur Clay.

He wasn't an old man either. He'd only turned 53 that year, and every memory I have of him was of a rosy-cheeked man full to the brim with life and energy.

Every memory save the final ones.

Mrs Wright was waiting for me when I got home to the vicarage, an archetypal Cotswolds limestone cottage next to Dad's church, covered in climbing roses upon which, in my childhood memories at least, the sun always shone.

Dad's housekeeper was a rotund woman of boundless enthusiasm and strong views who brooked no argument on any subject from anyone, from the Good Lord downwards. Owen had always referred to her as "Mrs Never Wrong," which I usually rewarded with a disapproving look and a smile I couldn't always suppress. He'd had a point.

"Oh, Beatrice," she said, opening the door before I'd gotten halfway up the little cobblestone path to the vicarage.

My heart sank beneath my tumbling stomach. Ever since I'd read her telegram, I'd been hoping Mrs Wright had been exaggerating. Notwithstanding, she was a woman who had downplayed every difficulty and calamity life had ever thrown at her.

But the look on her face confirmed my worst fears.

"Is...?" was all I got out before Mrs Wright shook her head, loosening a few, greying strands from her normally impeccable bun.

"He's upstairs..." she said, ushering me inside. The vicarage smelt of furniture polish, fresh flowers and the aromatic ghost of Dad's pipe, just as it did every summer.

After I'd taken off my coat and hat and put my little suitcase by the stand in the hall, Mrs Wright ushered me into the parlour, where Dad took tea and cake while listening to his parishioners' woes and worries. And scandalous gossip, as he'd often confessed to me with a theatrical wink.

"He's had a bad fall," she rapped a knuckle on her head, "fair knocked his bells to Timbuktu."

"But... he's going to be alright?" I asked, hope rising; a fall was nowhere near the top of the list of dreadful possibilities I'd been compiling since the previous night.

"It was a nasty one, but, on its own, nothing a few days in bed won't put to rights..." her voice was low, and her eyes kept darting to the ceiling.

"On its own?"

"Beatrice, your father hasn't been well for some time."

"But... he never said anything to me?" As soon as the words escaped, I knew why. He wouldn't want to worry me.

"You should go up and see him, but if he's asleep..."

I nodded my understanding.

"But what's wrong with him?"

The voice I spoke to on the telephone every Saturday from the telephone in Camberwell Green post office was the same one I'd known since childhood; cheerful, bright, quick and full of love.

But what the eyes couldn't see...

As I left Mrs Wright to make tea and climbed the stairs, I couldn't believe much could have changed since the last time I saw Dad three months ago on my previous visit home.

By the time I reached the top of the stairs, I realised the last time I'd come had been nearer to six months.

Guilt's spear ran through me.

How many times and in how many ways had Dad asked me to come home since then? However many Saturdays since the last time I came home. And each time I'd found a way to say no. I didn't want to come home and be reminded of Owen, so I'd batted each cheerful request away, too busy wallowing in my own misery to hear what might have been running under Dad's eternally happy voice.

I opened the door to Dad's room as quietly as possible, but he'd already heard me.

"Hello, kitten..." he said, struggling to sit up, "...I thought it was you."

I stood in the doorway. I barely recognised the man in the bed. He'd aged at least twenty years since I'd last seen him, becoming a frail old man, stick thin, hollow-cheeked and ashen-faced.

"Dad?"

He slumped back into the pillows propping him up.

"Kitten..." the way Dad smiled reminded me of a skull, "...I'm afraid I'm a bit under the weather..."

1952/53

Beauty is never anything more than a gift bestowed upon you by another...

Merry's words stayed with me for a long time, as truths sometimes do.

Owen made me feel beautiful.

Tom made me feel beautiful.

Frank made me feel... other things.

I told Merry the story of my life, most of it anyway, as we sat beside each other on bone-white driftwood. There was more to it than I remembered. I talked until the sun was sinking over the marshes.

"It's late!" I said, with a start. I would not get back to the Castle before sunset now.

"It is," Merry agreed.

I jumped to my feet. I didn't know if Frank would be home, but he wouldn't be happy if I wasn't.

"You can tell me the rest tomorrow."

"The rest?" I said, eyes bouncing between the honey-fringed clouds and Merry, whose skin seemed to glow faintly in the rich light of the lowering sun.

"There is always more than we think there is."

He was right, but what remained to tell were not things I should discuss with a strange man. Things I had not even told Reverend Vaughn, and Merry was, after all, only a priest when the wind blew from the north.

"Tomorrow..."

Merry rose to his feet. He was tall, broad, and strong looking, despite the grey in his beard and hair.

"Come back tomorrow, Lady Beatrice."

With that, he sat on the driftwood and turned his eyes to the sea.

"Goodnight, Merry..."

I walked back towards the Castle without glancing back.

Frank was home, but he barely noticed me, just a slow eye raised from his paper followed by a slower, knowing grin. He was fatter than ever. A huge, pallid mountain of flesh that grew day by day, week by week, year by year.

He didn't come to my room anymore, which was a great relief. He'd likely squash me as flat as a bug beneath a boot if he were still interested in doing his business with me.

I ignored him, he did the same in return. Things worked better like that.

The next day I walked along the beach again, but there was no sign of Merry or his driftwood.

Nor the next or the next.

I did not know what I felt about this.

It'd been a long time since I'd spoken to anyone about anything. Frank did his best to pretend I didn't exist, and I spent most of my time floating around the cottage or the shore.

In the end, I let it fade as day after day drifted away without sight or sound of Merry. The world turned, the seasons changed, and the voices on the radio blathered about things I didn't understand.

And Frank got fatter.

He rarely seemed to move from his armchair.

Sometimes I'd come in, and he wasn't there. And sometimes he was. But I swear I never actually saw him move. Save for his head, which lifted from his chest to stare at me with glassy eyes. He laughed every now and then for no reason I could see, a good-natured, pleased-with-himself chortle that chilled me to the core. Like he was looking at one of his paintings and considered whatever hideous mess he'd scratched, scraped and splattered over the canvas to be a particular triumph.

Occasionally, he cried. I didn't know why. I felt no need to ask. When he did, he sometimes held out his hands, pudgy fingers splayed wide. Perhaps it was his unrequited talent he wept for. Once in a while he said sorry through the tears. Vomiting the word up as if he'd eaten a bad egg. I had no idea what he was apologising for. There was a lot to choose from.

I spoke to Frank no more than he spoke to me. I just scurried away from his regard as quickly as possible. He didn't want anything of me anymore, it seemed. I'd become only something that amused or upset him from time to time.

Beauty is never anything more than a gift bestowed upon you by another...

Those words of Merry remained with me far longer than the expectation I'd ever see him again. They made me think of Owen; they made me think of Tom.

Maybe it is never anything more, I thought, yet it is still so much.

Everyone should get to feel beautiful once or twice in their life. And I'd had that, at least. Frank might have taken everything else, but I still had that.

The memory of being beautiful.

One day the following year, I came across Merry again.

Sitting on his driftwood, just as before, though I'd never seen it without him on it.

It was autumn again; sea fret hung about the beach, softening its familiar contours and hazing the horizon, so water and sky bled into one another.

It's a year to the day...

Of course, it was.

Mr Time was a tricky fellow. I'd been told so.

"My Lady Beatrice!" Merry boomed.

"Merry..." I smiled.

"Just Merry, there's still no wind from the north," he confirmed, licking a finger and sticking it in the air.

In fact, the air was utterly still. The water through the faint mist was flat as glass and dark as forgotten dreams.

"Another year," I said, sitting next to him.

"Or another day," a smile split his beard, "it depends on how you look at it."

His hair, beard, skin, and clothes were identical to the previous two times I'd seen him. As was the bleached tree trunk we sat upon. His eyes, however, like the sea behind him, were now as grey as a mouse's coat.

A trick of the light. Obviously.

"So... tell me more about Frank?"

Just like that. A year passed for me, a day for him. It was cool on the beach, but the chill I felt had nothing to do with the weather.

"Who are you?" I asked, ignoring his question.

"I am Merry. Nothing more. Nothing less."

"Unless the wind blows from the north?"

He conceded the point with a shallow nod.

"And when the wind *does* blow from the north?"

His head tilted a fraction to the left, "I bring gifts for the good..."

"So, you're really Father Christmas?"

He laughed, a hearty chuckle. The kind Santa Claus might make, in fact.

When the chuckle subsided, he said, "No, Beatrice, not like Father Christmas. My gifts are not at all suitable for children. They are not for the innocent..."

I said nothing, which is usually best when you do not know what to say.

Merry held out his hand and indicated the driftwood next to him.

"Tell me more about Frank..." he said, eyes as dark, deep and wide as the silent sea behind him, "...tell me more about the monster..."

1943

I had to get out of the Castle.

Frank's leave couldn't possibly have lasted this long, yet he was still here. No soldiers had turned up to haul him away to face desertion charges. Every day I awoke expecting him to announce he was leaving, I ended up disappointed with him still being here.

I had to get out and see Davey. If Davey was real, I wasn't insane. And if I couldn't find Davey, I could go to *The Green Man*, Angie, Bert and Wally could confirm my memories. If they existed, of course.

All I needed to do was get away from Grey Gull. And my keepers.

The certainty both Frank and my faceless companion were keeping separate beady eyes on me grew by the day. Another sign of madness?

Fighting down my growing frustration, I tried to play the meek little invalid. Rarely venturing from my bed, I forced down whatever concoction Frank managed to produce masquerading as food and argued about nothing.

All the time, trying to figure out a way of escaping my confinement.

The day after I'd seen Davey through the window, the sun shone brightly, and I told Frank I'd like to sit outside and take some air.

I was as sure a flash of suspicion burned the hazel in Frank's eyes a fraction darker than usual.

"There is a bit of a breeze, Sweetness," he said, "we wouldn't want you catching a chill on top of everything, would we?"

"I can't stay in bed forever."

"Oh, of course not! But till you're better, eh?"

He kissed my forehead before I could say anything else.

The lock turned with a particularly forceful click after he shut the door.

After a few minutes, I climbed out of bed and used the chamber pot that now served as my toilet. Frank changed it regularly. He brought me a chipped enamel bowl of tepid water to wash every morning and three meals daily. He was turning out to be a surprisingly dutiful gaoler.

I moved to the chair by the window.

The sea was calm; only the faintest ripple disturbed the surface as it lapped the beach. There was no breeze.

The lock on the door wasn't sturdy. I could break it with enough time and effort. Just not silently.

From my view point I could see Frank's studio. Normally, I'd be confident he'd spend most of the day inside, but currently, nothing was normal. Frank was checking on me too often.

He would have to go into Creethorpe for shopping sooner or later. Giving me at least a couple of hours to make good my escape.

In all my years here, I'd conjured excuse after excuse not to leave. The children, lack of money, nowhere to go, the daunting prospect of being alone in the big world beyond this brittle shore. In reality, it was always fear of Frank that kept me here. What he would do if he caught me, coupled with the belief he'd installed that I couldn't survive without him.

But now, finally, I had found the motivation to run.

I needed to prove to myself I wasn't insane. That, somehow, Frank had tricked me with those cuttings. Of course, I might be slipping further into lunacy, delusion and paranoia. But I wasn't going to sit in this room for the rest of my life, waiting to get better.

I was certain Frank would ensure I never got better.

Frank had left me a pile of books to occupy me. Inevitably, they included *Stalky & Co.* His idea of a joke?

I picked one up at random, sat by the window with it open on my lap and stared out to the distant horizon.

All the time listening for the front door to close. Frank always used the kitchen door to go to the Studio, Repository or other outbuildings. The front one only when he was heading into town.

Perhaps he wouldn't go today. But one day he'd have to. Had he been since locking me in the bedroom to get better? I wasn't sure, I hadn't been paying attention to anything at first, but I didn't think so.

I didn't know what day it was; so far had my mind drifted after reading those clippings, but I didn't think it was the weekend. He would have to go and buy food soon.

The sun arced across the sea, and I followed its dance with the clouds as the hours slipped by. Listening. The house remained quiet. I could do something practical, like pack a bag. But I didn't. I couldn't shake the feeling I was being watched and any preparations would give away my intentions. More paranoia?

Perhaps Frank had snuck away for the day, and I'd missed it. As far as I could see, he wasn't in his studio, which was strange. He'd never let anything other than Adolf Hitler keep him out of there before. I couldn't see why a sick wife would inconvenience his painting.

I imagined him sitting in the kitchen, hands folded in his lap, eyes raised towards the ceiling. Watching me. Or at least listening for my movements like I was listening for his.

My imagination, I decided, was something probably best not indulged too much for the time being.

Eventually, the sound of approaching feet broke the silence. I dropped my eyes to the book I wasn't reading.

After some rattling and fumbling, Frank unlocked the door, opened it and bent down to pick up the tray he must have placed on the floor to unlock the door.

The wild notion I could smash something over his head and make a daring Robert Louis Stevenson-style dash for freedom over his bleeding body flashed through my mind.

Although a little extreme, I filed it away for further consideration.

"How are we doing, Sweetness?"

"Quite good..." I said, putting the book down and conjuring my own smile.

"That's wonderful! I made tea, and some bread and jam. I'll bring your dinner up later when I can think of something."

"I can come down and cook; you don't have-"

"Oh, I don't think you're ready for that, Sweetness. Best for you to rest. Get better. We can't afford any more episodes..." he tapped his forehead with a finger, "...can we?"

The thought of doctors cutting part of my brain out appalled me or would have if I believed it. Did I believe it? If what Frank was say-

Stop that thought right now, Beatrice Clay!

You're not mad. And you can damn well prove it.

But could I?

The memory of those yellowing clippings from the *Eastern Gazette* floated behind my eyes again...

"Sweetness?" Frank was crouching down in front of me. I hadn't noticed him cross the room.

That probably wasn't a good sign.

I smiled, "Yes?"

"You... looked like you were elsewhere?"

Frank was holding my hand. I squeezed it, "No, I'm good. Really. Quite hungry, actually."

He beamed and squeezed my hand in return.

He's going to kiss my forehead again now, isn't he?

"That's it, Sweetness. Keep your strength up, there's a good girl."

Frank kissed my forehead, and then ruffled my hair.

I forced the smile to stay on my face.

"Perhaps I could have cheese on toast later? I fancy that," I said.

"I don't think we have any cheese left. Must be the mice!"

"Never mind, it doesn't matter. Whatever you make will be lovely. Thank you for looking after me, Frank. You've been so kind."

"What else could I do? I love you."

Frank looked sincere. He sounded sincere. He held my eye and didn't look one little bit shifty.

And yet...

"I love you too."

When was the last time I'd said that?

If such a thought crossed Frank's mind too, it didn't show on his face either. He just looked happy.

A stab of guilt.

I tried to strangle that with the memory of the thick, cracked old leather belt Frank kept hanging from a hook in the hall. Just for special.

"I'll get cheese tomorrow. We're getting low on stuff. The best cheese in Creethrorpe, what do you say to that, eh, Sweetness?"

I didn't say anything.

But my smile was wide, white and, for once, entirely genuine.

1919

Dad lingered for six weeks before coming down with the flu and dying on a grey day in September that felt more like January.

He kept telling me to go back to work and stop fussing, I said work was fine with me staying as long as I needed, and to stop nagging. There weren't many times in my life I lied to Dad.

I took my annual leave of absence entitlement and when that was used up and they told me to return, I resigned. Mr Hegley warned me, on a telephone line that did not crackle anywhere near enough to mask his annoyance and disapproval, that resigning without working my notice would result in unfavourable references.

I hung up on him, no doubt inflicting further damage upon my references.

If Dad hadn't caught the flu, he would have lived a little longer, perhaps, but not much. I'm not sure his end was any kinder for being quicker.

I did what I could, which was next to nothing. We talked when he was strong enough, and I read to him when he wasn't. I held his hand when even listening was too much for him. I cried a lot too, but never in front of him.

Dad would be more upset about seeing me cry than he would be about dying.

Still numb from meeting Frank and learning about the manner of Owen's death, those days passed in a hollow blur of disbelief, pain and supressed rage.

How could this be happening? To Dad, to me, to the world. It seemed so unfair, so cruel, so bloody unworthy of a loving God.

I hid all that from Dad as best I could. With everybody else however, I was generally rude, curt and dismissive. Dad was popular, well-liked, respected, his church one of the hubs of the community. People wanted to help, to pray, to visit, to do what they could even though nobody could do anything. If the doctors couldn't help, what would kind words, sympathy and flowers achieve?

Despite being so ill and so weak, Dad wouldn't turn anyone away. They'd troop up to his bedroom, or he'd bundle himself up and manage to make it down to the parlour. He'd find the strength, from somewhere, to talk about their concerns and difficulties. Because that was what he did, because that was who he was.

Irritation became annoyance became anger.

Partly it was for Dad, but largely it was for me. Every minute he spent with someone else, was a minute I lost. It was selfish, of course, but selfishness fuelled by guilt that I stayed away so long, wallowing deeply enough in my own grief and self-pity not to notice my wonderful Dad was dying.

"Don't blame yourself," Mrs Wright told me, one sunny afternoon after I'd chased a couple of Dad's elderly parishioners away like a yapping terrier.

"Blame myself for what?"

Mrs Wright gave me another disapproving look. The first had been for catching me smoking as I stood, only slightly furtively, outside the backdoor.

"For the world being unfair."

I didn't blame myself for the world being unfair. The world's unfairness had nothing to do with me. In fact, I was sure if the world had ever bothered to ask for my opinion, I would have put it right on any number of things.

The list of people I did blame, however, encompassed pretty much all of Dad's parish for giving him no peace. I also blamed Mrs Wright for not contacting me earlier.

Dad had been ill for a long time. As was his way, he never complained, never said anything, never asked for help, never slowed down. His parishioners, with all their petty problems, insecurities and concerns came first. By the time he went to the Doctor, there was nothing that could be done. A cancer was eating him away.

"The world is unfair," I said, pulling defiantly on my cigarette, "that's the way God made it."

"Don't let the Reverend hear you say such things," Mrs Wright said. Her words weren't unkindly spoken, but they cut all the same.

She meant well. I dear say everybody *meant* well, but every word I heard, every deed I saw, irked me more, Aside from the precious time I had with Dad, I became this curt, rude, short-tempered creature I barely recognised.

The Diocese sent Reverend Holland to take services and help run the parish. He was a young, plump man with prematurely thinning hair, a ruddy complexion and a nervous, almost ever-present smile.

He meant well too, I'm sure.

But he spent as much time drinking tea and having long-winded theological discussions with Dad as he did running *St John's*. Admittedly, Dad loved few things more than tea and long-winded theological discussions. He could literally spend hours debating what one particular line of the Bible *really* meant.

I also suspected Reverend Holland was keeping one of those beady eyes behind his thick spectacles on the fact *St John's* would soon have a vacancy. Churchmen could be as ambitious as anybody else.

If a plausible reason existed to think the worst of someone that summer, I would do my damnedest to find it.

The only person apart from Dad that I didn't find a reason to think the worst of was Frank Harryman.

Which was something I later came to think back on as bleakly ironic.

Mrs Hollister forwarded a letter from Frank enquiring how I was. He was worried about me. Which I found touching. I had no romantic notions about Frank, but his letter was kind, thoughtful and made me feel marginally less awful.

I wrote back the next day, explaining about Dad and that I was back home for the time being.

I'd given no thought to my future beyond caring for Dad. My job was gone and the likelihood of another one was remote given the abrupt way I'd left, coupled with the fact the country was now awash with young men looking for work after leaving the army. Women employed in the absence of men during the war were now expected to go back to the kitchen sink without any fuss, thank you very much for all your efforts, darling.

Frank's letters arrived like clockwork. He wrote well. I suppose it is easier to hide your true nature behind a pen than it is in person, but I thought him warm, charming and witty. Particularly as I could write to him when Dad slept, unlike other acquaintances, who might drag me away from the vicarage for tea, cake and idle gossip. Perhaps I needed a friend, one to whom it was impossible to attach any blame for Dad's illness, and Frank fitted the bill.

I had no desire to catch up, to learn who had blissfully married who and who had made a terrible mistake they would live to regret, who hadn't come back from the war and who had come back, but not completely. I found excuses to avoid the former friends I'd had little contact with for years.

In truth, I drifted away from my childhood girlfriends after falling in love with Owen. He had been the only friend I'd ever truly wanted and needed. No doubt that accentuated the sense of loss, the feeling of solitude, of the best of my life being lost, when he died.

It is foolish to become an island. They are so easily cut off from the rest of the world.

Near the end, Dr Sinclair wanted Dad moved to the local infirmary, but Dad wouldn't hear of it. He lived for the vicarage, his church, Hollscombe. He loved seeing the hills and the trees from his window. Or sitting in the garden with a cup of tea, listening to the birds and admiring his flowers.

"This is where God wants me to be," he'd say, with a smile that became ever thinner and harder to bear as the sickness ate him, "it always has been, and always will be."

Dad caught the influenza in early September. Spanish flu was killing people around the world in untold numbers, not just the old and the sick. Dr Sinclair, a shaven headed Scotsman who looked more like a boxer than a doctor, advised me to take precautions against catching it myself when he emerged from Dad's room.

"Being young is no protection if this is Spanish flu," he told me in a grave voice I paid little heed to, because Dr Sinclair said everything from how many sugars he took in his tea downwards in a grave voice.

Whether it actually was the Spanish flu or the more common or garden variety I do not know. In truth, Dad was so weak by then a cold would likely have done the job just as well.

I did notice Mrs Wright sniffing and red-eyed before Dad came down with it, but I could not bring myself to accuse her of infecting him, however much I might have thought it. Besides, it might have been from crying. God knows I did enough of that.

I can't relate those last few hours to you. I would like to say Dad passed peacefully from this world, but he didn't. I have never felt so helpless and useless in my life. There is no greater cruelty than having to watch someone you love suffer. Why God chose to inflict that on Dad, who was as good a man as might ever walk this Earth, I cannot imagine. I am equally clueless as to why he inflicted it on me too, so soon after losing Owen, and so soon after finally learning exactly how he died.

When Dad let out a final, wet, shuddering breath and his chest drew still there was no release, no mercy. Only tears and black despair.

I'm not sure they ever stopped.

1943

My heart lurched when the front door closed.

The rest of me stayed exactly where it was.

Frank said nothing more about going to Creethorpe when he brought my breakfast. He hadn't popped back with a cup of tea to let me know he was going. He'd passed over the opportunity to wet my forehead again and tell me he wouldn't be long.

That struck me as sneaky.

Perhaps he was standing outside, waiting to see if I'd make a dash for it. Or he just didn't want me to know I was alone and free to get up to mischief. Either way, it didn't strike me as the actions of the loving and concerned husband Frank was doing his damnedest to pretend to be.

I'd slept poorly the previous night, but at least it had been my own demons keeping me awake. My faceless companion remained silent. No, it was worry, fear and guilt, my familiar gaolers, who kept nagging at me.

Maybe I was ill. Maybe Frank did love me. Maybe if I escaped, I'd end up a wandering vagrant, cursed to live in hedgerows with no home, no money and no mind.

It was the kind of thinking that had incarcerated me here for twenty-three years with a cruel, abusive and violent man.

As best memory served.

My heart stilled after a while. But I stayed in the chair, the latest book I wasn't reading in my lap.

My eyes swept across the room. One keeper might have left the building, but what about the other? If my faceless companion killed Izzy and Tom to keep me here, then how kindly would it take to me climbing out of the window?

Fear. Worry. Guilt.

Always conspiring.

I waited five minutes. Nothing moved. No sounds arose from downstairs. Frank had not crossed to the Studio or any of the other outbuildings I could see from my window. He was gone. To Creethorpe. For cheese. Bless him.

I snorted at that and pushed myself to my feet.

The door was still locked. It wasn't a strong lock, though. Everything in Grey Gull was old and worn. The door rattled, but I had nothing to bash it open with other than my shoulder.

The drop from the window to the shingle, sand and grass wasn't great, but probably still enough to bust an ankle or knee if I landed badly. And my experience of jumping out of windows was sparse.

I dressed, packed a bag with what few things I needed. Finally, I went to the loose floorboard in the corner.

What if I imagined Owen too?

For a good minute, I stood, turning my bottom lip over between my teeth.

Eventually, I folded to my knees and pulled the floorboard up with shaking hands, frightened I'd find nothing but cobwebs.

Instead, I found everything my memory told me was there.

The photographs, letters, my engagement ring and the coffee can with my running away fund.

I flicked through the letters. The words as familiar as ever. I held them to my face. The aromas of paper, ink, dust and time teased my nostrils. In some tiny, miniscule fragment, they smelt of Owen too. Once, long ago, his hands had touched these fragile things. And amongst the mud, blood, terror and horror of that awful war he had poured his love into them.

And I smelt that too.

I placed the precious bundle in the dusty canvas bag, the money went into my coat pocket.

The sash window opened in jerky increments. Its screeches put the gulls to shame.

Sticking my head outside I found the day cool and overcast, the wind tiff enough to toss hair around my face. The drop looked further.

Luckily, I knew how to tie a decent knot. Francis and Simon had both been Boy Scouts and keen to practice their skills on whatever they could get their hands on.

I tied a sheet to the bed. And another to it and then another until I had a rope that reached within a couple of feet of the ground. I considered shoving the bed nearer to the window, but it was a heavy old beast and I could manage such a short drop without breaking anything.

After tossing my makeshift rope and bag out of the window, I sucked in several breaths. Everything was quiet. There was no sign of Frank or my faceless companion.

All I had to do was get out and shin down some sheets. Then I would be free of them both. Forever.

Standing there, I knew I was being a tad optimistic, but it was a heady feeling all the same.

I ducked under the raised pane and climbed after it, sitting on the ledge with my legs in mid-air. The only thing I didn't have were shoes. They all lived in the cupboard by the backdoor. My threadbare and ever so slightly moth-eaten slippers looked even more incongruous dangling from a window than the rest of me did.

Despite expecting to see Frank standing below, hands on hips, shaking his head, no one was about. Real or imaginary.

The drop to the ground seemed to have grown even more. Was this a good idea? I probably *could* batter my way through the door...

No. It would take more time. I didn't know how long I had till Frank came home, but I wanted to be well clear of Grey Gull by then.

I gave my rope a tug, nothing came apart, which was something.

Simon would have loved this as a boy...

That caught my throat. I twisted around and started easing myself down before it could rip through the rest of me.

As the sheets took my weight, something inside groaned. Just the bed shifting from the pull of the rope. Most likely...

I edged down a little, the sheet wrapped through my arms, my slippered feet against Grey Gull's salt-scoured wall.

A seagull laughed overhead. The wind played with my hair and enjoyed even more fun with my skirt. Perhaps trousers would have been sensible, not that Frank liked me wearing trousers, he-

Frank didn't matter anymore!

I was leaving him. At long, long last I was actually leaving him! Something I believed I'd never do, least of all by scrambling down a sheet out of my window. The thought made me more lightheaded than the view below my feet.

I steadied myself. *Concentrate!* I'd be going nowhere fast with a broken leg.

Carefully, I eased down a little.

Another creaking groan of protest came from the room, but the knots all seemed to be holding. I kept my eyes fixed upwards. I'm not afraid of heights, but there's something about hanging from a sheet that can really skew your perspective.

Looking up, the bedroom ceiling was visible through the open window.

A shadow moved across it.

I slipped a few inches. My heart skipped as I pendulumed from side to side. I clung to the twisted sheet more tightly.

When I looked again, the shadow remained, distorted and elongated, as if cast by a figure standing at the window. But nobody was there.

Just my imagination.

Or delusion.

Or something else.

I bit my lip and edged down further. The shadow shifted too, as if something bent to watch me.

"Fuck you!" I shouted.

Squawking laughter came back. This time it wasn't a seagull.

Stupid cunt, Bea, thy will never get away from me...

I scampered down the sheets fast enough to end up on my backside blinking up at the sky. One of my slippers had spun away, but I'd suffered no other damage.

Like a lonely princess I'd finally escaped my castle.

Princess was stretching things a little. Mad old queen was a lot closer to the truth.

I sat panting. The wind caught the sheets, making them flap. Nothing came bounding out of the window.

Gingerly, I got to my feet and hopped over to the errant slipper before brushing myself down. Once satisfied I was still in one piece – in body at any rate – I grabbed my bag.

Then stared at my slippers.

It was a long walk to Davey's shack. My old slippers looked like another few runs up the stairs would finish them off.

I didn't want to go back inside to get my walking shoes, but if my faceless companion had let me clamber down a sheet, venturing into the castle one more time shouldn't be too dangerous for our heroine, the mad old queen.

We seldom locked Grey Gull's doors. No one came out here and we had nothing to steal (unless you liked ugly paintings), so I expected the front door to be open. It wasn't. I walked around to the kitchen door. Frank had locked that too.

Just for your own protection, Sweetness...

"I bet," I muttered, "protecting me from the bloody gypsies, I suppose."

Talking to yourself. First sign of madness that...

I looked at my feet again. Then the kitchen door.

Both the front and back doors were solid wood. I'd never break them down. I could smash out a window and climb through, there were spare keys in the hall, so getting out again wouldn't be a problem.

"Damn it," I dropped my bag and scurried over to the tool shed. The fact my left slipper shot off my foot before I got halfway confirmed I didn't have much choice.

I wasn't going for a morning stroll to Dirkly Woods. After seeing Davey, I wasn't coming back. I doubted the slippers would get me there in one piece, they certainly wouldn't get me anywhere else.

Grabbing a hammer, I returned to the kitchen and began smashing out a window. The sound of breaking glass shocking the silence. Once the pane was out, I took off my coat and laid it over the frame. The window was too high for me, but I brought a small crate Frank was saving for something from the tool shed, stood on that, and managed to get through without slicing anything off.

Kicking off the slippers, I put my shoes on, wobbling against the table.

Stupid cunt, Bea, you'll never get away from me...

I jerked around. The taunt sounded hissed in my ear, but, of course, there was nobody there.

"I told you once, and I'll tell you again..." I said, crossing the kitchen to the row of hooks by the hallway door, "...fuck you!"

I snatched the key for the back door.

You can't leave...

I rammed it into the back door's lock.

"There's nothing you can do to stop me," I spat back over my shoulder, "if you could have, you would have!"

After unlocking the door and wrenching it open, I scooped up my bag. But before I could hurry outside, I found there *was* something it could do.

The sound of a baby crying floated down the stairs...

1919

I wouldn't see Frank again until the spring of the following year.

In truth, I wanted to run away from Hollscombe the day after the funeral, but the lack of anywhere to go coupled with the necessity of sorting out Dad's estate kept me in the Cotswolds well into the New Year.

The vicarage went with the church, though the Bishop, an old friend of Dad's from their Oxford days, who he always referred to as Bungy, said I could stay as long as I needed to settle Dad's affairs, probably to the chagrin of Reverend Holland whose feet had been itching to move in almost from the moment the first handful of soil went on top of Dad's coffin.

I don't remember much of the funeral. It didn't rain. That's about all I can say with any certainty. The rest was just a procession of faces gurning their sincerity.

I smiled, I nodded, I reminisced, I poured tea, I offered sandwiches. I accepted their sympathy like a despot receiving the tribute of their supplicants. A high priestess of grief, readily available for all to anoint with their tears.

Several bottles of sherry sat on the table and I kept wondering how I would feel if I downed the lot. Would it numb the pain? All I wanted to do was hide, cry and scream.

I settled for sneaking into the garden at every opportunity to chain smoke until I felt like vomiting.

Nice girls, particularly ones who happened to be a vicar's daughter, did not smoke at social gatherings. Even if you struggled to breathe inside for all the smoke from the men's cigarettes, cigars and pipes.

Later, after the last guest gushed their final commiseration into my slack, hollow-eyed, rictus-grinning face, Mrs Wright and I cleaned up. When everything was washed, dried and back in its place, I dug out one of the sherry bottles that had survived the wake.

I sat in Dad's chair and tried to drink it dry.

When I awoke in the morning, I found I hadn't managed to, though a fair portion of it ended up over my dress. I don't know how much went down my throat, but it was enough to hammer my head and churn my stomach.

Later, I decided this was actually worse than the howling empty pain of mourning, although, at least, it passed in a few hours. The grief, I feared, never would.

It didn't take long for people to stop coming to the vicarage. Either the penny dropped that I needed to be alone, or I'd run out of people to insult and offend.

Whenever I stepped outside, I would cross the road to avoid people, glaze my eyes and walk past them. I never returned a greeting with anything other than a pinched smile. Sometimes I didn't even make that much effort.

Mrs Wright tried to tell me people were worried about me, that I was loved here and everybody wanted to help. She got the pinched smile too. And told that with Dad gone there was no more need of a housekeeper until Reverend Holland took the place over.

That got me a pinched smile.

In the meantime, Reverend Holland took a room above the *Black Bull*, he didn't appear keen on the arrangement. He kept popping in on the pretext of seeing how I was coping and to offer comfort and support "at this most difficult time." I knew he was more interested in how I was getting along throwing Dad's life into refuse sacks in the hope he could get his flabby backside into the vicarage before the end of January.

Sorting Dad's things out wasn't something I intended to do with any haste, but the sight of those eager, magnified eyes blinking wetly behind his spectacles above his twitchy lips made me more determined to read every single scrap of Dad's paperwork. A minimum of twice.

My life constricted to nothing more than avoiding people, smoking, trying to master the art of becoming drunk and throwing Dad's life away.

I filled sacks, I burned papers, I sold furniture, I reduced Dad's life to dust and memories one drawer at a time.

By the time Christmas hoved into view, the house was virtually empty, the will had been executed. All Dad's worldly possessions were mine, save for some bequests to his favourite charities.

And I still hadn't quite got the hang of getting drunk.

Frank's letters arrived regularly, and I still replied to them promptly, though given my state of mind and, often, inebriation, I recall little of what I wrote.

Frank was spending time with an Uncle who was dying, they hadn't been close, but he was his only living relative and was staying with him in his cottage somewhere remote on the east coast.

Even in my stupor of grief and sherry, the synchronicity of our situations wasn't lost on me.

Unlike the rest of the world, Frank was enduring a similar ordeal to me. His relationship with his Uncle wasn't the same as me and Dad, but he was experiencing the same process as I had with his only living relative.

And he'd lost Owen too.

It made me feel closer to him.

We wrote about meeting again in London. I would be leaving the vicarage in February, Frank didn't expect his uncle to linger long, but he didn't want to leave him until the inevitable happened.

I thought of Frank sitting next to his Uncle's bed as I had sat next to Dad's – I saw him holding his hand, wiping his brow, trying to get him to eat something, to drink a little, to keep fighting, to somehow get better.

And that made me feel closer to him too.

I didn't know where I wanted to go after vacating the vicarage, other than I didn't want to linger in Hollscombe. The memories of Owen were still too raw and the memories of Dad cut even deeper. So, London was as good a place as anywhere while I figured out what to do with the rest of my life.

Mrs Hollister had let my room, but that didn't matter. With my inheritance from Dad, I could afford the luxury of a decent hotel, while I decided if I wanted to stay in London and look for work or something else.

I thought about buying a passage as far away as possible; Canada, South Africa, Australia, India or the Holy Land. Maybe I could travel around the globe and fill the emptiness inside me with all the marvels of the world.

Needless to say, I didn't.

I met Frank instead.

And filled the emptiness with something else entirely.

1943

The sound impaled me.

It was a trick. That was all.

Just like the taunting voice. Or the creeping figure in the corner of my eye that was never there when I looked properly.

It was trying to keep me here, to delay me till Frank came back and locked me in my room again. Or shipped me off to hospital so they could start slicing bits of my brain off.

The cries became more urgent, more distressed.

It *was* Tilly.

I knew the sound of her cries. Like my faceless companion's taunts, they'd haunted me for years.

My fingers opened and the bag thumped to the floor.

Slowly I closed the door, turned and walked across the kitchen, down the corridor and up the stairs. Each step I took faster than the previous one. By the time I reached the landing I was running.

The crying came from my bedroom, I skidded to a halt before it and tried to yank the door open, forgetting it was locked. The door rattled and the baby wailed on the other side of it.

"Tilly!"

I banged on the door, frustrated at my stupidity for both failing to bring the key and for believing a baby that vanished sixteen years ago could really be in there.

Neither stopped me from turning tail and flying down the stairs to the kitchen, where all the house's keys hung on hooks.

Save the one to my room.

Frank must have left it in his pocket.

I matched the baby's plaintive wail with my own anguished sob. Spinning around, my eye fell on the hammer I'd used to smash out the window. Grabbing it, I rushed back up the stairs, each cry cutting me far more deeply than the glass scattered about the kitchen ever could have.

I swung the hammer repeatedly at the lock, the door shook, but other than leaving indentations in the wood, the hammer did nothing.

The baby – Tilly's – cries grew louder with each wild swing. She was inside; she was reacting to the noise I was making. She wanted her mother, she wanted me, needed me.

I rained blows on the door in a snarling frenzy, aiming for the handle, but cracking the wood around it as often as not.

The world became a blur. Sweat slickened my skin and dampened my hair. My arm started aching, but nothing was going to stop me. My beautiful baby was in there. Returned to me.

For whatever reason my faceless companion wanted me to stay in Grey Gull so much it was prepared to return the baby it'd snatched. It was offering me a deal and I was happy to seize it with both hands.

It was nothing. I'd have sold my soul to the Devil himself in a heartbeat to get Tilly back.

Something cracked and groaned. I sucked in air and channelled everything I had into that hammer. I remembered Frank beating me, what it felt like to lose Owen, Simon, Tom, Dad. I remembered all those dark lonely nights staring at the empty spot in the corner where Tilly's cot had once rested. All those nights torturing myself, all those nights not knowing.

I screamed, I cried, I begged.

And above it all I heard my baby crying.

A sound I hadn't heard in sixteen years, but one I'd never stopped hearing all the same.

With a final splintering snap the door gave way and swung inwards. I staggered after it.

"Tilly!"

I dropped the hammer from my numb fingers and sank to my knees.

The room was empty.

But behind me, something laughed.

"Please..." I sobbed, "...give her back. I'll do anything you want. Anything..."

Grey Gull's warped, old floorboards shifted and creaked.

The clouds broke, light poured through the open window. Yet, a shadow still fell over me from behind, as if the sunlight refused to touch it. Elongated and distorted, too many angles, too many wrong turns.

A figure that forever hung sloightly on th' huh.

"I'll stay. I promise. Just give me Tilly back. Please..."

A hand fell upon my shoulder. Gentle, but cold. Tingling the skin beneath my clothes. Ice against flesh.

I kept my eyes on the window. I didn't want to know what those fingers looked like, though I knew they were too long and each would bend in ways no human finger ever could.

A darkness filled the corner of my right eye as I sensed it shift, not so much bending down to put its face next to mine as folding itself into some other distorted shape.

Air moved my lank hair; the winter breathed in my ear.

The child of thine, is the child of mine...

The words were a growl, a hiss, a belch. The words weren't spoken, they came on the thing's January breath to echo inside my mind.

"Please... is Tilly alive?"

Alive or dead, you will stay in my bed.

"No. I will go. If you can't give her back, there's nothing for me here!"

The grasp on my shoulder tightened, I could almost feel shards of frost penetrating my flesh.

If the child doth suffer, then so doeth the mother.

That came as a cackling, choking laugh. Frigid sparks burnt my ear. I cried out and flinched, but those wrong, twisted fingers dug deeper, stilling me.

"Is she alive? Please, just tell me that?"

The grip eased, but the hand started moving towards my face. The shadow in the corner of my eye darkened. I was shaking, part of me wanting to turn my head to see the thing on my shoulder. To know what crouched, folded behind me, even while understanding that if I did, my mind really might shatter.

Five points of ice pressed into my cheek. Bristles scratched my skin. Sharp as the Devil's tongue, wicked as his lies. Tears blurred my vision as that hand cupped the side of my face. The fingers so long they were wrapping around my entire skull like grasping tentacles.

A bitter breeze of a sigh ruffled my hair. The thing, my faceless companion, trembled.

Mine...

"No!"

Thou art mine Beatrice of Clay, yesterday, tomorrow and today.

I tried to squirm away, but that hand, now more like an enormous paw, squeezed my head till I squealed and grew still.

"What are you? Why are you doing this?"

Another hand came around me, seizing my left breast, squeezing and fondling. I kept my eyes on the window, though the sun was dimmer now. Shadow engulfed me, taking me within its foul cloak. Within itself...

Because thou art sweet, a heady, juicy, delicious meat.

The hand holding my head tipped it back. I stared into darkness. Then screwed my eyes shut. I had no desire to understand what I'd seen. The things moving within that looming shadow; nightmares and torments, fluttering, crawling, slithering in the dark. All coupled with a sense of overwhelming sadness and long slow time. Something ancient, something knowing, something full of sorrow, grief and pain. Things even the sunlight could not illuminate. Things best not seen. Things never meant to be seen.

Something pressed against my forehead. Lips. Wet, broken, frigid lips. So cold they burned. Lips coated with drool, lips curled into the darkest, bleakest of smiles.

Such a feast...

The lips withdrew, but not far, freezing breath shrieked across my numbed skin.

If thou leaves me, I will turn to slaughter. If thou leaves me, you will become lost like thy daughter.

The hands shoved me forward, hard and sudden enough to send me sprawling.

I laid there, eyes closed, my skin still burning from where it touched me, even through my clothes.

Distantly, just a sigh upon the breeze, came the sound of a baby crying. Tilly crying.

"If you don't give her back, I swear I will kill you!"

Feet shuffled, floorboards groaned. At least it didn't laugh at my threat.

But how can you kill something you can not even bear to look at? After all these years of hiding, here it was. The thing that took Tilly from me, the thing that killed Tom and Izzy.

Whatever it was.

I drove fingernails into my palms, ignored my thudding heart and dismissed the screams from the depths of my being that if I ever looked directly at this abomination, I really would go insane.

I pushed myself up onto all fours and forced my neck to turn and see the horror behind me.

To see my tormentor, my faceless companion, at long last.

"Sweetness..." Frank shook his head as he looked down at me, "...oh, what have you done...?"

1920

There was something different about Frank, but I couldn't put my finger on what it was. Perhaps the death of his uncle had changed him somehow. I decided it didn't matter. I was in such pieces the first time we'd met, it was a miracle I could even remember what he looked like.

Dad's death had certainly changed me. Smoking heavily and knocking back my drinks, if not with aplomb, then certainly unseemly relish.

"You didn't smoke before," Frank commented as I lit a cigarette.

"I did, just not in public. Now..." I shrugged.

I didn't really care what society thought nice girls, particularly nice girls who were a vicar's daughter, should or shouldn't do anymore.

Society deemed nice girls didn't open their legs for the man they loved prior to marriage as well, even when they were going off to war and likely to be riddled with bullets for king and country.

I knocked back my drink in one.

However many I drank, it was never quite enough to wash the bitterness from my mouth.

Frank's eyes followed my glass all the way up and all the way back down. Then he silently stood up and went to buy me another one.

Good.

I was trying gin tonight. I was curious to see if it was better at getting you drunk than sherry.

"Do you want to talk about... feelings...?" Frank asked.

It was a strange way of putting it, and he put it strangely. There was a hollowness to the words, like he was talking about something he didn't quite understand.

I didn't think too much about it. So long as he kept buying me gin, he could talk any damn way he liked.

"No, not really."

"You're... angry?"

I looked at him. Dark intense eyes stared back.

"Yes. I'm angry."

"The world is full of sorrows."

"It never used to be," I ground my cigarette out with a savage twist and resisted the urge to immediately light another. I drank more gin instead.

"It always was. You just didn't have cause to see it."

My eyes fixed on the table's wet circles, the ghosts of where our drinks had sat awaiting us.

"How do you stand it? The things you saw... over there."

"You got used to it."

"I watched Dad die. It was awful. But it was only once. How many deaths have you seen?"

"Too many to count or name. But I didn't love any of them..." a peculiar little smile curled Frank's lip beneath his sharply cut moustache, "Love makes sorrow stronger..."

"Better not to love then?"

Frank's only answer was to sip his beer.

I'd been in London for a few weeks, staying in a modest hotel in Pimlico while I figured out what I wanted to do with the rest of my life. Frank's uncle had passed away and I'd agreed to meet him. We were in a pub not far from my hotel.

Being surrounded by people felt strange after months of shunning everyone. I thought I'd grown closer to Frank over the course of our correspondence, but sitting across the table from him he seemed as much a stranger as anyone else in the smoky bar.

I knew, however, I needed someone. I was adrift and alone in a way I never had in my life. Dad was gone, Owen was gone. My old friends just reminded me of a life I once had that I'd lost forever.

I sat in my hotel room, all my possessions in a pair of mismatched suitcases, and imagined growing roots into the saggy springs of the room's easy chair. I stared at the sun-faded painting of a vase of chrysanthemums on the wall opposite, drinking myself into oblivion. Drinking until I became part of the tobacco-stained fabric of the room, absorbed and consumed till nothing remained of me bar the two cases I had found no reason to fully unpack.

It was not a healthy or appealing prospect. And the longer I stayed in that room doing nothing, seeing no one, the more inevitable that outcome seemed.

So, I had agreed to meet Frank and had even been looking forward to it as much as I'd looked forward to anything since Mrs Wright's telegram arrived.

I didn't want to talk about Owen, I didn't want to talk about Dad. Frank didn't seem inclined to talk about his Uncle, which I understood. Whatever he said he'd managed to grow accustomed to during the war, watching someone die via the slow increments of disease was a very different kind of horror to the one wrought by the battlefield.

He talked a little of the cottage he was going to inherit. Grey Gull. He made it sound idyllic. He was going to spend the rest of his life there painting, away from the noise of humanity. He wanted open skies and empty landscapes. He'd seen enough of what people did to the world.

I could understand that. It sounded romantic too.

More gin arrived. My head was starting to buzz.

I started talking more. I can't remember what about. Nothing of significance. Just the little, harmless things.

I laughed at something Frank said, or maybe it was something I said. It took me by surprise. A sound both alien and achingly familiar.

More laughter came. Perhaps unsurprisingly there was a direct correlation between the amount of laughter and the amount of gin.

A warmth spread through me, making me more comfortable in my own skin. My eyes started lingering on Frank's more and more. They were rather beautiful, and the way he looked at me hinted at all manner of things. He was deep. He was an artist. He was going to live in a windswept cottage by the sea. He looked, with some imagination and enough gin, a bit like a movie star.

At some point he moved closer to me. I think it was when he came back with another round of drinks. I'd long lost count by then. He leaned in more, his shoulder brushing mine.

It felt good.

I started noticing his lips as well as his eyes.

I'd only ever kissed Owen. Would Frank's lips feel different?

Distant flares of alarm and guilt ignited at such a thought, but I told myself Owen was gone and wasn't coming back.

Did I really want to be alone forever?

Yet more gin appeared.

The flares of guilt and alarm drifted off into the distance, became fainter, easier to ignore.

Even when Frank slipped a hand under the table and squeezed my knee.

I should have done something about that. Nice girls, particularly ones who happened to be a vicar's daughter, did not appreciate men they didn't know squeezing their knee.

Frank looked at me as his hand lingered on my knee. I made no move to shuffle away, I didn't shoot to my feet, I didn't slap his face or throw a drink over him.

Instead, I smiled back.

He squeezed some more.

I found I was enjoying the touch of his fingers.

In truth, I was wondering if I'd like them even more if the fabric of my dress and stockings weren't between his skin and mine. I'd had such thoughts before, of course, but only with Owen. Now I was having them about a man I hardly knew.

We'd been corresponding for a long time, but that isn't the same as knowing someone. Later, much later, when I had an abundance of time to ponder such things, it seemed Frank had talked very little of himself in those letters and what he had was just a skim across the surface, nothing of importance.

The letters had mainly been about Owen to start with, and later, me, interweaved with trivia, mundanity, a few observations, the occasional joke. He was no different in person, but between the gin, his hand upon my knee and those intense, burnt eyes I thought I knew all I needed to.

The choices we make shape our lives. Some good, some bad, some just licks of paint. I made a choice that night. The worst one I possibly could. And it broke the rest of my life.

Our glasses were empty again. Frank stood up, I thought he was going to buy more, instead he took my hand and smiled at me. Sitting there, looking up at him he seemed impossibly tall, a mountain I had to crane my neck to see the top of. Strong, broad, powerful. Something I could hold and anchor myself to before my pain washed what remained of my life out to sea.

He pulled gently on my hand. I got up. None too steadily. My hands rested on his forearms for a moment.

"Let's go..."

I nodded without knowing where we were going.

Outside, the cold air hit me as I struggled into my coat. Frank helped me straighten out a twisted sleeve. I giggled. Once I was in my coat, his hands did not leave me. Before I could button it up, he pushed me back against the wall. I didn't resist. He kissed me. Not a hesitant kiss, not a brushing of lips. He kissed me hard, tongue slipping into my mouth as he explored the body beneath my open coat.

I should have protested, refused, stopped him. He was kissing me in the street! He was running his hands over me in public, he was pushing himself against me for all the world to see. This was not at all the kind of thing nice girls, particularly ones who happened to be a vicar's daughter, allowed.

My hands and lips returned everything Frank was doing.

I could say it was the drink. That would be easy, but it wasn't. It was me. I wanted Frank in that moment, and I didn't give a hoot for the rest of the world.

I was scared and lonely. I could blame those things as easily as I could blame the gin.

But it wasn't that either.

It was just desire, lust, want, need. Call it what you like. Things I'd bottled up for years and denied myself, first by waiting for marriage, then for the war to end before I'd marry Owen, then through the empty, guilt-ridden months following Owen's death and now the raw, visceral pain of losing Dad.

I wanted a man, I wanted to be wanted. I wanted the things I'd briefly shared with Owen in our one night together. I didn't want to be alone.

Choices.

They can haunt you worse than any ghost.

1933

I went to St Luke's in Creethorpe most Sundays. When the children were old enough, I took them, too. Frank never came; he disapproved of God.

I tried not to linger after the service. Frank didn't like me going longer than I had to, and I was afraid he'd stop me altogether if I took liberties.

Long before the summer of 1933, I'd learned to do pretty much anything to avoid my husband's ire.

One Sunday in the June of that year, I'd gone to St Luke's with Simon (Francis was excused with a cold). It'd been a simmering, cloudless day, and Simon fidgeted throughout Reverend Vaughn's sermon on the importance of forgiveness. His bubbling energy was almost palpable; there was an entire world outside he could be rushing about exploring. Instead, he was stuck inside singing hymns and listening to an old man blathering about turning the other cheek.

I thought I knew a lot more about turning the other cheek than anyone else in the congregation, but I didn't say anything of the sort to Reverend Vaughn as we trooped into the sunshine afterwards.

I always sat in the back pew so I could be the first out of the door. This was only partly in order to get home quickly and keep Frank happy.

People still watched me.

A cold glance, a hard stare, a nudge and a nod.

People said little to my face, but you don't need to say a lot when your eyes said so much.

The woman who *lost* her baby.

Grey Gull had thickened my skin over the years. Still, I found it best to keep my distance whenever possible.

Not everyone was the same, of course. Or perhaps some were simply too polite to let suspicions squirm onto their face.

Reverend Vaughn always welcomed me warmly, chatted amiably, and never once looked like he wanted to spit at me. As a vicar, that was part of the job, but I was grateful.

Still, I liked to scamper straight off after Sunday service. Being in such proximity to so many people unnerved and unsettled me.

That particular Sunday, however, Reverend Vaughn had other ideas as I tried to scurry past him, mumbling my thanks for the service. Usually, I flashed him a smile as I went by, then kept my head down until I couldn't feel any more eyes boring into my back.

"Mrs Harryman," Reverend Vaughn beamed, clutching my hand in both of his, "how are you?"

"Well... thank you..."

The vicar, to my surprise, didn't let go of my hand.

"And young Francis... he couldn't come today?"

From anyone else, I might have thought questioning the whereabouts of one of my children carried implications, but I doubted Reverend Vaughn's interest went beyond our spiritual well-being.

"A cold. Nothing more..." I twitched a smile. Behind me, the congregation filed past, thanking Reverend Vaughn over my shoulder. Still the old man didn't release my hand.

"Poor lamb. Summer colds, so annoyingly inconvenient..."

"Yes."

I wanted to yank my hand away but resisted the urge. The Reverend was one of the few people in Creethorpe who ever smiled at me and looked like he meant it. He'd never crossed the road to avoid me, either. I didn't want to offend him.

Simon, however, had no such qualms and was already squirming to be free of the tie of his Sunday best.

"And how are you, Simon? Studying hard at school, I hope?"

Simon nodded.

"And do you know what you want to do when you grow up?"

"Racing car driver!" Simon jumped up and down, as he always did whenever a conversation veered close to the subject of motor cars.

"Oh, you like going fast then?"

Simon sliced his hand forward from his shoulder while making a whooshing sound.

"He's never still," I laughed with the Reverend.

Out of the corner of my eye, I could see Mrs Featherly swivelling her neck to look at us as she lumbered down the path. Reverend Vaughn wasn't the only one to have noted Francis' absence.

No doubt Creethorpe's most diligent chinwags would soon have another child murder chalked up to my name.

Reverend Vaughn raised kinder eyes to me, "I was wondering whether we might have a little chat?"

A chat?

Virtually nobody had wanted to have a chat with me since Detective Inspector Breaker stopped dropping in.

"Well... erm... Francis-"

"Just a moment, just a moment..." Reverend Vaughn still had my hand as he ushered me a few steps away from the ancient wooden porch covering the entrance to *St Luke's*.

Simon took the opportunity to hurtle over to talk to the Hardcastle boys. Like the rest of Simon and Francis' friends, they never came to Grey Gull. Mrs Hardcastle smiled at Simon as he barrelled over. As soon as her eyes flicked in my direction, the smile faded.

Reverend Vaughn was concerned for my well-being. Did I feel isolated out on the coast? Would I like to become more involved in parish life? There were lots of events coming up over the summer. You can never have too many hands, Mrs Harryman! It would be good for me. A chance to get to know the town better. And the town to know me.

I tried my best not to look too horrified.

He meant well, but...

I thanked him and made my excuses. Very busy. Husband. Children! And the house! Always tons to do with that place. It's the sea air. Oh, my goodness! All that salt. Corrodes absolutely everything!

Reverend Vaughn didn't put up too much of an argument. It was just an idea. But next year when the boys were older? Less of a handful.

Oh, yes. I'd think about it. Definitely. Certainly. Maybe. But thanks for asking!

I wondered whose idea this was. The Reverend's? His wife? Iris had a kind heart too. I doubted it was anyone on the Parochial Church Council. The churchwardens only seemed to tolerate me begrudgingly. I was the woman who'd *lost* her baby, after all.

Perhaps it was paranoia. Perhaps not. But I was relieved when the Reverend acquiesced to my polite refusals and let me escape.

After wishing the Reverend a lovely day and thanking him for everything, I turned and looked for Simon, eager to be away.

He was nowhere in sight.

I didn't panic, though part of me always tried to whenever I found one of the boys was not precisely where I thought they should be.

He wasn't amongst the dispersing cloud of worshippers heading off for their Sunday lunches and whatever real families did after church.

He hasn't disappeared. He really hasn't!

No one met my eye at first as I stood alone in my dowdy Sunday best.

Mrs Hardcastle noticed me, interrupting a furtive-looking conversation with Mrs Rice, she pointed around the side of the church.

He's with the Hardcastle boys, of course. Thick as thieves. I knew that!

I smiled my thanks. Mrs Hardcastle turned her back and moved her mouth closer to Mrs Rice's ear.

I could loiter, fiddling with my bag, or go and fetch Simon. I didn't want to drag him away from his chums, but we did need to be on our way. I had dinner to make. Frank didn't like it too late, even though he rarely ate much of whatever I served.

I went to find Simon. The sooner we left, the fewer glances would come my way.

It was quieter on the other side of the church. A large, neatly tended graveyard, bordered by a waist high dry-stone wall, vibrant flower beds, and a couple of gnarled old yew trees competing with towering oaks. Sunlight and shadow dappled lichen-mottled headstones. Bees buzzed, birds sang.

A tranquil place disturbed by three boys tearing around.

I seldom visited the graveyard despite attending church most Sundays.

The church services reminded me of Dad alive, the graveyard of Dad's coffin, descending into the ground's waiting maw.

"Simon!" I waved, "Time to go, darling!"

Simon, being Simon, suffered one of his sudden attacks of deafness and continued chasing the Harryman boys.

Or perhaps he couldn't hear me for their laughing.

I felt mean. There wasn't much laughter in Grey Gull.

I dropped my hand and wandered into the shade. Another five minutes wouldn't do any harm, would it?

I knew damn well Frank could get upset over a lot less than five minutes. But he wouldn't be angry with Simon; he'd only be angry with me. I watched the boys, blurs of laughter careening through the headstones.

Let him play. If I have to taste the belt for it... so what?

I'd be tasting it for something or other before long, it might as well be Simon's happiness.

I listened to the squeals of laughter and tried to file them away. Something to remember when Frank was...

I ambled, head down. Sticking to the shade. It was a sweltering day, and most of the walk back to Grey Gull would be in full sunlight.

A butterfly, just a common or garden cabbage white, flitted by in front of me and took my eye with it. It landed on a headstone deep in the shadow of a thick, twisted yew.

I didn't like looking at the gravestones too closely. They made me think of the slab of granite I'd chosen for Dad and how I'd anguished about what to have carved into it. Everything rang hollow, inadequate, and unworthy. Ultimately, I'd settled for the simple, unoriginal, but absolutely true *Beloved Husband & Father*.

The cabbage white fluttered off, leading my eye elsewhere.

Careful not to step on the neatly tended graves, I moved deep into the shade beneath the old yew tree. Despite the heat of the day, it remained cool here.

I stood before a plain headstone.

Hector Maurice Shackle.

1837-1913

A relative of Frank's uncle?

Frank's uncle died in 1919, not long after Dad. Frank wrote to me about caring for the old man in Grey Gull at length while I'd been in Hollscombe looking after Dad; we'd talked about it when we met *that* night... it had made me feel closer to him. So I'd thought through my haze of grief and alcohol anyway.

It must be another relative, that's-

My eyes moved to the next headstone.

Jane Shackle

1845-1881

Wife of Hector

There were other graves beneath the yew tree. Smaller ones. All girls. All dead before Jane in 1881.

He lied to me.

Frank had slapped my face many times by 1933, but standing before those graves, my face stung like he'd hit me again.

While I'd been caring for Dad, his uncle had already been dead for years; he'd already inherited Grey Gull long before he was in France with Owen. But why lie...

I knew the answer to that immediately.

To get closer to me. To win my trust. To make me think he understood what I was going through. He'd lost Owen too. He had to care for a dying relative like I had; he knew, he knew...

Bloody fool.

It had never struck me until I had to think about it, but how likely was it Frank would have cared for anyone? He barely bothered to clean his own arse!

I bit my lip. In the distance, Simon and the Hardcastle boys' laughter sounded only one step removed from screams.

Wife of Hector.

Would my life be reduced to that one day? A few words chiselled into stone.

Wife of Frank.

I should march back to Grey Gull and demand to know why Frank had lied to me.

But I wouldn't.

I should pack my bags, take the boys and leave.

But I wouldn't.

Just like everything Frank had done, continued to do and would do in the future. I would do nothing.

My eyes moved from the Shackle's graves to Simon.

As happy a boy as you've ever seen.

What would Frank do if I tried to leave?

My eyes returned to the children's graves.

What would happen if I didn't?

Tilly...

Frank had *never* hurt the children. He never would. I was sure of it. He had nothing to do with Tilly. And the boys' happiness was all that mattered. All that ever had and ever would.

"Simon!" I clapped my hands, "Come on, it's time we were heading home..."

Really, what was one more lie.

1943

"I never wanted it to come to this..."

Frank sat by my bed, hunched forward, hands clasped together, those oh so familiar burnt hazel eyes fixed upon his feet rather than me.

I didn't answer. Partly because I had nothing to say, but mainly due to the gag Frank had forced into my mouth. He'd tied both my wrists to the bed frame too. As soon as he left the room, I would start working on them, but they didn't have much give. Perhaps Francis and Simon had shown him the knots they'd learnt at the Boy Scouts too.

The window was still open. Frank had hauled up my sheet rope and tossed it in the corner. He hadn't bothered to remake the bed I'd stripped for sheets, though that was hardly my greatest current discomfort.

"I thought I could make you better. All this talk of monsters. I thought..." he sighed and raised his eyes, "...but Simon dying... has pushed you so far over the edge. I'll have to call the hospital now."

Those eyes lingered on me, accusation bright within them. I didn't know why. Either I was sick, or a supernatural monster who'd stolen my baby and killed my lover was haunting me.

Either way, I couldn't quite see what I'd done wrong...

I turned my head and stared at the ceiling. I assumed he didn't expect a reply.

The chair squeaked and Frank stood up.

It seemed he did want me to look at him though.

"I don't want to call the hospital, Bea, I really don't. But you were babbling about killing me. I never thought your illness would make you dangerous, but now..."

When I made to look away, I found his hand on my chin. Gently he turned my head back towards him.

Frank's fingers were clammy and warm. But beneath his touch, my skin still burned where my faceless companion had touched me.

I swallowed. Saliva kept filling my mouth.

He stroked my hair, "Once you've calmed down a bit, I'll take the gag out. I promise. But you were howling like a... like an animal."

He wanted to say loon then.

I lifted my left hand the couple of inches the rope around my wrist allowed.

Frank glanced at the door and back. He shook his head, "Don't want you trying to run off again, do we, Sweetness? Who knows where you'll end up... or what you might do. If you hurt yourself or someone else... that'd be on me, wouldn't it...?"

If thou leaves me, I will turn to slaughter. If thou leaves me, you will become lost like thy daughter.

"... no, best we keep you here until the doctors can see you. Didn't want them cutting you open..." he shrugged, "...but we can't go on like this. Look what you did to our home, Bea...? Maybe being lobotomised will work and we can go back to the way we were. Be happy again, without all this... *hysteria...*"

I wanted to strain on the ropes and scream at him but didn't. I guessed it wouldn't help convince him I was sane. Neither would lying meekly on the bed, but perhaps the doctors would be more impressed.

Doctors I had no memory of.

I'm not bloody insane!

The touch of my faceless companion's lips remained on my skin. If I looked in the mirror, I would expect to see their impression burnt into me. And what I'd seen in that instant it had loomed over me. That was madness. Swirling in the darkness and contained in the ill-drawn figure of a man.

What more would I have seen if I looked earlier? Tom and Izzy's souls trapped for eternity. And Tilly? Would I have seen her too. A swaddled bundle crying in a bleak, fractured plain of frost and sorrow. Crying for her mother. Crying forever.

If the child doth suffer, so doeth the mother.

I screwed my eyes shut. I hadn't looked properly earlier, but that's what I thought I would have seen. The thing living in Grey Gull was not my faceless companion, it was my torment. Perhaps the world's torment. A small piece of Hell with too long arms and legs that bent and folded like no arms and legs should. Not a man at all, but a vessel to contain grief, misery and suffering.

But by the time I'd found the scrap of courage I possessed, Frank returned and the thing had skulked back to the shadows. The shadows only I could see.

When I opened my eyes again, Frank had left the bed. He'd brought the canvas bag I'd packed with my paltry belongings and placed it on the dresser. His back was to me, head lowered.

"You won't be needing this," he said, "a small bag will do for the hospital. No point taking clothes, they'll have gowns for you to wear there."

Slowly he started unpacking the bag.

My heart began racing. A fear arose that had nothing to do with my faceless companion or the possibility I was insane.

Frank pulled each item out of the bag, clothes first, unfolding them, holding them up to inspect before depositing them to the floor.

I tried to call out, but only incoherent gargles escaped the cloth filling my mouth.

Once the clothes were scattered around his feet, followed by my toiletries, hairbrush and other bits and bobs I'd crammed inside, he stopped. Not because he'd finished or given up. But because he'd found what else was in there.

He pulled out the letters, photographs and my engagement ring. He placed them on the dresser, dropping the empty bag to the floor.

He ran a thumb along the stack of letters. Each in its envelope. I could not even throw them away, for each bore my name written in Owen's hand. A pink ribbon tied the bundle, though the colour, much like me, had faded over the years.

"You kept them all..." Frank said, head lowered, not looking around.

I stopped struggling.

The old Frank would be furious. He would have beaten me black and blue for keeping Owen's letters. But that Frank was supposed to be a conjuring of my lunacy, not the real man at all. But if this was the real Frank, then...

I watched him, not sure what I wanted to see at all.

Frank snorted, "Did you keep any of *my* letters?"

When I said nothing, he half turned towards me, perhaps overlooking the fact I had a cloth stuffed in my mouth.

"I thought you might have forgotten him..." Frank returned his attention to the letters, then fanned the photographs across the dresser before resting on his knuckles as he stared down at them, "...but it seems not."

"Where did you think you were going? Running away to find Owen, eh? He's dead, Bea. Has been for a long time. I'm not, yet he's still the man you want. If he hadn't died, we would never have been together. We wouldn't be here. We would never have had our children. Is that want you want, for them never to have existed. Is it?"

He swung around. His eyes burned, mouth a bloodless white line. He was shaking, too, trying to contain his rage.

Suddenly, he looked a lot like the old Frank again.

For a few silent heartbeats he stood still. Then he stomped across the bedroom and slapped my face, hard enough for stars to explode behind my eyes.

Much more like the old Frank.

Straightening up, he sucked air through flaring nostrils.

"Bitch," he said, "Think I'll leave the gag in after all. Harder for you to lie to me then."

I thought he was going to hit me again. And maybe next time it wouldn't be a slap. Maybe next time he wouldn't stop.

Perhaps he thought that too, because he whirled around, went to the dresser and scooped up the letters and photographs. Then came and thrust one of the photographs at me. Owen, in his uniform, stared back at me, frozen and unblinking. A moment of his young life forever preserved to remind me of what I once had.

"Winter's coming, be cold again soon. Always is here. Best I test the fire, make sure you haven't broken that too."

I tried to cry out, to beg him not to take all I had left of Owen. He smiled. A dark nasty smile I recognised well enough. He slapped me again and stormed out of the room, slamming the shattered door behind him.

My eyes filled with tears as his feet thumped down the stairs, but through my pain one thought cut through, like a shaft of sunlit on a bitter, stormy day.

I was not mad.

1953

I dreamt more in my latter years.

Or at least I remembered them better. Do dreams become more vivid as you get older? More vivid as everything else begins to fade? I don't know.

I thought I'd ask Merry. He had the air of a man who knew a thing or two about dreams. You only had to look into his eyes to see that. Something was fascinating about them; the more you looked, the more you wanted to, but, at the same time, the more apprehensive you became about just what you might see.

After all, who had eyes that shifted colour to match the sea?

I told him about Frank. Everything.

All he'd done, all I suspected he'd done, the way he'd made me feel, the way I had let myself become his prisoner, too scared of him to run away from this brittle shore of shingle and stone even during the times when he wasn't here.

How I lied to myself it was for the children, how I lied to myself it was for me, how I lied to myself I couldn't survive in that world beyond the marshes, that world of people and places, hope and possibilities. The world of dreams and nightmares.

When I finished, the sun was nearly set, just as it had the year before.

Merry is right; time is such a tricky fellow. Take your eye off him, and he scampers, scarpers and sprints, yet, watch him too closely, and how he dawdles, drags, and dallies.

"You must go," Merry said, looking at the sun, its light setting bonfires ablaze within his eyes. I assumed that was a reflection, but...

"Back there," my own gaze twisted towards the Castle, out of sight along the beach. The mist had risen. I hadn't noticed. Clouds stretched across the western sky in honeyed glowing smears.

It reminded me of one of Tom's watercolours.

"You can leave anytime you want," Merry said, "you choose not to."

I could only nod my head. Yes, I chose not to.

I faced Merry, legs astride the driftwood as if riding a horse. A rather unladylike pose. I couldn't remember throwing my leg over the log.

The dreams grew more vivid while I forgot what I'd done a few minutes ago. I looked at the fattening sun falling to the marshes.

A few hours ago.

"I don't know how to leave," I said.

"I have things to say. I suspect you will not care to hear them. But I shall say them. When the time is right. For now, you must go. We will continue tomorrow."

"Tomorrow? Or next year?"

Merry smiled and shrugged as if it mattered little. It was all much the same.

I stood. "Tomorrow will be…" I couldn't remember the year until it bobbed up before me, "…1954?"

"In some worlds, it will be 1954. In others, it will be… something else."

"I don't want to wait a year to see you again," I said, refusing to stand.

"You will wait for as long as you wish to wait. That is how you spend your days, Lady Beatrice…"

I didn't want to leave him. Being with someone, just talking, communing… it made the loneliness ache inside me like the ghost of an old wound rainy weather brought back from the dead.

My only friend. A man I saw once a year.

That was far too strong a word, but when you live in isolation from the rest of the world you took what crumbs life offered you and made a feast of them.

A tear pricked my eye, but I did not let it fall.

Instead, I turned and walked back along the shore, hoping Merry would call me back. But nothing came bar the screeching of the seagulls; a serenade sung by a lunatic chorus.

Frank was not home when I got back to the Castle. Which was something, at least.

I paced, listless and restless as the sea beyond the glass.

Later I dreamed of the Grey Place.

I dream of many things. Owen, Tom, the children, Dad, my own childhood. Things that were, things that could have been, half-remembered things, forgotten things, nonsensical things. I never dream of Frank. Not once, that I recall.

My only mercy, my only escape.

But, in those latter years, I dreamt of the Grey Place more and more often.

A dusty plain of ash speckled with small hills upon which the sun is forever setting without ever completely sinking below the distant horizon.

I am not alone here.

I walk with others, though I never see their faces. No one speaks to me.

We just shuffle through the dust. Feet kicking up a permanent mist, blurring and reducing us. Sometimes the sun turns the dust to the colour of blood, sometimes, the sun falls behind one of the hills for a while and the land returns to grey. It's cold in the shadows, so I try to move faster to find the sun again.

The other figures move through the dust in time with me, heads lowered, faces always turned.

I often see a soldier, head bowed, rifle slung over his shoulder. Every now and then it slips down his arm and he jerks it back up. Pausing for a second or two before picking up his muddy boots and ploughing on through the ash.

I think it's Owen, but I can't be sure. I call his name, I shout till I can taste nothing but the ashes and my own tears, but he never looks around.

Things lie in the ash. Bones, I think. But I don't like to look. Now and then I see skeletal hands poking out of the ground like dead, stunted trees bleached by the sun.

I walk. It is the only thing I can do. Along with all the others. Sometimes we circle one of the hills. Other times we plod from one to another and another. But we never climb them. Once in a while, there are figures atop the hills. Only ever one or two. They're the only ones not walking. They watch, cloaks flapping around them in the parched breeze. It hurts to stare up at them, so I soon drop my eyes back to my feet, watching them cut through the ash.

I don't know what it means. Probably nothing. Dreams are just dreams.

Even when you wake and find the taste of ashes on your tongue...

1943

Frank talked of doctors, hospitals and lobotomies. But nothing materialised.

He took the gag out for me to drink and eat, untied my hands to use the chamber pot. Both went straight back on when I was done. I spent my days praying for the military police to come and take him away, or for Francis to return from sea, or Diane to visit. For anyone, so they could see me tied and gagged.

But the war had not ended, it kept Francis far away and Diane busy doing whatever hush-hush work she did. I couldn't think of anyone else likely to come. Grey Gull received few visitors.

On the bedside table a little pile of blackened paper and ash taunted me. A faded pink ribbon sat on top.

My Owen.

It wasn't the only thing that taunted me, of course.

My faceless companion often came creeping about the room, whispering and laughing but never stepping forward to show itself fully.

Piggy, piggy tied and helpless, piggy, piggy mad and useless...

Occasionally, I heard Tilly too, crying in the distance. She sounded frightened, distressed, hungry.

Is there a worse thing for a mother to hear?

Perhaps. Though as I lay in my bed, wrists chaffed, mouth sore, none came to mind.

I continually worried the ropes, but never managed to do much save remove more skin.

Frank checked the bindings frequently, even in the middle of the night.

Sometimes, after retying and tightening them to his satisfaction, he'd stay and do his business on me.

The old Frank was well and truly back.

I filled my time trying to devise ways to escape, to rescue Tilly, to destroy my faceless companion. To kill Frank.

The first seemed ever more unlikely; the rest were fantasies. Dark but idle.

Time stretched, uncounted days melted into endless nights full of whispers and things that crept around the periphery of my much-reduced world.

One morning – at least I think it was morning, there was no clock in the room and Frank had taken to leaving the curtains shut – I awoke to find my husband standing at the end of the bed. He was turning something in his hand.

Owen's engagement ring.

Harder to burn than letters and photographs.

"How much you reckon I'd get for this?" he asked, holding the ring up between his finger and thumb for me to see.

I blinked. I wanted to scream at him, but it wasn't worth the effort.

"Piece of crap. Not as nice as the ring I gave you, but what do you expect? Owen was a cheap idiot. Still, might get enough for a few pints for it..." he shrugged and slipped the ring into the pocket of his waistcoat.

He wore a suit, I realised. Did that mean he was going somewhere?

"God, how he used to prattle on about you. Made you sound like the most wonderful girl in the world. Did my fucking head in. Never said anything about you being a headcase. Perhaps you weren't then," he shook his head, "but you certainly are now."

He shoved his hands deep into his pockets, "I was going to throw it into the sea but seems a waste if I can get a couple of bob for it. Have to get rid of it one way or another," his eyes drifted to the piles of ashes and the faded pink ribbon by the bed, "You need to learn the past is the past. Should have moved on a long time ago, Sweetness. I'm your man now. You need to know that. One and only. Forever."

Thou art mine Beatrice of Clay, yesterday, tomorrow and today...

I shivered.

Frank smiled and tugged at his waistcoat.

He was putting on weight again. That suit would have been baggy on him when he came back from London, now his stomach strained the waistcoat. How could you get fat so quickly on a ration book?

Frank came around the bed, untied one of my hands and took my gag out. I resisted the urge to bite him.

There was water and toast. Frank retreated and watched as I drank the water and nibbled on the toast. I didn't think I was gaining any weight.

"How long are you going to keep me like this?"

"Till you get better or till the doctors come for you."

"I am better."

Frank gave me a thin, I'll-be-the-judge-of-that smile.

"Don't you think the doctors will have something to say about this?" I held up my wrist to show the red bracelet of blistered skin decorating it.

"It's for your own good. And mine. They'll understand. You wrecked the house and threatened to kill me. Sometimes you have to be tough with the ones you love. Everybody knows that."

Actually, I'd threatened to kill my faceless companion, but I didn't see much value in trying to point that out to Frank.

"You need to piss?"

I shook my head.

"The rope's rubbing me raw," I complained, sores had erupted around my mouth from the gag too, but that didn't keep Frank from putting it back after he'd retied my wrist. He forced open my mouth, stuffed the cloth in and fixed a length of leather strap around my head to stop me working it out with my tongue.

Frank pulled back the sheet and tied my ankles to the bed too. Something he hadn't done before. After looking at me for a while he fetched a couple of leather belts. I feared he was going to beat me with them, but instead he strapped them around my arms, looped them through the bed frame and kept tightening till I winced.

Satisfied, he stood back and admired his handiwork. He'd always put the sheet back over me, but this time left me uncovered. I'd been naked for days. Saved on having to wash my nightgown, he'd told me.

He ran his eyes over my body, snorted and shook his head.

"Going to buy some proper restraints, be more comfortable for you. Owen's ring will help with that. Don't get no funny ideas while I'm gone. You won't get out of those knots; you'll just hurt yourself. Trust me, I know best, Sweetness."

He nodded and walked away, pausing at the broken door to glance back, "And please don't piss on the mattress unless you really have to, Sweetness, it's very unhygienic."

Then he headed off down the corridor whistling *It Had to be You*.

Once both Frank's whistling and footsteps disappeared into the distant hum of the sea, I started trying to loosen the ropes around my wrists.

Where Frank was going to buy his more "comfortable" restraints, I couldn't imagine. I doubted they sold such things anywhere along Creethorpe's sleepy Hight Street. However, it sounded like he would be gone for a while.

Whatever it took, I had to get out of here. No doctors were coming; nobody was coming.

After all, I was not the one who was insane.

1920

The Albion Hotel was a respectable establishment for respectable people. Whether or not you were a nice girl who happened to be a vicar's daughter was irrelevant. They did not allow unmarried women to bring men back to their room.

This concerned me through my fug of desire and gin as we walked from the pub to the hotel. A few hazy whisps of mist haloed the streetlights, coal smoke tainted the air. If I hadn't been holding Frank's arm so tightly, I'm not sure how many times I would have hit the pavement.

I'd given up on trying to fasten my coat, leaving it to flap open around me. It wasn't cold.

We paused on a street corner. *The Albion* was halfway down a terrace of identical Victorian buildings, all stern and disapproving behind their black iron railings.

I thought we'd stopped to devise a cunning plan to smuggle Frank into the hotel. Frank, however, had other priorities. His lips and hands were on me again, exploring, probing, pushing, squeezing, demanding.

Looking back, I'd like to think at least some part of me was protesting this, but I honestly do not remember. All I can recall is my own lust, an emotion I was unacquainted with. I suppose I must have felt similar things with Owen, but perhaps I choose not to give those feelings so base a label.

It was all so out of character I often wonder if Frank cast a spell upon me, something to dull my good sense and unleash desires I had kept bottled up all my adult life. This isn't as preposterous as it sounds, knowing what I now know. However, if Frank did ensnare me with some glamour, it was a trick he never had cause to use again. I've never suffered an ounce of desire for him since.

"How will-" I started to say when Frank finally pulled back a little.

"I want you," he said, explaining everything and nothing.

We walked again. My jelly legs just about kept me upright while my stomach, sloshing to the brim with little besides gin, rolled queasily. Other parts of my body were misbehaving too.

"How-"

"Leave it to me," Frank grinned.

I found this reassuring for some reason, stowed my worrying and went back to concentrating on putting one foot in front of the other without falling over.

A series of scuffed stone steps led up to the *Albion's* door; my heels clicked on each one in time as I wobbled up them. Confronted by the black lacquered door with its brass doorknobs, my worries bobbed back to the surface.

"We're not married," I hissed at Frank as if the fact might have slipped his attention.

Frank winked one of those burnt hazel eyes of his at me.

He took me inside, bold as the *Albion's* doorknobs.

I went with him, as much for fear I'd fall without his arm to support me. I kept my eyes down. My cheeks flushed as we approached the reception desk in expectation of the forthcoming humiliation.

I didn't look up until we sailed straight past it.

Nobody was there.

"Told you there was nothing to worry your pretty little head about," Frank's sharp little moustache twitched again as he stabbed the button for the elevator. I didn't recall telling him what floor my room was on, but once he'd hauled open the door, he pressed for the fourth floor without hesitation. I guess I must have.

I slumped against him as the elevator clanked and groaned. Frank cupped a hand around my bottom and fondled it. I knew I should tell him to stop, but I fumbled his lips instead. His other hand squeezed my breast, and I wondered if we'd make it to the room.

We did. Somehow.

We saw no one else on the way. Which, considering our scandalous behaviour, was just as well.

By the time I managed to find the lock with the key, my head was spinning as much with lust as gin.

I had enjoyed many daydreams about what losing my virginity would be like. They had all involved Owen, usually accompanied by scented sheets, rose petals, soft music (or perhaps birdsong from beyond sunlit windows) and slow, tender, beautiful exploration of each other before he finally, achingly, longingly, lovingly, ever so gently, eased himself inside me.

The reality with Frank was somewhat... *different*.

We fell into the room, stumbled to the bed, lost our coats somewhere on route, and collapsed into a tangled heap. I remember giggling at the absurdity. Frank started clawing at my dress.

I could feel his excitement as readily as my own. I remembered the one night I'd shared with Owen and wanted that hardness in my hand again but wasn't sure if I should. Was it something nice girls, especially ones who happened to be a vicar's daughter, did?

With Owen, everything had been hesitant. He'd put his hand inside my panties, which had been rather wonderful, but they had stayed resolutely in place. Frank had no such reticence. Pulling at my clothes, bra, underwear in a flurry of fingers, hands, arms, all the while kissing me, his beery breath playing over me.

Something ripped in the darkness as Frank tugged my dress off.

The room was cold. I wanted to get under the blankets, but when I wriggled, Frank pushed me down, and started bothering my bra, tugging the straps and biting my breast.

I cried out, but he didn't stop. In fact, it had the opposite effect.

Perhaps it was his frenzied groping, perhaps it was the weight of him on top of me, or the sharp nipping pain of his teeth on my breasts. Maybe it was the hand yanking my panties down, but suddenly, I wasn't so sure about this at all.

"Frank..." I gasped, "...slow down... please."

He pulled back a little, but only to drag my panties free.

I tried to sit up, "Maybe we should-"

"Don't be a spoil sport now, eh?"

He was tugging at his own belt, freeing himself.

The curtains weren't drawn. Streetlight stole into the room, giving Frank's face a sickly yellow wash.

He looked strange, alien, unreal. I was allowing him to have what I had denied the man I loved, the man I had known in the depths of my soul would never come home from the war to marry me.

What on Earth am I doing?

"Frank..." I sat up, resting on my elbows "...I don't feel right."

"Just the drink, you'll sleep it off," Frank was up on his knees; he pulled his trousers down but didn't bother taking them off.

"No... not the drink... this..."

Frank looked at me, his eyes dark hollows, mouth a black line.

"Don't worry, Sweetness," he breathed, "this won't take long..."

He lowered himself, pushing me back with his weight while one of his hands parted my legs.

"Frank, no..." I whispered in his ear.

When he ignored me, I tried to struggle, but he was a big man, strong and heavy. I felt trapped, claustrophobic, panicked.

What was I doing?

I slapped a hand on his back, "No, stop, *please!*"

My legs were apart, he was between them. His hardness pressed against my inner thigh...

"It's too late for no, darling," he panted, the beer and tobacco on his breath sour in my face. I attempted to wriggle away, but his arms slid under me, hands gripping my shoulders, coarse fingers digging in me all the way down to the bone.

Then he thrust.

"You're hurting me!"

And again. Harder. Going deeper.

Hot, tearing pain made me cry out, my own arm wrapped around him, holding fast as tears welled in my eyes.

Owen...

I forced my lips together to stop myself from crying out his name and begging his forgiveness.

Frank was grunting with each thrust, dark eyes consuming the world as the squeak of bedsprings and the slap of flesh on flesh filled the room, announcing my shame.

"I'm sorry..." I whispered.

"You're doing good," Frank said between grunts, thinking I was talking to him.

He was hurting me so much and each time became harder, deeper, faster, tearing another layer away from me, exposing all I was and ever had been to those black, hollow, empty eyes.

I don't know how long it lasted. As Frank promised, I don't think it was long, though it seemed an eternity. And in one way, it was. Long after Frank's final thrust, expulsion of air, and shudder, I remained trapped beneath his bulk, staring into those bottomless eyes, unable to move or breathe.

Lost to even myself.

From that night in the *Albion Hotel* when I gave myself away to an unworthy man for nothing, right up until the day I died.

And for many years afterwards.

1943

I cursed, using all kinds of words a nice girl, particularly one who happened to be a vicar's daughter, shouldn't know.

Not that there was much chance of making the seagulls blush with my vulgarity, even without the gag.

Sweat slickened my skin and I slumped back into my pillows. Everything hurt. Bedsores had begun to break out on my back and bum. Just how long had I been here now?

It felt like half a lifetime.

I turned my head and stared at the charred scraps and ash on the bedside table and wanted to cry.

The welling tears annoyed me. I snapped my head towards the curtained window instead. Owen had been dead for decades, I hadn't lost him again, just words and images, ghosts and echoes. I'd read those letters so many times I could recite most of them by heart. And I was never going to forget his face.

So, I wasn't going to cry. Not over paper and gold. I wouldn't give Frank the satisfaction of knowing how much his petty cruelty cut me.

I returned my attention to the ropes binding my wrists. Twisting, turning, flexing to loosen the binds enough to slip fee of them.

So far all I'd achieved was to make my wrists throb and smart.

I'm never leaving this room.

The thought slammed into me. I was getting nowhere with the ropes. Annoyingly, Francis and Simon's scout troop had never taught them how to get out of their clever knots.

Frank would never release me. He must know, after this, if he ever did, I would leave him. Perhaps he thought he could break me enough to ensure I stayed. Or his charade of being nice had broken him.

But I was not the woman he'd cowered for twenty-three years. The war had taken Frank away, and it had improved my life immeasurably. Then Tom showed me the possibility of happiness. The boys were gone. What remained to keep me in the Castle but ropes and belts?

Whatever games my faceless companion played, could I really believe Tilly was still alive? No, of course not. Had that thing spent sixteen years raising her, caring for her, feeding and nurturing her? Loving her? No. If it was more than some figment or delusion, some product of a shattered mind, then it was a monster.

And what would a monster do to a baby?

She was gone. Like Owen was gone. Like Simon and Tom.

The cries were nothing but a game. Or another rope to bind me to this bed, to this place, to this life.

I tugged against the ropes and belts. My cry softened by the gag. Nothing loosened, nothing gave.

And if I couldn't figure out a way to escape Frank's binds, I needn't worry about my faceless companion's ones. I wouldn't be going anywhere.

How long had Frank been gone?

Tracking the passing of time had become guesswork, the diffuse light in the bedroom hadn't altered much, but that was all I had to go on. A couple of hours, perhaps?

Both my wrists smarted and stung. The right might have even started bleeding, though I couldn't lift it far enough to check. No matter. I had to get out while Frank was away. Who knew how long it'd be before he left me alone for any length of time again. And with the shiny new restraints he brought home with him, it'd be even more difficult.

Don't give up! Keep working the ropes. You'll get out in the end.

In the adventure movies I had taken the boys to see on Saturday morning at the *Regal Picture House*, the heroes were forever slipping free of whatever fiendish bindings the dastardly villains had devised to tie them to a chair or a railway track.

In reality, things were much harder and slower. And a lot more painful.

I supposed I should be grateful Frank hadn't strapped me to a train line. The service was still quite regular despite the war. I'd have been sliced into pieces many times over by now if he had.

What *did* Frank intend?

That was a little wasp of a thought that kept buzzing around.

If there were no doctors, no hospital, no lobotomy – and the longer this went on, the more convinced I became I wasn't the one who'd benefit most from having my skull peeled open – then at what point did this stop being something to protect me from myself and turn into a crime. And the military police would eventually come for him...

A sound came from downstairs.

Was Frank home already? With his lovely new restraints?

Oh, darling. Did you get leather or steel? Pleeeease don't keep me in suspense!

I strained to hear, but nothing else came.

Maybe it was just the innocent creak of the cottage.

Or perhaps one of the less innocent ones.

I hadn't heard a peep from my faceless companion all day. I'd expected him to come a taunting as I laid naked, spread and helpless upon the bed, but there'd been nothing.

I tried to concentrate on the ropes, but I was exhausted, sore and beginning to give up hope. And if Frank was home, there was no point in hurting myself more.

Perhaps I should try to run when he changed the restraints. He wouldn't expect that, would he? Me, leaping to my feet and sprinting buck-naked through the marshes all the way to Creethorpe station. Sadly, Frank was bigger, stronger and faster, I doubted I'd make it to the bottom of the stairs, even if I hadn't endured days tied to a bed.

My head shot up.

Another sound. The familiar creak of floorboards. I'd heard it enough over the years. But whether it was Frank or my faceless companion I couldn't say.

Which would I prefer?

The husband who'd beaten and abused me for years and had now taken away my liberty on the pretext I was insane, or the faceless supernatural entity that had killed my lover and snatched my baby.

My head flopped back to the pillows.

Like choosing the manner of your own execution, it mattered little in the end.

I started at the ropes again on the off chance the monster wasn't human. I winced and bit down on the gag with discomfort and frustration.

Feet on the stairs.

Something coming towards me.

Did my faceless companion have feet? I didn't know, I'd never got much of a look at him, but it sounded like he owned some. A pair well suited to sneaking, skulking and tiptoeing around the periphery of my life.

It was more likely Frank. Which meant it was time to stop scraping the skin off my wrists and make like a good trussed up little wife again. Instead, I wriggled and twisted all the more. Was the left one easing a little? Or was that just my imagination. I did have quite the imagination after all.

No, I don't! I haven't imagined anything! I'm not the mad one, remember?

Would it be better if I were mad? A world where I'd lost my mind, when you thought about it, was much less frightening and unsettling than one where monsters really did sneak around, snatching babies and murdering lovers.

I concentrated on my left hand, tightening it into a fist before loosening it again as I turned it one way and then the other.

Beyond the confines of my bedroom, the footsteps finished climbing the stairs and were now moving about the landing. The more I listened, the less they sounded like

Frank. My husband had always been more of a thudder than a sneaker. My faceless companion, on the other hand...

Sod him.

He could creak all the floorboards he liked; I'd heard that part of its repertoire so often it wasn't as effective as it used to be. If I ever got the gag out of my mouth, maybe I'd suggest rattling some chains or wailing mournfully to mix it up a little.

The creeping about was starting to get rather old hat.

My left wrist seemed as tightly bound as before. Perhaps I had been imagining it loosening. I managed a muffled cry and threw myself back hard enough to make the bed rock.

The footsteps on the landing fell silent.

After a pause, the boots squeaked and the footsteps grew louder.

Did my faceless companion have squeaky boots? I didn't think so. And Frank certainly didn't. Neither of us tended to wear outdoor shoes upstairs.

So, if it wasn't Frank or my faceless companion...?

I started making more noise, bucking and crying out as much as the gag allowed, even if it did feel like I was going to choke..

The footsteps stopped outside. There was no handle to turn as Frank hadn't bothered to fix the lock I smashed with a hammer. All it took to open it was a push.

I fell still as the door swung inwards.

A head peered around the corner...

"Well, thas a roight rum owd dew, girl!"

1920

I had no intention of seeing Frank again.

After he awoke in the morning, with slow, groggy sighs and a phlegmy coughing fit, he wanted me again. I let him. I was hungover, embarrassed, ashamed and very sore, but it just seemed the easiest thing to do.

Once he'd had his fill he'd go, and I could forget about everything that had happened.

Perhaps if I'd simply told him to piss off, my life might have taken another path, or maybe it was too late and it made no more difference than making me sorer than I already was.

The second time, in the grey morning light, was, somehow, even worse. I could see more and I was no longer drunk. I stared up at his face, teeth grinding together, cords of his neck straining, burnt hazel eyes narrowing and widening in time to his thrusts, until I could stand it no more and moved my attention to the ceiling.

At least it didn't take long, which was as much as could be said for it.

He planted a wet kiss on my lips when done. His breath was vile. Then he rolled over and lit a cigarette, easing back down to smoke it with one hand behind his head.

I turned away on my side trying to stop myself throwing up.

"You'd best be away before anyone sees you," I managed to say.

"Why?"

"I don't want to be thrown out."

Frank chuckled.

"Only married couples are allowed here," I said, unable to keep the irritation from my voice.

"We will be married soon."

"Are we engaged now, then?" Sarcasm replaced irritation. I would soon learn not to speak to him in such terms and tones, but I was yet to meet the real Frank.

He chuckled again. Looking back, it was probably through gritted teeth, but I was too busy calling myself names to notice.

"Shall we go to the pictures tonight?"

"I don't think so."

He didn't say anything else till he finished the cigarette, then he turned onto to his side behind me and rested a hand on my hip.

"What's wrong, Sweetness?"

I didn't know where to start, so I said nothing.

"Bit tired, huh?" he eased himself up against me, "Long night we had."

He buried his face into my hair, I didn't know whether it was supposed to be a gesture of affection, or he needed to wipe his nose.

"Yes," was all I trusted myself to say.

"Pictures tomorrow night then," he patted my side, "I'll let you get some rest today."

He slipped his hand under the sheets and caressed my thigh and bottom. It dawned on me I was naked. Something I'd never experienced with Owen.

The thought of Owen made me squeeze my eyes shut as Frank continued to run his hand over my body.

I'd given away the one thing I denied the man I loved for nothing...

My throat thickened, I sucked air through my nostrils and shuddered.

For bloody well nothing!

I wasn't going to cry. Not in front of Frank, not in front of anyone.

Frank's hand stopped roving. He patted my hip again, "Don't think I can manage it again for a bit, Sweetness," he said.

It took me a few unsteady breaths to realise he'd mistaken my reaction for desire.

He fondled me a while. I don't know for how long; I was too busy trying to hold the fragments of myself together to pay any attention to such trivialities as time.

He sighed, kicked away the sheets and climbed out. I kept my back to him and hoped he'd think I'd fallen asleep. Perhaps I did, for when he put his hand on me again, he'd dressed.

"Get your rest, Sweetness, I'll see you tomorrow. Be at the *Rose & Crown* for seven," he lent in and gave me a stale kiss on the cheek, then ruffled my hair, "Don't keep me waiting, eh?"

"I-"

"I always knew we were meant to be together, right from the start..."

He left the room without waiting for a reply. I doubt he made it to the stairs before the tears finally got the better of me.

I went and had a bath after an hour of staring at the wall. I expected all and sundry to denounce me as a harlot the moment I stepped out of my room. No one did.

After scrubbing myself half raw and sitting in the water until it turned cold, I could still feel Frank, still smell him, still taste him.

I wasn't to know it then, but Frank Harryman was something I'd never be able to wash from my skin any more than I could wash him from my mind or soul.

I didn't leave the hotel till evening, when my stomach felt able to contemplate food.

The next morning, I checked out of the *Albion*, expecting sneers and knowing looks from the receptionist. There weren't any. He was polite, efficient and impersonal. He didn't ask why I was leaving early, which was just as well.

Perhaps it was written on my face.

I walked with the two suitcases that carried all my worldly possessions to the nearest bus stop and jumped on the first bus to appear. It trundled over Chelsea Bridge. I sat, glassily looking out of the window. It terminated in Putney, which I decided was far enough away for Frank to never be able to find me again.

After asking a couple of locals I found a nice hotel overlooking the river. I checked in for the week and went up to my room. I curled in a chair and watched the grey-brown waters of the Thames drift by until the night's gauzy veil descended over the world.

I spent most of the night awake, Owen's letters strewn around me, alongside his ring and photographs. I'd toyed with the idea of burning them and the photographs and selling the ring. I didn't deserve them; I'd tarnished Owen's memory.

All the stupid excuses I'd conjured for not wanting to marry him until the war was over, all the lies, all the petty fears. Selfish, ignorant, arrogant little girl!

Now I'd given myself away.

For nothing.

I hoped Owen's soul was at peace and so far away he could never know what I'd done.

In the end, I couldn't part with any of them. I might not have been worthy of his love, but they were the only things of worth I had left in the world.

I'd cried many times before reading those letters, but it had been a long time since I'd read them all in one go. Even when I could barely see them for the tears, I read every single one.

It was only later as I laid in the darkness hoping for sleep to take me, did it occur to me that in all those letters, Owen had never once mentioned the name of his pal, Frank Harryman...

1943

The first thing Davey did was throw a sheet over me.

Personally, I'd long since got to the point where the rag in my mouth and the ropes around my wrists troubled me a lot more than my nakedness.

"Dew yew wan' me git yew outta tha', girl?"

The gag muffled my profanity somewhat, but Davey got the gist.

"Whas this all 'bout then?" he asked once the strap and cloth were out of my mouth.

"Untie me, Davey! We need to be gone before my husband gets back."

Davey scratched his head, "Yewr husband put yew 'ere?"

"Yes… it's a long story. Just get me out of here!"

"Don't like to interfere between man an wife, can be messy, reckons…"

"There's nothing in the marriage vows about allowing your husband to tie you to a bed and gag you, Davey."

"S'ppose…"

Davey started on my wrist.

"Looks sore tha' does, girl."

"Stings a bit…" I muttered, holding my chaffed and bloody wrist up for inspection. "My clothes are on the chair in the corner," I told him once he'd got all the restraints off.

What I'd been wearing when Frank caught me still sat where he'd thrown them. He'd never been one for putting anything away. Like most of the chores in Grey Gull, that had been my job.

Davey brought my things and placed them on the bed.

"Oi'll wait outside, girl," he said, hurrying back onto the landing.

I tried jumping to my feet, eager to put as much distance between myself and Grey Gull before Frank came back. My legs, however, had other ideas.

My knees buckled and I had to sit straight back down or end up on the floor.

How long had I been in that bed?

I dressed slowly, sitting on the edge.

I must stink.

Frank had dabbed a flannel over me a couple of times and emptied the chamber pot when required, but the bedroom was a ripe old place now. I blushed and found I wanted to cry.

No time!

"Why are you here?" I called to Davey.

"Oi been worried. Nah sign of yew, and yewr owd man kept chasing me orf whenever oi came to see yew. Can't say oi like tha' one much. Cold owd bugger, reckons..."

"No. Me neither..." I said still struggling into my clothes.

"So, decided to watch yewr place, a bit sly like. Ain't seen hide nor hair of yew. When yewr owd bugger went to town oi came to see if yew wer' alroight."

"That was hours ago."

A pause followed the sound of a match lighting before Davey replied, "'bout thirty minutes, reckons. Wanted to make sure he weren't coming back 'fore nosing around."

Thirty minutes?

It seemed I spent forever working on those ropes after Frank left. I rubbed my wrists and winced. I had lost all sense of time.

Getting my shoes on proved the hardest part of my dressing ordeal. My head swam every time I tried to bend over and tie the laces. My thick, numb fingers didn't make it any easier either.

"Yew alroight in ther', girl?"

"I'm getting there. You can come in, there's nothing you shouldn't see on view."

"Reckons oi'll stay out 'ere if yew don't mind..."

I wrinkled my nose. It really was very stinky. I'd get the window open once I'd remembered how to tie laces.

Why? After you leave this room, you're not coming back. Are you?

My eyes darted to the corner where Tilly's cot used to sit.

Hot knives of guilt sliced through me.

Was I abandoning my baby by running away? Was she still–

If you don't go now, you never will!

Frank's the mad one, remember?

Laces eventually tied; I straightened up. Sweat dampened my brow from the effort. I ran fingers around my left wrist, wincing as they brushed the broken, blistered skin.

I am not insane.

Davey is not a figment of my imagination. Figments of your imagination can't untie knots. And if he is real, everything else is.

That realisation was a relief. No matter how much I'd told myself I wasn't a lunatic. The possibility Frank was right still lingered even after he'd reverted to his old self and all the familiar accompanying cruelties.

"How long has it been since you saw me, Davey?"

"'bout ten days, reckons... why?"

"I kind of lost time a little."

In gingerly taken increments, I pushed away from the soiled mattress. Once my head and knees firmed up, I took a couple of shaky steps and wrapped a hand around the bedpost.

"Wha' yew wanna dew now, girl?"

"Get out of here."

"Where yew gonna go?"

My fingers tightened on the bedpost. The thought of the long walk to get... anywhere was enough to make my legs buckle. I didn't doubt my strength would return, but right then, after all those days in bed, even getting down the stairs seemed a challenge.

"Yew alroight, girl?"

"Just taking a bit of time to get my legs working again. I'll be fine. It's like riding a bike!"

A phlegmy laugh came from outside.

Still not trusting my legs, I gave myself a little longer to get used to being vertical.

"The woman I went to see in London, Mrs St Clair, remember?"

"Oi remembers, girl. Ain't tha' long ago. Me bonce ain't tha' soft yet neither."

"She's dead. Died after leaving here in 1930. In a car crash..."

Davey shuffled his feet.

"I think... our friend killed her too. Killed her because she tried to warn me, tried to tell me something about Tilly. About her being taken. I don't know. She told her friend, a medium, she's dead too, but I spoke to her cousin. The things she told her... it sounds exactly the same as what we've seen."

More feet shuffling. Then another struck match followed by a cough.

"Evil owd bugger, reckons..."

"I don't know what to do, Davey. I've heard Tilly crying, the thing – our friend – talked to me... intimated, she was still alive. It said *if the child doth suffer, so doeth the mother.* What does that mean?"

The only answer was the creaking of the house.

I didn't know what wisdom old Davey Acorns could give me, but just saying the words aloud made me feel better. Made it feel less... crazy, somehow.

Taking a gulp of stale air, I let my hands slip from the bed. Whatever I did next, it had to be away from Grey Gull. Get back my strength, put my thoughts in order. Make some decisions.

With hesitant steps I moved around the bed. I ran my fingers through the ashes on the bedside table.

Hatred consumed me.

I wanted to scream. If Frank had walked into the room then, I think I would have tried to kill him with my bare hands.

Instead, I sucked it down and rammed it in the box with all the other things I'd had to find room for within my soul.

I stuffed the faded pink ribbon in my pocket. That was all I had left. I couldn't bring Owen's letters back any more than I could the man I'd loved so long ago, and every day since.

On the landing, Davey paced back and forth as he waited for me.

"Nearly done!"

It was only a couple of strides from the bed to the door. If I couldn't manage that, I might as well fall back into bed and wait for Frank.

There was still some water in a glass on the bedside table, I gulped it down. It helped wash a little of the taste of the rag from my mouth as well as easing my sore throat.

The bag I'd packed before sat in the corner; the clothes still scattered on the floor where Frank had dropped them. It was an effort to kneel, but I managed it and piled everything back in. My coat was on a chair, with my handbag. For some reason Frank hadn't bothered to go through it. My running away fund was still in my purse in the coat pocket. It wasn't much but it was something.

Right! Let's get out of here.

I took another breath and crossed the room. My legs still felt like distant relatives, but I took heart from the fact there was no wobbling or buckling.

Pulling open the door I hurried out, eager to be leaving Grey Gull.

The landing was empty.

The only sign of Davey was a roll up smouldering on the carpet runner.

"Davey...?"

A dark, malevolent giggle that came from everywhere and nowhere answered...

1920

I found a room in Putney, got a job as a barmaid, more for something to fill my days than to pay for the room, and tried to figure out what I wanted to do with the rest of my life.

I also drank quite a bit too.

Gin did nothing to help me decide my future, though it helped a little with forgetting my past.

The weeks passed in a hazy fug of drunkenness and denial. I managed to stay sober enough to not get sacked. I don't think I endeared myself to the landlord who would regularly take me aside to tell me to be "nicer to the punters."

As far as I was concerned, I was perfectly pleasant to everyone who came into the *King George*, but Albert expected fulsome smiles, frequent laughter and sufficient flirtation to keep his clientele coming back for more. If you knew some risqué jokes, all the better.

Besides a few boors and bores most of the men were nice enough, but each over long glance and clumsy compliment reminded me of Frank. Of his burning eyes, gritted teeth and straining neck cords. Of his weight, his smell and the feel of him pushing, pushing, pushing inside me.

So, I dismissed each look and ignored each compliment.

And if that didn't work, I dipped into Albert's gin when no one was looking.

Still, Albert kept me on. I worked hard, took every shift available and didn't scream at anyone. Despite my cool demeanour, quite a few of the men seemed to like me. Perhaps they saw me as a challenge. I don't know and didn't ask. The way I felt, I'd have happily spent the rest of my life in a nunnery. The thought of letting another man touch me again...

When I wasn't working or drinking, I sat in my room, reading, smoking, staring at Owen's letters and photographs or walking, watching the buds burst and flowers bloom as life returned to the parks, gardens and streets along the Thames.

As much as I tried to wash Frank Harryman from my life and memory, I couldn't shake the nagging certainty he was close. Countless times I looked up, turned around or opened my eyes and expected to see him, tall, broad, that thin razor cut moustache atop his lip, mouth curling into a smile that didn't reach his eyes.

Several times I nearly told Albert I was quitting and my landlady that I was leaving. Twice I went as far as packing my bags before talking myself down. Frank was as unlikely to find me here as he was anywhere else. Running served no purpose.

Of all the things that occupied my mind in Putney, the possibility I would fall pregnant after my ill-advised night with Frank rarely dirtied the horizon.

It was too absurd to consider. I did not love Frank; I did not even like him. He'd made me feel used and unclean. God would not, could not, be so cruel as to allow me to catch with child after one silly mistake, especially not after taking the love of my life from me.

God, of course, is not cruel.

However, I have begun to suspect over the years that he can get distracted.

I dismissed the non-arrival of my days. The emotional stress of Dad's death, added to the self-disgust I was heaping upon myself and the excessive gin-drinking, were no doubt responsible. The grief and self-disgust were monoliths too deep-rooted for me to shift. I could leave time to erode them. The gin-drinking, though, was all down to me.

For a few days I left Albert's stock in peace. I also ignored the bottle in my room that I kept in a suitcase under the bed for fear Mrs Briggs might take exception to renting her best room to a drunken harlot like me.

After a particularly trying Saturday, where three different men asked me out, another two pinched my bum and Hairy Harry Hawkins (a *King George* veteran who had his own stool at the bar and tankard behind it) asked me to marry him, I back slid a little on the sobriety.

By the Wednesday I'd back slid quite a lot.

By the next Saturday I'd forgotten all about my missed time of the month and the possibility gin might have anything to do with it.

I'd started feeling nauseous a lot too, especially in the morning. I put that down to too much gin and too many cigarettes and vowed to cut down again. But didn't. Probably because they were a good excuse as to why I was feeling nauseous.

My breasts started getting heavier and more sensitive. As far as I knew gin and cigarettes didn't make your breasts get bigger, but, whatever the cause, I wasn't pregnant.

I simply couldn't be!

I'd only had *relations* once! Well, twice if you counted the morning. How could I be pregnant?

I'm doubt I was the first young woman in the world ever to be struck by such a certainty. Nor the first to find out it only needs to be once.

When my days failed to arrive again the following month, and I was still waking up feeling nauseous, I started thinking about seeing a doctor. I obviously wasn't pregnant (I kept reassuring myself) but what if I had some horrible disease or condition?

I thought about talking to Maggie, Albert the landlord's wife, but decided against it. She'd probably jump to the wrong conclusion. I didn't want to risk losing my job when I obviously wasn't at all pregnant.

Just missing my days, feeling sick and suffering swollen breasts.

In the end, I went to the doctor to put my mind at rest and confirm it was something else.

Anything would do. I wasn't fussy. Just not pregnant!

Dr Jardine was a cadaverous looking Scot with yellow teeth, a widow's peak and the bedside manner of a man who had a hundred important things to do that I was keeping him from.

"You're pregnant... Miss Clay."

I blinked as if I'd been slapped.

"I can't be."

Dr Jardine looked up from whatever he was scribbling, "Are you a virgin?"

This time I didn't blink, though I still felt like I'd been slapped.

"No..." I told him in the smallest of voices.

"Have you had intercourse in the last three months?"

I nodded.

From the way my cheeks burned, I probably looked like I'd been slapped too.

"Then, you most certainly can be pregnant," he put his pen down and sat back to give me a significant look, "and you are, Miss Clay."

To be honest I don't remember much about the rest of the appointment, other than the disapproval dripping off Dr Jardine.

I was a fallen woman, a harlot, a jezebel. A wicked, selfish creature corrupted by sin and lust. A woman, as they say, who enjoyed the company of men.

Dr Jardine never said anything of the sort. But that was what I heard whenever he emphasised the word "Miss" from the far side of his desk.

At some point I left his office and settled my bill. I must have, but I don't recall. He may have offered advice, there were good Christian houses that took in the children of women such as me. He may have suggested them, I really can't say for sure.

The next thing I remember clearly was sitting in Leader's Garden, watching the river beyond the embankment. Putney Bridge was to the right, in the opposite direction the river curved towards Hammersmith. I could make out the football ground at Craven Cottage on the north bank.

I had a cigarette in my hand, a couple of inches of ash hung from it.

A woman walked past, holding the hand of a young boy.

She was looking down at him, smiling as he chatted away at a thousand words a minute. She looked happy. She was allowed to. I couldn't see her wedding ring, but I was sure it sat on her finger beneath her glove, declaring she was a good, virtuous, upstanding Christian woman.

Unlike me.

I dropped the cigarette and ground it out with my shoe.

What was going to become of me?

And my baby?

The Thames' grey-brown water pulled my eyes back to it.

There were worse options.

Yes, solve one sin with an even greater one.

What would Dad say about that?

He would know what to do. He always did. He'd put his arms around me, call me kitten and tell me exactly the right thing to do.

He always *had*, I corrected myself. The lump in my throat swelled so fast it threatened to engulf me.

I missed him so much!

A man walked by. Dapper in a pin-striped suit, greying hair and lingering eyes. He didn't smile.

A young woman crying in public. A broken heart or an unwanted swelling belly? The question flickered in his gaze; I busied myself searching for a handkerchief in my handbag to avoid it.

I was being stupid, self-indulgent, weak.

Get a grip, Beatrice, for goodness sake!

I had to stop thinking about me and do what was best for my baby.

For my bastard.

Slowly I climbed to my feet, left the little park and walked out onto Putney Embankment. The river churned beneath a sky as leaden as my mood.

In the distance a gull cried its lament.

You're a long way from home, I thought, peering back along the river, but the only birds I could see were a couple of mallards floating on the river.

I didn't know it, of course, but it was a sound I was about to become very familiar with.

1943

"Davey!"

Dropping my bag and coat I checked every upstairs room. All were empty.

Could he have gone downstairs? The old boards always made a racket, I would have heard him, but he must have.

The laughter hadn't come again, but I only needed to hear it once to know who it was these days. My faceless companion.

I clutched the banister at the top of the stairs. It was vibrating softly. Like the dresser had on the day Tilly vanished...

"What have you done?" I hissed, my hand springing away.

As usual, there was no response.

I tried to shake some reason into my skull. Perhaps Davey had gone to the toilet?

Then why drop a lit cigarette on the carpet? It was a threadbare excuse of a thing worn to patches, and Davey Acorns did live in a shed, but still...

"Davey!" I yelled down the stairs.

Nothing.

Tentatively, I touched the banister again. It was still thrumming. I'd learnt all of Grey Gull's quirks and idiosyncrasies over the years. This wasn't one of them.

I snapped my hand back to my side.

You need to leave and leave now!

I picked up my coat and put it on. Then scooped up the bag sitting in the bedroom doorway where I'd dropped it.

Where's Davey?

Downstairs. Please, God, let him be downstairs.

I made it as far as the top of the stairs.

A figure stood at the bottom, swathed in shadow.

It wasn't Davey.

Thou cannot leave me, ever...

The words came from no mouth.

It came towards me, the whole house reverberating to the thud of each footstep upon the stairs.

My eyes tried to make sense of it, but there was no sense to be found. I'd thought it a human figure, just one eschewed, all wrong angles and awkward turns, but it wasn't that at all. It had been my brain joining the dots to create something familiar. It was more a jumble of shadows, twisted, moving, restless. It had a head of sorts, faceless, long, bent forward as if it lived in a world where the ceiling was always too low for it. Limbs too, splaying, shifting, sometimes more than there should be.

"What did you do to Davey?" I backed off a step from the top of the stairs.

Davey's gone to play, over the hills and far, far away...

"Is he dead?"

He's not coming back forever and a day...

Black steamy bubbles escaped the thing along with those words and its gibbering laughter.

I hurled my bag at the monster slowly stomping up the stairs. I wasn't sure what good that would do, and it turned out it did nothing. Sailing right through my faceless companion it hit the bottom steps and rolled the rest of the way to the hall floor.

More laughter. High, grating, amused and not close to anything sane.

The thing was growing, filling the stairs with each step. Long spindly legs, replaced thick stumpy ones, becoming disjointed, insectile appendages. And within the darkness at its core, things moved. Trapped, like bugs caught in tree resin. Faces, forms, all screaming, all in torment.

"What are you...?" I heard myself say.

I am but sorrow and thou art my muse...

I turned and ran. Not that I could go far.

I bolted into Frank's room, crashing the door behind me. The key sat in the lock like it always did and I managed to still my hand long enough to turn it.

Beyond the door and above my own protesting heart, footsteps grew louder. I had a hunch a lock and a couple of inches of wood wasn't going to keep that thing out.

That something also warned me my faceless companion was no longer dancing around the shadows, taunting me before scurrying away. It was happy to show itself, happy to show it *was* the shadows.

I ran to the window.

It wasn't locked, but it had been opened so rarely during our twenty-three years here, it might as well have been.

Footsteps echoed outside. There was nothing sneaky about the way it was moving now. Slow and deliberate, it wanted me to hear it coming.

I put my shoulder against the frame and pushed hard. When it didn't budge, I pushed harder and swore at it.

There is nowhere to run, our time together has only just begun...

The footsteps halted on the other side of the door. For a skipped heartbeat I stood in the silence before slamming my palms against the old wood of the sash, trying to force the window up.

Squealing, it jerked up an inch. Cool moist air flooded Frank's bedroom. I got my fingers underneath and heaved, ignoring the protests of rope-raw wrists. More shrieks of protest, another inch or two of air.

Beatrice... Beatrice... Beatrice...

With every repetition of my name what sounded like a knuckle rapped upon the door. Each time a little harder than before.

I wanted to scream at it, but I didn't have the breath. There was nearly enough of a gap for me to squeeze through and... then what?

I wasn't going to be able to knot sheets together this time...

There wasn't any other choice. It wasn't that far; I might not break anything. I looked over my shoulder as the door shuddered and rattled in its frame.

But if I stayed here...

I got my shoulder under the window and we both shrieked at each other until it conceded defeat and shot up so suddenly, I had to grab the frame to stop myself tumbling out headfirst.

Perhaps it would have been better if I had...

Behind me, the knocking stopped.

Then the door opened on softly squeaking hinges.

And something came into the room.

1920

I didn't expect to hear back from Frank, but he had the right to know I was carrying his child.

Men, I'd often heard it whispered, did not always do the honourable thing when confronted with the circumstances I found myself in. I suspected that was even more likely when it came to men who got grief-stricken women drunk and took advantage of them.

Frank Harryman would no doubt screw up my letter and throw it onto the fire. Probably accompanied by a maniacal laugh at the thought I was so naive to think he'd lift a finger for me. Men didn't help women like me. They used them and threw them away once they'd taken their pleasure.

Of course, not all men are like that. There are good ones too. I'd had one of them myself and still had his engagement ring to prove it, but I'd been too scared of becoming a widow with a young child to marry him when I had the chance.

The irony felt like a world upon my shoulders.

My letter was brief. I apologised for not being in touch and said I needed to see him. The apology stuck in my throat, but it appeared on the paper of its own volition. I sent it to the address I had for Frank, not knowing if he had moved to his uncle's place yet. Part of me never wanted to hear from him. The part desperate not to be one of *those* women, however, was prepared to do almost anything.

As they say, you should always be careful about what you wish for.

The days passed slow and fast.

I wasn't showing, but I soon would. Then what? I tried not to think about it but managed to think about nothing else.

I had Dad's money, which I'd barely touched thanks to what I made at the *King George*. Was there somewhere I could go? It wasn't as if I had family and friends to embarrass. But I would be out of a job, and no one would employ me, my shame would follow me wherever I went, I...

The same thoughts span around my mind in an ever more frantic carousel of despair and desperation.

I'm not that kind of a woman, I'm not! How did this happen to me?!

"Sweetness..."

My eyes shot up. I'd been too busy running a tea towel around and around the inside of a pint glass alongside my thoughts to notice the man at the bar.

"Frank," I said, nearly dropping the glass I'd rubbed to a sparkle.

He looked the same as before. Which shouldn't have been surprising given it hadn't been long since he... since we...

And yet, he did look different, somehow. The same slick back hair, same razor thin moustache, same tall, heavy build, resting on hands spayed on the bar.

Or perhaps I was the one who'd changed and was seeing him through different eyes.

The eyes of a frightened, shamed and fallen woman.

The eyes of a woman carrying this man's child.

"I've been waiting to hear from you," he said. There might have been happiness in his voice or annoyance. Possibly both.

I put the glass down but kept hold of the tea towel.

"Thought you might have gone to your uncle's place by now."

Frank shook his head and leaned a little towards me, hands still on the bar, "I've been waiting for you, Sweetness."

"You have?"

"Of course, we're meant to be together..." he cracked open a smile, "...and love always wins in the end, so they say..."

He seemed to find that funny enough to splutter aloud.

Barry, who worked on the buses when he wasn't leaning on the bar studying the horse racing, looked up from his paper. He glanced at me as if to ask if everything was alright.

I smiled to show there was no problem.

Barry didn't look convinced, and neither was I.

He kept his eyes on us as he drained his pint.

"So they say," I agreed, returning my attention to Frank.

"Well, there you are," he nodded again, like he'd said something profound, "best get your stuff. We need to talk."

"My shift doesn't finish till seven; I-"

"You shouldn't be working here," he sniffed, casting an eye around the place like it was something unwholesome, rather than a common or garden local pub, "it isn't seemly for you."

Barry tapped the base of his empty glass on the bar, "Another pint of the usual when you've got a second, Bea, love."

Distaste flickered over Frank's face. When I moved to pull Barry's beer, he reached over and took my wrist. Not hard enough to hurt me, just surprise me.

"Leave it," he said, "you don't work here anymore."

"Frank..." I hissed.

He turned my hand over and put a small box in my palm.

"Open it," he said, releasing my wrist and straightening up.

I did as he said.

A simple band of gold sat inside.

"It was my mother's," he said, stuffing his hands in his pockets and suddenly looking nervous, "now it's yours. If you want it."

"Are you..."

"Proposing. Yes, of course, Sweetness. I love you. And I want to do the right thing. I know why you sent that letter. I've been waiting. I've known since we had our special night together. Before that, even. Some things are meant. It's in the stars, you and me."

When I did nothing, beside stare at the ring. Frank plucked the box from my hand, took out the ring and slipped it on.

His hands were cold. So was the metal encircling my finger.

"What do you say, Sweetness?"

Maggie joined Barry to watch us. I didn't know if they were smiling, scowling or looking worried for me.

I felt scared and uncertain, but one feeling pushed all the others aside.

Relief.

Perhaps I'd misjudged Frank. We were both drunk, both foolish. But now he was stepping up, doing the right thing when he could have washed his hands. He was taking care of me, and our baby.

I wouldn't have to face the stigma and shame of being one of *those* women after all.

All I had to do was say yes.

So, I said yes.

Which just went to show how wrong you can be.

1943

"Sweetness..."

I was torn between looking over my shoulder and jumping out of the window. Both options seemed bad, for body, mind and soul.

Perhaps it was cowardice, or maybe twenty-three years spent doing what that voice told me, regardless, but, in the end, I looked.

The voice had been Frank's and that's who I expected to see. The possibility of my own madness once more lapping at the shore of my sanity. I'd seen no monster on the stairs, Davey had never been here and I'd somehow managed to free myself from my bindings like a wild animal gnawing through its own leg to escape a snare.

I almost glanced at my arm in the expectation there'd be nothing but a bloody stump embedded with my own teeth marks.

"Sweetness..."

The voice called again, summoning me.

My head turned.

It *was* Frank.

But not at first.

For a moment, two figures stood there, one overlaid upon the other. One Frank, in his suit, belly bulging against the waistcoat, thinning hair slicked back, the same razor-thin moustache he always wore. The one that had once, briefly, put me in mind of a Hollywood movie star.

The other figure was the thing of my nightmares. The flickering, restless form of my faceless companion, repelling the sunlight to draw shadows around itself in curtains of black steam. Towering over Frank, head bowed to fit below the ceiling, limbs flaying in different directions and wrong angles, and within that darkness the tortured, anguished forms of others.

"Sweetness..."

In the blink before the two merged, I realised most of the shifting figures writhing inside the nebulous vessel of my faceless companion were women.

Frank moved forward, and my faceless companion moved backwards until only my husband stood in front of me.

"Who are you?" I asked. My right hand slipped into my coat pocket. Inside, I found the faded pink ribbon that had once bound all of Owen's words of love, hope and beauty.

I wanted to touch it one last time.

"Frank Harryman..." he said, frowning as he came to a halt.

"But what else are you?"

"It does not matter. We will be together. Forever. As I knew we would, from the moment Owen first showed me your photograph. Sometimes, you know what is meant to be when you see the one. You listen to the whispers. Then you do what you must do. Because love always wins in the end..."

His voice was as familiar as the one inside my head, yet it carried an echo, like someone else was saying the same words, at the same time.

"You cannot leave me, Sweetness. That cannot be."

I held those burnt hazel eyes. Familiar too. But now, as I stared into them, I saw other things. Shadows moving like smoke, and within those twisting tendrils, the ghosts of others. Tortured, trapped, tormented.

"Tilly...?"

"If the child doth suffer, so doeth the mother. 'tis only what is necessary. I had no choice. I did not know. I never have, and yet I do," his hand reached out and cupped my chin. Turpentine and paint. As always. But beneath, something else. I don't think I know exactly the right word for that smell, though I'd smelt it before, but one came into mind all the same. Perhaps not the right one. But close enough.

Brimstone.

"You killed her?"

Frank shook his head. Distantly something giggled.

"No need. I didn't know. He does what he must. I do not see. Usually. Only in dreams. Sometimes. And when I paint. Or look at what I've painted. *Really* look. I will remember this no more than I remember Owen..."

His hand slid to my throat.

"You will not stay. You cannot leave. There is only one solution..."

I squirmed away from him, trying to duck past and make for the door despite knowing I would never reach it.

Frank grabbed my wrist, nails catching the chaffed, blistered skin, making me cry out.

He yanked me back towards him, twisted me around and slammed me against the wall. My head swam, by the time the world came back into focus, Frank's hands circled my neck. His jaw tensed; eyes bulged.

He squeezed.

I tried to prise his fingers apart, but they were bands of iron constricting my throat. I tried kicking, wriggling. My knee sought his groin, but whatever I attempted there was no reaction.

I couldn't breathe, I couldn't speak, even as I tried to plead with him. Nothing changed in the set of his face. His eyes just grew bigger, darker. The shadows moved within them, a maelstrom into which I tumbled.

Darkness pulsed in the corners of my eyes. I could hear my heart, blood thumping in my ears. Behind me the sea crashed and called, the gulls, such constant companions over the years, fell silent.

I tried to edge towards the open window, but Frank held me firm. My legs began to weaken, my knees buckling. I slid down the wall. Frank followed me all the way to the floor.

I am going to die.

Panic clawed me. There was no calmness, no clarity, no release. Only the absolute certainty that I did not want to die.

I thought of Tom, Simon, Tilly, Francis, Dad. I thought of all the people I had loved and wished my life had been different, not wasted upon this man. This monster. Who I'd tied myself to through fear and weakness, who'd taken my love for our children and used it to tighten those binds.

Most of all, though, I thought of Owen.

Perhaps I would see him again soon.

As the light faded, I tried to call out to him, to look beyond Frank, beyond the burnt hazel eyes and all the things I'd never noticed sitting behind them. I looked beyond this world altogether. Hoping Owen was there. Looking for his smile, his hand, his love. Waiting for me. To tell me not to be scared, that there was something else, something better. That I was not alone.

I saw nothing.

Only the darkness, rearing above me, pushing past Frank, gathering itself to consume, to devour. To take me and destroy me.

But, even in that moment, I knew this was not the end...

Part Three

The Thing That Kills Sorrow

1954

After another year, the next day duly arrived.

The question of who Merry was worried the back of my mind. I told myself he was no one. An eccentric fellow with peculiar eyes, nothing more. A whimsical vagrant with a taste for the theatrical. I kept telling myself the same thing and ignoring the fact I didn't believe it in the slightest.

The days passed. Sometimes I counted them, sometimes I didn't.

An old calendar hung in the kitchen, all the days of the year laid out below a yellowing picture of two happy boys drinking Ovaltine above a legend promising, *It Keeps Them Fit and Healthy*!

I would stand in front of it, ticking off the days until 23rd October in my mind.

The calendar was for 1943. I kept meaning to throw it out and get a new one but somehow never quite managed to get around to it. The Ovaltine boys reminded me of Francis and Simon, which probably had something to do with not getting rid of it, even though it made me sad and wistful.

Frank remained as he always did. Sometimes there, sometimes not. Sometimes watching me, sometimes not. Growing fatter and fatter, although I hardly saw him eat a thing.

Occasionally, he'd shout at me. Something nasty and hateful blurted out of the blue, "Dumb bitch!" or "Stupid cunt!"

Then he'd settle back down with a throaty chuckle.

Why was I still here?

I didn't know.

Merry said I stayed because I chose to stay.

The sadness and sorrow binds you...

It was true. But I didn't know why I kept making that choice, other than I felt I couldn't leave. There was something I needed to do. Something I needed to finish. Something I needed to resolve. But no matter how many waves I watched roll onto the beach to dissolve upon its stones, I could not work out what it was.

The children were gone, I had never had any love for the Castle and as for Frank, he became more repulsive with each day I mentally ticked off that 1943 calendar. The only thing keeping me in Grey Gull was fear of what might become of me out in the world where you could not hear the sea constantly whispering outside your window.

But it wasn't just fear.

There was something else, I just couldn't figure it out.

Perhaps Merry would know.

Merry, I suspected, knew a great many things.

On the morning of 23rd October, I found Frank sitting in his chair, reading the paper. It wasn't that day's, but he was too lazy to go into Creethorpe and buy another. No paper boy would cycle all the way out here.

He didn't look up. He doesn't paint like he used to, mainly he just swells and festers in the corner. Perhaps he'd grown too fat to stand up long enough, maybe it'd finally dawned on him he was never going to be the great and feted artist he thought he deserved to be.

I left him, saying nothing.

Outside the sea was flat, the air still. The only movement, the gulls swooping along the wrack-line. I walked.

It never occurred to me Merry would not be there. It seemed like only yesterday I'd seen him last, yet another year had flown by. Little had happened. Little did. I was forgotten, as becalmed as the sea stretching out to the edge of the world.

Merry sat as he had the previous times, perched on that long, bleached piece of dead wood that was only here when he was.

He looked up as I approached, "Lady Beatrice!"

"Merry."

He whipped out a handkerchief and brushed down the driftwood before ushering me to sit beside him.

"There is no wind from any direction today," I said, easing myself down.

"Then, once, I am merely Merry," he grinned. The sea behind him was a hazy silver-grey. So were his eyes,

"Will I ever meet Father Merry?"

The lips beneath his luxuriant beard pressed together and he nodded, "I believe so. One day. He is eager."

This was the fourth time we'd met. Three years and a day had passed since the first, no more or less grey shot his beard and hair than they had then. A hard thing to be certain of given the way time tugs and distorts our memories, but I was sure enough. Once a man starts going to grey it does not stop. His youth washes away irrevocably, like the tide removing marks in the sand, it cannot be stopped. But not Merry. Perhaps next year he would look a little older, perhaps the grey would have thickened and the black diminished. But I didn't think so.

"Yesterday you said you had things to say to me. Things I wouldn't want to hear," I held those hazy silver-grey eyes, "I wish to hear them now."

I knew it wasn't really yesterday. It was a year ago, but as I sat with the sun warming my skin, it did feel like yesterday. And, I think, somehow, for Merry, it was.

"I have a niece," Merry said, sitting straight back and folding his arms, "she is impatient. Very impatient. A wonderful, kind-hearted girl who wants to save every lost soul she meets, but we all have our faults. With Moira, it is impatience. I was forever telling her, all things come in their own time. Good, bad, indifferent and any other flavour you can think of. Hurrying them along just burns the crust and leaves the dough uncooked."

He smiled and looked pleased with himself. It sounded like the kind of thing Mrs Hollister used to say.

"Did your niece ever listen?"

"To me?" Merry stabbed a finger at his chest, "Of course not! Young people, you know how they are?"

I nodded. I did.

"What did you want from your life, Beatrice?"

"Want?"

"Want. When you were young and all this..." he raised a hand and swept it out behind him, "...was just possibilities disappearing into the haze."

I didn't answer immediately. Instead, I thought of Beatrice Clay walking the lanes and hills of the Cotswolds. Where the sunlight falls dappled through boughs of shifting green and the birdsong that scores your day wasn't the maniacal taunting screech of seagulls.

"I wanted to be happy. Nothing more."

"And what makes one happy?"

"Love."

Merry raised both a tangled eyebrow and the corner of his mouth, "Is that all?"

"I think so."

"So, happiness is a gift you can only receive from another?"

"Like beauty?"

Merry laughed.

"Are we here to talk philosophy?"

The smile faded. He shook his head.

"Then, why are we here?"

He twisted on the driftwood, turning to stare towards the north, "We're waiting for the wind to change."

"And when it does?"

He turned back to me.

"I will offer you something."

"A gift?"

"A gift? Yes. And a precious one too."

"It isn't my birthday today."

"No, Beatrice, it isn't…" Merry stared at me so intensely I shifted under the weight of his regard. It felt like he was peeling away the layers of my skin and flesh to reveal what remained of my soul, "…today is the 23rd October. Today is the day you left this world…"

1954

My heart sank.

So, he was just a mad fool after all. Had my life become so empty that an annual conversation with a stranger was something I'd been prepared to invest with some... *significance?*

Merry's expression suggested he expected some sort of response.

The one I should give him involved getting back to my feet and showing him my back.

Instead, I said, somewhat archly, "In what world am I in now then?"

When Merry continued to stare at me, I looked pointedly back and forth along the beach, "It looks very much like England to me."

"Beatrice," he said, his voice soft, "you are dead."

I laughed so suddenly it came out more as an unladylike snort. It was not at all the kind of sound a woman of my years, particularly one who happened to be a vicar's daughter, should make.

"Don't be absurd."

"Your husband, Frank Harryman, murdered you eleven years ago. On this day. Although, in fairness, it was not all his own doing."

I gathered myself. Then I did stand up. All in all, today had not been worth the wait.

"Your body is at the bottom of the deepest mere in the marsh. In a hessian sack, weighted down with bricks and wrapped in lengths of iron chain."

He sounded serious, like he was reading something important from *The Times* aloud.

My mouth dropped open, but my feet did not seem inclined to move.

"There's a letter. Frank keeps it in that little bureau under the window in the drawing room. It says you've fallen in love with an American airman, and you're leaving. You're going to go with him to Kansas. You say you're in love and happy. You say sorry and ask Frank to forgive you. Whenever Frank shows that letter to someone, he cries. He's very convincing. As is the handwriting. It looks just like yours..."

Merry kept staring up at me, that waiting for a response expression still fixed beneath his beard and hair.

"Francis believed the letter and wants you to be happy. He's a smart boy and remembers what you think he never saw during his childhood. Diane, who is brighter still, was never so convinced. She knows how much you love your son. How much you'd want to see your grandchildren. Occasionally, Francis received a letter with a Kansas postmark; it never said a great deal beyond his mother insisting she was happy and missed him. Four years ago, he received a letter in another hand, saying you had passed away suddenly. He still cries when he thinks of you."

"You are quite mad," I managed to splutter, before heading back to Grey Gull.

"Francis is in great danger, Beatrice. So is Diane and your grandchildren. They need you."

That stopped me. I don't know why. It was no less ludicrous than anything else Merry had spouted, but perhaps it was the way he spoke as opposed to the words themselves.

When I looked over my shoulder, he had something in his hand. A piece of ribbon, dark and half rotten. He held it up. There was little to tell what colour it had once been, but I think it was pink.

"Sit down, Beatrice. I did tell you that you would not like what I have to say. But you should wait till I finish. If you don't, it will be another year before I can speak to you again. Frank is getting old; he does not look after himself. He will not live many more years. But the thing inside him will. And it wants your son. There may still be a chance next year, or the year after, but I cannot say for certain. I can do many things. Some wonderful, some terrible. But seeing the future is not part of my art."

Merry laid out the ribbon on the sun-bleached wood.

When I stayed on my feet, he leant forward, clasping hands together.

"Tell me, Beatrice, what do you do all day?"

"Do...?"

He raised an eyebrow, "Do? When was the last time you cooked? Bathed? Went to the shops? When was the last time you cleaned? When was the last time you talked to anyone besides me? When was the last time you did *anything?*"

It was a silly question. But before I could tell him as much, I realised that I couldn't remember.

"Beatrice, when was the last time you ate?"

"Why, this morning!" I blurted.

"Did you?"

Yes, of course, I remembered. I'd been at the kitchen table. Frank had eaten eggs, and I... and I... and I...

I could see Frank shovelling fried eggs and toast into his mouth. He was in a vest, which boasted the stains of previous meals and had long since faded to a sour grey, chomping away as I sat opposite. He'd ignored me like he usually did. Then he'd thrown the plate in the sink with the others and ambled off somewhere.

My frown deepened. Why was the sink choked with washing up? Why was Frank's vest so dirty. Actually, now I thought about it, the kitchen was a mess. Nothing was where it should be, the floor unswept, everything smelt of old grease and rotting vegetables. Frank never opened the damn windows to air anything.

But I do.

I do.

I sat back down next to Merry, despite part of me wanting to run away.

"I... don't understand."

"You don't remember doing any of those things, do you?"

I couldn't meet his eye, but I shook my head.

"That's because your body is gone," he nodded towards the marsh, "what remains, sits amongst the mud below the still water."

I swallowed and looked at the ribbon. Blackened with mould, interlaced with strands of green slime. It looked like it had been under water for a long time. One or two patches still bore a hint of pink. Like the ribbon that held Owen's letters together.

An image of blackened scraps of paper and ash flashed behind my eyes.

How long had it been since I'd read Owen's letters? I used to read them all the time.

How long had it been since I read anything?

"When was the last time you hugged your grandchildren, Beatrice?"

Simon and Hayley. Such sweet children. They didn't visit much. I never visited them. Francis and Diane lived in London. So far away. But they came to Grey Gull every so often. They played on the beach, they loved that. Diane would watch them, a faraway look in her eye. I would stand at her side. She never said much... the children... the children...

Something sick turned within me. Something slow and cold.

"Are you saying..." it sounded so ridiculous I couldn't utter the words without an accompanying smile, "...that I'm a ghost?"

"You are a soul without a body. You should not still be here, but you have been bound and chained. When your husband dies, you will pass on to another place. But it will not be the place souls should return to."

"Heaven?"

Merry smiled, "We are all part of everything; it is where we come from, it is where we return to at the end of all our everythings. Usually."

"I dream of a Grey Place, where people walk in the dust. I dream of it a lot..."

"The place of the lost, the place of the bound. It serves many purposes; some pass through, some return, some remain. Most never see it. Which is to their good fortune. Monsters live there too."

"It is not a dream?"

"Everything is a dream. Or a nightmare."

"You're being vague, Mr Merry. I've always found vagueness irritating."

Merry chuckled. Then the breeze tugged at his hair, pulling it about his face. Behind him, waves started to unsettle the previously becalmed sea.

He turned and pursed his lips. When he twisted back to me, he wasn't smiling.

"The wind, Beatrice," he said, "is finally blowing from the north..."

1954

I knew the place.

My meanderings had deposited me here many times.

Still, black water. The smell of rotting vegetation never left the air, even when the wind howled and rain poured. Reeds lined the water; the banks were steep. I'd sometimes sat here, eating a sandwich, watching the reed buntings, grebes, egrets and numerous other birds that fed, bred and died around the marshes.

I am not dead.

Merry stood beside me. The wind still blew from the north, so I suppose he was Father Merry now, whatever that meant.

I cannot be.

"You are down there. What remains, at least," Merry eyes did not move from the dark water.

"Why are you telling me such ludicrous things?"

"You still don't believe me?"

I didn't answer. I didn't want to. I should go home.

But I stayed.

I can't remember ever holding Simon and Hayley...

What grandmother never holds her grandchildren? Never speaks to her son or daughter-in-law. I couldn't even remember their wedding.

Did I have a tumour? Something growing in my head that was playing with my memories? It seemed more likely than being a ghost.

They want to cut your brain open, give you a lobotomy, Sweetness...

Frank's voice whispered with the reeds in the wind.

Perhaps I'd had that lobotomy. Perhaps I had been mad, after all, perhaps...

Merry bent down and pulled something from the long brown grass. A piece of flint brought up from the shore by one storm or another.

When Merry straightened up, he held the flint out in the palm of his hand.

"Take it," he said.

"Why?"

"Just do it."

I lifted my hand towards his, then pulled it away.

"I don't want to."

Merry cocked an eyebrow. The wind sharpened, teasing his hair. It still blew from the north.

"Beatrice. Take the stone. It's a simple thing. Anyone, even a child, could pluck it from my hand without the slightest difficulty," the eyebrow inched higher, "can you?"

He was right, of course. Just a small piece of flint. Easy peasy, pudding and pie.

"It's a trick," I said, raising my chin.

"I can do tricks," Merry conceded, "I'm quite well known for them in certain quarters. Some might go so far as to call it magic. This isn't one of them. Hold out your hand, Beatrice."

Despite myself, I found my hand outstretched. Merry placed his own above it and dropped the flint.

It passed through my hand and fell into the grass at our feet.

I snatched my hand away.

"A trick," I insisted.

"If you like," Merry shoved his hands into his pockets, eyes lingering on me before returning to the black waters of the mere. Despite the strengthening wind, its surface remained calm.

"Are you going to pull a rabbit from a hat next?" I laughed. Weakly.

Merry shook his head, "I don't have a hat. But my next trick will impress you even more."

Right then, I was a lot more scared than impressed.

"Really?"

"Yes. I can bring you back to life."

"I am not dead."

Merry pulled a face, "If you were alive, it wouldn't be much of a trick."

"I doubt your audience would notice," a bird flew fast across the mere, a marsh harrier, I think, though, I admit, I wasn't paying the attention to the wildlife I normally did.

"I can return you to your body until the sun rises tomorrow. You will have that long to save your son. It will be your only chance. It is something I can only do once."

"Save Francis? From what?"

"The Sorrowsmith."

"The... *what?*"

"The thing you've spent so many years seeing out of the furthest corner of your eye. The thing that killed your lover and the woman that tried to help you. The thing that took your baby. The thing that binds you to this world and feasts upon you."

I shook my head. I preferred the trick with the stone.

"And how..." I sighed, "...is this thing a danger to Francis?"

"When your husband dies, as he will soon enough, it will require a new host. It can live for a while without one, but not for long. It usually passes to a male of the same line, it can find another if it has to, but Francis will be its preference. And after it merges with him, it will change and corrupt him, as it did Frank Harryman when it passed to him."

"So, let me get this right. I am dead. My husband murdered me because he has a monster inside him? And that monster wants to take over my son next?"

"The Sorrowsmith did not want you dead. It has grown exceedingly fat on your sorrow. Your love for Owen James was so intense, it made your sorrow deeply powerful, delicious to the point of addiction. That's why it made Frank seek you out after the banquet it enjoyed in the trenches ended.

It did not want you dead, but it could not allow you to leave; it would have starved without you close. So, Frank killed you, and the Sorrowsmith bound your spirit to this place so it can continue to sup upon your sadness. Not as rich a fayre as when you lived. But it suffices until Frank dies and he moves to his new host. Then he will feast on all the sorrows he and Francis will bestow upon your daughter-in-law, Diane. And the pain of one generation shall pass unto the next."

"You know, you actually sound like you believe all this nonsense."

"You have seen the Sorrowsmith, Beatrice, many times. What is your explanation? Do you think you really were mad, or perhaps Grey Gull cottage is haunted and the Sorrowsmith is some simple, malevolent spirit rattling chains for its perverse amusement?"

I shrugged. I genuinely didn't know what to say.

"Let me tell you this, Lady Beatrice," Merry said, eyes suddenly fierce as cloud dimmed the wetlands around us, "in this world, it is not houses that are haunted..."

"And where did Frank get this Sorrowsmith from?"

"The same way he got Grey Gull. He inherited it."

"His uncle? Mr Shackle?"

"The one whose wife and children all died," Merry looked down into the mere, "yours is not the only body down there."

This is ridiculous! Stop listening to him!

Of course it was ridiculous.

But I still couldn't remember ever hugging my grandchildren, despite trying to throughout Merry's absurd ramblings.

My eyes fell to the flint poking out of the grass.

Pick it up!

I should go home, it was probably late, and if it wasn't, it soon would be. Frank would want his dinner...

Merry's regard weighed heavy upon me, though I wanted to look at them no more than I did that piece of flint.

When was the last time you made dinner, Bea?

A coldness crept through me. Spreading from my fingers and toes up through my arms and legs. As if my limbs had been lowered into freezing water. Well, perhaps not *freezing* water. But cold, black, still water, all the same.

I avoided looking at Merry or the piece of stone at my feet.

The mere below us was harder to avoid.

Silent and still. It was a place for swallowing secrets and keeping them down in its dark embrace.

This isn't real! It isn't!

I sucked in a breath. But did any air reach my lungs?

Before I knew what I was doing, I bent over and scooped up the flint.

Or I tried to.

I knew what I wanted to do. My fingers, hand and arm knew what to do. I could feel the cold, smooth flint, broken on one side to reveal its shiny, black interior.

I just couldn't pick it up.

My fingers moved around it, through it, tingling as they did so. But the stone remained in the grass. No matter what I did, I could not grasp it.

My knees gave way, and I fell to them. I feared I might collapse into a boneless heap at Merry's feet.

"I am sorry, Beatrice, truly."

I didn't think I could speak, that words would be impossible to summon from my mouth, but, in the end, I managed to choke a few up, "Who are you?"

"Someone who wishes to help."

I put my hands on the ground, fingers splayed wide. The grass, coarse and dry pushed against my skin, though not a single blade moved.

"So, you are like your niece, Moira?" I asked, looking up at him.

"No, Moira saves lost souls. I don't do that..." Merry shook his head, the north wind strong enough to flap his coat around him, "...I save the damned..."

1954

"What happened to Tilly?"

I hugged my knees as I stared across the mere. My knees, it seemed, were something I could still hold.

Merry eased himself down next to me, one leg outstretched, the other bent, both hands wrapped around his knee.

"The Sorrowsmith sent her away."

"She... isn't dead?"

"I do not know."

"Where did he send her?"

"Sorrowsmiths are not of your world, they're of mine, but they can cross between. This one did years ago. Many do. The game is greater for them here. He sent Tilly to my world to hurt you."

"Why?"

"What would make a mother suffer more than the death of her child?"

If the child doth suffer, then so doeth the mother.

I watched the mere; the wind had picked up enough to ripple the surface. It tugged at my hair too. I wasn't quite sure how that worked, but I had plenty of other questions to work through before I got to that one.

"Not knowing," I replied.

Merry nodded, "It would have greatly enjoyed your grief over Tilly's death. But the torment of not knowing what happened to her, whether alive or dead, stretched out year after year... "

"So... she could still be alive?"

"It's possible. But she was a baby when it sent her to The Fey; she could have arrived anywhere. I think it unlikely."

"Could you find her... please?"

Merry shook his head, "It is beyond me; I'm sorry, Beatrice."

The thought, the possibility, Tilly was still alive turned within me. I wanted to demand Merry got off his arse and went to find her. But I could see from the set of his face he meant what he said. And if he didn't, he wasn't going to admit it.

"And Frank?" I asked instead.

"What about him?"

"Did he know?"

"As hard as it may be accept, your husband is as much a victim as anyone else. The Sorrowsmith haunts him; he feels it and is aware of it but does not understand. That's why he paints it, over and over, though if you ever asked him, he would not see it in what he paints. All the suffering he ever inflicted upon you is at the Sorrowsmith's behest. Most of it he does not even remember."

"Can it be taken out of him?"

"No. They are entwined; they are one. It has lived in him for too long; it will not leave until your husband dies."

"And then it will... move to Francis?"

"Yes."

The questions were coming into my mind so fast I struggled keep up with them.

"But he never harmed the boys?"

"Because they are boys," Merry said, tilting his head, "it can only pass into a male host. Francis and Simon were its future, so he let you cherish them, despite the happiness they brought you stinging and burning it, but girls... girls are of no use. Girls are always expendable."

"That's why Frank always wanted more children...?"

Merry nodded.

"Boys to ensure it had someone to move onto, girls to..." I closed my eyes thankful I had born Frank no more girls.

"Why-"

He held up a hand, "Beatrice, we only have so long."

"So long?"

"Until sunrise tomorrow... remember?"

"Oh, yes..." I looked at the sky, clouds covered most of it now. I had no idea of the time, but it was gone noon.

"The choice is yours. I can leave you as you are..."

"And what would happen then?"

Merry pursed lips half hidden beneath his beard, "You will remain as you are, soul-bound to the Sorrowsmith so it can feed off your sadness. Until your husband dies."

"Then it will take Francis?"

"Yes. And the Sorrowsmith will subsume your souls within itself."

"Subsume?"

"Its final meal, you and Frank will both become part of it, you will add to its sorrows and be tormented by it for as long as it lives. And unless someone kills it, a Sorrowsmith lives forever. Sadly, neither of our worlds, The Fey or The Real will ever run out of sorrows."

"I saw… when I saw it… properly. Within the darkness of it, people, screaming. Women…"

"Those that have gone before…"

Jane Shackle, Frank's aunt. And God alone knew how many more before her. Going back for… years? Centuries? Millenia?

I held my knees more tightly, but they provided scant comfort.

"And if I… kill it?"

"You will return at sunrise to what you are now, but with nothing left to bind you here, your soul will go where it should."

"The Grey Place?"

"No. That is just a place between. A place for the lost and the damned. A vessel to hold the World's Pain. You will go where you should."

"Which is?"

"Something for you to find out for yourself."

"And Tilly-"

"Your daughter is gone," Merry said, before continuing in a softer voice, "you can believe she is dead or cling to the hope she survived. That someone found her, that someone cherished and raised her. It is possible. There is good in The Fey and there is evil too. There is also an awful lot of empty space…"

"The Fey?"

"My world. Linked to yours, The Real. Bound and weaved together, largely invisible to each other. The magical and the practical… but that is not important. Stopping the Sorrowsmith is. And time is against you."

"I have no choice, really, do I?"

"There is always a choice."

"The choice being to let my son be taken over by a monster who will torment my daughter-in-law and abuse my grandchildren."

I thought of Hayley scampering across the beach, giggling as she toddled in her big brother's wake, the sun making a halo in her mousy hair. My throat tightened, both at the thought of what the Sorrowsmith would do to her, and that I had never held her. Never talked to her, never made her laugh. I was a dead lady she'd never met. A dead lady who only lived in an old photograph.

"How do I kill the bastard?" I whispered.

"Sorrowsmiths do not die easily."

"Do you have… a magic sword or something?"

"There's no magic sword. No spell, no enchantment. No weapon forged by men or gods is capable of such a deed. Only one thing can ever truly kill sorrow. Do you know what that thing is, Beatrice?"

I looked down at his hands. He held a ribbon between his fingers, but not the decayed, blackened mould eaten one that had been in my pocket the day I died and had spent the last eleven years at the bottom of the mere we sat next to.

This one was so brightly pink it almost glowed in the dull light of the overcast sky.

When my eyes returned to his, I nodded and answered his question without hesitation.

"The only thing that can kill sorrow is love."

Merry smiled. And held out the ribbon towards me...

1954

I gasped and opened my eyes.

Then rolled onto my side and vomited. All that came up was black water.

I lay panting and shivering, screwing my eyes shut again. The light was too bright, far too bright.

My clothes were sodden, my hands and feet numb. Pins and needles cut the rest of me. My head throbbed; my mouth tasted of... I couldn't even imagine what. My heart raced, wild and erratic.

I waited.

For the sun to warm me. For the pins and needles to fade. For my heart to calm down.

Maybe I laid in the grass for minutes, maybe hours.

Eventually, things warmed, faded and calmed sufficiently for me to open my eyes again.

Everything was still bright enough to make me squint, but it wasn't unbearable. In stiff, uncertain increments I managed to push myself up and roll over till I was sitting.

I was by Cobb's Mere. One of the largest dotted amongst the wetlands. The day was overcast and dull, which surprised me as I'd thought it blindingly sunny. The wind was up, chilling the damp skin beneath my wet clothes.

The *north* wind. I thought, for some reason.

Why was I here?

Had I fallen into the mere?

I must have.

I tried to remember how I got here.

Nothing came.

Next to me I noticed a stone, a piece of flint. Instinctively I reached out and wrapped my fingers around it.

Whatever had happened, I needed to get home. I was wet through. Despite it not being an especially chilly day, the wind cut through me. If I didn't get out of these clothes and into something dry, I'd catch my death.

That made me giggle.

I didn't know why. Perhaps I'd been deprived of oxygen long enough to muddle my brain a bit. Or a bit more, if Frank was to be believed.

Climbing to my feet, I realised I only had one shoe.

Bloody hell!

I looked around but couldn't see it in the tall spiky grass surrounding the mere. Perhaps it came off in the water. The wind was chopping patterns onto the mere's surface. The thought of my shoe, lost in the mud the sunlight barely reached made me shiver more violently.

I tossed the piece of flint into the water, watching the circles of ripples it made in the water till they disappeared, imagining it sinking all the way deep, deep down to the bottom to rest next to my shoe.

Lord. I was acting peculiarly.

I kicked the other shoe off and picked it up. One shoe wasn't much good for anything, but there was a war on.

Wasn't there?

I shook my head and started gingerly back towards the beach, beyond the low scruffy ripple of dunes.

As I walked, I rubbed my wrists. Why were they so sore? Peeling back my sleeve I found the left blistered raw. I stopped. Frowning. The right wrist was the same. And around it was a bright pink ribbon.

It looked like the one I tied Owen's bundle of letters with, though it wasn't faded like that one.

Scraps of black, charred paper and ashes.

Owen's letters.

Frank burned Owen's letters!

Memories turned and twisted, mixing with the cries of waterfowl and the wind ripping through the rushes. I tried to grab their tails, hold them still, remember them, but they vanished too quickly.

One memory, however, kept returning. Frank, his face expressionless, but lips forced together in effort, cords in his neck standing out. And something in his eyes. Something dark and terrible.

My fingers touched my throat. It felt sore.

Frank killed me.

What a silly thought! Here I was, very much not dead. Albeit wet and cold.

I headed back towards Grey Gull, as fast as my feet allowed. My sock gave some protection, but countless stones and shells littered the path between here and the Castle.

Get dry, get warm, get my wits back. I'd had a fright, that was clear enough, but a towel, a change of clothes and a cup of tea would get my marbles all back in their box in short order.

I picked my way along the path by the mere and through the scrubby grass to the dunes. Cutting down the beach was a quicker way to the Castle than picking a route around the meres, reed banks and ponds of the wetlands.

The dunes are small here, hillocks crested with crowns of long grass. Once I reached the top, I immediately noticed two things. All the barb wire, tank traps and *keep off the beach* signs were gone. Secondly, there was a man sitting on a piece of driftwood. He stood up and waved at me.

It's Father Merry, the wind is still blowing from the north, remember?

I had no idea what that meant. My marbles were clearly still rolling around and very much not in their box. To my surprise, I waved back and headed towards him.

I tried to pick a route via the sandy patches of the beach, the shingle and pebbles were making me wince and wobble.

The man looked familiar, even though I'd never seen him in my life.

"This might help," he smiled, holding out my lost shoe.

I flashed a quick smile and took it from him. I wanted to ask who he was and how he'd come by my shoe, but my mind had gone quite blank.

Instead, I slipped my shoes on, trying to be as graceful as possible when hopping from one foot to the other.

When done and straightened up, the man asked, "How are you feeling?"

He had long hair, a beard shot with grey and eyes the same colour as the sea behind him.

"Erm... good, I think. I seem to have fallen in the water somehow. I'm not usually dripping wet," I laughed self consciously, pushing damp strands of hair away from my face.

I must look a complete fool!

"Thank you for finding my shoe, how-"

"It will take a little time for your mind to settle, Beatrice. The experience will not be pleasant, but it passes quickly."

"How do you know my name?"

"You will remember that, and everything else shortly. The corporeal and the spiritual are still reacquainting themselves."

"I beg your pardon?"

The man smiled. He opened his palm toward the bleached white driftwood trunk he'd been sitting on. When I stayed where I was, he placed his other hand on the small of my back and ushered me forwards.

"I'm not sure..." I shivered, the wind had its teeth out, chilling my wet bones.

"Please, forgive me," the man said, pulling off his brocade coat and draping it over my shoulders. The coat was neither thick nor heavy, but I felt warm as soon as it was about me.

Frank wouldn't be happy about me talking to a strange man...

...lips pressed together so hard they turned white, fingers so tight about my throat, hurting me, and his eyes, oh, God, I can see things in his eyes!

I blinked and found I was sitting on the driftwood, the bearded man next to me, legs astride the trunk.

"Do you know who I am?" the man asked.

I shook my head.

"My name is Merry."

"But the wind is blowing from the north," I said before I could stop myself.

"Indeed," he nodded and smiled. He had a good smile, I thought. Warm and friendly, "but Father Merry is so very formal."

"You're a priest?"

"I am many things. But we have already had this conversation, Beatrice, and we do not have an abundance of time."

"We have until the sun rises tomorrow," I said, again with no awareness I was going to say anything.

"Yes. And tomorrow always comes quicker than we expect," he ran a hand along the driftwood between us, a faint patina of whorls marked the bone white wood.

"We can wait until you are fully yourself or I can help you. The first option is easier, but it will take time. The second will not take long, but it will be unpleasant to the point of painful. The choice is yours."

"I have no idea what you're talking about."

"That does make it a tad trickier for you," he flashed white teeth at me, "shall I make the choice for you?"

"No!" I shot to my feet, heart suddenly pounding, "I need to get home. I don't know who you are, or why you have my shoe, or why I'm all wet. You're spouting nonsense at me!"

My head throbbed as if something was trying to get out of it. Or get into it. I made to storm off, but a wave of dizziness broke over me and I stumbled. If Merry hadn't darted to my side and grabbed my arm, I'd likely have ended up with a faceful of beach.

"Easy, Beatrice. Do not push yourself..."

His fingers stayed on my arm. I still had his coat over my shoulders. I should probably give it back.

"Only love can kill sorrow," I whispered, repeating the echo I heard.

I seemed to have developed a taste for spouting things I did not understand.

"And you have but a little time to do that," his fingers moved from my arm to my chin. Gently he turned my face towards him, his touch like warm sand against my skin, as if he was going to kiss me..

"I am sorry, but I think I have to make that choice for you, Lady Beatrice...

I knew I should pull away. To scream and run. This peculiar man, who I'd never seen before despite his nagging familiarity, had his hand on me. His face, close to mine, obscured most of the world. Sea-coloured eyes grew and brightened.

Patterns arose to swim in the deep grey rings of his irises. The same as the whorls on the driftwood, the same as in the faded brocade coat about my shoulders too, I fancied, without knowing why.

His hand wrapped around the back of my head, fingers pushing through the damp strands of hair the ever-fiercening wind was trying to toss hither and tither.

I cried out, frightened, and tried to pull away. I could not move. Other hands gripped my arms and legs. Impossible of course, but that's what it felt like.

The wind howled, the sea crashed, the whorls in Merry's eyes swirled and danced and dragged me down. Not into black cold water where old mud held the bodies tight and the sunlight never kissed, but a blue shallow lagoon, where the sun cast sparkles. Warm, lovely and nothing like the sea forever lapping this shingled shore.

"Ready yourself," a voice said from somewhere above the water.

The fear faded. I didn't know what Father Merry (for the north wind still blew) meant. I didn't want to know. I was floating amongst the restless patterns. I'd thought them random at first, things time, tide, wind and sun might carve upon an old, bleached piece of driftwood. But now symbols hidden within the whorls and lines emerged. Secret things, magic things, artful things.

Powerful things.

Pressure built against the back of my head. Father Merry's fingers. Tightening.

Then a storm broke.

Lightening seared through me. My body bucked and fizzed, my blood felt like steam trapped inside my veins, my eyes wanted to fly from their sockets, my limbs thrashed about me of their own volition.

Colours, bright, vivid, painful, ripped through the shapes and symbols swirling around them. Then they began to merge into images, into sounds, into things I understood.

Into memories.

1954

I opened my eyes.

A white, brown and unbroken cockleshell sat before the end of my nose.

I blinked.

The cockleshell remained.

I found myself sprawled on the ground. The wind tugged my hair, waves slapped and hissed against the shore. A gull shrieked with its usual manic urgency nearby.

"Merry?"

I sat up. Brushing away shell fragments pressed into my cheek.

The beach was empty. After climbing to my feet, I turned a slow full circle. Merry wasn't in sight, or that old driftwood trunk of his.

Patting myself down, I discovered nothing out of place.

"I am alive," I announced, "until sunrise tomorrow."

Then...?

Thoughts, emotions, fears bubbled and boiled inside me.

They didn't matter. Nothing mattered. I squeezed them down.

I had that long to save my son, my only surviving child, from the monster that lived within my husband. The Sorrowsmith.

That mattered.

My feet crunched the shingle, another familiar sound. I began to walk back towards Grey Gull.

How do I save Francis?

Only love can kill sorrow.

They might be true, but Merry had been somewhat sketchy with the detail.

I was alone. Tom was dead, Izzy was dead, Davey was...? I didn't know. He'd disappeared. Presumably the Sorrowsmith had dispatched him to the same place he'd sent Tilly. I hope he'd survived. Being a poacher and outdoorsman, he'd be much better equipped than a baby.

Of course, that was a long time ago.

I'd been gone for eleven years, after all.

I looked across at the dunes despite myself. Behind them, I knew, the black water of Cobb's Mere sat. Waiting.

Would I be back under those waters come the dawn?

More detail Merry had danced over.

I walked on.

How do I do this? How can I save Francis? Just how does love kill sorrow?

I played with the pink ribbon tied about my right wrist.

Something would come. I supposed. It had to, didn't it?

Otherwise, what did I do?

Jump out at Frank and cry, "Boo! Look who's back!"

And then, after he got over the undoubted surprise, he would murder me again.

My fingers moved from the ribbon to my throat. A necklace of bruises. Frank had never been much of a one for giving gifts, not the kind a girl likes anyway. I suspected I still wore his final one, vividly, circling my neck. Eleven years after he gave it to me.

A gull hovered above the breaking surf, searching for anything the sea might serve up.

I watched until my feet took me past it.

When I turned my gaze forward again, I found a man ahead of me, sitting on a bone-white piece of driftwood.

"Father Merry," I said once I was close enough for the wind not to steal the words.

Merry stood, pulling the wings of his faded brocade coat together and buttoning it to stop it flying about him.

"Lady Beatrice. You are fully restored? Mind, body and soul?"

Stopping before him, I nodded, "I remember."

"Splendid!" Merry beamed, "I'm glad it worked."

"There was a chance it wouldn't?"

"It's a very tricksy bit of art. Usually, I get it right..."

"I thought you'd deserted me?"

"Of course not!"

My eyes drifted past him, narrowing in the wind, north towards Grey Gull. Once the beach curved to the right a few hundred yards further on, the cottage would be visible.

"Then we go and fight the Sorrowsmith together?"

"Ah, well, not exactly."

"Not exactly?"

"Actually, not at all. I do not possess the weapons necessary for the task. You do."

"I do?"

Merry nodded, "Well, nearly all. You'll need this."

He produced a stone, perfectly round, sitting comfortably in the palm of his hand. He held it out.

It was the colour of diesel smoke. Although it looked pitted, it felt uncommonly smooth in my hand, as well as a smidgen heavier than I expected.

Turning it, I found a mark. A whorl, constructed of countless little circles of varying sizes as delicate as a spider's web, spiralled across one side. So faint I had to wiggle the stone until it caught the dull daylight before I could be certain there was anything there at all.

My eyes returned to Father Merry, "A paperweight?"

He smiled, "I think it might roll off your desk."

I tossed it from one hand to the other, "What is it?"

"A binding stone."

"Which does... what?"

"It will bind the Sorrowsmith to you and prevent it sending you to the Fey."

I stopped juggling the stone.

"Why would I want to bind it to me?"

"Once its host is dead, the Sorrowsmith will attempt to flee to the next."

"Francis?"

The Sorrowsmith is not physically strong. Without a host, it will wither and weaken quickly. It is the host that channels the sorrow, grief and pain it requires to live."

"So... the host must die?"

"Yes, Beatrice."

"I have to kill Frank?"

"There is no other way," he must have seen something in my face, as he added, softly, "he killed you, Beatrice. He is not really a man anymore, just a facet of the Sorrowsmith. A disguise the monster wears. Little of the man he once was remains."

"The Sorrowsmith killed me."

"They are one and the same now. For all intents and purposes."

I closed a fist around the binding stone and held it up, "So this will keep it close to me. It won't be able to go to Francis and then it will die."

Merry shook his head, slowly, "The Sorrowsmith will survive longer than the binding stone will work and longer than you will live. No. You will have to kill it too."

"How?"

"Only lo-"

"Yes, yes! I know. Only love can kill sorrow. But how?"

"You have to figure that out for yourself."

"Frankly, Father Merry, that isn't very helpful!" I snapped, "Why don't *you* kill Frank and bind the Sorrowsmith long enough for it to die? Surely, that is easier?"

"The Sorrowsmith will not die. It will become a husk, a dark seed that will bloom again when someone suitable finds it. And then it begins again. It needs to die. And only you can kill it. It is linked to you after all these years, it feeds from you, your sorrow, sadness, grief. All that has befell you since you met Frank Harryman. But if you pour love into that channel, instead, you will poison it. Weakened by the loss of its host it will perish. It will ruin no more lives."

"But how-"

"I cannot tell you, Beatrice. The love has to be true; I can't tell you how to find it. Only you can do that."

I felt like stamping my foot and throwing the binding stone at him. I didn't care about my life. That had ended eleven years earlier. The Sorrowsmith could do what it wanted to me. But Francis' life mattered. Diane's life mattered. My grandchildren – who I'd never been able to hold – lives mattered. More than anything.

But what if I bloody well can't work it out!

I wanted to scream at him.

But I didn't.

Instead, I dropped the binding stone in my pocket.

"You will know, Beatrice," he said. Perhaps reading my mind, though the expression on my face was probably clear enough.

For some reason he looked so pleased with himself it bordered on the smug.

The following silence was long and drawn out. I turned my face to the north, where Grey Gull waited for me, one last time. The wind gusted even harder, as if trying to push me back.

"Is there anything else?" I asked eventually.

"Good luck."

Frankly, I'd hoped for more.

But sometimes, you just have to work with what you have.

I nodded and continued down the beach to kill my husband and the monster who lived inside him.

1954

The sky darkened.

A storm was brewing. I would have known even with my eyes screwed shut. You would have hoped, on the last day of your life, the sun might shine. But the world seldom gives a damn for your preferences.

Merry said I would know how to kill the Sorrowsmith, but as the kink in the coastline that would bend the shore towards the Castle approached, inspiration still escaped me.

I didn't look behind. I knew, as much as I knew a storm was about to break, that neither man nor driftwood would still be there.

I was on my own.

Merry had brought me back from the dead and given me a chance to save my son. I suppose I should have been grateful. But gratitude was as sparse as inspiration as I bent into the wind and kept pushing my feet over the shingle.

The path skirting the top of the beach was easier going. However, I stuck closer to the sea and the ever-larger waves, spewing foam and showers of spray.

The sky ahead grew biblical. Bruised and beaten. The temperature was falling too, the wind trying to rip my still damp clothes from my body. Under the circumstances I guessed I needn't worry too much about catching a chill.

The shoreline began to curve.

Towards the Castle, towards the darkest swathe of sky.

Did the coming storm have anything to do with Merry and what was happening, or was it just a fitting coincidence?

Another thought I shoved away.

Did inspiration come more readily to an empty mind?

I listened to the wind and the surf. Everything else I ignored.

Particularly the part of me that wanted to turn and run.

I didn't want to see Frank. The man who'd murdered me. I didn't want to see the Sorrowsmith again. No desire for vengeance spurred me on. Only Francis, Diane and my grandchildren.

If I was to die, again, which Merry told me I must, I did not want it to be in vain. But if I couldn't work out how to destroy the Sorrowsmith, then surely it would.

Frank was just a man. Old, fat and not in good health. Inspiration in dealing with him would come. But the Sorrowsmith...

Only love can kill sorrow.

But how?

If I killed Frank and not the monster inside, the thing would take Francis. A dark seed, Merry said. Even if I weakened it, that seed would remain. Francis would come to Grey Gull after his father's death, and then it would take him.

Without killing the Sorrowsmith, I would be doing nothing but hastening the day when it took my son and made him like his father. A man who would bestow sorrow and grief upon Diane and the children to feast on her misery. As it had feasted upon mine.

I kept walking.

The coastline turned and I turned with it. The sea snarling to my left, the wind howling in my face.

The Castle came into view.

A brittle grey shell on the dark, brutal shore, cowering beneath furious skies.

Between Grey Gull and me, a figure stood watching the sea, coat flapping about him. At first, I thought it was Merry, but as I drew closer, I could see the coat wasn't long enough. There was no driftwood around either.

The beach wasn't always deserted, however, with a storm approaching, it wasn't the weather to be hanging about admiring the view. The sea was darkening to match the sky, only the ribbons of white-topped waves breaking the deep, ominous grey.

My feet took me on.

I could have cut inland to avoid the stranger – it wasn't Frank – but I carried on, stride lengthening, heart quickening, stomach tightening.

The man was young, hair cropped short. So engrossed by the angry sea frothing out all the way till it met the equally unhappy sky, he did not notice me until I was close enough for him to hear my shoes crunching shingle over the pounding surf.

He half turned his head to me. He was gaunt, cheeks hollowed, streaks of dried mud dirtied the left side of his face from temple to jaw.

He wasn't wearing a coat at all, but an army tunic, unbuttoned. The wind ripped it back, exposing a soiled shirt underneath. Familiar eyes lingered on me as a frown and a smile fought for control of his features.

The smile won.

His head tilted, as a single uncertain word escaped lips I had never ceased dreaming about.

"Bea...?"

I stopped. The wind tore at me, water hissing as the sea sucked each wave back into itself through the shingle. My heart pounded harder.

"Where am I?" he asked, the smile flickering as I stood staring at him.

"Home..." was all I could say.

Then I flew the final few yards and nearly knocked him from his feet.

He never said anything, but his arms came around me, tentatively at first, then he was hugging me as hard as I held him.

At that moment, during the last day of my life, that was all I wanted.

The stink of stale sweat mixed with the acrid bite of what I assumed was gun smoke. I pushed myself harder against him. My throat thickened and the sob that burst from me sounded like a wounded animal. I struggled to stay upright, my knees wanted to buckle. All of me wanted to buckle.

But through my body's convulsions and my heart's joy one thought rang clear.

Merry had been right, I worked it out.

My inspiration had arrived.

The only thing that can kill sorrow is love.

1954

He looked more confused and befuddled than I must have when I'd awoke on the beach.

I suppose it wasn't really surprising. Owen had been dead even longer than I had.

We sat before the sea, shoulders against each other. He held my hand so tightly it was almost painful. And completely wonderful.

He looked different. Not the same young man I'd known. Not the one that stared out of those precious photographs Frank burned. Not the one I waved off at the train station knowing, wrongly as it now turned out, that I would never see again.

The war had hollowed him. Those hard terrible months before he died. The softness was gone from his face, gentle lines hardened to sharp edges. Save for his eyes. They were as beautiful as ever.

At some point it dawned on me I must look ridiculously different to him. I'd been forty-seven when I died. As far as I could tell Merry had given me back my life, but not my youth. Which was something I considered a bit of an oversight when I thought about it.

Perhaps Owen hadn't noticed in his shock and confusion. Or he was still too much of a kind-hearted boy to comment. Whichever, I doubted it had anything to do with ageing well.

Several times he started talking. On each occasion it sounded a lot like a question, and I'd stilled it with a sssshh and a finger against his lips.

We had until sunrise. And some of those hours would, I feared, be hard ones. Still, we had enough time for the questions to find some patience. So, we sat before the snarling sea, the wind whipping hair and clothes, spray tainting the air.

It was not the perfect moment for lovers to sit upon a beach. The damp and chill seeped into my bones, but we didn't have the time to wait for a sunny day. We had to make the most of it, so, sod the bloody weather.

Owen twisted to look at me, his eyes moist. Perhaps due to the wind. It looked like another question was brewing. I would have much preferred a kiss, but I looked more like his mother than his fiancée now.

"Where..." he began, then stopped to shake his head as if a wasp was stuck in there somewhere. His shoulders slumped, "...I don't understand any of this, Bea."

How *did* I explain it?

I looked at the sky. The rain was holding off, but it was so dark it could not be far away. And when it came it would do so in buckets. I couldn't guess where the sun was.

"We were both dead. Now we are not. A man, who you might think of as a wizard as I don't have a better word, has brought us back to life. When the sun rises tomorrow, we shall both be dead again. There are things we have to do before then."

As explanations went, it was thin. But we didn't have long.

Time flies, after all.

Slowly I pushed myself to my feet. Owen jumped far more easily to his and helped me the rest of the way up. Ever the gentleman. He'd always been good with old ladies...

I laughed, and he looked at me strangely.

"I died in 1943, you in 1916. That's why I'm slightly older than the girl you knew."

"You look beautiful," he said, even sounding like he meant it, which was quite an achievement.

My fingers found his, like they always had. Some things you never forget.

"I remember dying," he said.

I nodded, the wind tormenting my hair, "Do you remember how you got here?"

"I remember being shot. Can see the bas- bugger's grinning face. Remember the pain, being scared, begging, crying out. Remember knowing I'd never see you again. That hurt worst of all," he squeezed my hand, I squeezed back, "knowing I'd let you down."

"Let me down?"

"By not coming back. Like I promised."

"You came back, Owen. You came back!"

"Yeah..." an oh so familiar grin spread across his face, "...I did!"

I looked sharply away. I wanted to cry again.

"After that?"

He shuffled feet over shingle; his boots looked a few hefty stamps away from falling apart.

"Walking..." he said, so quiet the wind almost stole the word, then he shook his head again. Another wasp, "...through dust and ash... the sun was always setting... others were there, but I could never see them... not properly... couldn't talk to them... just walked... seemed like forever."

Hesitant eyes found mine, "Was I in hell?"

"The Grey Place. I was there too. Behind you, I think."

Owen's eyes widened, a hand reaching out to cup my face, "I never knew... sometimes I thought I heard your voice... but it was..."

I put my fingers against his. I'd forgotten how Owen's touch made me feel. How could I have ever forgotten such a thing?

"It's not Hell; it's... some kind of purgatory, limbo... a waiting room. The Sorrowsmith sent our souls there, whe-"

"Sorrowsmith?"

"Did Merry not explain any of this?"

"Merry?"

"Long hair, beard, sea-colour eyes, faded blue brocade coat. Might be mistaken for a vagrant if you didn't know better..."

Owen shook his head.

"He brought you... us... back from the dead," I sighed, "I thought he might have introduced himself under the circumstances."

A raindrop, fat and cold, hit me square between the eyes. The universe's – or perhaps Merry's – way of telling me I should be shaking a leg. If not both.

I tugged Owen in the direction of Grey Gull.

"I'll explain on the way."

Owen tugged me back and pulled me close. We stood, nose to nose, eye to eye. I'm not sure for how long. By the time he kissed me, however, the rain, in many, many buckets arrived to drench the world.

I couldn't have cared about anything less.

1954

We were both breathless by the time we tumbled into the potting shed. It turns out being dead is not the best way for you to keep in shape.

The potting shed was the smallest, least used, and most distant of the dilapidated outbuildings in the Castle's orbit. Neither Grey Gull nor I were well suited to gardening. Little grew here, while my fingers had never been green, though I managed to coax a few summer blooms in the Castle's lee. My paltry collection of pots, bulbs and tools lived in the "potting shed."

Frank never came here. It was far enough away from the house that our voices would not carry, even without the rain hitting the roof like a manic drummer having a fit.

Musty shadows hung dim and cool inside. Water dripped through several cracks onto half-rotted floorboards. We found a corner and hunkered down together amidst the competing scents of dry earth and damp air.

I wiped rainwater from my face with a moth-eaten hand towel before giving the soggy rats tails of my hair a cursory rub. When I handed it to Owen, he turned it about his hands, eyes not leaving me.

The downpour curtailed my explanation as we'd sprinted towards the house. Frank wasn't much of a one for staring out of windows, and few overlooked the potting shed. I thought the chances of him spotting us slim.

I wondered if Frank was missing me. The sad little ghost who'd spent the last eleven years not even realising she was a ghost. When I thought about things, it still seemed absurd. Respectable girls, particularly ones who happened to be a vicar's daughter, did not believe in ghosts, let alone fantastical creatures that ate your sorrows.

The Church of England did not approve of things like that.

It fed from me!

Anger and nausea turned inside.

I bit them down. Finding Owen's hand helped. More than a little.

"Why are we here, Bea?" Owen's thumb moved back and forth over my knuckle. I didn't know if he meant in the potting shed or something more metaphysical. The confused look was back on his face, still, under the circumstances, I thought he was coping admirably.

A drop of rainwater clung precariously from the tip of his nose. I had an urge to kiss it away. I resisted and took the towel from his other hand to dab it off.

That made Owen smile.

Dear Lord, I've missed that smile so much!

I sucked in a breath.

"To kill my husband," I said, deciding it best to plunge headfirst into the deep end.

"Oh," was all Owen said. Perhaps he'd been hoping for something more romantic.

"This will take a long time to explain. We don't have a lot of time. So... let me talk. No questions till I'm done, right?"

"You're the boss."

"I'm very glad you still remember that."

Another smile.

I have till sunrise tomorrow to spend with the love of my life. Oh, bloody hell! I don't want to talk about Frank and his wretched monster.

I swallowed. Would this be easier if I wasn't looking at him? Perhaps. But my eyes weren't going to go for that. They were far less certain about who the boss was.

The light in here was arbitrary even on a sunny day. The one little window as much dirt as glass. Wind whistled between the ill-fitting planks but brought little daylight along for the ride.

It wasn't a good place for reading, but the gloopy dimness was probably flattering. Something to be grateful for if I'd brought Owen here for flirting or seduction.

But, of course, I hadn't.

The words came slowly at first. Owen shuffled closer, perhaps not catching them all over the hammering on the roof.

I cried when I told him about Tilly, and again when I got to Simon's death. I blushed when I told him about Tom and struggled to keep his eye. His hand never left mine, the pressure increasing whenever I faltered. I told him about the Sorrowsmith, about all the things that had been sloightly on th' huh ever since I'd moved into Grey Gull four years after he died, I told him about Izzy, Mutt Harris and Davey Acorns. I told him about Francis and Diane, the Jewish girl my husband never approved of, but my son loved with a fierce, consuming passion that reminded me so much of how I felt about Owen. I told him about the grandchildren I'd never held. I told him about Merry, who saved the damned and had brought us back from the dead to keep my son and grandchildren out of the Sorrowsmith's clutches. I told him about the life I'd had here by the sea, about the things my husband had done to me. The sadness and sorrow, the pain, grief and humiliation that I had only recently discovered had been at the Sorrowsmith's behest. I told him what would become of us if the Sorrowsmith lived, how we would be subsumed and endure the rest of that monster's life trapped in torment and damnation. I told him how my husband tried to trick me into thinking I was mad to keep me from running away. I told him about my murder. I told him about the strange limbo I had lived in not realising I was but a ghost, soul bound by the Sorrowsmith so it could continue to feed from me.

I told him everything.

Everything except who Frank Harryman was.

That came last and of all the things I told Owen, that was the hardest.

Owen had gone to war and died. I'd made no vows and even if I had they would have been only until death do us part. I wished fervently I had made those vows and caught with his child. My fear and weakness kept Owen's wedding ring from my finger and denied him the one thing in all the world he wanted. Me.

Still, it was not that I had, after a lengthy period of mourning, married another man that made me feel guilty. Nor did my spectacularly bad choice of husband embarrass or shame me. No, it was simply that Frank had been Owen's friend and comrade that bound my tongue.

I sat in silence for a while. My throat dry, listening to the rain and hoping for Owen to say or do anything to delay me having to deal with that one last fact.

"Who is this man, your husband?" Owen asked, offering me no respite.

"He..." I groped for the words. I squirmed and shifted on the floor next to Owen, hard enough for the potting shed's floorboards to protest beneath me.

Finally, I had no choice but to vomit up the truth, "He wrote to me after the war. He fought with you, was with you at the end. I met him, I had no feelings for him, but... I... was lonely, heartbroken. Dad had just died. I got drunk... I... wasn't thinking. It was only once. I got pregnant. I..."

I couldn't look at him. I'd given Frank what I'd refused the man I loved despite knowing he was going to die. It had always shamed me, but saying it aloud cut me deeper than I could ever have imagined.

When Owen said nothing, I raised my eyes. I expected to see hurt, anger, confusion. Instead, a faraway look I couldn't name haunted his eye.

"Frank Harryman...?" he said, voice blank and terribly devoid of anything. Sometimes the absence of emotion can be so much worse than any rage.

I nodded, "He told me how you died... I... I..."

Now something did flash in Owen's eyes. It spread across his face, distorting it into an expression I'd never seen before on him. One I wouldn't have thought him capable of.

Hatred.

"Owen..."

He still held my hand, though his grasp went limp.

His mouth twitched.

"He lied to you," Owen said.

"He has lied to me for our entire marriage, I-"

"No," Owen snapped, "he lied to you about how I died."

"How do you know?" I asked. I hadn't recounted Frank's account of Owen dropping his rifle as they retreated from the German trench and jumping back in to retrieve it.

"Because..." Owen said, "...I doubt you would have married him if he'd told you he killed me..."

1954

"I never liked him," Owen said over the rain beating on the roof, "there was always something off about him. Never did or said anything particular. But there was always *something...*"

My hand was over my mouth. Each word Owen spoke ripped me deeper, like a shower of razor blades, slicing me to shreds.

"...I thought it was just me at first, but no one else spent much time with him either. When you rely on lads for your life, you want to be close to them. To know they'll have your back when you need it. But Harryman was always on the outside, looking in. The other thing I never understood was he always looked so damn healthy. Glowing, almost. The rest of us looked like... dunno what... but bloody awful. No sleep, dodgy food, driven half-mad by the guns, eaten by fleas, lice, rats. But him? No, Harryman always looked like he'd stepped out of one of them spa places fancy folk go to."

"A lot of sorrow in war," I managed to say.

Owen rolled his bottom lip between his teeth, nostrils flaring, "I remember we would often talk about our girls. Or just girls. Some lads were married, some had sweethearts, some had no one but the French girls who'd be... nice to you for a few francs. Some of the things lads said were stupid, shit, boasting, nonsense. Some made you laugh out loud like you were in the music hall. Some near on broke your heart...

Harryman never said much about women himself, but he paid a lot of attention when we were. Watching, listening, concentrating. He was always first in line when someone passed their photographs around.

He took an interest in you straight off. So much so I stopped talking about you when he was lurking. Sometimes he'd come slithering up when I was on watch, and as often as not, he'd start asking about you. On my charitable days, I just thought he was lonely, didn't have a girl back home. Other times it gave me the creeps," he snorted, "Goes to show you should always trust your instincts."

I remembered Merry telling me Frank had sought me out after the war because the Sorrowsmith knew how strong my love for Owen was. The only way the monster could have known that was because of how strong Owen's love was for me.

The deepest love brings a happiness like nothing else, but the greatest potential for misery comes with that love. Heartbreak, loss, bereavement, grief. Sorrow is the price we suffer in return for love. Frank... the Sorrowsmith used ours to create a feast that sustained it for decades.

Owen blinked. I felt like all the blood had drained from my face. Perhaps it had. He reached up and peeled my hand from my mouth. Then he held it to his and kissed it.

"Owen, I'm so sorry; I-"

He shook his head, "We haven't got time for apologies, have we? Nor getting sour with each other. I love you. Always have, always will. Even in my grave, I loved you. It ain't you I have a grudge with."

"What... did happen?"

Owen's account of the attack on the German redoubt atop Ancre Heights was a lot different to Frank's...

"Halfway up the hill, I found myself face down in the sh- erm... muck at the bottom of a crater. Think a shell went off nearby... Can't remember if I meant to dive down there or lost my footing and fell..." he rapped a knuckle against his head, "...must have taken a whack to the noggin... dazed myself for... a bit... don't matter. Not important. When I got my wits back together, I looked around, expecting to see other lads with me. There'd been a group of us together, working our way through the wire. Cutting, running, taking cover... but there was no one. Or so I thought to start with."

He wiped his knuckles across his mouth, eyes not seeing me.

"A flare went off, turned night into day. That's when I saw him. Just sitting there on the slope of this crater, legs stretched out, one foot over the other, casual as you like, staring at me with a smile on his face. A right smug one, too.

"Harryman?" I called after spitting the dirt out of my mouth.

He didn't say anything at first, just kept staring at me, sitting there like he was taking a little breather from a nice Sunday stroll. Except there was a body right next to him. Bits of one, anyway. Don't know if it was one of my mates. Not a lot left to... sorry, rambling. It's all a bit jumbled up in here," Owen pointed to his temple.

I managed a watery smile and waited for him to go on.

"I thought he'd gone doolally. Saw plenty of that. Lads who just stopped, like a broken clock. Something inside their head snapped by the... by the *everything* of it all. Shouted at him to get his stupid head down before Fritz blew it off.

"Nice hole you've found for yourself," Harryman said once he joined me at the bottom, "cosy, like..."

"Don't get too comfy," I said, rolling over and brushing myself down to make sure I hadn't taken any shrapnel.

"Why not?" he asked.

"Can't sit it out here, can I? Get done for cowardice," I said.

"Shoot you will they then, Farmer Boy?" he said and laughed, right loud, like he'd sunk a dozen pints down the pub on Saturday night and thought he'd just told the best joke ever.

Farmer Boy, that's what he called me. Nicknames usually stuck over there, we all had em, but he was the only one who called me that. Always said it like it was about the funniest thing he'd ever heard, the fu-"

I think Owen was going to use words he considered inappropriate for my ears but stopped himself. He needn't have held back. As far as I was concerned, he could use any word he liked about Frank.

"I asked him if any of the other lads were close by.

Harryman just shook his head, right slow. And then he winked and grinned. Like all the slaughter around us was just some grand wheeze.

I never liked him, but down in that hole, there was something else about him... something *really* off...

Dunno how long we stayed there. It was deep enough to keep us safe from the gunfire, at least. I never was a hero or a coward. All I wanted to do was stay alive and come home to you.

My normal instinct would be to stay safe, keep my head down. No one wants to run at a machine gun unless you have to. I wouldn't have hid in that hole till they sounded the retreat, but I wasn't in no hurry to go again, especially with just the two of us to work our way through the wire. But something about being so close to Harryman was making me want to charge up the hill at Fritz sooner rather than later.

The guns eased a little. I waited. Ignoring my itchy feet, the way I could see Harryman staring at me, the way he made my skin crawl.

"Heard from your girl?" Harryman asked like the conversation was flagging over a couple of pints.

I ignored the question. Weren't the time or place for idle chatting.

"Time to go," I told him, "before Fritz sticks another flare up."

"What's the rush, Farmer Boy? Nice and snug here, just like being in your own grave..."

I thought I saw something in the corner of my eye then, like there was someone else in that hole with us. I turned, expecting to see another one of the lads joining us, or maybe Fritz creeping up, but there was just Harryman, still staring at me, still grinning like a loon.

"We should go," I said again. I wanted to get away from him and the way he was looking at me, but it weren't like walking off down the street.

"Ever think of what'll become of her if you don't make it back?" he asked.

"This ain't the place for a chat," I said.

Harryman shrugged, "Why not? Passes the time till they call off the attack. We ain't getting nowhere near Fritz."

"Not if we sit here all night, we won't."

A machine gun went off then. Hate them things, The noise they make..."

Owen rapped his knuckle against the potting shed floor, hard and fast enough to make me jump. He gave me a distant, apologetic smile.

"...someone screamed out in the dark, close to us. One of ours...

Harryman kept staring, "Must think about it," he said.

"Think about what?" I snapped.

"What will happen to Beatrice if you don't make it," he said.

"Nothing to think about. I'm going to make it; we're going to get married, and I'm going to spend the rest of my life forgetting all this shit..."

Harryman sniggered, like... I dunno... can't say I'd ever heard a laugh quite like it.

I scrambled up to peer over the rim of the crater and see what I could see before we got our act together. That's what I told myself anyway, though I just wanted to get away from Harryman. I didn't like the way he was behaving, really didn't like hearing your name on his lips either...

You had to get yourself ready for the next ten yards, twenty yards, however far you could go before Fritz spotted you, to make yourself do the exact opposite of what every bit of you wants to. But Harryman was making my feet itch to go. Which was something I'd never felt before.

"Clear as it's ever going to be," I said, sliding back down beside him.

"After you..." Harryman said.

I got up into a crouch, readying myself. I tried to push everything to one side. No room for thoughts or distractions. Move your feet, get to the next piece of cover. Stay alive. Summoning up whatever the hell makes a man think running towards people trying to kill you is a clever idea. I heard Harryman shuffling. Didn't look, didn't want to look.

Some lads give you strength. Some take it. Harryman was always a taker. He was the last person in the world not wearing a spike on the top of their helmet I wanted to be stuck in a hole with. And there I was. Stuck in a hole with the creepy git.

I sucked in some air even though it tasted of..." Owen curled his hand into a fist and licked his lips. He was shaking, remembering. The horrors of the trenches or the horror of what was about to happen. Probably both, "...dunno, can't even say. Death and madness is the closest I can think of. Yeah... that's what a battle stinks of... tastes of..."

He was silent for a good long while before continuing.

"I prayed, hoping to hear the whistles calling us back to our trenches. But nothing came.

"Ready?" I asked Harryman.

"It's high time, Farmer Boy..." he said.

I spat - supposed to be lucky for some reason - and then started up the crater's slope. Ain't many rules in No Man's Land, but one of em is when you start moving from cover, don't stop till you're behind the next bit. I think I only managed a step or two before the churned-up earth gave way under my boot, and I went down on one knee.

"Farmer Boy!" Harryman hissed.

I looked over my shoulder, thinking it was a warning about Fritz or... something. That's when he did it. Stuck me with his bayonet... once, twice... three times... I think."

Owen's hand moved to his back, around where the kidneys are. He twisted to show me. His tunic was darker there, beneath the mud. He found a tear with his finger and pushed it through the hole, then a second one just above it. His hand flopped away before he could find a third hole. Ashen-faced, he turned back to me.

"Owen..."

"I screamed, went down. Thought it was a German bullet at first... then Fritz put another flare up, and I saw it all. The bloody bayonet in his hand, grinning from ear to ear, enough to split his face clean open if it was a quarter of an inch wider, trembling like he'd just got out of the sea on Christmas morning. Clear as day it was under Fritz's flare, except for Harryman's eyes. They were still black as the pit. Like the light couldn't reach that far..."

I'd dropped my rifle when he did for me... I made a grab for it, but he was faster... or I was slower. Tried to stand. Went down... all the strength gone out of me."

"Why...?" I knew why, but I couldn't think of anything else to say, and I needed to say something.

His eyes found mine.

"Because of you."

When I stared at him, he shrugged, "He laughed as I slid back down to the bottom of the crater. He told me you were gonna be his girl now. How he was going to... do things to you... how he was going to make you cry... how he was going to make you suffer..."

I tried to reach for his hand, but he pulled it away and curled both his hands into a fist.

"The pain, Bea... I can't describe it. Never was much of a one for words; you remember my letters, right?" he found a smile, then shook it away, "but his words

399

hurt me even more than that bayonet did. He was standing over me, dancing from one foot to the other. Mad as the march hare. Snorting and laughing, waving that bayonet about. All I could do was pray Fritz got him because I knew if he got away, he'd do terrible things to you, Bea..."

Owen pressed the balls of his hands into his eyes, "Can still see the bastard. I couldn't move no more, tried to... tried to... do something, anything. I knew I had to stop him but couldn't... I couldn't...

"Love to stay and see you cry, but gotta run, got a girl to catch, after all," Harryman giggled, then bent over me and pulled out the photograph of us I always carried in my tunic..."

Owen's fingers brushed his breast pocket.

"...I tried to stop him, I did, Bea, I did! But I couldn't..."

I reached over and took his hand. This time Owen didn't pull it away.

"...Harryman held the photograph in front of me.

"C'mon, one last peek at your bitch! Gonna remember the look on your stupid face now every single time I fuck her. What a picture! How about that, eh? Yes, sir! How about fucking that, Farmer Boy!!"

I tried to snatch it back, screaming at him, but he pushed me down and put the photograph in his pocket. Then he raised his rifle. Before he shot me, I remember that something... the darkness was rushing in. I didn't have long, even without the bullet coming my way, but before he finished me, there was... someone else there. Someone folded up and wrong, no face and features, but there all the same. Like looking at two people at the same time. Except one of them wasn't a person.

I heard one last thing just before Harryman shot me, but it didn't sound like him. Didn't sound like anyone. Just one word..."

"Mine..." I said.

"Yeah," Owen frowned, "How'd you know?"

"The Sorrowsmith. I spent years listening to it whisper. It often told me that. Amongst other things..."

"The world went black. And then grey. Just dust and ash and crunching bone beneath my boots. And all I could think of was you, suffering, the man who murdered me and what he was doing to you."

"The Sorrowsmith sent you to the Grey Place, bound your soul there so it could keep feeding from you, from your pain. Until Frank dies, and then it'll subsume you within itself. Like everyone else it's caused to suffer in Frank's lifetime. Like everyone else in its previous hosts' lifetimes."

"How'd this happen to us, Bea. What did we do wrong?"

"Wrong?"

"For God to punish us like this. Was it that night in the hotel when..."

"No!" I shook my head hard enough for damp licks of hair to lash my face as I leaned forward, "This isn't anything to do with God."

"Then why?"

"There is no why. It's just... rotten luck. None of this would have happened if you'd joined the navy."

"So, it's my fault?"

"Of course not! You're a victim. I'm a victim. Even Frank's a victim. He didn't choose to inherit a monster from his uncle along with this house. And my son, Francis, will be the Sorrowsmith's next victim. If we don't stop it. Before sunrise tomorrow."

Owen wiped a hand over his face.

"I don't understand any of this..."

"Neither do I. But that doesn't matter."

"Killing the Sorrowsmith does."

I nodded.

"And how do we do that?"

"Only love can kill sorrow."

Owen didn't appear convinced.

"But... we have to kill Frank first."

The smile that turned his lips made him look like someone I didn't know at all.

"And how do we do that?"

I'm guessing the smile that then turned *my* lips made me look like someone he didn't know.

"Any damn way you like..."

1954

I didn't want to leave the potting shed.

We snuggled together in the driest corner, between some old boxes containing God knew what and an ancient table repurposed to hold my collection of cracked and broken pots.

Owen's arm was about me, my head rested on his shoulder.

While we talked about killing a man.

Later, as the rain eased, I said, because I felt I had to, "I never stopped loving you..."

Owen didn't say anything but twisted to kiss the top of my head.

We needed to go, but after half a lifetime apart, every fibre of my being wanted to stay where I was. Just with fewer clothes on.

That was something I shoved from my mind as best I could.

"I'm sorry we never married. It was stupid; I was sca-"

This time Owen lifted my chin, our lips met.

Part of me flushed and glowed. Part of me worried about what it was like for him, kissing this middle-aged woman who bore a faint resemblance to a girl he'd loved long ago. Another part of me thought it was a convenient way to avoid apologising for something I really should apologise for. Mostly, however, I was lost in the wonder of what life might have been if I'd spent it with this man.

When our lips finally parted, Owen pursed his and tilted his head forward till our foreheads touched instead.

"We don't have time for apologies, Bea. We don't have any need for them either. We both made mistakes. That's just being human. Dunno how or why its happened, but we got to be together again. At the very end. Doubt many people get magic like that."

He was right, of course. He often was, which I remembered could be vaguely annoying at times.

"Frank lied to me about lots of things. Everything, I suppose. Some of it I knew, some I didn't. Never worked out any of the why till Merry told me about The Sorrowsmith. Now it makes sense. Frank told me he inherited this place after the war, but I found his uncle's grave years ago and saw he died in 1913. Frank had the Sorrowsmith in him when we met, when he was in the trenches with you. I suppose the Sorrowsmith must have had a grand old time in France, all that misery and suffering..."

"Explains why Harryman always looked so healthy out there," Owen said.

I snorted and raised my eyes to the cobwebs in the ceiling.

"I never asked Frank why he lied, but Dad was dying then, and he said it to make me feel closer to him when I was vulnerable. That he was going through the same thing I was. Lies, lies, lies... I was such a bloody fool."

"None of this is your fault, Bea. It's all on him. Harryman."

"No," I shook my head, "It's on the Sorrowsmith. And it's on us to make sure that thing never does this to anyone else. We have to do this," I said, pulling away. I run a hand through the short bristles of his scalp. I missed his messy curls.

Owen nodded and jumped to his feet, then helped me to mine.

I hate feeling like his bloody mother!

His fingers brushed my cheek and he looked at me the way he always had.

"How do we do this?" I asked once Owen's hand dropped to his side.

"Leave Harryman to me," he looked around the potting shed, spying a mallet hanging from a nail by a rough string loop.

He gave it a few practice swings before whacking the palm of his hand with it. He shrugged and looked at me, "This'll do..."

I swallowed and pictured Frank's face, empty and emotionless, as he'd strangled me.

Killing Frank should be the easy part. It'd take more than a mallet to dispatch the Sorrowsmith. And we couldn't begin to tackle that monster with Frank still alive.

Don't be so squeamish.

I couldn't help but wonder if the real Frank Harryman, the one that existed before he came to Grey Gull to collect his inheritance off his uncle, Mr Shackle, was still in there somewhere. His soul waiting to be subsumed into eternal torment along with the rest of us.

I supposed he was. In the long, strange years after my death, Frank would sometimes sit and weep, staring at the hands that had squeezed the life out of me. I hadn't understood why, but now I thought I did. But there was nothing we could do for him. Save ensure the Sorrowsmith died, so we didn't end up spending eternity screaming together.

I shoved the potting shed's wonky door open on the sodden world awaiting us. Low grey clouds and a weeping sky. The rain had relented some but remained heavy. How much of the gloominess was due to the thickness of the cloud and how much to the lowering of the hidden sun I didn't know. We could have been in the shed for thirty minutes or five hours.

Whichever, time was passing.

"This way," I flicked my hand and hurried towards the house. The wind rattled anything not tied down and bolted, covering the wet slaps of our feet. Beyond Grey

Gull the sea snarled at us as if it knew what we were about and didn't like it one little bit.

Frank would either be in his studio or the comfy chair in the kitchen. He didn't paint so much these days. If I could trust the hazy recollections of my latter years floating about Grey Gull unaware of my own death anyway.

I headed for the house at a half-run. Owen padded after me, mallet in hand. It would have been helpful if Merry had seen fit to return his rifle and bayonet with him, but maybe I was being pernickety. There were plenty of things you could kill a fat old man with, after all.

My stomach gave another queasy roll.

For God's sake, he murdered you both!

I led Owen down the side of the house to the front door.

It dawned on me as we approached that just like Owen was missing his rifle, I was missing my keys. Merry had conjured us back in the clothes we died in, but nothing else. Did his magic not do that, or was it an oversight?

The front door was rarely locked when I was alive, there was even less chance of me running away after I died. Still...

I wrapped my fingers around the handle and tensed as it turned. I pushed the door open.

Hi, honey, I'm home! I've got such a big surprise for you, do come quick!

I resisted the urge.

Just.

The Castle was its usual quiet, gloomy self. Only the mournful tock of the hall clock greeted us. It said quarter to five, though it'd never been diligent when it came to timekeeping. It'd never bothered us enough to get another. We seldom had trains to catch.

Neither monsters nor old men were in sight.

I glanced at Owen. He nodded. He looked grim and serious, which I suppose the situation warranted. Our souls, as well as my son, daughter-in-law and grandchildren's lives were at stake. Still, it was an alien look that suited him poorly. I much preferred the mischievous smiles I remembered from my long-lost youth.

I made to lead us down the corridor to the kitchen. Where I expected to find Frank slumped in the disintegrating armchair in the corner of Grey Gull's warmest room.

Owen put an arm across me and shook his head before pointing at himself. He wanted to go first. He was being the man, being chivalrous, protecting me. It was a long time since anyone had done that.

I pushed his arm down and hurried towards the kitchen.

I didn't need any of those things anymore.

It was sweet, but Frank was my husband, my problem, my mistake. I wasn't going to hide under Owen's coattails or shy away from what we needed to do.

Besides, I found myself quite keen to see the expression on the bastard's face when his murdered wife walked, bold as brass, into the kitchen.

Maybe he wouldn't bat an eyelid and just demand to know why I hadn't gotten dinner started yet.

But I doubted it.

The floorboards protested beneath our feet. Grey Gull was not a house that leant itself to sneakery. A powerful gust set all the windows of the sea facing side of the house rattling hard enough to make us both pull up short.

I'd lived half my life (and all my death) here, but the Castle's propensity for breaking silences with sudden noises was one I had never become used to.

The shadows waited thick in the hallway. I'd always found them oppressive even before I'd worked out some of them hid monsters. I expected the Sorrowsmith to coalesce out of one of them, but nothing moved as the door to the kitchen loomed.

I gave Owen a significant look. I should have told him I thought Frank would be in there, but it was too late for words. Wherever Frank was, I didn't want to give him any more notice than I could that the journey he'd sent me on hadn't been one-way after all.

The door was solid and plain. Like everything in Grey Gull, it bore the scars of years past. It also creaked and moaned like an arthritic grandmother struggling to climb from her bed.

I took a deep breath. Owen tried to move ahead of me again. I shook my head and he looked a dash confused.

Had I been so assertive before? Of course not; I hadn't been assertive during my marriage either. If I had, maybe I would have found the courage to get away from Frank.

The things dying teaches you. Who would have thought?

Deciding the time for skulduggery and creeping about was past, I threw aside the door. Ignoring its protests, I marched into the kitchen.

As I expected, Frank was sitting in his favourite chair. Close enough to the fire to keep warm, far enough away from the worktop, sink and stove that I wouldn't disturb him with all my silly cooking and cleaning. When I was still alive, anyway.

His head didn't turn as we crashed into the room. The big table sat between us, as well as all the sundry rubbish piled atop it. In fact, the whole kitchen looked like a refuse tip. Even with the excuse of being dead, how hadn't I noticed?

"Harryman!" Owen shouldered past me, mallet raised, unable to contain himself.

I scanned the room for a handy carving knife in case the mallet wasn't up to the job. Nothing was in sight. The days when everything was neat, tidy and lived in a logical place had clearly ended years ago.

"Bea..." Owen yanked my attention back.

He'd rounded the table and still held the mallet over his head as if about to swing for the big prize at the fairground. But he'd come to a halt, wide eyes looking at me over his shoulder.

I came up next to him.

He lowered the mallet. I lowered my jaw, though somewhat more slowly.

Frank sat in his favourite chair by the fire, staring vacantly into space.

At least I'd found my best carving knife.

My husband had used it to open both his wrists to the bone.

1954

"He knew we were coming."

"How?"

"I guess someone told him," I reached forward and closed Frank's eyes. They were still the colour of burnt hazel, but no fire remained in them.

"Bastard!" Owen spat, hurling the mallet across the room.

I dragged a chair out from under the table. A pile of sweat-soiled clothes sat on it. Probably awaiting every other garment Frank owned before being washed. Or maybe Frank just turned the pile upside down and started wearing them again from the top. He'd never been much of a one for chores.

I tipped the clothes onto the floor and slumped down.

"Why?" Owen demanded, starting to prowl the kitchen.

"Why what?"

"Why kill himself? Why didn't he fight?" Owen sounded disappointed to the point of resentful.

"It wasn't his choice," I plonked elbows on the table and pushed my face into my hands. Despite sleeping for eleven years, I felt impossibly tired.

When no reply came from Owen, I looked over my hands.

He was staring at me.

"Merry said the Sorrowsmith was tied to his host – Frank – till he died. It must have sensed we'd returned and were coming for it. It made Frank sever the link between them so it could flee to its next host."

"Your son?"

I put my face back into my hands. They smelt of something faint and ripe, I realised.

"Yes."

A chair scraped on the floor. When I looked up, Owen was sitting beside me, crouched forward, brow crumpled.

"So... what do we do?"

I stared at him. I wanted to cry. I wanted to kiss him. I wanted to pick up the mallet and start whacking him with it.

"*Do?* Nothing, Owen, we can do nothing! Francis and Diane live in London, her aunt sold her a house in Golders Green. I've never been there, though when I close my eyes, I can see it anyway," I snorted and shook my head, "It doesn't matter. The

Sorrowsmith is heading there now. Even if we could get there before sunrise, it's too late. It'll be inside Francis..."

The words hit me one at a time. The realisation hollowing me out. Why had Merry bothered? Might as well have left me at the bottom of Cobb's Mere and Owen in his French grave.

I turned my eyes on Frank, resenting him as much for being dead as I ever had for being alive.

"Should we not try to get to your son's?" Owen offered.

"And kill him?"

Owen didn't hold my eye.

"Even if we could... there'd be no time left to deal with the Sorrowsmith. I suppose it would jump to my grandson immediately and... oh, God..."

I felt sick. Sick and useless.

We sat like that for a while, only the distant clunking tocks of the hallway clock competed with the sea and weather to break the silence.

Despair, heartache, grief washed over me. Sorrow had been the accompaniment to my life here, and it seemed it would continue throughout my final night on Earth.

The expression on Owen's face suggested he desperately wanted to say something but had no idea what. He put his hand on top of mine, which helped a little.

Eventually, he got up and went to stare at the blurry grey world beyond the window.

Frank continued to sit in the corner, waxy, ashen and glassy-eyed. Blood from his slashed wrists darkened his lap. Should I do something? Throw a sheet over him? Generally, you did that to furniture rather than corpses, but there wasn't much point burying him.

In the end, I got up and headed for the drawing room. When Owen lingered at the window, I called him.

He looked so bloody young! He was twenty-two when he died and still possessed the gangly frame of a boy. Strange I'd forgotten that, or never noticed in the first place. You couldn't see it in the photographs I'd cherished for so many years.

Owen pulled his eyes from the sea and followed me. The shadows stank of dust and stale air behind the undrawn curtains.

But at least there were no corpses in here.

I yanked the curtains open; the light was fading. Bruised clouds still squatted on the horizon. Night was coming. Our last.

Owen's arms came around me. When I didn't pull away, he kissed my temple. Gentle and tentative.

His closeness, after so many lonely long years, soothed me. I closed my eyes and tried not to think of anything, floating on the sound of the rain, floating on the impossibility of Owen's presence.

"What happened?" Owen asked.

"Happened?" I kept my eyes shut.

"With the war? Did we win?"

"It lasted till November 1918, the Germans surrendered in the end. So many lives were lost. Then twenty years later, we did it all again," I sighed, "hopefully, we've finally learnt our lessons, else they'll be another one around 1970."

"1918..." Owen muttered, shaking his head behind me, "...I wonder if I'd have made it if it weren't for... him."

"Should have joined the navy," I said, "would have been a lot safer."

"Always wanted to see the world."

"Since when?"

Owen kissed my head and stroked my hair.

"I look old enough to be your mum," I said, arching my head back towards him, my smile growing. His fingers found their way through the damp tangles to my scalp.

"You look nothing like Mum," he reassured me, lowering his lips to my ear.

I swallowed. My heart was quickening as a heat rose within me.

"I'm old. Frumpy, fat and old. I-"

He silenced me by kissing my ear. I trembled.

"You'll always be me Bea. I told you that enough times, remember?"

And I did. One of those daft little sayings sweethearts think up for each other and never say in front of the rest of the world.

Be me Bea...

Such a silly thing. Such a wonderful thing.

For a few heartbeats, beyond my closed eyelids, the dappled Cotswolds sunlight fell upon my face through those ancient green boughs once more.

Owen breathed in my ear; his arms tightened about me. One hand found my breast and cupped it gently. The fact it was somewhat saggy and less impressive these days didn't seem to affect his ardour.

Be me Bea.

I turned my head, he leant forward, lips finding mine.

The birds sang in the hedgerows, the wind kissed the barley, we sat on top of Cleeve Hill looking out all the way to forever and I was again a young woman in love. I'd found my way back to Camelot after all.

I shuddered.

And so did the house.

My eyes snapped open.

"What's that?" Owen stepped back a fraction, though one hand stayed on my shoulder, "An earthquake?"

"No," I said, spinning around as the rattle of crockery and picture frames faded back into silence once more. I smiled at him, "it's not an earthquake. It's the Sorrowsmith. It's still here..."

1954

The binding stone sat in the palm of my hand.

When Merry had given it to me, the whorl was so faint I could only see it clearly when the light hit it in the right direction. Now it glowed like molten gold ran through it.

"Pretty," Owen said. Raising his eyes to mine, "What is it?"

"It's why the Sorrowsmith is still here."

Owen looked blank. It was one of his most endearing expressions, it had always made me want to hug him.

"The stone binds the Sorrowsmith to it. It's linked to me, it still feeds off my sorrows. It must have killed Frank while we were in the potting shed. When it felt... something else coming off me, it knew what was happening and tried to escape to Francis. But it couldn't flee because it was already within the stone's influence."

"And the wizard who brought us back to life gave you that."

"Yes, Father Merry."

Owen frowned, "He's a catholic wizard?"

That made me giggle.

"Don't be silly."

Owen shrugged and sat back in the armchair; the cracked old leather squeaked in rhythm.

"If we don't kill this thing – the Sorrowsmith – before we...?" his eyes moved to the darkening window.

The nights drew in quickly in October. I didn't check the clock above the unlit fire.

I turned the binding stone over in my hands. Francis was safe, for now, at least.

"The binding stone will keep it here for a while, but the.... magic won't last forever. Without sorrow to feed on, it will... hibernate. Become a dark seed and wait for a new host to come here."

"Your son?"

I nodded, "It can take over others. It would have done if Frank had died in the trenches, but as a link already exists, a male relation to its previous host is a better, easier, fit for it. If I understood Merry right."

"So, we have to kill it before we die?"

I'd explained this already, but I suppose it was a lot to take in.

"Yes," the glowing whorl was rather hypnotic. If I stared at it long enough, I could see the gold threads within the stone moving. I shoved it back into my pocket.

"How?"

"The only thing that can kill sorrow is love."

"Yes, I remember that... but Bea... *how?*"

I turned my bottom lip between my teeth. I stood by the window, back against the wall, wishing Merry had been a tad more specific about this bit.

"The Sorrowsmith has been feeding off me for years, growing fat on the sorrows Frank inflicted on my life. That's why Frank got so big without ever eating much. There's..." I waved my hand, "...an umbilical cord connecting us if you like."

The leather under Owen's bum squeaked some more.

"But now it isn't receiving sorrow through that cord. Or pain, sadness, grief... it's getting..." I smiled at Owen, "...love. That's why the house shook. It was like you having to eat something really bitter and unpleasant. Like one of your mum's puddings."

That earnt me a look, followed by a begrudging smile.

"Our love will be enough to kill it?"

"I do love you an awful lot," I said, shuffling my feet and suddenly feeling like I was that seventeen old riding to Camelot again.

"I love you too."

Looking seventeen was a much easier feat for Owen to pull off.

He blew me a kiss which I caught with a laugh.

The smile on Owen's face didn't last long, "So, the Sorrowsmith is going to what? Sit around and wait to die?"

"Merry said it isn't physically strong."

"But it was strong enough to kill... your American friend. And that woman."

"Tom and Izzy," I nodded, "they were both driving. It appeared next to them and seized the wheel. Shock and fear probably made them crash as much as anything."

"So, as long as we don't drive...?"

A drawn-out creak floated in from the hallway. A sound I knew well. I'd heard it many times over the years.

"What was that?" Owen asked, eyes darting to the door as he rose from the chair.

"It isn't hiding anymore," I said quietly, "it knows we know it's still here now."

Owen joined me by the window, together, we watched the door.

"It's very good at creeping and only being seen when it wants to be. I'm not sure what else it can-"

What sounded like plates breaking cut off my words.

"Throw tantrums?" Owen suggested.

My arm slid around Owen's waist; when he looked down at me, I stretched and pecked his cheek, "It can't hurt us. But we can hurt it."

"It spent a long time hurting you."

"Frank spent a long time hurting me, and I allowed my love for my children to keep me here and endure it," my fingers brushed the stone in my pocket; it felt warm, like it had been sitting in fierce summer sunlight all day, "but now it's the one that's bound and..." my lips moved to find his, "...I'm the one hurting it."

We kissed to the serenade of smashing crockery.

1954

We dragged Frank's body to his studio. It seemed the most appropriate place.

He'd grown fat to the point of corpulence over the years. Not from cakes and pies, but my sorrow. Swelled and bloated by the Sorrowsmith's gluttony.

It wasn't far, and the rain had thinned to drizzle, but we were both as wet from sweat as rain by the time I threw a paint-soiled sheet over the corpse.

I didn't like the idea of Frank being in the house with us, and we were both hungry. I suspected making food with him sitting in the corner would sour the romance of our last meal on Earth.

His armchair was dark with blood, and Owen manhandled it outside. A ripe smell still dirtied the air, but that was as likely from the state of the kitchen as Frank's corpse.

The mess offended me, but I wasn't going to spend any of the precious hours we had left doing housework. I wanted to be as happy as possible until the sun rose. Both for selfish and practical reasons.

"Is there anything to eat?" Owen asked after dumping the chair and washing his hands. He was still capable of concentrating on more mundane matters.

When I looked at him, he shrugged, "It's still a long time till dawn."

"There must be something, though whether there's anything to eat it off is another matter," I glanced at the smashed crockery carpeting the floor.

The Sorrrowsmith had been silent since we'd left the drawing room. Perhaps it was sulking.

I found some bread, cheese and apples. Plus a tin of spam and another of prunes that looked like they might have been in the cupboard since the war. My sorrows alone were enough to provide a healthy balanced diet for both Frank and the Sorrowsmith. My husband had never been much of a one for eating. I'd often wondered how he'd gotten so fat when he never ate more than a sparrow.

In hindsight, one of many things it might have paid me to have given a little more thought.

"I love spam," Owen beamed, eyes actually lighting up.

There were also a few bottles of beer. His grin spread wider when I held them up. I opened one and found a couple of glasses with nothing growing inside.

We returned to the drawing room with our feast (the kitchen really was too smelly). I lit as many candles as I could find. Twilight was deepening and there wasn't much point in saving them.

I was going to fetch trays so we could eat off our laps, but Owen took a throw from one of the chairs and spread it on the floor.

"Let's have a picnic like we used to."

Surrounded by the glowing tongues of candles, we hunkered down together with our meagre fayre. Not that the food mattered; a king's banquet wouldn't have made me any happier.

Something growled in the distance.

Owen raised his eyes, but I just bit a chunk off an apple.

We talked of nothing and everything as we ate and drank. Beyond the candles, the dusk darkened to full night. The thought I would never see the sun again barely scratched at the corners of my mind.

Tomorrow didn't matter.

I had till sunrise with the love of my life, my son was safe, I was free from Frank, and the monster that had lived within him was dying.

Noises came from time to time. Groans and moans. Creaks and cracks. But, other than that, the Sorrowsmith didn't make an appearance.

We sat, shoulder to shoulder, conversation and eating regularly interrupted by lingering kisses. I grew warm and took off my coat; Owen did the same with his tunic.

I took out the binding stone and placed it before us. The house shook hard enough to make the candles momentarily dance.

"It doesn't like that thing," Owen said.

"Good."

The golden whorl of circles seemed fractionally less bright. Its power was finite. When it faded back to the faint mark it had originally been, the magic would be spent.

The Sorrowsmith had to be dead by then. If anything remained, it would persist. The dark seed Merry warned me about, waiting for Francis to come, as he inevitably would when he learned of his father's death.

Waiting to ruin more lives.

Was our love great enough to destroy the monster by then? To poison whatever it had for a heart?

I assumed it would be. Why else would Merry have summoned us back to the world?

I pushed the doubts aside. I had never stopped loving Owen, despite all those long years without him. It was strong, it was powerful. It had survived death itself. It *would* kill the Sorrowsmith.

"We should get out of these clothes," I said once the house quieted again.

Owen raised his eyebrows and grinned.

"They're still damp," I said, laughing and picking at my skirt. In truth, they were nearly dry, but the thought they were what we both died in still nagged me.

"You got used to being wet in the trenches."

"We're not in the trenches," I jumped to my feet and scooped up one of the candles.

His eyes moved to the door, "That thing's out there."

"It can't hurt me now."

Owen didn't appear convinced. He nodded at the binding stone, "Take that with you."

"Why?"

"Maybe its magic will protect you."

"It binds the Sorrowsmith to it; it doesn't keep it away."

Owen pursed his lips, "Hasn't been near us while you had it with you."

He was right, but I left it all the same.

I wasn't scared of the Sorrowsmith anymore. And I wanted the thing to know it. Once your monsters stop frightening you, their power over you fades.

The candle made my shadow dance around me as I went up to my room.

There was still a bed but not a lot else. The other furniture was gone. My belongings, my books, clothes, the chipped porcelain vase I sometimes put flowers in, the pencil sketch of a sheepdog, the stern photograph of Mum and Dad that made them look like mannequins. Even the collection of seashells I'd harvested from the beach with Francis and Simon. All gone.

The house looked like it hadn't been cleaned since the day I'd died, but Frank had found the time to erase me from Grey Gull like I was a stain.

I stood there for a whole minute, candlestick moving back and forth.

Why was I surprised?

It meant nothing, but it was a hard reminder that I'd been dead for a long time.

And soon would be again.

This time for good. Erased, rubbed away, extinguished. Thrown out with the rest of the rubbish.

It made me want to go and drag Frank from his studio and dump him in a mere. To gather up all his awful paintings and have the biggest bonfire this coast had seen since the Vikings last visited. I want-

Something moved behind me.

Although, of course, these days, I knew exactly what the things that snuck about the shadows were.

"I'm not afraid of you anymore."

I meant it too.

But seeing the empty room hurt me in a way I hadn't expected.

A tasty snack for the Sorrowsmith.

I turned around. I didn't spin or whirl. Just slow and steady.

Nothing moved bar the candlelight.

"Enjoy it," I said, walking briskly along the landing, "that's the last thing you're getting from me."

The stink that greeted me in Frank's room was quite unspeakable. However, after a bit of rooting around, I found some old things in the back of a wardrobe that smelt of nothing worse than mothballs. He'd probably grown too big for them decades ago.

They wouldn't fit me, but at least they were dry. I stripped and left my damp things in a pile. The underwear followed.

Thou art old and fat, no man wants that.

"What do you know about desire?"

I slipped on one of Frank's shirts and buttoned it up. It was long enough on me to be a dress. Sort of.

He is young, you are...

The Sorrowsmith's words dissolved into black giggles.

"He remembers who I am," I pulled a jumper over the shirt, "So do I."

To believe the lies thou tell, say them loud enough to yell.

"Cheap insults in bad rhyming couplets? Is that the best you can do?"

Thou disgusts him now, thou are just a fat and sorry sow...

I snorted, bundling the rest of the clothes, and grabbing the candle, "It seems it is!"

I took a couple of strides onto the landing before realising I couldn't see anything.

The candle still flickered in my right hand, but only darkness stretched in front of me.

Thou are mine...

I took a tentative step forward.

Thy child is mine...

When I stepped into nothing, I took another step.

In the distance, a baby cried.

I stopped.

Break the stone, and I will bring her home.

"You must be getting desperate. That doesn't even rhyme properly."

The crying grew louder, closer.

Tilly.

My baby.

The darkness shifted, swirled, coalesced.

A figure emerged to loom over me. The Sorrowsmith.

With a bundle cradled in its too long arms.

Part of me wanted to try and snatch her from the monster's grasp, but I forced myself to stay where I was. This was a trick. I knew that, even if my heart and soul didn't.

Set me free, and I will leave her be.

"So you can take my son again?" I intended to say that with a derisory laugh, but nothing else came.

Frank's clothes tumbled to my feet. I managed to keep hold of the candle. Just.

The boy will be alive, the baby will survive.

The Sorrowsmith had always been made of shadows, coiled and cloaked in darkness, but now, as well as swirling around it, the shadows rose off it, like hot water on a cold day.

It was dying.

I just had to keep on killing it.

And give no credence to its lies.

"And let you destroy Francis' life like you did Frank's? Destroy Diane's like you did mine? Destroy Hayley's like Tilly's? And when Francis dies, you'll take his son then. Won't you? I know what you are, I know what you do..."

The Sorrowsmith didn't reply. Instead, it shifted spindly arms. All wrong angles and impossible joints, tilting the swaddled child till I could see a small, round, pink face looking back at me. Tilly blinked and squirmed. A tiny hand reached out towards me.

I wanted to run to her, to rip her from the monster's twisted grip and hold her close to me. Take her in my arms and press her to my breast. To keep her safe. I yearned and longed for her, as I had every day since she went missing.

My baby. My beautiful baby.

I had thought, just a little while earlier, that I could love no one more than Owen. But of course, that was nonsense.

A mother's love is like no other.

My feet inched me forward, my hand reached out.

Thou must destroy the stone...

The Sorrowsmith moved back into the darkness and I cried out, a wrenching, guttural cry that tore through me.

Before the creature disappeared, the shadows, I noticed, had stopped steaming from its body...

1954

Owen hurtled up the stairs.

I hadn't moved, though my free hand clutched the banister. I think I could still stand without support but wasn't confident enough to try.

"Bea?"

Owen put down his own candle before wrapping his arms around me. I was shaking and didn't break from his grasp until I'd stopped.

"What happened?" Concern creased his young face.

I swallowed and looked over my shoulder as if the Sorrowsmith might be lurking behind me.

"I saw it..." was all I trusted myself to say.

I scooped up the clothes and let Owen lead me downstairs.

Once we were back in the drawing room I fell into a chair and downed the remainder of the beer.

"You want me to get another?"

I nodded, "All of them."

Owen's fingers brushed my shoulder before he padded off to the kitchen.

My eyes snapped to the binding stone. The whorl faced upwards, its golden spiral glowing in the candlelight.

Don't be a damn fool, Beatrice Clay. Just you don't!

Intelligent women, particularly ones who happened to be a vicar's daughter, knew the promises of monsters were not to be believed.

I sucked in a breath.

And if the thing was telling the truth? Then what? I would die with the sunrise. I would have Tilly for a few hours. And the Sorrowsmith would be free to visit ruination on God alone knew how many more generations. Maybe all of them.

Still, I found I had picked up the binding stone all the same. It still felt like it had spent the day sitting directly under a blazing hot sun.

I was still holding it when Owen returned cradling beer bottles.

When I raised an eyebrow, he shook his head, "Didn't see anything. Maybe he doesn't like me."

That won him a faint smile as he filled our glasses.

"What did he do?"

I preferred to think of the Sorrowsmith as an it, but I wasn't going to argue the point. He passed the beer; I took another hearty slug while Owen perched on the arm of the chair.

I traced the length of the golden whorl with my thumbnail.

No secrets, Bea. We don't have long enough together for that.

"He showed me Tilly."

"Oh, God," Owen's hand found my shoulder.

"Said he'd give her back if I destroy this," I lifted the binding stone, even though I was pretty sure Owen knew I wasn't talking about the beer.

"You're not thinking of..."

"Of course not," I dropped the stone into my lap.

Owen looked down at me. My eyes stayed on the stone.

"When did Tilly disappear?"

I paused to add the eleven years I'd been dead to the total.

"Twenty-seven years ago..."

Owen's hand moved back and forth, warmer than the stone in my lap.

"She'd be a grown woman by now. It's not possible."

"A monster that feeds upon my sorrow isn't very likely either," I muttered, sipping my beer.

"Did this Merry bloke say anything about what the Sorrowsmith did to Tilly?"

"Sent her to another world. The one they both come from. The Fey, he called it."

"So... she can't still be a baby. Can she?"

I shook my head. I'd told myself the same thing. Usually, when someone confirms something you'd already worked out, it made you see the truth of it. Strangely, Owen's words didn't help any.

Owen shuffled and bent forward to put his glass on the floor. Then he curled his arm around my shoulder.

We sat in silence for a bit, I leaned into him, resting my head against his chest while I tried to get my thoughts back in order. I didn't work out much besides Owen really needed a bath.

"Why don't you change out of those things," I said edging away from him.

He eyed the clothes I'd dumped on another chair, "Dunno if they're gonna fit."

I ran a hand down myself, "They're the latest fashion. Dead men's attire is simply all the rage."

"Looks better on you," he glanced at my bare knees. The grin widened further when his eyes returned to me.

Thou are old and fat, no man wants that.

The smile faded in the echo of the Sorrowsmith's taunt.

Owen kissed me before grabbing the clothes and going into the hall to change. Which was kind of sweet.

Of course, he was right. Tilly couldn't still be a baby. Could she? No matter how many times I told myself that, I couldn't shake the idea I might be able to hold my little girl again.

Until sunrise.

And then?

I would be dead, leaving the Sorrowsmith to do whatever it wished.

When Owen came back, Frank's clothes hung from his frame. Still, at least they were clean. Sort of.

"What do you reckon?"

"Very dashing," I said, before the binding stone pulled my eyes back to it.

"How do you feel, Bea?"

"Feel?"

"Yeah, right now?"

He perched on the arm of the chair again.

"Confused," I admitted, "Conflicted."

"Sad?"

I nodded.

"Isn't that what this sod wants?"

I nodded again.

"The Sorrowsmith doesn't need you to do a deal, does he? Doesn't need you to destroy the binding stone. It eats your sorrows. So, if that's what you're feeling..."

My hand found his. He was right. The seed the Sorrowsmith planted in my head was something it hoped would bear dark blooms and bitter fruit. Enough to keep it alive till dawn. And then...

Tilly was gone. A long time gone.

This wasn't about her. It was about Francis, Diane, and the children. And all their children yet to come.

I looked beyond the ring of candles to the black rectangle of the window.

Love, joy and happiness would kill the Sorrowsmith. Nothing else. To find those things, even with the long-lost love of your life, was not easy when confronted by the certainty of your own death in a few short hours. But that was all I had. All we had.

Owen stroked my hair. I tilted my face towards him. His eyes were dark, liquid pools. How many times had I stared into them? And how many years had I yearned for them.

"Are you afraid?" I asked.

"Of dying?"

I nodded.

"Nothing is as scary once you've done it. I'm trying not to think about it, but... we're here for a reason, I guess."

Yes, we were. Merry brought us back because we shared a love capable of destroying the Sorrowsmith and saving the souls of others. As well as our own. How often did those circumstances arise? How long had Merry searched for the weapon we possessed? The thing that kills sorrow.

"What are we going to do, Bea?"

I reached up and touched his face, "Those clothes look ridiculous. I think we should go to bed so we can get rid of them."

Owen smiled, then kissed me.

When our lips parted, he whispered, "You know, it's funny, I've suddenly forgotten all about dying..."

1954

I insisted we bathed.

Owen wasn't keen. You know how boys are.

We hauled the tin bath inside and heated water on the stove for it. Grey Gull had never been a place of modern convenience.

Several times the distant cries of a baby tugged at my heart. If Owen heard them, he never reacted. Perhaps forthcoming business too fully occupied his mind, but I don't think so.

My faceless companion was a trickster. It had changed those old newspaper clippings I'd kept inside *Stalky & Co* to make me question my own sanity. Had it conjured something real, or just played with my senses, so I saw something different from what was actually under my nose?

I didn't know, and I wasn't going to ask.

I concentrated on matters at hand.

It had always been a chore to persuade Francis and Simon to get into the bath. Owen was cut from the same cloth. Boys. Again.

I told him it would be prudent to save time and get in the bath together. It was a trick I couldn't use on my boys, but it worked a treat on Owen. The grumbling stopped immediately.

"Step outside for a minute," I said, when the bath was ready.

The kitchen wasn't the most romantic setting in the world, even without the unholy mess and bloodstained floor where Frank's armchair had sat. I'd spread candles around the room. Beyond the house the sea sang quietly upon the shore. It was the best I could do in the circumstances.

After pulling Frank's jumper over my head, the shadows in the furthest, darkest corner coalesced into a familiar figure, head stooped to fit beneath the ceiling.

You are fat and old-

"Yes, yes! So you said before."

My fingers hovered above the buttons of the shirt. I raised my chin and kept my gaze on the thing that for so many years had only skulked in the furthest corner of my eye.

I let my hands drop away and crossed the room towards it.

"Bea...?" Owen called from the hallway.

"Stay there for a bit..." the Sorrowsmith's eyeless face tilted as I approached it, "...my love."

Like old, bad air escaping a bottle, a hiss filled the room.

I stopped in front of it, staring into the darkness where things moved. Where things writhed. Faces and forms. The subsumed. Those who had gone before, Frank's forefathers and the women, like Jane Shackle, whose sorrows this creature had devoured. Others too. The souls it had taken and sent to the Grey Place to walk plains of dust and ash until the host that killed them died and their torment could begin in earnest.

Were Tom and Izzy in there now Frank had died? Had they walked beside me in the Grey Place as Owen had?

The Sorrowsmith shifted. Without a face it is harder to tell, but it seemed uneasy, shrinking away from me, as if my direct regard troubled it.

The shadows of its form bubbled, dark steam rising off it again.

I smiled.

"Why don't you strike us down, Mr Sorrowsmith? That would solve all your problems, wouldn't it?"

It twisted, twitched, folded itself, retreating as far as the room allowed.

"But you can't, can you? You are a feeble, pathetic thing. The only physical strength you have comes from your host. With Frank gone you have nothing but your taunts and lies. The poison you've dripped into my ear for decades.

But I am not afraid of you anymore.

You are going to die. You are going to blight no more lives. I am the last of the women you have tormented. There is no more sorrow in me for you. Only love," I leaned in close enough for the blackness of it to fill my vision, "I suspect you won't like the taste of that half so much..."

Thy weak and puny heart cannot tear my sorrows apart.

The voice was a low rasp, dripping with malice.

So what?

Sticks and stones...

It had nothing but words now.

I would not show it fear. This thing lived off negative emotion. Not only sorrow and sadness, but grief, anger, jealousy, hatred. I was sure anything it could conjure in me would feed it. Help it survive until the sun rose, even if just as a withered husk awaiting however long it might take for its next host to arrive.

I half turned to the table. Between the scattered candles, the binding stone sat, adding the soft glow of its golden spiral to the candlelight.

"Why don't *you* take it? Why don't you smash it to pieces, eh?"

It shuffled itself but made no other reply.

"You can't even do that, can you? You're already reduced to rattling and shaking, creaking and creeping without Frank and I to sustain you. You no longer have the power to get rid of us to The Fey, like you did Tilly and Davey. Can you still break plates? I bet you can't."

I took another step forward. I wouldn't even need to stretch to touch the thing.

"You're weak now. Like I used to be. Weak and dying," I cracked a smile, "and that makes me so, so happy..."

The Sorrowsmith convulsed, spitting droplets of darkness from it like an overheated frying pan.

Slowly, I unbuttoned Frank's shirt, as big as a tent on me. Then let it slide off my shoulders and fall to the floor.

"I am old and fat. Or at least older and fatter than I once was. But I don't care. I'm going to spend the night with the love of my life. People don't often get second chances. Dead people even less. This is the happiest night of my life."

I smiled at the Sorrowsmith, then turned my back on it and walked naked to the bath.

I didn't look back till I'd put one leg in the steaming water.

"Stay if you want. After all the things you made Frank do to me, it doesn't bother me in the slightest. But when Owen joins me..." I put a hand over my heart "...I'm going to be so full of joy and happiness. You might find it all a bit uncomfortable."

I climbed into the bath. The water was hot as blazes, but I was damned if I was going to wince.

He won't want thou saggy old bones...

When I looked up, the room was empty.

"Fuck you..." I whispered back.

Then giggled.

It wasn't at all the sort of thing a respectable woman, particularly one who happened to be a vicar's daughter, should say out loud.

But it felt bloody good all the same.

1954

I didn't quite know where to look when Owen started to undress.

I know where I *wanted* to look. But that wasn't the same thing at all.

With Frank, there had never been a dilemma. I'd always avoided his pale, bloated, fleshy body. With Tom, much to my surprise, I rather enjoyed the looking. With or without clothes. I'd been too conflicted, by guilt, desire and embarrassment during the night Owen and I shared in the *Agincourt Hotel* back in 1916 to know what to do with any of my faculties.

But I was not that girl anymore. Even if Owen was the same boy.

"I thought I heard voices," he said, playing with the buttons of Frank's baggy shirt.

"Happens more than you might expect here... Come on! There's no need to be shy," I slapped the water in case he had any reticence about jumping into a bath with a woman old enough to be his mother.

I stamped down on the little tremor that thought provoked in my belly. Was nervousness a negative emotion? Probably not the Sorrowsmith's richest fayre, but I didn't want the bastard stealing so much as another breadcrumb from my larder.

"I'm not being shy," Owen said, rather shyly from where I was, "it's just... I've waited all my life... for this."

"To jump into a bath with a naked woman old enough to be your mother?" I said, before I could stop myself.

"You'll always be me Bea," he undid a few buttons, "told you that..."

He glanced up from his hands. His eyes lingering on the exposed parts of my breasts, already glistening with moisture. They were nowhere near as perky as the last time he got a peek at them, but Tom had been happy, so I wasn't going to worry about it. Worry was definitely a negative emotion.

I held out my arm towards him, "Then best we don't waste any time, eh?"

"Yeah..."

The shirt came off. His skin was starkly pale compared to his face, tanned by a long-ago French summer. His ribs had never been so evident.

He fussed around with his trousers. There were no underpants beneath. I dreaded to think what state his army ones would have been in. He hurried over to the bath in a somewhat unnatural fashion, hands cupped before him.

"Why don't you bring a beer?" I suggested as soon as he began raising a leg over the rim of the bath.

His eyes flicked to the table.

"Oh."

His blush made me giggle. Once, long ago, I'd been prone to a giggle. But it wasn't a sound Grey Gull had heard often over the years.

I hoped it felt like a knife in the Sorrowsmith's gut.

That was probably a negative emotion, too, but I was only human.

After making Owen scamper naked across the kitchen to fetch the bottle, he scurried back, still in an unnatural fashion. I did toy with the idea of sending him back for a glass but found myself too keen for him to get in.

The bath was an unfussy, functional thing of cold dented metal that had likely lived here long enough for several generations of the Sorrowsmith's victims to have used. It certainly wasn't designed for two.

The squeeze, however, was delightful. And once Owen settled himself down at the other end, our legs entwined deliciously.

We talked, passing the bottle back and forth. Actually, I did most of the talking, Owen mainly stared at my breasts in a way that was meant to be discreet enough for me not to notice.

Boys.

And he really was still a boy.

The love of my life, returned to me. No older than when I lost him. There came a moment I had to turn away, my throat tightening. In the distance the sea broke on the shingle shore. Once or twice, I heard a baby's cry in the pause between each wave.

My conscience or the Sorrowsmith's last throw of the dice?

Happiness, joy, love.

I could let nothing else trespass upon my "weak and puny heart."

"I love you," I said abruptly, interrupting Owen.

He smiled.

I remembered that smile. Slightly shy, slightly aware, more than slightly infectious. Completely wonderful.

"I've loved you from the moment I saw you," he said, "I'll love you until the sun rises tomorrow. And long after."

"You always had a way with me, Owen James."

"I wish I'd never gone to that bloody war."

"I did tell you."

He tilted the bottle toward me, "As much as I hate to admit it, you were usually right about everything."

"*Usually?*"

He laughed. And so did I.

The water rippled around us.

My eyes darted to the shadows beyond the candlelight. No figure lurked there.

"He isn't happy, is he?"

Owen reached forward to pass me the bottle. I let my fingers find his, more interested in him than the beer.

"It's dying."

"How old do you think he is?"

"Very," I said, finally taking the bottle from Owen's hand and sitting back. "There are so many people within it. I saw them. I saw their suffering."

"And our love is enough to kill him?"

"Our love is enough to..." I struggled for the right words, when I couldn't find them, I settled for, "...do anything."

"I think so too..."

We stared at each other before he asked, "What will happen to them?"

"They'll be free..."

I didn't know any such thing, but whatever became of them, it would be far better than internal damnation and torment encased within the Sorrowsmith.

"And us?"

"The same."

When Owen reached out for the bottle, I handed him the soap instead.

"The water gets cold quickly."

With a rueful grin, he started soaping himself. The water was turning dark. French dirt, I supposed. Though I was in no position to cast stones, I'd had eleven years in the muddy bottom of a mere.

The thought made me shiver. I found Owen's leg and ran my hand up and down his calf. It was warm, reassuring, alive.

The idea that we would both be dead come morning tried to force its way into my mind, quickening my heart and wrenching my stomach.

A negative thought.

You can stop that right now, Beatrice Clay!

Still, it couldn't prevent me wondering what would become of our bodies the second time we died. Me to the black water, Owen to French dirt? I hoped not. After spending so many years of our lives apart, I wanted our remains to stay together in death.

But that wasn't the important thing.

"What are you thinking about?" Owen asked. He was holding out the soap.

He didn't seem to have spent much time cleaning himself, but my thoughts had distracted me from paying due attention.

Francis and Simon would never wash themselves properly without my beady eye on them. They'd have had potatoes behind their ears if I hadn't kept on top of things.

What is it with boys and soap?

"Nothing," I said, "Just mesmerised by your dashing good looks."

"Happens," Owen tossed the soap in my direction. It disappeared into the ever-darkening water with a plop.

"Hey!"

Once I'd recovered the bar, I washed myself diligently. A good lather and plenty of soapy bubbles.

Owen watched me. Perhaps he was looking for tips.

Something like that, anyway.

Several times the water shimmed and shook. The Sorrowsmith expressing its displeasure. Was it dying so quickly it could do nothing else?

I leant forward and grinned.

"What are you doing?" Owen asked, eyes following me.

"Making sure you've cleaned the most important parts."

He licked his lips, "You've changed quite a bit, you know..."

"I'm a mother. I often had to clean my boys."

Admittedly not the part I began working the soap towards, but the principle was much the same.

Was I seducing Owen?

I'd never seduced anyone in my life. It seemed absurd. Respectable women, particularly ones who happened to be a vicar's daughter, did not stoop to seduction. It was very un-British. The Church of England didn't approve of that sort of thing either.

Still, I found the idea thrilling. Among other things. And that was a positive emotion. Anything the Sorrowsmith would choke on was good.

"Just stay still..." I said, cocking an eyebrow.

He nodded.

And I cleaned. Slowly.

With lots of lather and soapy bubbles.

"I don't know why you made a fuss. Bath time is fun!"

Owen emitted a peculiar little noise. I don't think he was trying to speak.

The tremors running through the water were all our making now, though I fancied a few rattles from the shadows were not.

I edged further forward and put my lips on Owen's, careful not to neglect my cleaning duties. I'm very thorough. The Castle was always spotless when I was alive.

"Bea..." he managed to say, but I kissed him harder to stop anything else. His arms were about me. I let the soap slip from my hands and, after I'd ensured I'd rubbed away the suds from the skin I'd been washing, my arms curled around him in return.

It wasn't necessary to be *too* diligent. I wanted our last night on Earth to be a long one.

There was as much water on the kitchen floor as the bath by the time I pulled back. In truth, a tin bath is not best suited, in either comfort or practicality, for such larks.

"Perhaps we should have an early night?"

Owen only nodded. I'm not sure he was capable of speech, though that might have just been from the pressure I was putting on his diaphragm.

We eventually extracted ourselves from the bath in dripping, giggling, rather undignified and utterly delightful increments.

I'd laid out towels, a sorry threadbare collection Frank had not added to in the eleven years of my physical absence. A chill haunted the kitchen, it was autumn and the mercury often falls rapidly after the sun at this time of year.

I fumbled a jumper over my head. Despite my newfound role of seductress, the thought of running (as well as wobbling, jiggling and bouncing) naked up the stairs was a bit too much. Perhaps in time I-

Silly thought.

I had no time. Neither did Owen, who was still towelling himself down, back to me.

I grabbed his hand and pulled him to the door.

"Steady on! Ain't got anything on yet!" he laughed.

"So what?" I snatched the towel from his hand and flung it away.

Frankly, there was a lot less of him to wobble, jiggle and bounce. There never had been, but army rations had left him spare to the point of gaunt.

It only took a quick kiss to overcome his resistance and we were soon charging naked through the house.

"How come you've got something on?"

I spun around the balustrade and mounted the stairs.

"Owen!" I turned on the step and put both my hands over my chest in mock offence, "I'm a vicar's daughter! Remember?"

The step I was on put us at eye level. His arms came about me again. We kissed and his arousal – his almost sparklingly clean arousal – pushed against me.

I felt decadent and wonderfully wanton. Kissing a naked man on the stairs of my house. But so what? There was no one to see. Save maybe the Sorrowsmith. And I hoped that bastard was watching. I could feel the happiness glowing off my skin.

I hope it burned.

1954

Of course, the bed wasn't made.

Given the throes of passion, the swirling emotion and decades of lost love, you might have thought I could have overlooked that.

"Leave it, Bea."

Owen certainly did.

"It doesn't matter," he insisted, manoeuvring me to the bed. There was a mattress. This was sufficient for Owen.

I flattened each palm against his bare chest and pushed him gently back.

"Seriously?"

"We've waited this long. Let's make it nice, eh?"

The room, stripped of my paltry belongings, was spartan. Dust hung in the stale air. The bed had creaked and sagged eleven years ago.

It would take more than a few sheets to make *nice*.

Still, this would be our first time and our last. Sheets and pillows seemed a minimum requirement.

"It won't take long, we want to be comfy," I wriggled out of his grasp, leaving him looking more than a little awkward. An erection is such a peculiar thing when you think about it.

I did my best not to think about it.

"Fetch candles," I told him, deciding to give him something to do to take his mind off matters.

The bedding was still in the same cupboard on the landing. Frank had done little in the way of reorganising while I'd been dead. I bundled up pillows and sheets. They were as musty as everything else, but at least nothing appeared stained.

Despite my years lying dead at the bottom of Cobb's Mere, I hadn't lost the knack of making a bed double quick.

By the time Owen returned with more candles, wearing Frank's shirt and trousers again, the bed was all but done.

"You've dressed. Going somewhere?"

"Didn't seem right, standing around with everything..." he made a sweeping gesture "...hanging out."

That made me giggle.

Then the wind howled hard enough to rattle the window.

"Just the weather this time," I said, when I looked back to find the smile gone from Owen's face.

"This feels so odd," Owen sighed.

"Which part? Returning from the dead, the monster that feeds off our sorrow or the bad weather?"

"The weather. Obviously."

Outside, the rain was coming in sheets again.

"It'll pass..." I straightened up, "...well, I've made the bed, so I suppose..."

This seduction business turned out to actually be quite fun. Something else they glossed over at Sunday School.

I held out my hand and he came to me.

Around us, the wagging tongues of candles danced in the draughts, while the wind keened a wild lament outside. Every so often I thought I heard a baby crying, but each time seemed fainter than the last.

The Sorrowsmith was dying, losing its power to conjure and deceive. It couldn't hurt me anymore.

Owen was hesitant, uncertain. I was no expert when it came to lovemaking. What I'd endured with Frank had nothing to do with love and Tom had been but a brief release from my loneliness. Still, as far as I knew, Owen had died a virgin.

I wasn't going to let that happen a second time.

I put my arms around his neck.

"I love you,"

Such a simple thing to say. Three little words. So easy. It can mean nothing, or it can mean everything. As with most things that happen between two people, it's what you put behind those words that counts.

"I love you," he repeated, his lips hovering over mine.

You are old and fat...

A voice on the wind told me. There was, I thought, a hint of desperation and a lot of pain. Like a dying man in a hospital bed raging against the injustice of it all.

"Does it bother you I'm old and fat now?"

He ran his fingers through the hair around my face.

"You're not old or fat. You're beautiful. Always were. Always will be."

To be fair to Owen, he made a pretty good fist of sounding like he meant that. Good enough to make my heart, as old and fat as it was, melt a little bit more.

Something screamed in the wind. Though, you had to be listening for it to hear it.

"Dance with me..."

"Dance?"

"We never danced enough... just imagine the music."

We started to move together, toe to toe, nose to nose, heart to heart.

"I could whistle..." he said, eyes staying on mine.

"I'd rather you didn't. Better to dance to the wind."

We probably looked a sight in our ill-fitting dead man's clothes, dancing around a dusty bedroom to the discordant rhythm of a storm. But I didn't care what we looked like. It's what we felt that mattered. The greatest orchestra in the world's fanciest ballroom couldn't have made me happier.

At first, only the howling wind and rattling windows serenaded us, then the squeaking floorboards as we span faster about the room before our laughter drowned out every sound in the universe. Even the plaintive cries of the dying Sorrowsmith

Our last dance dissolved into a kiss, and we eased onto the bed. At some point, not long after, we tossed aside Frank's clothes, leaving only bobbly, old linen pressing against our skin. Apart from each other's.

We talked a little, we kissed a lot. And touched, caressed, explored. We did all the things we should have done a lifetime ago.

The occasional bang and crash reached our ears, but the few times I looked, nothing stood in the candlelight. After a while, I stopped looking.

Do I need to describe everything that happened that night?

I don't think so.

If you possess an imagination, this is an opportune moment to use it.

As I may have mentioned, I'm a vicar's daughter. We don't kiss and tell. Well, I've rarely even kissed, though I'm sure not every vicar's daughter is the same.

Between the fumbling and rolling about, we whispered, we giggled, we laughed. On occasion, we made other noises.

Is saving the best night of your life until the last night of your life to be recommended? Probably not. But as the clock climbed towards midnight and then fell into the smallest hours, I knew a happiness I hadn't known since the long-ago days before the war came. Back when I'd lived in Camelot. And certainly not since Frank Harryman and the Sorrowsmith entered my life.

A cold breeze played across my sweat-slickened skin several times during the night.

Perhaps it was another draught, but it felt more like an icy breath.

The Sorrowsmith's last exhalations, I concluded, concentrating on the important business of kissing the love of my life.

With only a few hours to live, sleeping seemed a waste. Though at one point, still wrapped together, I did fall into a doze.

"It seemed mean to wake you," Owen said later, lips brushing my forehead.

Some of the candles had blown or burned out, deepening the shadows about us. The wind and rain no longer pounded the Castle. Everything was quiet.

"What time is it?" I asked.

"I'd prefer not to know."

"Do you think if we stopped all the clocks...?"

"Not sure that'd keep the sun from rising."

"No, suppose not..."

"We got a gift, Bea. Best not be greedy, eh? It never ends well whenever someone tries to bend the rules in a fairy tale."

I remembered that, on very rare occasions, Owen could almost have you believe he was quite wise.

I loved remembering the thousands of little things about him I hadn't realised I'd forgotten.

We lay and listened to the deep silence together.

"Do you think it's gone?" Owen asked.

"I don't feel any sorrow inside me."

"Let's hope it was enough. I'd feel better if we saw it go in a blaze of light with some big loud explosions. More final. More certain."

I agreed. Instead, I nuzzled him and breathed in his ear what I did want to feel inside me.

I didn't want to think about the Sorrowsmith anymore.

It was gone. It was over.

1954

Given the cold, and the circumstances, you might have thought we'd have stayed in bed for the remainder of our lives.

Instead, we sat together on the beach, facing east, blankets around our shoulders.

Behind us, Grey Gull and its outhouses burned. The warmth carried a little, but I didn't want to get too close.

Owen hadn't been sure about firing the house, but I'd always hated it. My prison. Despite all the rain, Frank had an abundance of turpentine to get things started.

The storm passed in the night, leaving the air crisp enough to steam our breath. However, for some reason, dying in bed didn't seem right.

Of course, I was burning Francis' inheritance, but it was worthless, and more importantly, I didn't want him here, in case, somehow, the Sorrowsmith survived the night, and a fragment remained buried in the shadows awaiting its new host.

A little pang of grief cut through me at the thought I'd never see my son or his family again, even if he hadn't seen me for eleven years.

But I did what I did every time grief, sorrow or pain tried to find a way to burrow into me. I reached out and found Owen's hand.

The eastern horizon wasn't black anymore, the darkness softening to a deep, rich blue reflected by the sea.

I rested my head on Owen's shoulder.

"Bea-"

"Ssshhh," I thought everything was as perfect as it could be, given we would both be dead again in under an hour. Better to listen to the sea kiss the shingle.

"Bea," Owen said again, not taking my subtle hint.

When I didn't respond, he moved a little away, took my chin in his hand and raised my head so I was looking at him.

"Is this important?"

"I think so."

"Go on then."

"Will you marry me?"

I was going to laugh until I noticed he wasn't.

"You've asked me this before."

"It was a long time ago. And I don't think it counts anymore," he lifted my left hand. It still sported Frank's wedding ring.

I snorted. I'd quite forgotten about that.

Pushing myself to my feet, I twisted it off and hurled it into the sea, emerging out of the receding night.

Owen's eyes followed me back down to the shingle.

"I'm recently widowed," I explained, pulling the blanket back around my shoulders and snuggling up against Owen again.

He took my hand, sliding his fingers between mine, "I love you, Beatrice Clay. Will you marry me?"

There was no joking in his voice. I'd both accepted and refused this proposal before. I wasn't going to refuse again.

"Yes, Owen James, I will marry you."

He kissed me and hugged me hard enough for it to feel like it mattered.

When I opened my eyes again, the sky had brightened further. Only the brightest stars remained in the east. I could make out clouds smattered over the sea. They would soon start catching the first golden light of the coming day and take on all the colours of creation. It promised to be a beautiful sunrise.

We didn't have long left to live.

"Might have trouble getting a church in time," I said, eyes returning to his.

"That's not the important bit."

"It isn't?"

"The saying yes is the important bit. Everything else is just... confirmation."

"I suppose."

"I don't think I've ever been happier."

I couldn't help but laugh. Owen laughed too. We'd always been good at laughing together. I reckoned that was an even more important bit.

We kissed again for quite a while.

And ended up flat out, entwined between the blankets and pillows we'd brought.

The gulls were waking up, their cries competing with the sea and the crackle of the burning house upon the shore.

I cried out a few times too. So did Owen.

Afterwards, we held each other limpet tight, and I kept my eyes screwed shut, face against his chest. Light pressed on the other side of my eyelids.

"How do you think it will happen?" Owen asked.

"Happen?"

"When the sun comes up. Do we... keel over and die? Do we vanish in a puff of smoke. Do we-"

"Think about living, not dying," I said, finding his lips without the need for my eyes.

Then I sat up.

The east was a blaze of colour. Gold, silver pink, peach, blue, grey, purple, red.

Owen did the same, and we stared at the dawn.

My hand found his. We both squeezed tightly and waited for the sun to appear above the sea.

"What a spectacle, eh?"

My head shot around, though I was not entirely surprised to find a man standing there, one sandaled foot resting on a bleached bone-white driftwood trunk. Behind him, smoke sullied the western sky from the still-burning buildings.

"Father Merry," I said.

"Oh, the wind isn't coming from the north at all; in fact," he grinned and stuck a finger in the air, "there's not a breath of wind at all. The world is wonderful after a storm, don't you find? The light is so much... cleaner."

I wrapped one of the blankets around me. Partly to protect against the sharp dawn air, but mainly because I wasn't quite dressed.

"Erm... how long have you been here?"

"Oh," he shrugged and pulled a face, "not long. Just breezing through. As is my want."

Owen's head moved closer to mine, "This is the wizard?"

"The one who brought us back," I nodded.

"We haven't been introduced, my apologies," Merry bowed, "we have met, but you weren't fully alive at the time, so I don't expect you to remember."

Owen climbed to his feet. I followed, Buttoning and adjusting as I went.

"Thank you," Owen said.

"Oh, I am the one who should thank you," Merry looked over his shoulder at the burning remains of the Castle, "dispatching a sorrowsmith is no mean feat, I can assure you. A love that can kill sorrow itself..."

"It's gone?" I asked.

"They're tricksy things. You can never quite be certain. But, yes, I think so."

Owen shoved his hands into his pockets, "We didn't really do much."

Merry's beard cracked to accommodate his grin, "On the contrary, young Owen. What you did was very hard. Love, true, deep and complete love, is not as common as one might think. Beatrice loved her children; she loved Tom Dupree too.

But the Sorrowsmith could withstand that love; it left a bitter taste, but it didn't harm it, and it could twist that love and use it to hurt Beatrice all the more. Make her sorrow sweeter. But you two together, well..." Merry first rubbed his hands and then held them out towards us.

Owen curled an arm around my shoulders. My heart was beating slightly faster, the greying smoke rising from the Castle was taking on a golden tint. My throat thickened, but I resisted looking around.

"I've waited a long time to find a love capable of killing a sorrowsmith..."

"Why?"

"Because I save the damned. And because a sorrowsmith once did my family great harm..." his eyes hardened, "...my motives are not entirely altruistic when it comes to those monsters."

"And Francis is safe. His family?"

"I believe so. Your love was too strong for the Sorrowsmith to endure, weakened as it was without its host and neutered by the binding stone. It's dead. Gone. Today is a day with one less sorrow in it. We should rejoice!"

Merry clapped his big hands together.

Francis was safe. Diane and the children. I squeezed Owen's hand. That was all that mattered.

"Is there any way you-"

"No," Merry snapped Owen off, "absolutely not. It took a tremendous effort to bring you two back from the dead for as long as I have. It's given me a grey hair or two, I can tell you. No. It's time," his eyes, which were now golden rather than sea coloured, drifted beyond us, "almost..."

"Just another day!" Owen protested, "We want to get married, if-"

"No. Even if I could, tomorrow... it would be the same. Just one more day. Everybody wants one more day. They always do."

He held out a hand, "The binding stone, you still have it?"

Nodding, I took it from my coat pocket. The whorl no longer glowed; the circles of gold had faded into the grey stone. I handed it to Merry, who turned it over in his hand, mumbling something before dropping it onto the beach.

"All done," he smiled.

I risked a peep over my shoulder. The clouds scattered along the margin between sea and sky were afire.

I pulled Owen close and held him as fiercely as I could.

"I love you," I said.

How many times had I told him that? Both to his face and to his photographs over those long years without him. Not enough, not anywhere near enough.

"You'll always be me Bea," he whispered back, burying his face in my hair.

And he was right.

I always would be.

We stood together, waiting for the sun to rise above the sea.

And the light to fade.

Epilogue

I fell in love with Owen James on 23rd October 1911.

Which turned out to be forty-three years to the day before we both died for the second time. I assume I fell in love with him the same day in my first life, although I shouldn't take such things for granted.

After all, I already knew I would fall in love with him by then.

The memories didn't come immediately. But by my tenth birthday, they were pretty well formed, though they did, and still do, tend to come and go, ebbing and flowing. Much like the sea.

They came in dreams and nightmares at first. For many years I would often awake at night, crying. The worst of my nightmares rousing Dad to my bedside in his pyjamas, hair tousled by sleep, the scent of pipe smoke almost as comforting as the arms he rocked me with.

"Nothing but a silly nightmare, Kitten," he would whisper.

Sometimes he asked about my dreams, but, as I never said anything about the man with the burnt eyes who hurt me, the monster in the shadows who drank my sorrows, a baby I couldn't find despite her crying or any of the other things, he didn't often ask.

And I've never told Dad about the dreams of him dying far too young.

As I grew into my teens, the certainty hardened that these were not dreams and nightmares but memories.

Memories of great sadness and memories of a love so strong it could kill sorrow itself.

However, the memory of love is not quite the same as being in love.

To be honest, when I first saw Owen after Dad and I arrived in Hollscombe, I was somewhat disappointed. He didn't really cut the romantic figure of my dreams. A man I would love beyond death and through to the other side. A man I would love so intensely it would be able to kill a monster.

But then, it isn't easy for a boy to cut a romantic figure when he's eleven.

I decided, perhaps, my memories were faulty. Or not real at all. Though things I remembered do keep happening. Both in my little Cotswold life and the greater world to come.

Owen never seemed particularly interested in me. We sat on different sides of the classroom, and our paths seldom crossed. Sometimes I watched him, wondering if he shared the same dreams as me.

He caught me staring at him once when my mind had wandered even further than usual. On that occasion, it had gone all the way to memories of the final night of our previous life.

When my mind snapped back, I realised Owen was no longer engrossed in the doorstep sandwich his mother had hacked for him that morning. Instead, the sandwich hung in mid-air as he stared across the little courtyard playground outside the village school.

His hair was a mess of dark curls. One unruly lick bobbed above his eye in a rather dashing fashion, his lips, which a moment before I'd been remembering the touch of against my breast, curled into a half smile that lay in some not quite definable place between cocky and sweet.

That was 23rd October 1911. We were both fifteen years old. A Wednesday. Grey and damp without any real rain. Funereal, was how Dad always described such days.

And that was the day I fell in love with Owen James for the second time.

As I sit at my window writing these words, I know that in a few days time Archduke Ferdinand will be assassinated in Sarajevo. It will plunge the world into war. I know this because I have lived this life before.

Why am I able to live it again? I do not know. Perhaps it is a gift from Merry, his magic couldn't keep us alive beyond that last sunrise in 1954, but it could give us our time over again. Or perhaps this is how the universe works, and we all get to repeatedly live our lives over, maybe until God decides we've got it right, and it is some legacy of Merry and the Sorrowsmith that has somehow kept my memories intact. Or maybe we did not defeat the Sorrowsmith and the eternal torment of being subsumed within that dreadful creature is to keep living your life over, repeatedly experiencing all the sorrows it inflicted upon you.

Then again, I could just be mad after all.

However, if the Archduke is assassinated on 28th June 1914, as I recall he will, I will discount that possibility.

Owen has no recollection of our previous life. I've nearly told him many times, but... well, how would *you* react to such a tale? So, no, I haven't. I've told no one.

Apart from whoever finds these words.

But I will pay heed to my memories. Whether living your life again is a blessing or curse remains to be seen, but I will not walk the same path. I will not make the same mistakes. I will never let love make me weak again.

And Owen will not be joining the army.

I cannot stop him signing up, but if I have to hit him on the head and drag him there myself, he will be volunteering for the navy. There will be few naval engagements in the war to come. With a little luck, he will never see a German.

And, more importantly, he will never meet Frank Harryman.

Does the Sorrowsmith exist in this life? If it is Merry who has made this possible, I presume not, if there is some other explanation...

Perhaps one day, when the war is done, I will take the train to Creethorpe. I will walk out across the wetlands to look for a cottage standing on that brittle shore where the constructions of men have never been welcome.

And if I find a man with burnt hazel eyes and a stack of paintings of something he cannot see but knows is there...

But I don't think I will.

I will marry Owen before he goes to war and bear his children. If there is a girl, I will call her Tilly, and the boys will be Francis and Simon. Hopefully, I will be lucky enough to have to think of some other names as well.

There are sorrows a plenty in this world still and I will taste them again. We all do. But I will know love. I will fill my life with it, give it with all my heart, and receive it as the blessing and wonder that I know it is.

Because, in the very end, the only thing that can ever kill sorrow is love.

Books by Andy Monk

In the Absence of Light
The King of the Winter
A Bad Man's Song
Ghosts in the Blood
The Love of Monsters

In the Company of Shadows
The Burning (Novella)*
A House of the Dead (Novella)*
Red Company (The Night's Road Book One)
Precious Things (Novella)
The Kindly Man (Rumville Part One)
Execution Dock (Rumville Part Two)
The Convenient (Rumville Part Three)
Mister Grim (Rumville Part Four)
The Future is Promises (Rumville Part Five)
The World's Pain (The Night's Road Book Two)
Empire of Dirt (The Night's Road Book Three)

Hawker's Drift
The Burden of Souls
Dark Carnival
The Paths of the World
A God of Many Tears
Hollow Places

Other Fiction
The House of Shells
The Sorrowsmith

The Burning and *A House of the Dead* are currently only available by subscribing to Andy's mailing list. If you enjoyed this book and want to read more of Andy's work, why not join?

Please visit the following sites for further information about Andy mailing list writing and forthcoming releases:

www.andymonkbooks.com
www.facebook.com/andymonkbooks

The House of Shells

If you enjoyed *The Sorrowsmith*, try *The House of Shells* another standalone novel set in the same universe.

Would you give up your world for love?

An illicit romantic getaway. A remote cottage. A deserted beach. A vanished lover. A house that can't be escaped. A place that can't possibly exist. A love that will cost everything.

The remote and secluded seaside cottage was the perfect location for a romantic break, especially for a married man having an affair. But when Jack Orford's beautiful young lover disappears he finds that the House of Shells is impossible to leave and the beach is not as deserted as it first appeared...

Trapped, stalked and alone, all of Jack's worlds are about to be turned upside down.

Printed in Great Britain
by Amazon